Jove titles by Daniel Stryker

COBRA
HAWKEYE

COBRA

DANIEL STRYKER

JOVE BOOKS, NEW YORK

COBRA

A Jove Book / published by arrangement with
the author

PRINTING HISTORY
Jove edition / November 1991

ISBN: 0-515-10706-9

Jove Books are published by The Berkley Publishing Group,
200 Madison Avenue, New York, New York 10016.
The name "JOVE" and the "J" logo
are trademarks belonging to Jove Publications, Inc.

PRINTED IN THE UNITED STATES OF AMERICA

10 9 8 7 6 5 4 3 2 1

1

Day 1: Near-Space

Cleary's aerospace plane was ninety seconds into a correctional rocket burn when all his cockpit electronics went dead.

"Was it something I said?" he asked Rowan, his copilot, and got no reply.

For a moment Cleary thought he'd blacked out. He couldn't see anything in the pitch dark around him—that was right for pilot blackout. But he could feel the vibration of the rockets thrusting the X-NASP, America's experimental national aerospace plane, toward the corona of the Earth below.

He could hear his pulse in his ears, and his respiration, with more clarity than he should have had if he were blacking out. And anyway, Cleary usually could manage, even in blackout, some little bit of vision at the center of blackout's tunnel—a spot of consciousness and control that made the difference between a good test pilot and a great one.

Also the difference between a live test pilot and a dead one.

"Hey, Rowan?" he tried again. His voice sounded like a croak to his ears, as if he had his head in a bag instead of a com-helmet with sophisticated electronics, but he could hear himself speak. He just couldn't see anything. Not anything.

Something slammed into his right arm: Rowan's fist, demanding his attention. And he heard, dimly, "What the fuck's wrong, Cleary?"

Helmet electronics weren't working, he realized. That was why Rowan's voice was so far away. And that was why he couldn't see squat. His heads-up display was kaput.

"Yeah, I can't see shit," he said hoarsely into his com system, with a sinking feeling that it wasn't going to be working either.

He manually retracted his visor and there wasn't anything to see out there beyond it either: The whole cockpit was black. The NASP didn't have windscreens, or windows of any sort. Everything it could see was ported in electronically to its consoles and to his helmet's redundant display. And everything that kept its human pilots alive was routed through the artificially intelligent life-support/pilot interface.

Rowan was a moving shape he could sense but couldn't hear or see. Throttle controls, the stick—everything had that dead feeling of nonoperational equipment. Cleary was beginning to gasp for breath. He wasn't getting the oxygen he needed.

That probably meant that nothing in his helmet was working— no electronics meant no life support, no coms.

Still, gasping or not, he was a test pilot: He had regulations to follow, a reputation to maintain. Cleary sent a regulation Mayday to Mission Control, trying to ignore the fact that he couldn't hear the staticky sound of a com circuit when he tried.

Once he'd done that, Cleary stopped playing by the book because the book was written for pilots who still had systems interfaces. And he couldn't seem to remember what the book said to do in a situation where you had none. . . .

What if this unresponsive bucket of bolts started tumbling?

Last night he should have gone out and gotten drunk and brought home some girl from a local bar, or seen how fast his hot new sports car would go, instead of being a good boy and packing it in early because he'd fought so damn hard to get this flight and he wasn't about to screw up his physiology at the last minute. Space Command physicians were so damn picky about who flew their multi-billion dollar babies . . . especially when those babies weren't built by the lowest bidder, but as part of a black project under tight security. . . .

The X-NASP program was officially called NOMAD these days. The Nomad he was strapped into was Cleary's ticket to the fastest lane of the fast track, and America's ticket to strategic supremacy in space. He really didn't want to be one of the unsung heroes mourned by Air Force Space Command. . . .

When he realized how shallowly and fast he was breathing, it occurred vaguely to Cleary to unlatch his mask and reach for the emergency oxygen. The suit-system was intimately connected to the X-NASP, so if both were down, this was a massive systems failure. Maybe so massive that it didn't matter if he talked out loud or kept trying to raise the guys back at Colorado Springs, because the cockpit voice-recorder was probably down too.

Real massive failure. As in deadly. He pulled the emergency air-pack out of its bracket and shouldered it. Only after he'd taken a couple of greedy, gasping breaths did he think to take off his now-useless helmet so that he could yell at Rowan and Rowan could yell back. Without oxygen, a brain doesn't function as it should.

"Rowan, get me some backup power." Cleary's fingers were clumsy as he fumbled for the unlocking mechanism on his safety harness. Then he stopped himself. He wasn't going to leave his controls. If there was any way to get power back up here, Rowan would find it. He had to figure out how to get his systems to come up live.

Anyway, he wasn't in real great shape to go fumbling around the back of the flight deck. You didn't leave a testbed with nobody in the hot seat, to fly itself . . . or to tumble nose-to-tail into disaster. The roaring in his ears might be just the unstoppable rocket burn or some weird physical response of his body to rapid pressure and gravitational changes in the cockpit. . . .

Rowan was saying, "—now trying to manually connect the backup batteries. No automatic emergency power—"

What the hell was wrong with the plane's emergency systems? Cleary tried emergency cutoff procedures for the rocket burn. No response.

He tried three com systems, including an automatic beacon. He couldn't get a light on that console to save his ass. He kept flipping switches and looking for power, somewhere. Just because you didn't have lights didn't mean you might not have power to restart systems, he told himself.

He kept seeing the plane as if he were outside it—an elongated teardrop with him and Rowan inside, heading for a final rendezvous with Earth. Nomad had suicide switches—electronic circuit breakers that sacrificed themselves to protect the electronics behind them—to shield the space plane's circuitry from damaging electromagnetic bursts. Sensing a destructive incoming pulse, the switches should have fried, shutting off the equipment (hopefully in time) to save it. If that was all this was, he'd be able to get everything back up and running.

Eventually. If crucial suicide switches hadn't failed. If he had the right replacement circuit boards.

Cleary and Rowan had flown together long enough that they could almost read one another's minds. "Maybe," Rowan called from somewhere aft, "replace enough boards to shut down the rockets before we—"

Before they careened, out of control, out of the space envelope that ended fifty miles above the Earth and into gravity and the stratosphere, where they would start crashing for sure.

Cleary wanted desperately to leave his seat and go help Rowan find . . . something. He was still free of his harness. Habit and years of drilled-in command procedure kept him there, staring at the blackness in front of him and feeling his way along familiar control panels. This was what it would be like to be blind. He felt around for a flashlight.

Bad luck multiplies. The flashlight wouldn't work. He told himself all he had to do was change its batteries. But it scared him more than he was ready to admit. Yet. He changed batteries. The light still wouldn't work. He found a spare light, with no batteries in it, and a fresh battery pack, and put them together in the dark with trembling hands, maniacally concentrated on the simple task. The second light worked fine; that was even scarier.

If there was no automatic emergency power, then the suicide switches that protected the X-NASP's electronics *had* failed. But all of them? At one time? Massive systems failure, including running lights and life support, wasn't the sort of contingency against which testbeds like the Nomad were normally protected. And there was the flashlight.

A tiny glow blossomed to his rear: Rowan had a flashlight lit, back where Nomad's big systems emergency batteries were. Cleary called back, "So?"

"So I'm workin' on it." Rowan sounded half strangled. "Had to find a fucking flashlight that worked first."

Oh, man. If you get pulsed, anything electrical that's connected gets fucked. . . .

Cleary said, "Need me back there?" like he wasn't scared shitless now. Still breathing his emergency air, he played his flashlight's beam over the magnificent technological achievement that was the X-NASP's control suite. The second flashlight still worked. That was comforting.

"Nah, stay put. I almost got these emergency power supplies connected," Rowan grunted. "How's it up there?"

"Dead," Cleary said. Once they had emergency power . . .

Lights came on. A few, here and there: backup battery power. The console didn't spring to life. Nothing self-tested. No views of space beyond, or the Earth's curvature, or the ground toward which they were headed, came up in the monitors.

"Controls still dead," Cleary said in a flat, attenuated voice. He needed to void his bowels. But there was no time.

"Now what?" Rowan's muffled question was faint, from behind him, but so inexorable that Cleary winced.

Cleary twisted around to look at Rowan. The copilot's face was white over the elastic of the emergency oxygen mask cutting into his cheeks. His black brush of hair sparkled with sweat.

Rowan's pale eyes seemed to swoop across the distance and stare into his. Cleary had to say something. He was the pilot, the mission commander. Rowan waited for an answer.

Fighting nausea, Cleary replied, "Now we replace every circuit board we can: first the life support, then enough control boards to stop those rockets." As he spoke, he turned back to the inert control console and resumed trying restart procedures. But he didn't have much hope. Not the way things were going. It took more than bad luck to fuck up this royally. It took something actively malevolent.

His body was telling him he was in real trouble: nausea, grainy vision, elevated pulse rate. Pilots like Cleary didn't even feel alive until they were in a little bit of trouble. With his inboard, human systems reacting like this, his biological computer was telling him he was in deep shit. He couldn't let Rowan see that he was flapped.

Cleary never flapped. That was how he'd gotten this assignment. He dated Death for a living and courted Disaster on the weekends. But he'd never been in a depressurization emergency coupled with a control emergency.

Firsts, he told himself, were what testbeds were all about.

Go slow. Don't rush. One switch at a time. Think it out. Get home in one piece.

They had to replace lots of circuit boards to get this particularly complicated space plane running again. Replace them in time. Before the X-NASP reached the edges of the atmosphere and fried her pilots as she broke up in an uncontrolled descent, way too fast. At least he couldn't contemplate how nasty a death that would be, for the pilots or the spacecraft. He didn't have a single working computer on deck.

And then he admitted it: They *had* been pulsed. His dry mouth eased as some relay in his brain clicked over from quandary to problem-solving. The Nomad had been attacked.

Never mind that he hadn't felt it. His battery-powered flashlight had. And he was sure as hell feeling it now. Rowan had a wife, a kid on the way. So did lots of other guys. Having a technical emergency to report was a whole different thing from having an aggressive action to report—one that pulsed even flashlights with batteries to death.

Something in Cleary that he called hysterical strength settled into place. He wasn't going to let whoever had done this get away with it clean. Somehow, he'd let the ground know what had happened.

He stopped methodically flipping switches and checking systems and just stared at the pool of light his flashlight was throwing. He had a hypothesis. Now he needed to make sure he was right. Dead flashlights weren't enough proof.

Normally, any of these shut-down modules would restart when he fired one up. The suicide switches were there to shut down a system in time to allow you to restart it when a naturally occurring pulse was gone. But this wasn't anything natural, so that wasn't happening. . . .

"Rowan, give me the boards for the com circuits—whatever I can replace up here."

He needed to make sure that Space Command knew what had happened, in case he couldn't stop those rockets in time.

A hostile, directed, electromagnetic pulse, or a series of them, could have done this to him—to the Nomad. The thought of being shot at and not knowing it made him breathe quicker as adrenaline pushed his metabolism. A pulse beam could have destroyed every piece of working or connected electronics on the X-NASP, if the pulse was quick enough and strong enough to get past the suicide switches.

Could have, but hadn't necessarily. These were new technologies. And who the hell was the enemy up here anyway? Every space-going nationality was working together on Space Station Freedom: the French, Canadians, Japanese, Germans, Italians— even the Soviets these days. And the Soviet Mir station was way out of Nomad's line of sight, which you'd need for electromagnetic pulse.

But there were lots of spacecraft up here, plenty of satellites and modules, within range. If he'd had a targeting computer that was working, or even helmet electronics, he could have determined who'd been in line of sight himself. But he didn't have any of that.

He had a soft, tiny, temperature- and pressure-sensitive human body encased in an unresponsive, runaway single-stage-to-orbit vehicle that wasn't going to stop until it ran out of fuel or until it burned up in atmosphere—and that was all he had.

Except for his reasoning ability and his peculiar responses to danger, the combination that had put him in this seat in the first place. On any piece of equipment where the suicide switches had worked, Cleary should be able to restart his systems, no harm done. But not if his X-NASP had been attacked by some sophisticated EMP (electromagnetic pulse) source with lots of pulse power. The only way to truly harden something like the Nomad against an EMP attack would have been to build a Faraday cage into its skin. And weight considerations just didn't allow for that. So he was right, as far as he could tell.

Somebody had fucking shot at him. And Rowan, and the American program, he reminded himself.

Somehow, Cleary felt a little better. At least this systems failure wasn't something endemic to the X-NASP. Now if he could tell somebody on the ground his theory, he could get ready to figure out how he was going to save the Nomad.

The test pilot in him still couldn't be convinced that anything justified leaving his station. Rowan was back there, doing all you could do in close quarters. EMP only destroyed electronics that were running. . . .

Cockpit lights came on, flickery emergency lights.

"Nice work, Rowan," he said.

"Thank you, sir," Rowan said breathlessly, from what sounded like far too far away.

Probably stupid to talk. If they'd had EVA (extra-vehicular activity) suits, they could have stretched their time, maybe left the Nomad to crash on her own and floated around waiting for a pickup from somebody, with a few hours of air to spend. And they'd have had the com systems in the suits.

But they didn't have those suits, because they weren't scheduled for an EVA and every ounce of weight counted in expensive test programs. Ought to tell somebody they should have them next time. They could punch out anyway, once they reached high sky, but he was breathing the oxygen now that was meant for him to use during a high-altitude emergency punch-out. . . .

Cleary realized he was panting—using up too much oxygen too fast because he was so damn pumped up. Or because he was getting the pilot's equivalent of the bends. He wondered how his partial-pressure suit was doing, and whether his whole theory of EMP attack was just some product of stress-screwy blood chemistries, carbon dioxide, and oxygen mixing in ways a human wasn't supposed to endure.

So he kept doing what he was trained to do: trying to restart one system after another, patiently and carefully testing everything he could, every way he could.

He forgot about Rowan until a couple of replacement boards appeared in his peripheral vision, which was too grainy for his liking.

He took them, and went to work helping Rowan snap them in. Done, he said, "How're we doing on rocket burn?"

"We'll run out of fuel eventually." Rowan slid into his own seat, beside Cleary.

Not before they were dead. "Cute. You ready to try a restart from scratch?"

"Try coms first," Rowan said diffidently, pale and unsmiling. His faded blue eyes met Cleary's. "Don't want to waste power—or time."

"Be my guest," said Cleary. The fingers of his right hand were already moving on the console as he put on his helmet left-handed. Might as well assume they'd fixed everything that was wrong.

By gut reckoning, he didn't have a hell of a long time to regret a bad decision if he'd made one. At their rate of burn, the uncontrollable Nomad was going to hit the atmosphere with all the finesse of a ballistic missile, and nowhere near the survivability.

He didn't realize that he was smiling when he heard the staticky sound of a live circuit and Rowan sending his Mayday laconically to the ground controller at Consolidated Space Operations Center, then to Edwards, then on open frequencies in every mode he could think of: You couldn't be sure where you were, so you couldn't be sure who'd hear you.

By the time Rowan had broadcast their situation so that anybody on the ground or in space could respond, Cleary had a live heads-up display and, hopefully, a fighting chance.

He hardly heard Rowan as he went through the procedures that would test his ability to control reentry.

Because his electronics, now that half of them were working, were telling him that was what he was facing: reentry procedures.

It was too late to pull up out of the atmosphere and try again, even if he was sure he could.

He burped one attitude thruster and it responded.

Then he said, still so concentrated on his task that Rowan seemed a million miles away: "Whoever you get, tell 'em I'm going to put down in Sri Lanka, if I can manage it."

"*What?* You can't be—"

Then Rowan looked at the data that Nomad was showing them.

"Christ. Look, I'm not sure if anybody's hearing me, Cleary."

"That's okay. I'm not sure I'm going to be able to make any kind of landing. You got a better idea, Rowan, I'll be glad to hear it."

Cleary's voice was nearly a murmur. The Nomad was a single-stage-to-orbit vehicle, and if there was any kind of vaguely acceptable runway he could reach, it was going to be in Sri Lanka.

If Rowan wasn't busy trying to raise somebody to talk to, he'd have seen that himself.

Then they were both too busy to worry about broadcasting their emergency.

They were living it. Maybe somebody had heard them, maybe nobody had. But Cleary wasn't worrying about telling the world that the Nomad had been EMP'd any longer. He had enough power to tell his own black box, and if he didn't make it home to talk about his troubles, the black box probably would.

That was the thing about equipment: It was recoverable. Even if it was eighty percent destroyed, it could tell you something. People weren't so lucky.

Then they ran out of space and hit the envelope of the stratosphere, and the Nomad bucked like a wild horse.

Cleary's head-up flickered, but it didn't punk out on him. His electro-optical sensing system brought him exterior information, including terrain mapping.

He was looking at nearly two thousand miles of ocean and terrain and praying like hell that he wasn't going to run out of rocket fuel just at the critical moment, when he needed to stabilize his attitude.

Once they had air, they had a rougher ride, but they could use the Nomad's air-breather capabilities. The scram-jets had to be eased in; the process of turning a rocket ship into an air-breather was still experimental.

In the best of flights, this was the moment when Cleary's mouth got dry. Not only were you heading into turbulence and out of the space envelope, you were asking the Nomad for the most intelligent assistance it could give you.

And he and Rowan were doing that with equipment that had been pulsed.

It made your eyes ache to concentrate that hard. His ears blocked and produced tones. His arms fought the controls. Rowan swore and they came out of a rough patch, upside down, praying that the Nomad would hold against the stresses of an insane maneuver.

Once the Nomad wasn't threatening quite so loudly to break up under their hands, and the nose temperature reading was down low enough that Cleary wasn't glad he couldn't see the nose because it was probably melting, Rowan said, "Cleary?"

"What, Rowan?"

"That was the worst ride I've ever had. You want to estimate ETA for Sri Lanka Control?"

Then Cleary realized that he'd been hearing Rowan talking to various unhappy ground types for the last little while. Very unhappy ground types.

"Fifteen, twenty minutes. Tell them I want lots of foam on that runway. Full emergency procedures. And tell them I don't want to go around twice."

Landing this crippled bird in the Third World, somewhere it wasn't cleared to be, was going to be only the next leg of Cleary's all-time worst flight. He still had to explain what had happened up there. But until he made that landing, he couldn't be sure he'd be alive to do it.

"When you get a minute, Rowan," Cleary said with a tongue that seemed sandpapered, "I need a secure channel to Space Command Intelligence."

He wished to hell he didn't have to tell them what he thought had happened up there, this way, right now. But he did. Just in case he couldn't manage a landing that he and Rowan could walk away from.

2

Day 1: Cheyenne Mountain, Colorado

Aleksandr Shitov, of the First Chief Directorate of the KGB, blinked owlishly around him at the American citadel called Cheyenne Mountain Complex, and cursed his luck, his fate, and his enemies back in the Soviet Union—or what was left of it.

If not for those enemies, he wouldn't be here, in the bowels of the American defense complex, waiting like any other piece of shit for the walls to close in about him and mash him to a pulp.

Somehow, his blood's enemy, Levonov, had engineered this posting of Shitov to the United States. Shitov had thought he had won his war against Levonov. But Levonov had arisen from his crypt and now Shitov was in America, holding the hands of visiting Soviet dignitaries on this tour of Imperialist majesty, while Levonov was home in Moscow, marshaling his forces for a return to power—the power of Shitov's current position in the KGB's First Chief Directorate.

No Soviet leader had ever retired from power; all had died in office except one, who'd had the poor judgment to go on vacation without his colleagues—and he had been made a nonperson. Power and absence were equally dangerous to beleaguered, overworked KGB functionaries in this new era of *glasnost* when the KGB was the most reviled of Soviet institutions. The Executive President was a dictator, the people were murderous in their anti-Communist fervor, and Shitov—

Where was Shitov? Was he home, with Shitova waddling by his side in her sable, taking his accustomed seat at the ballet and making his claim upon whatever future was left to them, preserving whatever comfort bold action could ensure? Was he masterminding the retrenchment of Soviet intelligence from his comfy desk in the new KGB building? Was he securing his sources of raisin pumpernickel on the black market and the open market, such as it was, and doing his bit to bring about the gold standard by demanding his bribes in gold and buying Shitova all the gold he could?

No, he was not. He was here, where no Soviet official had ever dreamed to be (except under deepest cover), under a mountain of rock and behind tons of metal doors, getting the sanitized tour of America's might reserved for her most inanely naive of citizens.

And in payment for this "honor," whenever he had completed his tour and was home again, he would drive a stake into the heart of that vampire and one-time friend, Levonov. Peace might be reigning in the world, but between them, the Cold War had become the Hot War. There could only be one survivor in such a war.

And that survivor would be Shitov. He had a plan for turning this exile-in-disguise into a triumph. He had asked for and received permission to consult with the highest levels of the American intelligence community on a possible bilateral agreement to pool resources against terrorists.

Since terrorists in the Soviet Union, these days, were everywhere, if Shitov managed this, he would have power that the subsequent, quiet assassination of a minor KGB functionary named Levonov could not endanger.

He kept envisioning the moment when his faithful Estonian and Bulgarian operatives would swarm over Levonov's Zil as Shitov's mortal enemy drove about the provinces. Levonov the reformer would soon be Levonov the cold corpse, lying unremarked behind some local police station. It was the old way, the right way, the only way to deal with traitors.

So absorbed with his Muscovite enemy and his greater vision was Shitov, he barely had time to be depressed by the magnificence of the Americans' electronic command center. Accompanying the director of the USSR's Baikonur Cosmodrome on an underground tour through Cheyenne Mountain was no way to gather useful information, or else the Americans would never have let them set foot in here. All that they were seeing was a display of overt American might.

And a tasteless one, considering the plight of Shitov's embattled country. If it were the American Administration that was in such straits instead, then it would be a pleasure to be here.

But the Americans knew what the rules were for their society, and no Communists had ever known that. To serve the new government, Shitov might have to give up his Party allegiance. Levonov had already done so. But Levonov had less to lose, if the military decided that things were moving too fast, or the progressives decided that things were moving not fast enough, and one or the other put a bullet through the hairy ear of the Executive President, who had just voted himself Czarist powers, and was now changing the very constitution that ensured that the Soviet Union would endure as a Communist entity—or as any entity whatsoever.

Around Shitov, men were scurrying back and forth—American men in uniform and men in white, talking and laughing to one another as no Soviet functionaries would have dared to do in the presence of their superiors.

The director of Baikonur was surrounded by American agents: by generals and CIA men in disguise, by scientists who ruled over a destructive power unmatched—these days—anywhere in the world.

It was a sad thing to be an ex-equal, an ex-threat. This Shitov well knew. If it would have made any difference to the fate of his country, he would have come in here wrapped in plastic explosive like a mummy and detonated himself upon these Western oppressors, like the terrorists who now were Shitov's main concern.

For the first time, seeing America's underground war rooms, he understood the frustration of Third World boys who were willing to "bomb themselves" upon their enemies. But Shitov was no Third World boy. He was a Third World man, from a country with nuclear weapons once the envy of the whole world. And his enemy was, alas, no longer America.

His country was no longer worthy of American fear and hostility. This, all the Americans' kindly assistance and helpful openness clearly said.

"What?" he responded churlishly when some American called his name. His English was good, but he hadn't been paying attention. His own troubles were simply too pressing. He must pay attention. He must make this trip a weapon in his private war, a sortie that brought him back to Moscow triumphant, with all the intelligence he needed to put an end to Levonov, once and for all time.

Shitov squinted up at the tall man awaiting his response and again said, "What? I did not hear. My English is rusting, you see." He pretended to be a poor linguist, and they pretended to believe him.

The tall man in uniform had sandy hair and a mustache and a physique that Shitov had never had, even when he was a colonel in his country's air force, as this man Pollock was.

Pollock was also the Space Command Special Operations Chief, which meant he was an intelligence professional. Thus, professing a bond of brotherhood, Pollock had become Shitov's personal guide.

"I was just reminding you that we've got to leave soon for our meeting with the Commander in Chief for Space—CINCSPACE."

"Ah, yes, Sinkspace. If it will be my opportunity to display our new cooperative spirit against the terrorists on the ground, I will like it." There was a tension in Pollock's nearly handsome face that Shitov had not seen there previously. He looked closer. Yes, the muscles around the man's eyes were so tight that the eyes themselves were nearly obscured.

"You'll like it, I promise, *Sekretar,*" said Pollock.

"Something, I see down there by all the agitation—is not quite . . . regular, is this so?" Behind Pollock, where the Baikonur director stood transfixed before a great electronic display of the world, surrounded by Americans, those Americans were suddenly whispering in each others' ears and their flunkies were coming and going too rapidly. "You wish to have our Baikonur *rukovodyted* and myself out from under your feet? Something is happening, I think so."

"*Sekretar*—you can ask your questions in the meeting that's next up on our agenda—it's all community folks."

"It will be the intelligence community staff from your Space Command, and myself, yes? Then you may count on me for whatever help my country can give in this moment of your crisis." He arranged his cheeks in a smile and moved off toward the group milling before the gargantuan, colored display of the world.

Pollock followed. "*Sekretar.*" Pollock caught up in three long-legged strides. "We'd be greatful for your help, of course. Did you ever hear the joke about your President asking ours for one hundred thousand dozen condoms for the Soviet Army, all at least twelve inches long?"

"Only if it is the one in which, before your nation sends ours this much-needed aid, you mark each condom as medium," Shitov said.

"Actually, the version I heard, we mark them all as small."

The Air Force Space Command colonel stopped stock-still and put a hand on Shitov's arm. "Let me ask you something, privately," he said in a low tone.

They were on the stairs descending to the central command floor of the huge information-processing bay. No one was within earshot. Here was something interesting, perhaps even something useful. Shitov's fisherman's instincts had not been in error. When you see fish schooling, as they were down below, there was always good fishing. He wetted his lips in anticipation. "Ask as you would ask a brother, *Polkovnik* Pollock. You know we are now so full of cooperating spirit we cannot even keep our deepest thoughts to ourselves before your hospitable persuasion."

"Yeah, well. We have an incident to discuss in our meeting—one that'll bear on an official, overt, and public announcement by the German ORTAG space agency that they're declaring a thousand-mile territorial limit around their space assets. You still want to sit in on this meeting, in the spirit of intelligence-sharing and *glasnost* and everybody's asses?"

"You Americans." Shitov shook his head in wonder, and because what he had heard made him dizzy with implications. "You are so direct." Crazily so, or foxily so. Shitov's heart was racing. Oh, Levonov, eat your heart in shame and envy. The luck of Shitov was returning.

Being in the right place at the right time was often the difference between life and death, or between triumph and failure, or between opportunity and dishonor. This was a moment that never would have been Shitov's without Levonov's schemes to destroy him. "If your CIA will be there, I will be pleased to participate openly and freely." To the extent of his mandate, and perhaps a little beyond. The Executive President was constantly preaching initiative. Shitov was determined to take some. "Of course, one might wish to consult with one's superiors."

"We can give you a secure line, and all our intelligence services happen to have people here right now—because CINCSPACE is here." Pollock proceeded carefully, despite his bravura American machismo.

"Then let us go boldly into this meeting, Colonel Pollock. What for are we waiting? Surely the Cosmodrome delegation is safe from penetrations by both our enemies, in your sanctorum?"

"Great. Come this way then," Pollock said with a dip of his head that broke eye contact.

If Shitov believed in reincarnation, he would wish to be reincarnated as an American, so that he could do whatever he wished and say whatever he wished and still not starve to death in Gorki or be shot in the head for it. All the Americans risked was failure, not death in response to failure.

At least, so it seemed to Shitov until he arrived at the above-ground office of CINCSPACE at Peterson Air Force Base and there saw the grave faces of a half-dozen men sitting around a table. The gray pall in the room was a pall of death, and Shitov nearly forgot the wonder of being here, of having such a landmark meeting, because of the dark atmosphere in the room. But he had been in many such rooms.

And this was Shitov's chance to turn everything to his advantage. Once he'd been introduced to the Commander in Chief for Space, he realized that his luck was even better than he had suspected. This was Leo Beckwith, the redoubtable admiral with whom Shitov was well acquainted on paper, from his work in the past.

Someone, probably at Levonov's request, had withheld the information from Shitov that Beckwith had this week been promoted to the highest level of U.S. Space Command. Levonov had meant this to be a stumbling block for Shitov, who was briefed to meet with Beckwith's predecessor.

But no matter. Shaking Beckwith's hand, Shitov said, "It is a pleasure to meet with the man who helped Bright Star from becoming Brilliant." This reference to a conflict-averting crisis in the Middle East, on which Shitov had also worked, raised Beckwith's eyebrows. "It's always a pleasure to meet a well-informed ally," Beckwith said, and offered Shitov a seat next to him.

"My Ops Chief says you're comfortable sitting in on this," Beckwith said to Shitov under his breath as both men pulled their chairs to the table.

"It is precedent-setting, in a time when it is necessary to set the proper precedents," Shitov replied. "If I have information that will be helpful, I will give it—although I may have to consult with Moscow Center before I can give detail in depth."

"Understood." Beckwith nodded, and started introducing Shitov to, "my CIA, DIA, and NSA liaisons," and his various chiefs among the four-headed hydra that comprised the consolidated United States Space Command.

All of these were fine-looking, well-fed Americans with good teeth. Each had the shiny skin tone of the properly nourished, and every one had a clean suit or uniform with unfrayed collar. Even the admiral's aide-de-camp, who scurried in with coffee and tea and sweet rolls, was elegant and in perfect trim. And the room itself was a fine conference facility with flickering video monitors and secure phones, and smoked glass windows through which the corridors on either side could dimly be seen.

But what mattered was not money here, not even firepower or governmental security. What mattered was information. All these fine young men with their computer-printed briefings were evidently relying on a twenty-four-hour broadcast news service to make their judgments.

The CIA man got up and, as if to prove this, ran a videotape of the news segment about to come under discussion.

The news reader proclaimed, on the tape, the German pronouncement, and then told the American people more about ORTAG, the German space agency, than any Russian citizen knew.

The video scene shifted as reaction was solicited from foreign press secretaries. First from the British, who were the most anti-German of any people but the Poles, and the most worried about repercussions of reunification; then from the Poles themselves.

Lastly, the tape showed the United States government spokes-woman, who said, "Space is an internationalized zone and, according to the Outer Space Treaty of 1967, outer space cannot be made the territory of any nation. The fiction that a registered space object such as a platform or a satellite can be treated as territory on Earth is clearly invalid. Therefore, the United States refuses to recognize any unilateral claim by any nation to territorial boundaries or limitations in space outside the physical extent of that nation's space construction."

The CIA man, who was impeccable in a dark jacket and tan pants, froze the tape with the spokeswoman's mouth still open. "There we are, gentlemen. You now have all the background we have."

"Surely not all," Shitov said under his breath. This was a matter of overt information, public knowledge. Shitov was only slightly disappointed. He knew, he was beginning to realize, much more about this situation than he at first had suspected. Let the overt collection materials be discussed, and then Shitov's moment would come.

These smart young men discussed legal ramifications of space law at length, until Shitov had drunk three glasses of tea and could ask to use the bathroom. As he expected, Pollock, not the CIA man, took him.

When he was through at his urinal, he said sorrowfully, "Your CIA liaison is afraid of me."

"He's not near your—he's got no parity in rank," Pollock temporized. "We don't know what to make of all this," he added very carefully, "and we were hoping you could help us."

"I shall call Moscow now."

"You bet," Pollock said with a boyish gratitude that Shitov at first didn't understand. But as Pollock led him to a small office with a bulky secure phone and made his connection personally, the American colonel said, "To save time, I'd better tell you now. We think the Germans shot at one of our space assets today, right after their announcement."

"Shot? Asset?" This was the true information, which had been withheld in the more public meeting, although Shitov was not yet sure precisely why.

"Shot: pulsed, we think. How the hell could they do something like that? We're not sure they have that capability. Are you?"

Fishing expedition.

"Now I know the question," said Shitov in his workaday voice, which made Pollock blink and stare. "I will see what I can give you for an answer. But you must leave the room."

"I'm gone," Pollock said with a shrug, and handed him the phone. "I'll be right outside."

Of course the room was bugged. And of course, whether Pollock spoke Russian or not, someone would translate the entire conversation, secure phone or not, later. Shitov harbored no illusions. So he framed his inquiry carefully, and made his request narrow and specific. Still, such a request soon got him to the KGB Chairman himself, who was at first gruff and doubtful, and then gleeful at the opportunities for trading information with the Americans that Shitov promised.

"Do this for me, *Glava*," said the Chairman, "and we will all benefit. If it can be as good for us as you say, I will put it before the Executive President personally."

Now all Shitov had to do was turn an opportunity into a bonanza.

He couldn't wait to get back to the meeting, in which, during his absence, he had no doubt that everything salient had been discussed that could not be discussed with him in attendance.

Let it be so, for now. Things would change. He would make them change. The one glimmer of hope in these dark days of realignment was that the USSR would stumble into the loving embrace of America. Russia's very size and raw materials made her still a worthy ally, and the possibility of an aggressive United Europe worried everyone who could not be a part of it.

And America could not be that.

When the sharp eyes of Leo Beckwith, the Commander in Chief for Space, fixed upon him, Beckwith asked, "Can you shed any light on our problem, *Sekretar* Shitov?"

"If you would like me to talk to your trouble, Admiral, you must define it."

"I thought we'd done that," Beckwith said and his square, tanned face hardened. "Pollock?"

"What are the capabilities of the Germans, in your opinion, to produce an electromagnetic pulse sufficient to destroy electronics in space, aboard fast-moving spacecraft?"

"Ah, fast-moving spacecraft, eh? I hope no condolences are in order. I have permission to talk to you about this." He turned to the CIA and DIA and NSA men, sitting together, trying to seem as alike as peas in a pod. "You officers of my fraternity must promise me that this gift of ours to you will begin a greater cooperation— on this very enterprise. We will work with you, and you with us, as closely as we can, to set a pattern for future work."

The one in the middle, whose name was Ford, said, "I can match that, for my people."

Then the other two chimed in that they could offer assistance as well.

"Then listen, and do not make conclusions yet. We have sold these Germans—openly and in accordance with all rules of commerce, through an American-registered foreign agent—three of what are known as MHDs—"

The one called Ford groaned and rubbed his jaw, smothering a curse and hiding his expression.

Pollock shifted in his seat to glare at Ford.

From all this, it was clear to Shitov that Ford was the technical expert present, at least so far as Soviet technologies were concerned.

"The MHDs are Magneto Hydro Dynamic generators, each capable of generating a gigawatt, as you say, of power," Shitov continued expansively. "Any one is small enough to be carried on a truck, and thus boostable into orbit. Given that the power requirements are the most difficult part of what you are discussing as a hypothetical weapon, then I am saying to you that the Germans certainly have the capability to generate such power in space. They have *our* capability to do so."

Ford said, "Couple that with a few refinements, and you could have a switchable weapon—high-power laser to EMP. Even to high-power microwave. So let's say they can—hypothetically, thanks to *glasnost*—do what we're assuming they did today. What's the point, and who exactly are they? The German government isn't admitting to any aggression."

Ford was asking the question generally, but he had already traded some valuable information back to Shitov: The Americans had the technology to make a switchable weapon from such a power source. Nor was this a slip. Ford looked up at him with disturbingly intense eyes, almost as a suitor might look at a woman.

Pollock said, "We don't have anything except public statements, so far. But maybe *Sekretar* Shitov might want to expand further?"

They were pumping him, and he was letting them. He was trolling for their attention, and they were rising to his bait. It was time to change the game, up the stakes. "What else I have to say is not technical. And I think, given what I know of the American intelligence community and the military, that the rest of the political speculation I could add should be discussed only with your Commander in Chief and one trusted advisor." Shitov clasped his hands in front of him on the table. "Terms, I think, must be better spelled out for this information-sharing, before it goes further."

Beckwith said, "That's it, gentlemen. Ford, you'd better stay. The rest of you, reconvene somewhere else. And tell my ADC to hold everything but a Presidential directive until we come out of here whenever we're damned good and ready."

Shitov was not surprised that the man whom Beckwith had asked to stay was Ford. Dalton Ford's dossier had come across Shitov's desk in the past. On one occasion, an *apparatchik* of Shitov's had worked directly with the dark-haired, lean counterintelligence officer now sheafing his papers on the other side of the table.

Ford would be the right man to hear the KGB's suspicions and confirmations that a new German-Japanese-Italian axis was forming that could threaten both America and Russia as nothing since the Second World War.

But one must go slowly. One must not seem to be telling tall tales, or trying to frighten the Americans unnecessarily.

So when Pollock, the last to leave, had assured Shitov that he would "be waiting to take you to lunch when you're done, *Sekretar*," Shitov leaned forward and said directly to Ford: "So, what is the truth of it, Comrade Ford? Was there human kill? What was this spacecraft? And is it destroyed?"

Ford turned to the admiral. "Sir?"

Beckwith folded his hands in an unconscious imitation of Shitov's posture. Good. This meant that rapport was established with the admiral at least.

Beckwith had a fine movie actor's face with a shock of white hair that made him look avuncular, and he knew it. He leaned toward Shitov confidingly. "*Sekretar,* we're going to ask you to leave your delegation and tell your story in Washington, right beside me in a couple of high-level meetings. Given the proper responses, I can assure you of interagency cooperation such as neither of our countries has ever dared before. But you've got to give something positive to go in with besides the MHDs, which don't, by themselves, make your country look like the best friend we've got."

"And you, Admiral, must tell me if you have a crisis situation that might involve my country in escalating hostilities."

"Ford, how do you want to say this?"

"Sir? Okay. Let's say"—Ford, too, leaned forward and folded his hands—"that we had a test craft with normal EMP hardening—suicide switches—and that we lost half the electronics on that craft, although we recovered the craft intact. So we've got proof that something happened. We think we know what happened. With your help, *Sekretar,* we'll be able to at least postulate how it happened. Now we need ammunition, because it's going to get nasty, behind the scenes. The Germans sure as hell aren't going to admit to doing anything to a spacecraft of ours within twenty-four hours of their proclamation. We're not going to admit that they did either. No reason to support their suspicions that they got past our defenses."

"Your broadcast Mayday did that," Shitov said flatly.

Admiral Beckwith grunted.

Shitov kept his eyes on Ford's face. It was the face of a field man, traced with tiny lines. It was the face of a borzoi, raptly awaiting instructions. Shitov continued. "I was privileged to call Moscow when your Pollock escorted me to the pisser. So I know what you need to cover over. And I am about to tell a story that will remind you of a children's scary tale, and which you will not like believing. You are right to assume that the German government will not admit to having done anything to your X-NASP."

Hearing the designation of the Americans' most beloved secret spacecraft pass Soviet lips, Ford sat back and unclasped his hands.

Beckwith squinted at Shitov and said, "We can't confirm or deny that kind of potshot, Mr. *Sekretar.* I can't talk to you about any specific spacecraft until after we go to Washington."

"So we will go. We will go because of my scary tale—because the German government did not do this thing. They only succumbed to pressure to try floating a legal position. They are not in control of this situation. A faction of theirs, combined with a Japanese faction and an Italian faction, is deeply committed to certain goals. Among these goals is the control of near space. In the Formosa Sea, at their launch platforms under Italian registry, they have been preparing." Shitov shrugged. "Everyone is always preparing. So we have information on them, because we too are always preparing. For the right considerations, even this suddenly very valuable information we will share with you."

"Oh, shit," Ford said, shaking his head imperceptibly.

But Beckwith, a much older, more professional person with years more experience, said, "If this conversation continues to be informative on this level, you can write your own ticket, wherever it doesn't impact the internal security of the United States, I'd be willing to bet."

"I'll take that bet," Ford said.

"And I too will bet alongside Admiral Beckwith. So you see, in more ways than one, our interests are converging."

"How many of those MHDs did you say you'd sold the Germans?" Ford asked.

"I did not say. Enough, Mr. Ford, to consider nonnuclear electromagnetic pulse as a future danger in space from which all of us must be ready to defend ourselves. I must convey my country's congratulations that none of your crew were killed during your space plane's encounter." Again Shitov shrugged. "If we shared more information, think of how many man-hours could be saved, Mr. Ford."

"I'm a slow learner. You say it's not the German government?"

"What government?" Shitov scoffed. "The reunifying coalition of redissolving semi-entities? The Germans say they wish to have a European Germany, not a German Europe. What this tripartite coalition wishes is something entirely different. And since a technological superiority is in the hands of multinationals with a shared objective, we cannot—should not—expect the German government to do any more or less than it needs to survive. As my government does."

"And mine," Beckwith said, standing abruptly. "Let's go see if we can muddy some water in Washington, gentlemen, before somebody jumps to the wrong conclusion. I'm satisfied that we can have the rest of our talk while we're airborne."

And so, Shitov thought, I am off into the belly of the whale. If I emerge from it successful, I will buy Shitova a gold bracelet from Tiffany's to wear to the ballet. Levonov, enjoy your last days. When I return home from America, I will have the Americans in my pocket and your head on my plate.

3

Day 2: Kirtland AFB, New Mexico

Mackenzie hadn't been on the ground at Kirtland ten minutes before he began worrying about the effect of residual radiation on any children he might want to have in some distant future, if he ever got any sleep and got out of this crazy-ass business. This close to White Sands wasn't anyplace you really wanted to be, not if you hadn't settled down yet or even donated to a sperm bank.

But nobody else seemed worried about their nuts out here on the glaring flat that reminded Mackenzie of the northern Sahara or the northern Nevada covert test strip. There were plenty of brains clustered around the crippled X-NASP that had come in under cover of darkness, piggybacked on a NASA 747. As if there were any way to preserve security now that the X-NASP was out of the black bag.

The nerd contingent from NASA's Ames Research Center at Moffett was here in force. There were three NASA planes parked over on an auxiliary runway's apron. The California longhairs and cowboys from those planes were in the middle of what Mackenzie recognized as a turf battle with the honchos from Kirtland's Space Weapons Center and USSPACECOM in Colorado. Standing out in the open sun, the sunstruck lot of them were gesticulating and tapping clipboards and pointing at the black space plane that had caused all the trouble.

They looked like a bunch of Third World gestapo arguing over a dead cow with voodoo signs on it.

Around the plane were parked test vans and trailers from every vested interest, including Los Alamos National Lab and Mackenzie's people: Space Command had sent down its own test team from Falcon to back up Kirtland's claim that the ailing Nomad ought to be torn down right here, where it was based.

And Mackenzie was here to reinforce USSPACECOM's claim to autopsy rights on the X-NASP's dead black boxes. Falcon Air Force Station housed the 2nd Space Wing, and supported DOD manned spaceflight programs. Plus, because it hosted the National Test Facility for the Strategic Defense Initiative, Falcon's 2nd Space Wing pilots flew the officially nonexistent squadron of X-NASPs.

Nonexistent until Cleary and Rowan fucking landed this one in Sri Lanka.

Mackenzie wandered around, sweat cap's visor pulled down low, wishing his polarized aviator glasses would polarize some more, trying to figure out what the hell he could do to help things here. As USSPACECOM's S-3 for Low Intensity Conflict, Terrorism, and Special Operations, Mackenzie wasn't sure his expertise was relevant. He was truly certain that the opinion of a Special Forces major wasn't going to carry much weight among all these high-ranking gourmet troubleshooters.

Exactly what low-intensity-conflict angle USSPACECOM saw here hadn't been explained to Mackenzie. All Conard, the Army Space Command intelligence officer, had said was, "Find some. Since the Nomad was subject to attack, we need to know whether it was meant as harassment or an attempt to destroy."

Conard was a light colonel with an Army-first attitude, and an abrasive by-the-book bastard to boot. So somewhere in the book it must say that Mackenzie's job description had to be represented here.

What good he was going to do among all these senior scientists and four-stars, he couldn't imagine.

Plus he was wrung out, dead tired, and just coming off an actual emergency, the type with lives on the line and men on the ground, that he'd been supporting in person, halfway around the world, the way he was paid to do.

The crippled Nomad had had to be flown in from even farther, or all this would have been squared away before Mackenzie got to this particularly hot chunk of desert. Not that Mackenzie minded desert. He just minded like hell being where he was superfluous when he'd been jerked out of something not, to his way of thinking, finished enough. He might still be needed to make sure that his payback team on the ground in Tunisia got *off* the ground in good order. . . .

"Sorry," he muttered, having managed to bump into somebody because he was looking down, into the cool of his own shadow, rather than where he was going. It took a real artist to collide with another human being in the middle of nowhere, but if you were as tired as Mackenzie . . . "Sorry."

"It's okay. I was hoping to run into you while we were both here." The voice was deep, amused—and female.

Mackenzie looked up at last, despite the sun's glare.

"You were?" he asked lamely, jamming his hands into his back pockets. Even in the punishing light, what he could see looked good. Tall, slim, in tan coveralls that hugged a tiny waist, she had broad shoulders, dark straight hair in a ponytail, and a tan that reached all the way to the sunglasses hiding her eyes.

Civilian clothes meant she was some kind of science type. Science types—especially attractive female ones—didn't usually seek him out. For a minute he thought wildly, what if she's press?

But then, she couldn't be. Not here, where security had determined the landing site. "You're Major J. H. Mackenzie, right?"

"James Harry, yeah. And you're . . . ?"

"Pettit, from DARPA. We've been corresponding a little lately. . . ."

Christ, one of the Witches of DARPA: the legendary, punishingly intellectual female contingent from the Defense Advanced Research Projects Agency who now were overseeing or "dual-tracking" the research technologies supporting SO/LIC (Special Operations/Low Intensity Conflict)—which meant that guys like Mackenzie were at their mercy.

Mackenzie took a step backward. His mouth got gummy and he nearly yawned as his body went from semi-rest state to combat readiness. You bet he'd been corresponding with this bitch, trying to convince her that he needed some special hardware he couldn't have unless her office agreed it would "significantly improve the performance" of his organization's piece of the low-intensity-conflict, special-operations, drug-interdiction pie.

"Yeah, I guess I owe you a letter, Ms. Pettit."

"Never mind that now." She came the step forward that he'd moved back, and indicated the Nomad with a flick of her ponytail. "What do you think?"

"I think . . . I have to get a closer look." Mackenzie wasn't great at this particular sort of low-intensity conflict. "We'd like to keep it here and tear it down ourselves. I'm just here to say that to whoever'll listen."

"I'll listen. I need to sit down with you anyway."

Oh, man. This was weird. This woman had been giving him more trouble than an apartment house full of Muslim commandos. "My boss is right over—"

"Let's go look inside the corpse. We can talk there."

Mackenzie wanted to find Conard. Conard deserved this woman. But Conard was still huddling with the rest of the brass. "Seen Cleary?" he asked, resigned to following the DARPA woman's lead. "Or Rowan? I haven't since I got here."

"In the green trailer. Debrief. I've got to talk to them too. Get some subjective take on what they thought."

He almost asked her if she were cleared for that; but of course she must be, the way she was acting.

Up the ramp and into the plane she led him, as if this X-NASP were her personal property, helloing the techs working there by name.

This testbed wasn't much different from any other X-NASP—except this one had a lot of its guts hanging out.

Pettit, stepping over snaky utility light cables, sat at the copilot's station, and gestured to the other seat. When he didn't move, she took off her sunglasses. "Quit staring at me, Major Mackenzie."

She had this eagerness on her face he couldn't understand. And her eyes were as sharp as the claws he knew she had.

"Sorry. I don't know what we're doing in here."

"I want to make you a proposition."

Why not. He sat in the other seat. "Okay, ma'am."

"Joanna. Since you're here in New Mexico, why don't we get permission for you to stay an extra day? We've got something at the Lab I'd like your opinion on—something right up your alley."

"I'm still tailing out an oper—" He stopped. He looked away from her, to see if anybody was within earshot. There wasn't anybody else. But he shouldn't have said even that much.

"I know," she said. "They were serving lemon sorbet at nine o'clock last night, between courses to clear our palates, and all I could think of was what those guys were eating, out there, in the middle of that—situation. I thought it was finished. Heard it went perfectly."

"The objective, yeah; we got that. But it's not done for me until everybody and every piece of equipment's home."

"I know that." He couldn't tell if she were defensive or angry. But she was really built, for a DARPA witch and one of his most concerted pains in the ass stateside.

He tried to keep his eyes on her face. "I'm not saying you don't know. I'm just saying I don't make my own decisions about where I'm supposed to be." He couldn't seem to make anything he said sound friendly.

"I'll buy dinner. Don't worry about permission. I need to have you here. Who's here that I should talk to?"

"Conard, the Army intel light colonel. And I'll buy dinner, Ms. Pettit—Joanna—if you clear it for me to stay." He'd better not rebuff this, especially when he didn't know what "this" was. If he could make peace with her, everybody would be winning.

"Fine. Deal." She shook hands with him, more firmly than anybody not trying to prove something needed to do. "Meet me at the green trailer in ten minutes. I want you to introduce me to Cleary and Rowan."

And she was gone. Mackenzie leaned back in the pilot's contoured seat and realized he still had his dark glasses on. He took them off and rubbed his eyes. Well, here was something he could do, anyway, to justify this junket.

You had to meet the enemy head-on in life, if you couldn't sneak up on them. He began wondering if she'd snuck up on *him*, and was still wondering when she met him in front of the debrief trailer, all smiles.

Joanna Pettit, civilian DARPA employee, was really a fine-looking animal, and if his mind weren't sending him such conflicting signals, he'd have been figuring how he could see the rest of her, every inch the cinched coverall was hiding. But this was one dangerous woman, dangerous to his performance and the performance of any special operations team anywhere that depended on the equipment whose procurement had to be routed through her office.

He said, "So what did Conard say?"

"He said okay," she replied with another toss of her head that made her ponytail furl. "But he wants to debrief Cleary and Rowan privately, so we can't talk to them yet."

" 'We'?"

"Me in my official capacity. So you and I can leave now, according to your Lieutenant Colonel Conard—go down to the Lab and get started. You'll both be staying the night, and he'll want to tell you where to meet him tomorrow."

So "we" was the whole of DARPA. My, my. The government—at least Mackenzie's part of it—was going to have a rough ride adjusting to civilian females in high positions. He grinned and she demanded, "What's funny?"

"Nothing." At least nothing that he could tell her. There were positions and positions. "I'll go get my orders. Where will you be?"

"The black Porsche over there behind the flight line—it's dirty, but it gets me where I want to go."

He realized that some of her bravado was awkwardness, but she couldn't feel any more awkward about this than he did. Porsche. Shit.

He had to salute a lot of brass before he could zero in on Conard. "Sir, did that woman talk to you?" He put his hands in his back pockets and ducked his head a little to go eye-to-eye with Conard above his sunglasses.

Conard took Mackenzie by the arm, walking him off a little way from the main-event huddle. "Mackenzie, you go with that DARPA woman. She's from the Tactical Technical Office. You give her whatever she wants until I come to get you in the morning. Leave your whereabouts with the Lab service."

"Colonel Conard, I thought I had a job to do here—one important enough that I had to leave an ongoing—"

"Whatever she wants, Major Mackenzie; that's an order. You and I know what's happening here. This is going to take longer than we thought." Conard, fairer than Mackenzie, was getting one mother of a sunburn out here.

Good. "But we're keeping the plane, sir? You don't need me to talk to anybody?"

"Not now, Mackenzie."

"What about—" Mackenzie stopped. No good arguing. "Sir, do you know what she wants to talk to me about?"

"New equipment. Something they want you to like. If you like it, something they want you to test, or at least help them test. That's all I know, but I'm sure no one's wasting your time, Major." Conard's cynical, warning comment hung in the air between them.

Mackenzie saluted his way out of there. He hated this part of his job. Nobody seemed to care about his special op except Joanna Pettit, and she cared that it had ruined the taste of her sherbet.

How come she knew about an operation in progress anyway? Mackenzie had been in the field long enough to realize he'd better not discount Pettit because she was a woman—not in any particular.

When he got to the black Porsche, which was dirty and a couple years old, she was inside, and the air wafted coolness out of it as she opened his door for him.

"Okay?" she asked.

"Okay," he said, feeling as if he were dreaming. "We can make it breakfast, instead of dinner, so far as Conard's concerned."

"Great. You're going to love this, I promise."

"Could be," he said, settling his head against the leather highback so that he could watch her breasts as she wheeled the little car over the desert sand.

"Major, you'll need more leg room. To push your seat back, reach down and to your right and you'll find control wheels."

When he didn't follow her crisp instructions, she reached one-handed over his lap to show his fingers what to do. And for an instant, her upper torso was lying on his thighs. All his systems reacted. He folded his hands in his lap as soon as she'd straightened up.

Maybe it was a good idea, all this, but maybe his reactions weren't. He was from the "kill it or fuck it school" of special operations, and he wasn't sure doing either to Joanna Pettit was a flamingly great idea.

And she was bossy. "Put on your belt. Physics are different for Porsches, but not that different."

The speed she made on the open road, once they found their way off the base, had to be designed to test his nerve. But he didn't care if she crashed him in a car, as long as she killed him instead of maiming him.

He said that.

She looked at him out of the corner of one eye. "Are you always like this?"

"Only when I have men on the ground and I'm not with them."

"That car phone's secure. Be my guest."

You bet it was. This woman had a cellular Secure Telephone Unit and a carte-blanche mentality. Once he'd called in and asked careful questions that wouldn't tell her anything, he began to relax and wonder whether she'd had an AIDS vaccination. Maybe he'd get lucky.

"Everything's okay with your people, Major?"

"Yep."

"Would you like to talk over what we've been corresponding about?"

"Nope. I made my case. The rest is up to your people."

"Our 'people' need to know that what you're asking for will perform creditably into the next century."

"Those laser rifles are good enough for the Marines. They're user-friendly weapons with multiple antipersonnel, antimatériel applications. The Brits are selling them openly to anybody with cash—anybody. We're going to come up short against them if you won't—"

"We're looking at laser rounds for conventional firearms instead," she said in a tight voice.

Exasperated, he looked out the window. You couldn't face tits like that and argue for a weapons procurement. "I made my request. I want them—and not optical radiators for regular rifles or super-acid rounds for forty-millimeter guns—in case we have a space-control application. In any space combat, the current mission definition says we've got to 'provide freedom of action for friendly forces' "—he closed his eyes to recite the rest but still saw her breasts—" 'while, when directed, denying it to the enemy.' These days, that could include hostilities in near-space and I want something on hand for pilots like Cleary, something that won't violate the integrity of pressurized modules."

"You don't need that yet."

DARPA witch. Despite the air-conditioning, he was beginning to sweat. "If I had them now, we could use them in very special cases on the ground, for this or that Delta or Team Whatever operation that USSPACECOM's supporting or advising techni-cally. For certain applications, like blinding enemy optics, I can do it easier and cheaper with a hand-held weapon than I can with space-based resources. So it saves the government money if we hand out the occasional cheap rifle instead of needing to do complicated, expensive—and revealing—things with satellites." How much simpler could he make this?

"I still don't see it. We gave you all that expensive, complicated equipment for a reason. We need to see how it works and when it doesn't. If you don't use it, we don't find out."

His body wanted to convince her physically to do what he wanted—anything he wanted. He looked back at her, and saw the speedometer of the little car was in three figures.

"If you know as much as you imply," he said carefully, "you know the sort of thing I get called in to do. You know that sometimes I'm on the ground with these folks. If you know that, you ought to know I wouldn't ask for anything—nothing extra to hump—that somebody in my position, with his ass on the line, might not really need."

Then he stared at the ceiling, just breathing. There was nothing else he could say—at least, nothing that he *should* say.

Pettit didn't want to talk anymore either. She put in a tape, and he must have gone to sleep.

He dreamed about trying to get her out of a half-bombed-out building in West Beirut, but he needed a laser rifle to do it, and she hadn't signed off on the paperwork. He got her, in the end, but she was dead in his arms, and stinking of roast flesh and feces because the Muslims had used the old hot-poker-up-the-rectum trick to see what she'd tell them.

He was carrying her body down the stairs, wondering where the rest of his team was, when some terrorist jumped out of the stairwell shadows and grabbed him by the arm.

He awoke to a startled cry, with his hand crushing hers—which was on his left arm. He was sweating and his breath was coming in short, harsh gulps. He let her go right away. "You startled me."

She was rubbing her wrist, her eyes wide above her hand. "I can see that."

He couldn't see much else. It was dark and they were sitting in front of a big, squat building sparkling with lights. "Let's go check in and then we'll get dinner."

"Ms. Pettit, I thought you wanted to show me—"

But she was out of the car. It was a Los Alamos National Lab facility, all right. She signed them in and went somewhere while he waited, looking at boring magazines. When she came back, she was radiant with pleasure, smiling widely. "They'll be ready for us as soon as we've eaten."

Checking back out, she told the desk that they'd be eating at her motel. It sounded provocative to his ears.

During dinner, she told him what she had. "An exoskeletal powered suit that'll take numerous weapons platforms, has four hours of power and life support, and is com-capable beyond anything you've ever seen."

He'd heard rumors, of course. There were plenty of rumors. "Oh, yeah?" he said. "You've got it there?"

Despite himself, he was flattered to be brought in on this. He had a good reputation, but so did lots of other guys who'd led A-Teams. Of course, he was the only techno-commando around with a Space Command slot.

"Only for use in the lab, so far. And something else: virtual prototyping. That's what I want your reaction on."

"Virtual what?"

"Simulations. Very special simulations. Almost like an aircraft simulator. I'm really glad we ran into each other, Major Mackenzie."

"Mac's fine." No need to get too personal.

"All right, Mac. I need somebody to take this the rest of the way, all the way to field test. We'd have to borrow you for a week at a time for some temporary duty. But we really like this project. NASA likes it too. All we need is the input of someone with the experience to know what a man who's got to use it will need."

"Maybe I'm your boy," he said softly. She was beautiful in the dim light of the dining room, but he didn't care about that anymore. Or at least he told himself he didn't, blinking away visions of X-rated temporary duty.

The simulation, or whatever it was, could be not only a career-builder, but a lifesaver. Or it could be the worst boondoggle since the Stealth bomber.

An hour later, Mackenzie was looking at the most daunting array of electronics and hardware he'd ever have the clearance to view.

He said, in a low voice he reserved for life-and-death decisions, "You people've got to be crazy. Nobody'd weigh themselves down like that. It's too heavy. You couldn't jump with it—"

And then stopped himself. NASA was involved. This thing, which looked from the outside like Robbie the Robot, was basically for space applications. And for twenty-first-century special forces applications like the one in his dream: when you weren't going to live through the projected mission, without exoskeletal armor.

He forgot all about Witch Pettit, for a time, and about the lab and the cachet attached to being here, and everything else.

He just kept running his hands over that huge thing, shaped like a man but badder, and wondering what it would be like to be inside it.

4

Day 2: The Pentagon, Washington

The surreal circumstance of squiring a KGB colonel through the Pentagon's halls, while at the same time sorting possible responses to the X-NASP incident "on the fly," made Beckwith dizzy when he thought about it.

So he tried not to think about it. That was easy when you were in landmark meetings with a Russian in tow. It was harder between those meetings. Shitov was soaking up information like a sponge. The USSR was really getting its rubles' worth out of this KGB man's trip here.

Shitov caught Beckwith looking at him and said, "My friend, do not be worried. We will convince your superiors that whatever we must do will be worth the price."

"*Sekretar,* I wish you wouldn't read my mind."

"If you would call me Al, I will like it. And see my point: Both governments are much alike at the moment, yours and mine. When my country gives you the supporting information on the New Axis power bloc we know is forming, your representatives will be roused to sympathy, and sympathy will lead to action."

"Is that what you people call this—group? The New Axis?" Shitov had this way of dropping his most explosive bombshells in urinals and hallways and in the back of speeding limos. Spooks were spooks, the world over, Beckwith supposed. But it made things more difficult when you never knew if the canny Slav had another rocket left in his pocket.

"We are calling them that—in Russian, of course—in Dzherzhinsky Square, but not in the new KGB building. It depends on who is talking—how old is the officer doing the assessment, how much fear he has of saying something . . . unhealthy for his career. But we are calling this the German, Japanese, Italian coalition: Gee-Jay-Eye, everywhere we speak of it. Which, of course, has been until now only among ourselves. And that only after we had sold these MHDs and began finding out what it was they were going to do with them."

Beckwith's eyes squeezed shut of their own accord. He forced them open. "This isn't going to play well in some of our . . . penny-pinching Washington quarters, Al." Calling a KGB colonel by a diminutive chosen to sound familiar to an American ear wasn't an act without its own implications. Shitov was a master player.

Beckwith hoped his own expertise in this kind of game was up to it. At the CIA, they hadn't been certain it was. But Shitov had fallen into Beckwith's lap, and now Beckwith was going to play horsie. "If you're right, *Al,* and not just fielding some ploy to expand your own power base in space at our expense, then we've got to convince our people and yours to support aggressive countermoves."

Beckwith was acutely aware that, a discreet ten paces behind, their trailing entourage (a veritable herd that included NSA, CIA, DIA, and a dozen more representatives from lower-profile acronymic organizations that made up the Intelligence Community) had fallen silent and was listening as hard as it could.

Good. Beckwith wanted witnesses to every word that came out of Shitov's mouth.

"When you say 'we,' if you mean cooperatively with my country, then of course I cannot commit beyond my own mandate. But we can certainly ask at our highest levels, if your highest levels wish to ask."

Beckwith began to perspire.

They reached the end of the corridor, and his ADC darted forward to open the door that led into the secure sanctum of The Tank, where the Joint Chiefs were waiting to take Shitov's historic deposition and, if things went badly, Beckwith's scalp.

Beckwith believed the Russian. Whether anyone else would was now out of his hands for the moment.

The flags in the room were all hung with battle standards. Some of the men around the long oval table had fought in some of those wars, but none had fought in all of them.

A long tradition meant a great deal of inertial respect for tradition. The challenge that Leo Beckwith had seen in the U.S. Space Command was that he was making new traditions, for a future whose safeguarding would be a task vastly different from anything that had gone before.

So when the pleasantries were over and the Chairman of the Joint Chiefs rubbed his dark hand over his face and asked Leo to summarize the purpose of this landmark meeting for the record, Beckwith was ready.

"Chairman, sirs. It is the opinion of the United States Space Command that we are facing a situation without precedent, that could easily escalate into full-scale hostilities in space. I have brought Colonel Aleksandr Shitov, of KGB's First Chief Directorate, to testify supporting the following conclusions and recommendations:

"First, that one of our experimental single-stage-to-orbit spacecraft, a Nomad, was fired upon with a non nuclear electromagnetic pulse generator in near-space *while the German ORTAG space agency publicly announced its intention to defend a thousand-mile territorial limit around its assets in space.* Secretary Shitov will discuss the technical feasibility of this with you at length.

"Second, subsequent to this event, we recovered the plane and have evidence to support our thesis. That thesis is as follows: De facto control of space is already in the hands of whoever fired that weapon, unless we have the will and ability to counter covert aggression. Debate about space territoriality and legality may be a smoke screen and delaying tactic that will allow this group to consolidate its power."

Looking from chief to chief, Beckwith counted one scowl, one frown, and two deadpan expressions. Aides scribbled notes and two passed them to their chiefs. The SOCOM representative met Leo's eyes briefly and steadily, then looked away.

Beckwith continued: "My recommendations are as follows. The U.S. must consider this shoot as an unprovoked attack, announce it publicly, and demand a meeting of the UN Security Council, having first assured ourselves of Soviet support and concurrence. Simultaneously, once you've satisfied yourselves that Secretary Shitov has valuable information, I would like to ask that this foreign intelligence official be allowed to address interested members of the National Security Council.

"If, as Secretary Shitov says, the U.S. and Soviets can together demand reparations and an apology—as well as immediate disarmament of whatever manned platforms are in space under German registry—from the German government *alone,* we may be able to break this multinational coalition apart before it becomes too strong to do so without overt and massive confrontation.

We should demand cessation of attempts to enforce territorial boundaries in space, and support those demands with a Space Control mission or series of missions, which my service is ready and able to mount."

One of the men across from Beckwith muttered something, maybe a groan, maybe a grunt of assent. Beckwith couldn't tell who, or what the noise meant.

He plunged on determinedly, mouth suddenly dry and his pulse as loud in his ears as his words, reciting exactly what he knew he must say, though it felt to him almost as though someone else was speaking: "An initial covert mission is ready for your consideration now, and implementable in stages when and if the need arises." Beckwith took a deep breath. "If there are no questions, I'd like to turn the floor over to Secretary Shitov."

The Chairman looked long and hard at Beckwith before he said in a velvety baritone, "I should have known you'd come in here guns blazing, Leo. Okay, gentlemen, I know we've all got questions, but let's hear what Colonel Shitov has to say first."

And they were rolling. Beckwith reached into his pocket and got out a clean, starched handkerchief as Aleksandr Shitov rose to address the American Joint Chiefs of Staff.

5

Day 3: Tokyo

Osawa was a happy man. So happy that he was feeling expansive. He would take Rutger Schliemann out on the town in a celebration that the huge, pale German would never forget.

Osawa was worldly. He knew of the perversions these Germans found delectable. But in Japan, women were . . . still women.

Osawa's white stretch Mercedes was custom-built. It had every creature comfort. In it, he picked up the German, who ran his sausagelike fingers through straight, taffy-colored hair after ducking into the car.

Schliemann said, "Ah, I see you have the best taste in automobilia, Osawa-san."

Osawa despised this condescending German pig, but this pig was the pig of all their dreams. "We are after only the best, from all over the world—and beyond it," Osawa purred. "Together, our enterprise will command the finest of everything and put it to the best use. What news from your country?"

Its doors closed, the Mercedes accelerated smoothly, bearing them into the night. Reservations had been made at a very special place for tonight. Tonight was not a night for factionalism. Osawa struggled with his own feelings of revulsion, of superiority, of disdain. These Germans always smelled of garlic and onions; it got in their sweat, and they stank from meat and sausage and spices too alien to ever be forgiven by a Japanese nose.

So that would make this evening all the more delectable.

Rutger Schliemann said, "Thus far, the uproar is as we hoped. There is much stamping of legal feet. The Americans and the other mongrels are worried. The Canadians chatter at each other

in two languages, but at no one else. The Italians are holding firm
alongside us—as we knew they would."

"As they must," Osawa said. These Germans were proud of
their racial purity, but they overstated it. They had been overrun
too many times by too many foreigners. They were flawed. This
one had green eyes. And the Italians—that was even a sorri-
er race.

"As we assured you they would, Osawa-san. We know our
dago friends well."

"Well enough, let's hope," Osawa murmured. Only the Japanese
had the purity of blood that ensured clarity of vision, strong purpose, and unified action. Japan would industrialize space and make
Mars its own while these huge, smelly people were stumbling over
each others' silly prejudices and trying to pretend that they could
cooperate. Only Japan had the will, the concentration, and the
Five Hundred Year Plan.

"Don't worry about the Italians, Osawa-san," Schliemann
assured him too confidently. "They love complaining loudly
and beating their breasts."

"Good," Osawa said. "As long as there is open debate, and
legal process, we are adhering to our timetable. And about your
government's *internal* soul-searching?"

"There is confusion. There is discomfort." Schliemann again
raked his lank, greasy hair back from a high forehead—a habitual
gesture. "But our men are well paid and well placed. It is a matter
of due process in our governmental organs. ORTAG has said what
we wished it to say. We are now releasing the first block of funds
to them. With those funds, three more of the manned free-flying
platforms will be assembled, and one additional MHD component
will launch this evening, on schedule."

"We should have the MHD component here, for our engineers
to copy," said Osawa uneasily. On this, the Germans had not
been fully cooperative. They knew their power resided in their
ability to acquire the Soviet MHDs, as the Japanese had not, for
some reason, been able to do. Osawa suspected that the Germans'
exclusive contract with the Soviets contained an exclusionary
clause that forbade the Germans to further transfer the Soviet
technology to Japan.

"We have been through this. We cannot alter our agreement—
the technology resides with us. You understand, Osawa, that this
is to everyone's benefit." The German frowned at him.

When asked, Osawa's German co-venturers had said only that
they could not transfer the technology to Japan because the Soviets

had sold working units while maintaining proprietary rights. And the Germans were afraid of the Soviets, still. Privately, Osawa thought that the Germans were more afraid of the Japanese, and were holding the MHD technology hostage to assure Japanese cooperation.

"I understand. And tonight is a night for celebrating. Soon we will be able to do whatever we please in space—including take apart one of the MHDs—when we can afford to waste one. But now, this night, I have a special treat for you."

Outside the window, neon streamed by. "What kind of treat, Osawa-san?" The German was uneasy. Sometimes Japanese entertainments, such as Japanese men enjoyed, were too confrontational for outsiders.

"We are going to a special club, with special women, who do special things. You do like women, I recall," said Osawa in a smooth and only slightly teasing voice. This German liked anything that he could wrestle to a standstill, including large animals.

But never had Schliemann seen what Osawa was about to show him. When the Mercedes reached the club, Osawa said, "After you, friend. The name of this place translates, roughly, to the 'Golden Palace of Sexual Harassment.' I am sure you are going to like it."

The German turned his huge head. "As long as I'm not the subject of the harassment."

This German had been long climbing the social ladder in the Orient. Osawa briefly regretted some of the things that he and his cohorts had done to Schliemann in the past to test the man's mettle and his loyalty.

"No, no, Schliemann. This is a man's world, and the women within are all mongrel women: Japanese-Western mixes, and Thai women, and Chinese women, and Mongolian women. You know as well as I that such women have tiny wombs and that their slits are sideways. Come, I will show you."

Up the stairs where neon rolled like waves they went, and there was much obligatory bowing and scraping when Osawa presented himself. His compartment was ready, he was assured. Once they were led beyond rice-paper screens and facing the most delectable of sights, the German stopped in his tracks.

"It's an office! We're—I mean, have we made a—have I mis . . . ?"

Once Schliemann subsided, Osawa took the fore. "Indeed, it is an office." The huge dolt could not smell the food, and the oils, and the tang of fresh sex on the air? Probably not. Germans had terrible noses, for all their size.

"Come and let us find some secretaries." Down they walked, onto a floor full of cubicles and small offices in which young women labored. Some sat before computers. Some made coffee. Some wore dictation headphones. Some were doing filing. All had short skirts and pert breasts.

Osawa led off briskly. He knew where he was going. He customarily used a corner office. It was more expensive, but better. "You can work all night here too," he called back to the German. "We can keep tabs on our project as we enjoy ourselves."

As he moved among the secretaries and assistants, he looked for new ones, ones he had not used before. He saw a man bend down over a desk and touch a woman on the shoulder. She picked up her notepad and followed him. Too bad. She had a nice ass.

"Keep an eye on their office numbers, Rutger," Osawa advised. Already, his pants were full.

When he reached the corner office, which he had rented for the evening at great expense, he thrust open the door to it triumphantly. "Regard!" he told the German behind him, who was flushed now, with bloodshot eyes that seemed uncomprehending.

"Come right in. Look around."

First was the anteroom, with a receptionist typing and a black leather couch. She looked up at him, bowed, smiled, and scurried to open the inner door. Rutger was following uncertainly.

"Look here, Osawa, I'm still not—"

"Fax. Phone. Desk. Conference table." Osawa was muttering. "Good. Very good." He put down his things. "Now we need staff." He smiled, taking pity on the floundering German.

"Watch." Osawa sat behind the desk and punched a button, bringing up a headline service on the computer. "Good. All is peaceful. Now we will find our staff and get to work."

Up, and out, and prowling among the women. When he found one typing assiduously into a word processor, he reached down over her shoulder and squeezed her left nipple, hard.

She kept typing, head down. He heard Rutger come up behind him, still asking what was going on.

Osawa reached down and cupped the woman's whole breast. She made a typing error. With his other hand, he reached over farther, and pulled up her skirt. Beneath the skirt, she wore garters and stockings.

He said, "Fix that error in your typing," as his hand opened her. Her typing slowed. Her chest began to rise and fall as he twiddled her clitoris. Around, other women were giggling.

He let go of her breast and smoothed down her skirt, twirling her chair around. She was eye-to-eye with his zipper.

She reached to unzip him, but he slapped her across the face. "Don't be greedy," he told her, and pushed her head against his zipped fly, where she gnawed gently at the fabric of his pants.

Grabbing her by the hair, he raised her up. "Here, Rutger, I've got a typist for you," he said, and pushed her at the German.

Then he walked down the corridor, pointing at two women he'd never seen before and telling them, "Get into my office. Bring tea, and saki."

Then, at a closed door, he pushed it open, conscious that Rutger was behind him, his "typist" in tow. Here was an executive secretary, very expensively attired, with an assistant of her own. "Come into my office," he told her.

But when that one got up tardily, he said, "I have changed my mind." The woman blinked in distress, and said, "Please . . ."

"All right. Order food and we'll see."

He came out of that room and said, "Rutger, are you getting the idea?"

Rutger was nearly panting.

Wandering back through the women at their work stations, Osawa saw Rutger stop before one of them, spin the woman out of her chair, and expose himself to her.

Germans were irremediably crude.

But that was nice, tonight. Before Osawa went inside his office to await his staff, he spied an additional girl, who was filing. He walked up behind her.

He touched her cheek with a finger. She stiffened.

He pressed himself against her buttocks. She fussed with her files.

He lifted her skirt over her ass, in front of all the other women. This variation was purely thanks to the German's crudity. Because he was enjoying himself, he called out, "Rutger, do not ruin your long night too early."

He slipped his hand up the buttocks of the file clerk, and slid it between her legs, rubbing until her hips began to move to the rhythm he dictated.

Then he pulled down her hose in a swift, rough movement, so that it caught her around the knees.

She had stopped pretending to file. She was hugging the cabinet now. His masterly touch had made her so hot she was rubbing her clitoris against the corner of the cabinet.

He massaged her buttocks some more, and when he touched her pubic hair, it was soaking wet.

He giggled to himself, and put his knee between her legs. She rubbed herself along his knee, fucking herself on it, until he stopped her.

This one, when he turned her, hugged his waist and dropped to her knees in a submissive posture, her thighs spread around one of his legs, so he let her suck on him awhile before he brought her up and fucked her on his hand, disdainfully, while she writhed and cried out and bit at her own breasts for all her girlfriends to see.

He left her unsatisfied, and she sank to the floor.

He was ready for his main course.

In his office, his staff was assembled. The executive assistant wore an expensive cream-colored suit.

He went right to her and said, "You are pretty today," and, standing eye to eye, started unbuttoning her blouse.

When he heard Rutger come in, he had the executive assistant's breasts exposed.

"Take your skirt off, roll your hose down to your ankles, and sit on the conference table," he told her.

"Rutger, would you mind attending to the conference while I check the computer?"

Now he was burning to get a woman's lips on him. He sat in his chair, behind his desk, and called one of the typists to kneel before him. She buried her head in his lap and he allowed her to nuzzle his cock. "You," he told the next one. "Bring me tea."

When she did, he reached up under her skirt and grabbed her by the hair, pulling her crotch to his face for a moment before he put his fingers in her.

When he looked up, the big German had dropped his pants and was trying to enter the asshole of the executive assistant, who was crouched on the conference table, presenting her buttocks to him with her head down and her groans muffled.

The sight of the big German reaming the once-proud executive assistant nearly made Osawa lose control. He took his hands from the tea-server and put them in the hair of the woman between his legs.

"Now you may unzip my pants," he told her, and as her mouth made contact with his penis, he reached back up with both hands to grab the tea-server's tits and pull one toward his mouth.

When the final explosion came, he barely remembered to jam the choking secretary's mouth down to his root, he was having such a good time watching the crude and clumsy, but giant,

German tearing the executive assistant apart. Who would have thought that the German could draw blood from the woman's ass.

The tea-server's muted, pathetic little cries of unsatisfied passion as she fucked herself on his arm were almost drowned out by the executive assistant's screams.

Osawa vowed to bring his German friend along more often. He'd finally found a use for the big, clumsy man with the giant penis.

As his passion receded, he realized that the executive assistant wasn't moving, or screaming anymore, and that the phone was ringing.

He didn't bother to zip his pants. The tea-server handed him the phone.

The call was from a cohort, saying that they all must meet in Berlin right away.

"Why?" Osawa asked the agitated Italian.

"Because, you fool, the UN Security Council has called an emergency session to discuss . . . things. So we must discuss them too."

"Do not panic," Osawa said sternly. "Rutger and I will take my jet. We will be there before you are."

Hanging up the phone, he shooed the women out. If Rutger had truly damaged the executive assistant whore, things might get complicated on so tight a time frame. He went to look, arranging himself.

At least the woman was conscious.

And Rutger was already headed for the executive washroom. He had heard Osawa's end of the phone call. His stream of curses proved it.

Osawa left generous tips all around. If the German had been so violent with the executive assistant that Osawa was not welcomed back, the German would suffer.

But right now, they must get to Berlin. Only Osawa had the vision to keep the coalition on track if members started panicking.

He called his pilot and told him to file a flight plan. He must be in Berlin, holding the hands of his compatriots, as soon as possible. Emergency session of the UN Security Council!

If the German ORTAG conspirators panicked, or if their jobs were suddenly at risk because others panicked, Osawa could lose everything. It was too early for such a session. This was not as he'd planned.

He must find a way to regain the advantage, to set the tempo of events. He must make sure that the Germans dared not back down from their position.

"Hurry, Rutger. You can beautify yourself on the way!"

6

Day 3: Washington

Captain Jefferson "Sonny" Cleary was getting as drunk as humanly possible, in a Washington hotel bar across from the ABC television studios. He kept trying not to be angry about the way the Congressional committee had treated him this morning.

But he wasn't succeeding. Even in closed session, you couldn't tell folks what they couldn't understand. So Cleary had been left trying to explain that the flashlight he was holding up—the first one, which would never work again because it had had batteries in it when the Nomad was pulsed—was clear, low-tech proof that it wasn't his fault that the Nomad had nearly crashed.

Nobody on that committee of fat, pasty politicians seemed to be able to understand that if there was something fatally wrong with the X-NASP, somebody like Cleary, whose life hung in the balance, would be more than happy to tell them the truth.

In fact, more than one of his nation's elected officials had insinuated that Cleary would lie to them—under oath yet. As if he could afford a perjury trial on his salary. Or had some kind of goddamned death wish.

The only wish he had was that when this was over, he and X-NASP could both get themselves back in the air and off the grounded list.

He'd tried to tell them that. So had Rowan, who as copilot sure as hell didn't have anything to lose by telling the truth.

But you couldn't convince a bunch of technophobes looking for a scapegoat that you weren't one. And Space Command didn't want Cleary talking about hypotheses. So, although he could theorize that the Nomad had encountered an overwhelming

46

electromagnetic pulse, he'd been encouraged not to "speculate for the record" about how come that pulse had happened to bathe him, his copilot, and their testbed with all that crippling power.

Now that the first day of hearings was over, Cleary was morosely drinking himself into what he hoped and prayed would become a stupor. Maybe he could get drunk enough to forget that he was grounded until the mystery around the Nomad mishap was solved and he was absolved. Fat fucking chance. You couldn't get that drunk.

Those Congressmen were after his scalp. He'd finally lost his temper when Norden, the head of the special Congressional inquisition, asked him, "Captain Cleary, are you expecting us to believe your assertion that there was no human error on anyone's part— not in development, construction, or operation of this spacecraft— in the face of the fact that you and your copilot nearly lost your lives, as well as a billion dollars worth of government equipment during a routine test?"

"Yes, sir," Cleary had said quietly into the mike before him.

"Because"—Congressman Norden had smiled like a crocodile—"if you are, I'm afraid you're not making your point very well by holding up a two-dollar flashlight—or, if it's government issue, perhaps I should say a two-thousand-dollar flashlight. Would you explain to us—this time in English—why you and your spacecraft weren't prepared to handle this contingency?"

"Because," he'd said (and now he wished like hell he could turn back time and unsay it), "it wasn't a normal contingency." He'd felt like a puppet, as if somebody else was working his controls. "You don't prepare for abnormal contingencies like repeated pulses in the gigawatt range. It's not like sunspots. It's got to be done *to* you. And as far as 'routine test.' Sir, people like me are paid less than you-all spend on mass mailings every year to strap our butts to testbeds that—by definition—can kill us every time we take them up. There's no such thing as a 'routine test' of an experimental vehicle. I kind of thought folks realized that when Challenger blew up years ago."

By then Walsh was kicking him under the table. And he knew he should shut up. But he was trying to talk himself out of the mess he'd talked himself into.

He should have known better. Congressmen couldn't fly testbeds and test pilots couldn't win in a verbal war against the best word-jockeys in the government.

He just wanted somebody to tell him he wouldn't be grounded

permanently. He wanted to prove that there was nothing wrong with the Nomad.

And he sure as hell wanted to come out of that building without having destroyed his own career, as well as Rowan's, and the whole X-NASP program, which should never have become the subject of a Congressional hearing, no matter how closed.

If he and Rowan had been lucky, they'd have crashed the Nomad and died with the program. It was tough to be a walking ghost, a plague carrier, and a guilt-ridden grounded pilot all at once.

Glumly, for the third time in as many rounds of drinks, Cleary admitted to himself that there was nothing Colonel Walsh, the Space Wing Commander who'd come out here to run interference for Cleary and Rowan during the hearings, was going to be able to do to fix what Cleary'd done today.

Walsh had done all he could. It was Cleary's big mouth that had screwed up everybody's damage control.

Colonel Walsh, beside him at the bar, said, "Sonny, don't take it so hard. It's a closed hearing. Everything was classified. If it doesn't leak, we're okay."

"I won't believe that until somebody tells me I can fly again," Cleary said, staring at the mirror behind the bar and his reflection in it.

Cleary didn't belong here. He wasn't trained for Washington power games. He needed a shower and a shave, and he needed some open space to work off all this emotion: wild country and high skies. He needed to be up there in a thin atmosphere where God could sort out whether he was too dumb to fly a plane or not.

Maybe he could get Walsh to find him some nearby unit on night exercises and an airplane to jump out of, if nobody would let him fly one. But there was no chance of that. If he got hurt, the circus on the Hill would have to be postponed.

This bar was long, polished, elegant, and civilized. Like all of Washington, it made him claustrophobic. As certainly as it was the wrong place for what Cleary and Rowan needed, this chi-chi D.C. watering hole was the right place for the impression that Colonel Walsh wanted to make.

Walsh wanted them to keep their heads up and show they weren't guilty of anything. Let people see they weren't afraid. That they hadn't done anything to be ashamed of.

Except nearly crash a testbed. And they were afraid. At least Cleary was—afraid he'd never get back in another X-NASP.

Pretending everything was A-okay would have been easier if Cleary and Rowan weren't a circuit of misery and fear making each other worse every time they locked glances. So they weren't looking at each other.

They were looking at their drinks, their hands, and their memories. And trying not to look at this situation as a cruel and unusual dog-and-pony show, with them playing dog and pony.

Walsh had them booked into the hotel whose bar this was. Most of the people in here, at five-thirty, were probably not newsies or TV types—just tourists. But tourists got CNN in their rooms and read the papers.

Cleary had never been more off balance in his life. He couldn't even get drunk, it seemed.

"How come we can't go to our rooms, sir? I can feel people looking at me and I don't fucking like it," Cleary said, knocking back another shot of Jack Daniel's and reaching for his beer chaser.

"Easy, Cleary," Walsh said. "We sit here another little while, until after the evening news."

The Space Wing Commander had circles under his eyes like fresh bruises. Colonels don't like public flaps; public flaps keep colonels from becoming generals. They'd all gotten bruised at today's closed hearings—first in the Russell Building and then . . .

Cleary refused to remember. He wanted to lose track. In one day, starting at six this morning, he'd met more brass than he could count. He'd looked the Secretary of Defense straight in the eye. He'd gone head-to-head with more elected officials than he'd ever dreamed of meeting in his worst nightmares.

"Easy it is, sir," he said. And, to his drink, "But it ain't."

Rowan, on his far side, was talking to some woman. Leave it to Rowan to pick up some blond bimbo in flat shoes to make himself feel better. If Rowan's wife heard about it, Rowan wasn't going to feel better enough to make up for the hell he'd catch.

And Walsh wanted *Cleary* to take it easy? As Rowan and the blond girl slid off their stools and headed for a couple of chairs by the window, Cleary added, "I'm fine. I'm just great. It's not every day you get your ass grounded, get grilled by a bunch of Congressmen looking to hang you, and chased down the Russell Building steps by reporters. I'm just great. Maybe I'll go into politics next."

"We'll get you through this and back where you belong," Walsh promised as if he could do it. "You're just grounded temporarily—until we trace the trouble and get the profile down. But you've got to do better with these Washington honchos tomorrow. Pilot or not, you're just a worker bee, like the rest of us. So calm the hell down, Sonny. You're acting like this is a witch-hunt. It isn't. Yet. Those Congressmen have their jobs to do too."

Cleary could feel the flush crawling up his face.

Walsh was a big, grizzled guy, with years of working the system engraved on his face. That face was beginning to swim before Cleary's eyes. Cleary hadn't been able to eat breakfast—his stomach hadn't been present and accounted for. He hadn't had time for lunch. And now Walsh was intent on critiquing his performance because, tomorrow, they were going to have to do the same thing all over again, for the Senate.

"I've been putting my ass on the line my whole life, and I've never faced an environment that hostile before," Cleary said. "Sir." It sounded too angry, and too full of complaint, and it came out from between gritted teeth. He went back to what was left of his beer, staring at his hands. He didn't want to look at Walsh. He sure as hell didn't want to look at Rowan, who was going to get his Irish self laid, which somehow made Cleary feel even more alone.

This was Cleary's fuckup, if there was some fuckup for anyone to call his own. He'd found that out this morning, when the Congressmen started grilling him. Like there was some way a pilot could have avoided the kind of problem Cleary'd had up there. . . .

"Until we're through this, you'll face a lot more of that. And you'd better do better than you did today, Captain. Until we find the source of the trouble, you and Rowan are our only on-site experts."

"We gotta reverse-engineer the failure. The diodes and the current. See what fails when. If we reverse-engineer the failures," Cleary told his drink, in what he hoped was a cool, collected way full of reasonableness and patience that he just didn't have today, "and we find out I'm right—that the Nomad was EMP'd by a hostile power, then where are we?" Where was he? His whole damned career was hanging on the uninformed opinion of a bunch of folks who wanted to flush him down the toilet so they could say that what happened had been just pilot error.

Which it sure as hell wasn't.

Then he realized that Walsh wasn't listening. Walsh was talking. To somebody else.

Cleary looked up and saw a manicured guy his age, with a

woman in tow who seemed vaguely familiar—short, Oriental, and pretty the way a doll is pretty.

Cleary watched their mouths move for a minute and realized he was probably drunker than he ought to be. Walsh was gesturing from Cleary to the woman, and she held out her hand.

Gold Rolex and pearly nails, and he shook it.

Then he heard her say, "I see you don't watch much network news, Captain. I'm Carla Chang."

She was responding to the blank look on his face. He tried to say something, but all he could think of was, "Yeah, well . . . Ms. Chang . . . my work gets me up pretty early and keeps me out pretty late. Or did."

Wrong thing to say. Walsh winced and shook his head. The guy with Walsh had a satisfied look on his moon face that mixed somehow with Walsh's wince and made Cleary realize that, at the very least, he should let go of this woman's hand and, probably, punch out for his room before the tension he could feel jumping between the four of them got any worse.

He was about to excuse himself, saying he had that additional round of hearings scheduled for tomorrow. But Walsh was saying something to the guy with the glib smile, and Cleary heard the words "what the Congressman wants . . ."

Then he remembered the moon-faced, smiling guy from the long hazy day of endless smilers with deadly eyes.

And the Chang woman was asking him, "Captain Cleary, can you explain to me what you meant just then when you were saying that the Nomad was EMP'd by a hostile power? What's EMP exactly? In terms a layman can understand."

She *couldn't* have heard him. Could she?

"Jesus," Cleary said slowly, shaking his head. He felt as if he'd just punched out of some crashing bird and was free-falling, waiting for a chute that might or might not open to decide if it would save him. "Did I say that? I was just bullshitting, ma'am— I mean, just speculating idly."

He cast a desperate look at Walsh, for help. But Walsh was huddled with the Congressional aide, elbows on the bar, staring at the wood as if it was going to save them all once Walsh read some message there.

"Let's have a drink, Captain," said Carla Chang, who was some kind of network newsie. She turned to the bartender. "Give the captain another round, and I'll have the same."

Cleary was drunk enough to wonder what she'd do when she saw what she'd ordered—Orientals and Tennessee whiskey were a volatile mix. She hopped up on a bar stool beside him. He wished Walsh would let him know what he was supposed to do. She was pretty as she could be, and he kept trying to remember her name.

"Now, Captain," she said as their drinks came, "you were telling me about EMP."

She knew how to say it—she didn't pronounce each letter separately; she said "emp."

He said miserably, "I can't talk to you, ma'am. Ask your friend the aide there—those hearings were closed. Everything on the record's got to come out of the USSPACECOM Public Affairs office. Maybe you'd like to get with—"

"We've heard from other sources that what happened to your test craft wasn't your fault, Captain. That it wasn't pilot error."

"It was anybody's fault. Not the . . . testbed's either. Stuff happens. That's what test programs are about—to find out what can go wrong so we can fix it."

"We've heard, Captain, that your spacecraft was attacked by some new weapon. Don't you think the American people have a right to hear about it? What's your opinion? You're the eyewitness. You're being all but accused of incompetence. What's your side of it?"

What's it to you, lady? Want to suck my dick?

"Colonel Walsh!" Cleary almost shouted. "Can you help me with this?"

Whatever Chang knew, it was too much. And Cleary couldn't make his tongue work. He'd never been more frightened in his life, not even when the testbed was crashing and he figured out why.

This time the threat wasn't a faceless enemy with an invisible beam weapon.

This time, the threat happened to be a ninety-pound woman. If Walsh thought Cleary could handle this shit, Walsh was wrong.

This little-bitty newswoman could get him in enough trouble here that he'd never get to fly another testbed, no matter how the hearings came out. His hands were shaking as he reached for his drink, using the excuse to cast Walsh an imploring look.

Walsh's back was turned to him: *Handle it yourself, Sonny.* Cleary's reputation said there was nothing he couldn't handle— in the air or in space. On the ground, he was washing out pretty bad these days.

He kicked back the shot. "Sir, did you hear me? This reporter here's got questions I know I can't answer."

Walsh finally broke away from the Congressional aide, and said, "Come talk to our friend Mr. Duvall, from Congressman Norden's office, Sonny."

Saved by superior rank. Relief washed over him so that he felt limp and weak. Getting off the bar stool was hard enough, shaken and tipsy as he was, that he didn't bother trying to disengage politely from Carla Chang. The bar had filled up some. He jostled her as he tried to obey the colonel's order. He didn't look back.

And he didn't realize how angry he was until Duvall, the Congressional aide, touched his sleeve and started telling him, "It's all right. She's all right. She's on our side. My boss wants to get the whole story out, unattributably, that's all—now that some of it's on the evening news. And you did great."

"*Did?* Story? I didn't—" How did this guy know what was on the evening news when it hadn't even aired yet?

"Oh, yeah, sure." Duvall smirked. "You just happened to be saying the right thing when we walked up. I've got to hand it to your Space Wing Commander. You leak a whole lot better than you disseminate. You guys are cooler than—"

Then, finally, Cleary understood. This aide's boss, Congressman Norden, had leaked part of today's testimony to Chang and now was setting up to blame it on Cleary.

Leak. After all he'd been through.

Cleary didn't even think before he hit Duvall, the moon-faced Congressional aide, square in the nose. And then he hit him again, for good measure.

Duvall flipped backward off his bar stool, bounced off two women as he fell, hit one in the crotch with his heel, and landed on his back, tripping a passing Indonesian waiter, who fell on top of him with a tray of drinks.

As Duvall swiped at his nose with his hand, Chang saw the blood and said in a deathly cold voice to the bartender, "Call the police, will you?" before Duvall came up off the floor and lunged at Cleary.

And then it got real strange in that nice, quiet, upscale hotel bar, what with people scrambling and women screaming and the Congressional aide running at him like some kid in a schoolyard.

You just didn't expect to be in a fistfight in civilian clothes in Washington. Not with a TV anchorwoman there, calling directions to guys who came from somewhere with cameras . . . Still, when someone hits you, you hit back. When someone runs full-bore into you, head down, you whack him across the back of the skull with whatever's handy. . . .

Rowan grabbed him from behind, saying, "Whoa! Come on, Captain, cool out!" and not letting go.

Walsh, arms outstretched, was between Cleary and Duvall, telling the aide, "Calm the hell down. You started this, trying to set one of my people up."

But Cleary remembered most vividly the wail of an approaching police siren, and a feeling of vertigo. And the big Oriental eyes of Carla Chang, as she flashed in and out of his field of vision, talking to a microphone she held and then to two guys with cameras, who followed her as she ran out the door.

He knew she was going right across the street. That bothered him more than the police wanting to handcuff him. More than the Congressional aide wanting to press charges. More than Walsh telling Lieutenant Rowan to stay the hell out of this and go to his room—right then.

And telling Cleary: "Just don't say anything else, okay? We'll have you out of this in an hour."

Then Walsh left Cleary with the cops and went into a jurisdictional huddle with somebody in civilian clothes.

They wouldn't let Colonel Walsh ride in the police car with Cleary. You got real offended when you were all pumped up and a little too drunk and somebody forcibly pushed your head down so they could shove you into a police car. He didn't remember anything but the ceiling of that car and his own breathing, all the way down to the police station.

The guy they fingerprinted and photographed with a slate number was somebody else. He was completely detached. In the last few minutes, he'd managed to jeopardize everything he cared about. If they wanted to put him in jail and leave him there, he wasn't sure that was such a bad idea.

He was sick to his stomach, but he couldn't throw up. They stuck him in some kind of group cell with a bunch of unhappy souls, some more screwed up than he was. He could feel the swelling in his eye by then, where the Congressional aide had landed a lucky punch. He couldn't see much out of that eye and what he could see was fuzzy. If his eye was damaged, even if Walsh was right and they could get him out of this, he was grounded forever.

Hell, he was probably grounded for eternity and ever anyhow. That woman had heard what he'd said, but that wasn't the trouble. That fucking staffer had leaked everything they'd told the Congressional committee to the news types, or she wouldn't have been there in the first place. So was it Cleary's fault, all this?

You fucking bet it was his fault.

The least they could have done was give him a private cell. Three of the black guys in his cage wouldn't let him be and his head was aching.

But he couldn't start any more trouble. He had to trust that the colonel would find him and get him the hell out of here. He had to trust Walsh.

And anyway, they'd need him for the Senate hearings in the morning. He didn't think the Senate would be content without a piece of his hide. So he told himself it would be all right. Just like Walsh almost said.

And it was all right, eventually—if you could call the appearance of Dalton Ford anything like all right.

Space Command's dual-hatted DIA honcho looked like somebody who'd come to get his rottweiler out of the pound after it had mauled a three-year-old girl.

"Asshole," Ford said to him judiciously as they walked down the steps toward a gray sedan. The stars were all double in Cleary's vision. Ford was double too: a Joint Command type that didn't waste time on anything that wasn't crucial. Even if half the stories about Ford weren't true, the remainder comprised the dark underbelly of history.

"Thanks, Mister Ford," said Cleary.

"Don't thank me, Captain. You aren't out of the woods yet. And the bears down here eat rambunctious boys like you for breakfast." Ford was a civilian DIA employee attached to U.S. Space Command. Ten or twelve years older than Cleary, just as fit, Ford had the jump-ready look of somebody who'd never really stopped thinking like Special Forces. He was certainly carrying a weapon under his windbreaker, and he shook his short-cropped head at Cleary. "Get in the car."

In it, Dalton Ford stared Cleary up and down, leaned back against the seat, and said, "You know, kid, I always wanted to do what you did today." A slow grin broke out on Ford's even-featured face. "Now that we've got you out of jail, let's see if we can't go get you out of trouble." He started the engine.

Squinting out the window, Cleary realized they were headed out of the District. "I've got to go back to my hotel. Rowan and the Space Wing Commander, Colonel Walsh, are waiting—"

"Just relax, okay? We're going to get you through that Senate hearing tomorrow by giving you enough classified poop that nobody's going to dare to leak anything. Walsh and Rowan will catch up with us. Meanwhile, start trying to get your head clear enough to think. I want you to talk to some people about what kind of reverse-engineering might zero the problem."

Zero the problem. Did everybody know? "What happened with the leak? Does everybody know what I—"

"Did? Yeah. Said? No. We did some damage control. There's a rumor that some kind of aggression or sabotage was involved in the X-NASP mishap. The worst of that's admitting the X-NASP exists at all. But we'll handle it. They don't know one plane from another, most of them. We'll try showing them the X-31; it's got a high-altitude top end. As for the rest . . . There's a story that one of our guys had a fistfight in a bar." Ford's left shoulder twitched. "Tough shit. Maybe it's okay it leaked. But now we've got to close ranks. Don't worry, Cleary. We're all in this together. But it's time you told somebody what happened—somebody who's capable of evaluating what you're saying."

Cleary had already been debriefed at the crash-landing site by what seemed like most of the government—anybody who'd had half a reason to claim access. Ford's scary legend was full of echelon jumping and weird interagency connections. "I don't want to talk to any—"

"I'll be right there with you. We'll get you through this. I know what it's like to be cornered."

Cleary leaned his throbbing head back and stared at the ceiling. "I just want to be able to fly again, when all this is over, okay?" He sounded like a kid asking Santa Claus for a new bike, and he knew it.

But Ford said, "Okay, Cleary. You got it."

And somehow, against all reason, Cleary believed what Ford said. Even though he knew better. Just because it was Ford who was saying it.

7

Day 3: Los Alamos National Laboratory

Five years ago, Joanna Pettit would have slept with this Major Mackenzie, James Harry, at her earliest opportunity. Maybe she would have engineered an opportunity.

But not now. The last thing she needed was a distraction, and she couldn't risk slumming in the ranks. Control was everything when you'd reached Joanna's position in life. You couldn't afford a wrong move, or a poor decision.

And Mackenzie was clearly a poor decision for someone as determined as she to reach her full potential, not squander her energy and attention on a storybook love affair with somebody who thought his life was a reasonable thing to risk on a regular basis.

As she set him up for a run in the virtual prototyping bay with the hard suit, she kept reminding herself of all the trouble this Mackenzie had made for her during their correspondence phase.

The suit was formally the Future Infantry Fighting System—FIFS—but everyone connected with it knew what it really was: a ticket to a high-level Washington job, even a masthead slot in some technological forecasting think tank. Mackenzie's name had popped out of her DARPA computer three times as she'd searched among low-intensity-conflict specialists for the right candidate to field-test the FIFS prototype.

And then she'd seen his name on the Nomad invitation list. Now she wished she hadn't. How could anybody as bright as Mackenzie be so fit? Or so infuriating?

"Ready, Mac?" she said into her slate mike. She was sitting in the glassed-in control room. Beyond, Mackenzie was suited up in the test bay full of carefully wired and precisely constructed obstacles: stairs, gantries, scaffolding, and even a wind tunnel.

"Ready," came Mackenzie's voice through the speakers mounted on her control console. He looked like anybody else in the FIFS gear. That was a relief. Pettit sipped coffee before she toggled her keyboard.

Up came a menu of simulation choices. She grinned nastily. He thought he was ready. How badly could he hurt himself, really, in the simulation bay? When the project was ready to be fielded, men like Mackenzie would have helmet-mounted computer displays that allowed them to run a "virtual reality"—an accurate computer version of whatever their mission parameters would be—as they flew toward their target. They'd see on their heads-up displays everything intelligence could determine might be at the site of their operation, and be able to alter what they saw.

Currently, the test version offered computer-generated scenarios that were displayed onto the visor of the suit's helmet. In combat, those displays would carry real-time command, control, communications, and intelligence data—seven, plus or minus two, data streams—up to the operator's threshold of comprehension.

If you ported the suit's wearer too much data, his performance suffered. If you didn't send him enough, he could lose his life and the suit. The program managers were still trying to determine what information a wearer needed to see, what he needed to hear, and what could be imparted by a cuff on the suit that gave little shocks or pulses.

Pettit didn't like the cuff. But she did like the idea of seeing just how much Mackenzie could handle with minimum training. "Now, we've gone over everything, and you're clear on what's going to happen, right?" she asked him as she chose a simulation of urban conflict in a Third World venue.

"Yep. Let it rip."

She did. She monitored what he was seeing on a high-definition CRT. As if looking through his eyes, she saw what Mackenzie saw displayed on his helmet's visor: a simulated alley leading to an apartment building's back stairs, instead of a test bay. A superimposed logistical grid, with letter/number designators. Two simulated companions, who were blips on his helmet's display.

When he started moving through the simulation, her heart raced. They'd worked so hard on this equipment, she was suddenly afraid he wouldn't like it.

Then the view she had of buildings and the alley changed as Mackenzie got the hang of maneuvering in the heavy, exoskeletal powered suit. She heard him grunt, and she heard his breathing quicken.

She popped up a readout of his physiology: pulse rate, blood pressure, galvanic skin response—the works. She could replay the test results later, but right now she wanted to know how he was reacting.

When the numbers came up, Pettit leaned forward and broke into his com system. "Mackenzie, do you copy? Talk to me?"

He was nearly at the stairs already. "Yeah, I read you." His voice was very quiet, a whisper.

She realized then, from the tone of it that this virtual reality was real enough to elicit from Mackenzie all the physiological responses of someone accustomed to using whisper mikes in real life-and-death situations.

"I want to—" Mackenzie muttered. Then: "There, I've got it."

He'd quadranted his helmet-mounted display. Using the command and control "Associate" they'd adapted from a pilot's artificially intelligent targeting system, he was taking a close-up of the simulated doorway behind which his target lay. Despite herself, she was impressed by how quickly he was learning.

But then, it was the program that should get the credit.

The operator was just a testbed for this system. He said, "I need to do this with weapons." He grunted, and she realized he was at the head of the stairs, crouched down, and fumbling with the control box she'd given him.

He began asking for a stream of modifications. She said, when he was halfway through, "We want you to reach the target, remember? Punch in the—"

He crashed through the actual door, shoulder first, rolled through to the other side, then tumbled off the edge of the scaffold.

The screen in front of her showed a dizzy spin and she nearly closed her eyes. She heard him hit the ground, and tried to ignore his curses and the heavy breathing.

As her screen righted itself, shimmering through every one of its information-gathering modes in a four-color overlay, Mackenzie said breathlessly, "This thing's too fucking heavy. When you hit, you hit real hard."

Pettit could hear anger, and what might have been pain, in his voice. She said, "If you've broken any—"

But Mackenzie was up and moving. The suit had to be capable of righting its wearer. They'd wondered how the servos would handle heavy punishment, but never tried anything like what Mackenzie was doing with it. In the simulated "basement" he now saw in his visor display, he was moving jerkily.

She said, "If you've hurt yourself, please stop. All these tests are on the record, for us. Even this one. I can't—"

"There." He grunted. The screen showed that he'd ordered a flash-bang grenade simulation. Then the screen whited out. He moved forward, fast, using a non-real-time floor plan until the simulator could give him a visual scan.

She sat back, and realized her own chest was heaving. They'd never had anybody like Mackenzie test this equipment.

Somebody said from behind her, "Who the hell is that?"

She jumped in her seat and her head snapped around so fast that pain lanced up to her jaw. "Jack, hi. That's Mackenzie, from USSPACECOM. I thought when we had the chance we ought to try FIFS with the kind of soldier who's going to use it."

"If he keeps pushing that system like that, we're going to have to rebuild it from scratch," said the program's senior scientist.

"But look what he's done. . . ."

They almost forgot about Mackenzie, still moving through the simulation, until he said, gasping for breath: "Okay, enough. I can get to the pickup point alive without all this hash. How do I clear this screen anyway?"

She told him. "And come on in. I want you meet FIFS's daddy."

"Tell him for me this doesn't mean squat without real weapons—and real downloads from spaceborne sensoring platforms or command-and-control sources."

"Come in and tell him yourself."

Then she looked through the glass, into the bay, and realized how slowly and carefully the man in the suit was moving.

"Jack, I think he's hurt himself."

"It's possible, certainly. If he went against the power curve of the suit—tried to push it beyond its reaction speed. Or if he crashed around in it. After all, this is the NASA model, meant for—"

"He fell off a scaffold in it." She was up out of her chair.

"I'm sure he'd have said something—" Jack called after her as she made for the door and the program scientist slipped into her seat.

"I'm not," she muttered.

In the simulation bay, Mackenzie was struggling out of the suit by the time she got there.

He had the helmet off. His face was pale.

"Here, let me help you," she said brusquely.

She was nearly afraid to help. He was as white as a ghost.

"Thanks." He wiped sweat off his lip. "This thing could use an air conditioner."

"It's got life support and climate control. I just didn't—"

They got him out of the suit. He was soaked in sweat. And he leaned against the wall with a grunt when he gingerly put his weight on his left leg.

"You are hurt."

"Maybe I cracked a rib and pulled a couple muscles. I wasn't expecting it to drop me on my back like some damned turtle, and then get me up. I think I was pushing when it was pulling." He bared his teeth, but it wasn't a smile.

She felt terrible. She fumbled with the suit, arranging it on its rack. "So you don't like it."

"I like it better than getting dead," he said softly, in that same voice he'd used during the simulation.

She looked around at him: His T-shirt and slacks were soaked and his tanned arms were trembling. "If you like it, would you be willing to work with us on it?"

"Only if it gets more real-world. I want to use it with real weapons, real coms, and real data dumps—just in case this thing ever gets fielded." He took a step away from the suit in its rack and her before it.

Again, he grunted. He was awkward, trying not to limp.

"Let's get you to the infirmary and see—"

"I thought you had some scientist type that wanted a verbal report," he nearly snapped.

"I do, Major Mackenzie. Let's go."

Without another word, he hobbled off toward the door. If he wanted to perspire and pretend he wasn't in pain, that was fine with her. As long as he didn't give the program a bad report.

She caught up with him and said, "This way. If you want to try it with real weapons, as you say, I could probably come up with one of those laser rifles you're so in love with."

"Bribe time? I've got to go back to Colorado in a few hours, remember?"

He was angry because he was hurt, she thought.

"We'll talk about it," she said quietly. "This way." And then, just before she led him in to meet Jack, she said, "You did us a real favor. We've never had anybody do that sort of thing with one of the prototypes. . . ."

"What sort of thing? Fall on his ass? Anytime you want somebody to fall off a ladder, lady, I'm your guy."

Then she realized it was his own performance, as much as the pain, that had Mackenzie in such a bad temper.

"Mac—"

"Look, could we get through this and go get some coffee or something?" He cocked his head at her. "You know, you look really worried about this. Don't. I'm fine. It's fine. Your toy'll get a good report from me. Okay?"

"Okay. And we'll try it with real weapons."

"Honey, I can't wait," Mackenzie said in a raspy voice.

Relieved, she opened the door and motioned the limping soldier to precede her. Once Jack had finished asking Mackenzie questions, they'd go see if he'd done himself any permanent harm.

He'd done the program a world of good. Pettit was determined to see Mackenzie assigned to the FIFS program for as long as they needed him. No matter what it took.

But later, when he'd had his ribs taped, his right leg X-rayed, and been discharged as fit for light duty by a frowning infirmary staffer, she was no longer so certain that having Mackenzie around was wise.

He wanted to look at her program notes, and was determined to input operational benchmarks. He had lots of ideas and she didn't like any of them, because they were looking at the notes at her place and she'd somehow been talked into making sandwiches and coffee.

When he grabbed her as she went by his chair in her kitchen, she froze. She just couldn't move.

She couldn't think what a proper response would be. Her first impulse was to hit him over the head with the dirty plate she was carrying.

That wasn't right. He was hurt already. And it was her fault. And he'd grabbed her by the waist, from behind.

She turned around, saying, "Look, Mac, we—"

He was still sitting and he pulled her against him. His other arm went around her and his breath was hot against her thighs.

She was determined that nothing like this was going to happen. But she wasn't sure how to stop it. His hair was ash blond. She grabbed some.

He said, "Ssh, come here."

She dropped to her knees, to explain to him why this couldn't happen.

There were beads of sweat on his upper lip and she remembered he was hurt. His eyes bored into hers and he said, "Just don't say anything, okay? Let's see if we can't solve this problem we've got."

He had that quiet tone, the one she'd heard in the simulation bay. He slid his hand down her, and between her legs, watching her intently the entire time.

She couldn't look at him. She couldn't, somehow, break away. She dropped her head onto his shoulder and just breathed. She ached wherever he'd touched her.

She knew she shouldn't let this happen. It was going to ruin everything. "You're hurt. . . ."

"We're both going to feel a lot better."

Somewhere at the edges of her sensing, he was unzipping her pants and pulling them down. She couldn't possibly be letting this happen. She wasn't going to let this soldier pull her down on top of him, on a chair in her kitchen, with her shirt up above her breasts and her pants still tangled around one ankle.

He wasn't even wearing a condom, for God's sake!

She couldn't seem to get control of anything happening to her body, and then the tip of him entered her, and she just came down on him, hard, and locked her arms around his neck. If it hurt his taped ribs, good. He'd asked for this, and now he was going to get it.

He seemed nearly to stop breathing. "Unless you want to set a land speed record, you just sit perfectly still," he said.

"Uh-uh," she told him, finally thoroughly and completely in control. "You just do what you're here to do, Mac," she told him, and leaned backward until he groaned and lunged out of the chair, lifting them both onto her kitchen table for one final, explosive moment.

"Damn, Pettit . . ." he whispered into her hair.

She brushed her hair from her face and said, "I don't know. Weren't we talking about deep, mutual cooperation, about an hour ago?"

He clearly didn't know what to do, or say. She said, "Go clean up. Let's watch the news. Maybe there's an update."

His eyes shifted across her face quickly, intently, as he got off her and straightened up, then ducked his head to put on his clothes.

But she'd seen the uncertainty, the raw confusion, and the vulnerability there.

"It's fine," she said, sitting up. "You were fine. I'm just not feeling like cuddling on the kitchen table."

Was she going to have to coddle him? She knew, then, that she'd been right to avoid this. They were too different. Did he expect her to swoon? Proclaim or demand an oath of undying affection?

He was awkward all through the interval of dressing and he couldn't meet her eyes.

So she said, "Come here. Let's see what the headlines are. I've got the twenty-four-hour service." She sat on the couch in her living room.

He came and stood over her, hands in his hip pockets. His head was down, his eyes lowered. "I—could I take a shower?"

"In a minute. Look, Mac—"

"Harry."

Now he would tell her, for the first time, what his friends called him. Okay. "Look, James Harry. This doesn't mean anything good unless we can handle it without spoiling our working relationship. Do you understand?"

"Yeah." He nodded gravely. "I—should I apologize or something?"

So he didn't understand. "Sit, will you?"

He sighed and sat.

"I just can't afford any emotional firestorms right now. I'm deeply committed to my career. But I'd do it again, in a second, as long as you understand what I'm telling you." Cowboy. Oh, Lord, save me from egocentric males with blue-collar backgrounds.

"I just think . . . usually I'm the one that says more or less what you're saying."

"Well, this should be a novelty and a relief then. We'll get you back to your hotel as soon as you've showered—"

The headline service was showing the UN Security Council. She reached beside her and thumbed the remote's volume.

The announcer was saying, "Council's resolution of censure." Then the newsreader came back on and began another segment. This one was about German space development.

"Shit." Mackenzie sat now, shaking his head. "It's really getting tense."

"You think that was in reaction to the X-NASP incident?"

"You know of any other emergency meetings of the Security Council going on, except the one about the German territoriality claim for orbital assets?"

Then she remembered he wasn't as dumb as he looked. "No, I don't. And yes, it's tense."

"But not between us, okay?" He reached out and touched her cheek.

In the flicker of the TV tube, his angular face was almost handsome and his whole body seemed to quiver, so concertedly was he staring at her.

"Not between us, no. That is, unless you won't cooperate with us on the FIFS project."

"The way things are going, I'd be crazy not to. It's going to be in my best interest to be the guy who's operationally trained on that thing if this space dispute keeps up," he said judiciously.

But he wasn't teasing, or even smiling slightly when he said it.

All the hairs rose on her arms and she rubbed them. "I guess that's true. So I'll make the arrangements?"

"I'd like that a whole lot," he said, and leaned forward to kiss her.

Maybe this wasn't as bad a mistake as she'd first believed. As Mackenzie's arms went around her, she thought she could feel him shiver.

But maybe it was she. Or maybe it was pain from his cracked ribs. He almost cracked hers, he held her so tightly.

Men. If she lived to be a hundred, she'd never understand them intellectually. But her body understood Mackenzie's body just fine. Better than fine. She hoped to hell that understanding wasn't clouding her judgment.

8

Day 4: Space Station Freedom

Standing erect in a space suit on the free-flying manned maneuvering platform as he steered the open space-truck away from the station behind him and toward a distant target, Dietrich looked like a kid on a homemade scooter.

But he didn't feel like a kid. Kids didn't have to worry about anything. Kids didn't have the fate of the world in their hands. Kids didn't need to depend on undependable equipment, made by incompetent nations, failing in the near-vacuum of empty space and killing them. Kids didn't have to worry about power failures, power overloads, circuitry burnout, meteor strikes, or life-support screwups on their scooters.

And kids didn't work for ORTAG, the German space agency. Every kid on Earth dreamed of spending a night on Space Station Freedom. If their dreams suddenly came true, they'd piss their pants in fear.

There were 5,780 items on Space Station Freedom that might require EVA or servicing by astronauts, and Dietrich was sure that every one of them was going to fuck up on his watch. Dietrich couldn't decide if he was more frightened when he was inside the underpowered, multi-fucked-up station where he wasn't cocooned in NASA-spec life support, or when he was outside, like now, on an EVA where everything that could go wrong invariably did.

EVA stood for extra-vehicular activity, but the American term didn't convey what it was like to spend every other day of your tour outside the multinational space station doing expensive, time-consuming, and dangerous missions that were the direct result of poor planning by the American primary contractors.

But that was what he was doing. Dietrich was supposed to be an astronaut, not some glorified mechanic in a space suit trying endlessly to fix by hand what the telerobotic servicers couldn't handle. Dietrich toggled the controls of the free-flying platform, a console and laptop-sized screen on a stalk before him at the platform's front.

Attitude jets responded. The platform picked up speed.

The manned free-flying platform was of German manufacture. When you were alone out here, too far from Freedom to get back by yourself if it failed, that thought was your only comfort. At least his country's equipment tended to perform as advertised. Not like American equipment. Or Canadian equipment.

The Canadian-made telerobotic manipulators and general servicers should have been performing more of the maintenance on Space Station Freedom. Should have been, but couldn't—yet.

Dietrich blinked down at his control panel and toggled through a navigation check. His booted feet, clamped onto the grid of the control station as you'd clamp your feet to skis, were beginning to cramp. If the telerobotics program were further along, he reminded himself, then Dietrich's real job would have been harder.

For sabotage and covert action, you needed opportunity. Currently, the Canadian telerobots could handle only about a quarter of what continually went wrong on Space Station Freedom. So Dietrich had his opportunities. So many of them that it seemed as if he'd last slept years ago.

All he did was EVA. He EVA'd every other day, and even when there wasn't a schedule, he found an excuse to get outside. Never mind that it scared the shit out of him. Never mind that he couldn't get used to it. It was what he'd been boosted up here to do.

He was so nervous around the other astronauts and mission specialists on Freedom that he was actually beginning to prefer the clearer danger of the free-flying platform and the unforgiving cold of orbital space. When he was on an EVA, nothing he said could ruin anyone's plans. No tic under his eye could betray his fragile nerves, and get him sent home prematurely. No case of the sweats could escalate into something else, so that he began muttering about the space plane he'd pulsed. Dietrich knew he was talking in his sleep. So he was trying not to sleep on the Freedom. When he knew he had to sleep, he used his science specialist's status to go over to the German power experiment module. At least there, he could sleep without worrying what would happen if he said something he shouldn't.

So, Dietrich just loved EVAs. If it weren't for all the scheduled and unscheduled maintenance EVAs plaguing Space Station
Freedom, Dietrich's German bosses wouldn't have had an excuse
to boost the MHDs up here.

The MHDs were a quiet German comment on the poor planning
of Space Station Freedom, which had enough power to sustain
itself, but not enough to serve any operational purpose. So Germany had magnanimously reached into its back pocket and pulled
out the first gigawatt generator, donating it to the good of multinational cooperation in space. Without ORTAG's Soviet-made
MHD, Space Station Freedom would have been substantially less
functional.

And without men like Dietrich, the spare MHD in its discreet
parking orbit wouldn't be a covert threat to anyone or anything.
Knowing that every hour of EVA work should take, on paper,
2.3 plus 1.7 hours to perform, Dietrich's ORTAG bosses had
seen an opportunity too good to pass up. Frequent maintenance
EVAs gave Dietrich all the slack necessary to make various
"adjustments" to both MHDs that no one on Freedom would
ever notice as out of the ordinary.

The Americans and Canadians and French had so many of
their own problems that they had no time to worry about what
"ordinary" performance specs for the MHDs might be.

So Dietrich wasn't afraid of the Americans or anyone else
discovering what he was doing out here for half of his "K factor" EVA time. K factor was American jargon for the inherent
uncertainties in any repair task. Dietrich had dubbed it the Klutz
factor.

K might as well stand for kamikaze, the way things were going
on the ground, what with the UN Security Council resolving to
censure ORTAG and the Germans basically telling the Council
to go piss in the wind. Dietrich tapped in an additional course
correction with a single keystroke. He'd made this run so many
times, he could do it in his sleep.

Sometimes he thought he was doing it in his sleep. When you
slept, you dreamed. If it weren't for the clamps on his boots,
Dietrich might have floated away one of these times, just dreamed
his way into oblivion, a tiny, space-suited figure drifting slowly
toward nothingness. He could hear the wind lulling him, a soft
sighing in his ears. . . .

His own breathing. He started awake, and hit his head against
the inside of his space helmet. Awake now, all right.

There wasn't any wind up here to speak of, unless you wanted to count solar wind, or an ill wind. Somebody was hailing him.

"Ja—yes?" he said in his com.

"Just checking, Dietrich. You didn't call in your 0300 report—"

It was Jenkins, the American watch commander, a Space Command soldier who kept a watchful eye on other nations' mission specialists.

He couldn't say he'd dozed off. "Jenkins—Commander, go tend your own sheep, okay?"

"Look, Dietrich—whatever's going on down on the ground isn't anything to us, right?"

These Americans. All transmissions were logged for the record. "Yes, of course. Is there some problem I can help you with?" Asshole. Go ahead, talk politics on the com line. Only Americans were so boorishly blunt.

"Ah—we just had a power fluctuation, and you're our power specialist. . . ."

"Fluctuation?"

"Nothing much. A few KWs. When will you be back?"

Another half hour to get there. Three hours sleep. Two hours back . . . "By dinnertime. Okay?" His tension sounded like irritation. He didn't want these Americans getting too curious. "Unless you need me to look at your fluctuation?" Unless you need somebody to hold your hand, fool. . . .

Dietrich had to live in close quarters with the Canadians and Americans, as well as with the Italians and Japanese who were currently manning Freedom. So he didn't want to be caught, or even questioned, while he was tweaking the "spare" Magneto Hydro Dynamic generator to perform its next mission. But the Americans, especially, never admitted to anything being truly a problem if they could help it. Everything with them was understatement. They had their high-tech machismo to protect.

"No, you go ahead. We're fine here. See you when you get back. Freedom Control, out."

Freedom Control. That was who the Americans thought they were. But perhaps not for much longer. Not if the coalition was successful. Not if ORTAG held its ground. Not if Dietrich's MHD was used to best advantage.

Suddenly, he wanted desperately to be there with it, to touch it, to check its every function, to make sure it was all right.

The spare MHD floated in a parking orbit of its own, not connected to the station, housed in a German-only module labeled as a science experiment.

Some experiment. If the German contingent hadn't overtly saved everybody's bacon by boosting up a previous Soviet-made MHD to give additional juice to the underpowered station, Dietrich's MHD power experiment station would never have gone unquestioned. As things stood, this one was logged as "supplementary power source" under German registry.

Since it was orbiting free, nobody else went near it. Since the decree of territoriality, nobody could, uninvited.

You had to use a free-flying manned platform to get to it, so no one could drop by casually, unannounced and uninvited. And Dietrich wasn't handing out invitations. When you were the sole caretaker of a virtually automated electromagnetic weapons platform, you didn't have foreign nationals over for tea. In the unlikely event that the main MHD that ORTAG had donated to the Freedom project failed, this one would have to beam energy to the station, or be cannibalized to provide replacements. That was its rationale for being here.

But here was so far above the Earth, anything could happen. And probably would. Given the new German decree of territoriality, nobody had any right to come near the German power experiment—except Dietrich. If anybody did, he'd been told, he must do whatever was necessary to preserve security.

EVAs were more dangerous than they used to be. But Dietrich understood what was required of him. He was a member of the German "Green" environmentalist party. He knew what was worth saving, and what wasn't. The Earth was overrun with a pest called man. Like a cancer, man was destroying his host, the beautiful blue-white planet below. Greed. Lust. Lies. Shortsightedness. All of these must be managed by strong-willed, farsighted people who were able to rise above their animal needs and plan for the future. The Americans, the Canadians, the rest—they'd had their chance and failed.

They'd had their day and failed. They'd had their turn, and fouled the Earth.

So Dietrich didn't mind being the man who'd fired the first salvo in the new war. He just minded being treated like a cog in the machine by those below, on the ground.

If there was truly a new era coming, those like him, who protected and policed near-space, were the ones who'd secure it. Not fat cats in UN meetings.

But Dietrich harbored no illusions. He would be, in history's eyes, no more than one of the men who flew the *Enola Gay* over Hiroshima. If that. He didn't care. He didn't want to be famous.

Or infamous. He didn't really want to kill American pilots.

But he thought he had. He was sure the Americans were lying, that their Nomad had been totally destroyed by the MHD's beam weapon. He had seen it, speeding helplessly toward the atmosphere. But then he'd lost sight of it. He could not have too many electronics on his science station. Otherwise, his country could not claim, if discovered, that the Americans and their allies were misconstruing the use of the equipment onboard.

Dietrich's free-flying platform was so near the MHD station that he could see it clearly. Half of it was in shadow, half in the light. Like all their fates.

Seeing it, he became anxious to be inside. Once he parked the manned platform and got inside, he could relax. Sometimes he thought that his fate and the MHD's were one.

Perhaps they were. The next time the Americans ventured into the zone of German territoriality in space, that fate would be tested. Until then, Dietrich was merely a mechanic, keeping Armageddon's machine running like clockwork.

If below, on the beautiful Earth, someone wanted the clock to strike midnight, they would tell him so. The codes were pre-arranged. Otherwise, the targeting electronics on the MHD would never be turned on Space Station Freedom, but only on aggressors into its zone.

If worse came to worst down there, Dietrich and his two German cohorts would be told to move out to the MHD station permanently. They had a week's life support. In a week, the whole world could change.

As he used his reverse thrusters to slow his approach, so that his platform could bump gently against the power station's docking port, Dietrich wondered if worse would ever come to worst. He doubted it, when he was awake.

He only believed it in his dreams. But dreams were the only thing that ever changed the world. History could attest to that. Dietrich's dreams of dead pilots had nothing to do with history.

But every time he slept, he kept seeing their faces.

He felt the bump as the free-flying platform docked, and his whole body shivered with relief. Once he had his feet out of the locking clamps, he'd feel better. He wasn't truly any more afraid of going to sleep than he was of staying awake.

Or of being asked to shoot down another spacecraft. What were they thinking down there, anyway?

If the men who made the decisions could see the Earth as he saw it, they might make different ones. But they couldn't, and

Dietrich could only do what he'd been trained to do. You had no choice, in space. In space, any error was deadly.

That was why he was glad when he had crawled inside the tiny MHD experimental station and pressurized the module so that he could take off his suit.

Somehow, whenever Dietrich was out of his space suit, he felt better. And whenever he was around the MHD, he knew where the real power was. Right here. In his hands.

9

Day 5: Peterson AFB, Colorado

Ford had said, "Leo, let me take Shitov along with Cleary, back to Colorado Springs." Poker face. Soft voice. Letting CINCSPACE Leo Beckwith know just how much Ford wanted Beckwith to back him.

And Beckwith had looked out over the Potomac and said, "Shoot your shot, Mr. Ford."

Ford had never seen anything like the strategic paralysis gripping Washington in the wake of the German declaration.

Beckwith was a heavy hitter, and Beckwith was nearly out of options.

You didn't like to wonder about competency in Ford's business. You liked to believe that everybody was tending his piece of turf. You liked to assume that the highest levels knew what the hell they were doing.

You didn't like it when the Commander in Chief for Space turned to you and said, "Mr. Ford, I'm going to do my best to convince the National Security Council not to wait too long to act on this, but I don't know how successful I'll be. Congress wants to ignore this and let the chips fall where they may. We can't afford a war, or even a warlike posture, anymore."

Ford had known something like that was coming. Now, hours later as his plane taxied in to Peterson, he still couldn't get that conversation with Beckwith out of his mind.

Sure, American interest in space was at a low ebb. You bet, the Congress was unwilling to offend the Germans, the most muscular player in the European community and a major shareholder in the globalized aerospace industry.

But you didn't want to think that budgetary constaints could make U.S. default in space a real-time possibility. Ford had tried his best for Beckwith, even meeting with the President's National Security Advisor. But it did no good.

Everything was economics, these days. The U.S. was feeling the pinch. Ford had lost his temper and suggested to the National Security Advisor that they were going to end up the Portugal of the twenty-first century.

And the National Security Advisor had looked at his wristwatch, saying, "That may be, Mr. Ford, but the time I have for you is about up."

Ford knew when he'd screwed up. You didn't lose your cool when you were tap-dancing at those levels. You didn't say what you thought. So he'd gone back to Leo and they'd talked about it until Ford's throat was sore.

"Don't worry, Mr. Ford," the admiral had told him. "We've still got our rubber on the road here. I'll see if I can nudge some sort of workable consensus out of the Administration. I know I can get the Joint Chiefs to find a way, using space law as it applies to low-intensity conflict, to mount a power-projection mission."

Leo just didn't quit. But Ford had a bad feeling about this one. "Without declaring war?" he'd asked softly.

"Mr. Ford," Beckwith had said to him, suddenly wide-eyed and hard-voiced, "you don't declare war when you do low-intensity conflict."

And Ford had felt like an ass, hurrying out of there. He knew that. Everybody knew that. He was too tired to think straight, that was all.

On the plane, he'd listened to Shitov tell a crestfallen Cleary cheery little Soviet morality tales. Shitov acted as if Cleary was his own country's wayward pilot. This situation was making Ford think he'd fallen through the looking glass into another world, where everybody's job descriptions were reversed.

In that other world, Cleary was a Soviet son in need of KGB support, and Ford was some kind of government lackey who was having trouble moving his bureaucracy into line.

Once they'd landed, and Cleary was handed over to Pollock, the AFSPACECOM Special Ops Chief, under a gray sky, Ford kept telling himself he'd feel better.

But when that happened, Cleary said, "Thanks a lot, Colonel Shitov. I really appreciate you spending all that time with me. And you too, Mr. Ford."

So, maybe it was better to be a KGB colonel who told you war stories than a civilian DIA man who got your ass out of jail.

"Cleary," Colonel Pollock snapped. "Go wait in my jeep."

The kid headed for the jeep without another word, eyes downcast and shoulders hunched against the coming storm.

Pollock looked Ford up and down. "Nice trip, Dalton? You're cleared for your Soviet jaunt, by the way. Orders just came through." The Air Force Special Ops Chief's sandy mustache drooped disapprovingly.

"What?" Ford said, and couldn't help but turn on Shitov. "Shitov, if you—"

"I would have told you, Mr. Ford, but I did not want to get your hopes up high until the arrangements were made by my government and yours."

"You sonofa—Colonel Pollock, you wouldn't happen to have those orders on you, would you?"

Pollock did. Ford read them, shaking his head. "Do you know how much you could've saved my government, Colonel Shitov, just in jet fuel, if you'd told me about this beforehand?" He caught himself.

Pollock was smirking when Ford looked at him. "Got in a little over your head this time, did you, Mr. Ford?"

"Mr. Ford is justifiably surprised," said Shitov, with that way he had of letting you know that a KGB colonel was a whole lot heavier than an American military colonel.

"And so am I. Your Admiral Beckwith has done us a great service. This Space Command of yours is a fine utility of your government policy," said Shitov for Pollock's benefit. "If only, as with my country, the men in it could remember that we are all on the same side, things would be much simpler."

"And what side's that, Colonel Shitov?" said Pollock in a slow, warning drawl.

Ford didn't want to have any more of this discussion on the apron. It felt like lightning was going to strike down out of those gray clouds any second, but Ford knew it was the tension between Pollock and Shitov.

"The side of harmony, peace, and forward motion, *Glava* Pollock. You know as well as I that my government must prove to yours now, quickly, that we were not responsible for the crippling of your space plane. Because as you must also know by now, our equipment was involved."

"You can say that again."

Ford said, "Look, Pollock, just back off, okay?"

"No, Mr. Ford," said Shitov. "These things must be said so that they can be answered. It is like ghosts. If you have a ghost in your house, and you do not admit it, everybody thinks there is something . . . funny . . . going on. You are nervous. Strange sounds and lights are heard and seen. People begin to whisper. Soon you are thought to be running a secret organization out of your attic. But in truth, you only have a ghost under your eaves. And as soon as you bring in someone to exorcise the ghost, then things get back to normal. At worst, people will say, 'Oh, crazy Shitov, he believes in ghosts.' But they will not say, 'That Shitov, he is a traitor and a liar.' "

"What the fuck?" Pollock muttered.

Ford knew what was happening now. "Colonel Shitov is trying to say that if he shows us the equipment in question, and some sensitive communications, we'll understand that the Soviets are on our side in this. Nobody wants a disastrous result from technology transfer."

"Exactly so," Shitov said loudly, clapping Ford on the back so hard he stumbled a step forward. "You Americans are now facing your own high-tech weapons in the hands of your Third World tormentors. We know the feeling. And since, together, we have created most of these low-intensity-conflict problems we share, we say, let us solve them together."

"The USSR created them, you mean."

"So, if we did, *Glava* Pollock. That was then. We made a mistake. But now, any terrorist problem you have, low- or high-tech, is a problem we are glad to help you with. Mr. Ford understands this. So Mr. Ford has been invited to my country to see what information we have that may be helpful. Surely this is no cause for distress on your part, since your government's highest officials have sanctioned it, Colonel Pollock."

Ford grinned and let Pollock twist until he thought of an answer to that one.

After too long a pause, Pollock said, "I'm not in a position to comment, *Colonel* Shitov, on what the involvment of Soviet equipment in this dustup could mean. But Ford, just tell me before you leave—is Cleary all straightened out with the D.C. authorities?"

"Assume it's taken care of, Pollock, until I file a report."

"But he's—"

"He's most concerned with you people grounding him. See if you can straighten that out for him, will you? And keep him away from reporters." You could only say so much, in front of Shitov. Pollock ought to know that.

Ford turned his back on Pollock and faced the KGB man. "I suppose, Colonel Shitov, that we'd better get our things together and get going."

The Soviet Union. Ford couldn't quite believe it until, once Pollock had stalked over to the waiting jeep and driven away, Shitov looked at him with twinkling eyes and winked.

"You see, Mr. Ford, you have been worried that your government and mine are not efficient any longer. Do not worry. Where it counts, we are still the superpowers."

"I hope to hell so, sir," Ford muttered. He wasn't convinced that a cozy trip to the Soviet Union with Shitov was any kind of good idea, but nobody'd asked him what he thought, and his orders had Leo Beckwith's signature on them.

The least Leo could have done was to warn him. The Soviet Union. Baikonur, the Soviet Cape Canaveral. The times, Dalton Ford told himself, sure were changing.

He just wasn't sure they were changing fast enough. Leo wanted the Soviets to have a clean bill of health. With the number of Cold Warriors still in this government, that was going be nearly impossible to accomplish, even if the MHDs that Ford were to inspect all said *Made in Japan* on them.

10

Day 6: Los Alamos

Mackenzie couldn't figure how Pettit had done it. But here he was, assigned to temporary duty—and her—still testing this FIFS suit.

He didn't know which of the two, her or the suit, made him more nervous. Things were getting so hot, so fast, over the German space territoriality decree, that Mackenzie had a sneaking suspicion that this was a real-for-real training mission, not merely a tech tweak.

If they had this suit, they'd use it. He wasn't sure he wanted to be the first guy to test its fighting capabilities in microgravity.

The damn thing wasn't exactly glitch-proof. He knew the weight wouldn't be a problem later, but now it was heavy and it hurt his ribs—and his left leg—to move in it the way he thought he should.

And he had Pettit's voice in his ear too much of the time. It was bad enough trying to become accustomed to the man-machine interface—the Associate expert system that downloaded targeting and command-and-control information into the suit and brought it up as an image on his heads-up display—without being distracted by her. Pettit was one high-power distraction.

The suit took dumps from the Global Positioning Satellite System, laser targeting codes from any digitally interoperable source, and fire, command, and control messages—all without verbal communication. So you wanted to look, not listen. It also had navigation and a three-dimensional data base, because it was meant for use in space more than on the ground.

You could mount any number of weapons systems on this exoskeletal powered platform, in zero-G, and you had yourself a discrete suit/soldier system. But Mackenzie couldn't quite imagine them actually deploying this prototype—and him—in space. He kept telling himself that this just happened to be the NASA model and they were training him on it because that was what they had. When deployment was imminent, he'd find out he was going to get his butt dropped into the Bekaa, in a ground-pounder's version, to look for hostages, or some such.

They couldn't seriously be getting him ready to use this thing in space. Could they?

This equipment sure seemed serious. Mackenzie had access through the helmet-mounted display to everything from head-steered forward-looking infrared and compatible night-vision systems to a target-handoff, digital-communications terminal.

He felt like somebody'd transplanted his brain into a fighter aircraft, for a while, as he tried to use the Associate expert system to give himself some sense of what kind of cueing he'd like when, and what sensor packages were helpful in which situations.

His helemt's integrated visor-display could show him a targeting grid, with blips and data, or a terrain map, or location information—strength and type of enemy—but required different protocols for each data stream.

All of which meant that Mackenzie's awareness tended to telescope down into a color-coded world of graphics icons that had very little to do with the acronym-heavy descriptions of each suit capability.

Miraculously, he was beginning to get the hang of it. He found himself, during one pass through the scenario bay, windowing a clear vision oblong in the center of his faceplate, running time-to-target display counting, using a synthesized target lock-on as if he had a live laser rifle in his gloved hands.

But he didn't. They didn't want him messing up their high-tech simulations bay.

He had to assume that everything he dry-fired electronically, from shoulder-launched missiles to "smart" pistols with electronically targeted heat-seeking rounds, really would work.

And Mackenzie hated to assume that anything would work, unless it had worked in real-time.

His suit's climate control worked in real-time, which was a blessing. So did the life support; he ran an hour in the suit without any air-intake from outside.

But he just wasn't an astronaut. And Pettit kept asking him questions that broke his concentration.

"Pettit," he snapped finally, "do I look like a test pilot to you? Do you think your record could live without a moment-to-moment of how I feel about this equipment so I can goddamn get the feel *of* the equipment? Unless, of course, you're planning to come with me the first time I deploy in this, so I can use this stuff the way you'll have trained me—with Mommy's voice in my ear the whole time."

She didn't say one word. He thought he could hear her breathing, but he wasn't sure.

At least this time, when his helmet showed him a long green swath of terrain with enemy heat-signatures sprinkled on it, he could pay attention to the goddamn C & C graphic without having her ask him if he'd like a little more magnification.

Because if he did, he could get it from the Associate program, by toggling through or even trying the internal voice-activation.

"More," he said to it softly.

It gave him too much. "Half," he told it. That was better. The blips of simulated people looked more like real infrared images of people that way.

He toggled back to blip-and-designator mode as he moved forward, stifling the impulse not to creep, the way he really would through jungle, because this wasn't really jungle and because Pettit was watching.

He kept asking himself where all this command-and-control download was going to come from, if he humped this gear in a space application, but he couldn't find an answer on his own.

When he'd finished the jungle scenario, he was panting and his suit whirred as it tried to cool him. There was just no way that "powered" meant easy. The servos that made the man-shaped suit respond to his movements were still slow to react to him.

Pettit had said it would get better. Maybe it was getting better, but he was getting better at moving in the suit too, so he didn't notice.

The FIFS suit had to "learn" him just the way he had to learn it. He wanted to sit down in it, but he was afraid to. The most trouble he had with it was getting up from a sitting position, or a prone position. When he tried, he was so far ahead of its motion sensing that it felt as if he were lifting weights with every muscle in his body.

"What?" Pettit said in his ear.

"What yourself."

"You're all wound up. Is something wrong?"

They could monitor his physiology in the control room. He wondered if they could in combat, or if there was some damned black box in the suit that did, the way pilots' conversations were monitored in an aircraft.

"Pettit, can we try some space simulation—just in case?"

He heard a long pause in that particular kind of grainy silence that indicates an open mike.

Then she said, "If you wish, Major Mackenzie," in a very controlled and professional voice.

He should never have grabbed her the other night; he knew that now. He knew it then, really. But his body hadn't believed his mind, and now there was this awkwardness between them that was only going to disappear if he fucked her again.

But she wasn't about to let that happen, and he knew she was right. So they'd really screwed up, for two people who were working together on something as crucial to James Harry Mackenzie's life as this suit might just be.

He said, as the display on his helmet began to flicker and turn to static, "Hey, Pettit? Not now—just sometime soon. I need a break. So does this unit. What's its power pack—six hours? It looks to me like it's time to change it."

"We put the twelve in this morning. But come in," she said, her voice deepening with concern. "You shouldn't be able to notice any power drain."

Maybe he hadn't. Maybe he just wanted to piss in a standard urinal. Maybe he wanted to flex his shoulder muscles without his suit thinking it was time to raise his arms.

Once he'd gotten out of the suit, he limped into the control room and said, "How does a guy wash out of this program anyhow?"

She said, "Sorry, I'm not sure you can."

Maybe if Mackenzie wrestled her to the floor there and then . . .

She said, "We've got the spaceborne simulation ready. We'll have to change your weapons grouping, though."

"To what?"

When she began to tell him, he wished he'd never asked. These folks were serious about deploying this thing—and him—somewhere, sometime soon, or they wouldn't be so item-specific in their equipment list.

You didn't run A-Teams and not recognize a shopping list when you heard one.

He stopped her recitation and said, "You want to level with me, honey?" as neutrally as he could, leaning against her control console to take the weight off his sore leg. "We're going to go play space war in this thing, aren't we? Real soon now?"

"How do I know?" she flared. Her face flushed, right up to her eyes, which slapped him across the face and then wouldn't meet his. "We're just . . . getting ready to take an opportunity if it presents itself."

"Don't I have to volunteer?" He kept thinking maybe she'd remember that he was a human being. She'd been punishing him ever since he'd gotten his hands on her.

"I think that's taken care of, don't you?"

"I sure as hell don't." He got up, jammed his hands in his back pockets, and started to pace around the room. "The least you could do is ask me nice."

"Someone named Ford called here," she said levelly, "and gave whatever authorization was necessary. That's all I know."

"Fucking Dalton," Mackenzie said. But he wasn't really surprised. He could ask to see whatever Ford had sent, but he didn't bother. Except: "Dalton leave a message for me?"

"Yes," she nodded. Her lips were tight. Her chest was heaving. He remembered how she looked without her shirt on, and then closed his eyes for a second.

Then he realized that she thought he really might balk. He could have pressed the advantage—maybe, but she was holding out Ford's note: *Have fun, Mac. You can thank me later—D.*

He put Ford's fax in his pocket. "You know, I could get dead doing this burn-in for you and your program."

"It's your program, Major Mackenzie—remember? DARPA just supports Special Operations Command, and you are the high-tech pinnacle end of that command." Her nostrils flared. She licked her lips. "You wanted all these fancy toys. When we wouldn't give you your whisper mikes and laser rifles and what-all, you were making my life miserable."

And I'm not now, right? He couldn't look at her anymore or he was going to lose his temper. He said, "Let's get that space scenario run, as soon as I piss. Then we're going out to eat with that list of yours—you and me—and we'll pare it down to something a man can be expected to need wherever the hell it is you think I'm going."

"I can't tell you—"

"And don't tell me what you can't tell me. You just don't get it, do you? In order to do my job, I have to know what that job is. It's what I'm trained for." Not entirely true, but there was no way he was going through another day like this with Pettit.

There was only one cure for her problem, and he had it on him. He just had to convince her that she was in need of a good fuck. And since she and her agency were giving him one, he was going to interoperably and responsibly return the favor.

He couldn't make things any worse than they were now between them. Probably better. Damn, he'd tell her he loved her if it would help.

Maybe he did love her—they way you loved anything your life depended on. But one way or the other, he was going to get the projected mission parameters before morning—out of somebody.

And Pettit was the most likely source of everything Mackenzie needed and didn't have right now.

Which just goes to show, you should never grab some woman rocket-scientist in a kitchen if you aren't ready for one hell of a lift-off.

One of these days, Mackenzie was going to learn better. But he hadn't. Not yet.

If he lived through whatever Pettit's people and Ford's people had in mind, then he'd swear off women. Or combat. One of the two. If he could just figure out which one was the most hazardous to his health.

Mackenzie was absently watching her fiddle with her damned control console, and all of a sudden he said, "Look, can we have a truce? For the sake of the mission?"

And she looked up at him, eyes very bright. "For our own sakes," she said. "I promise, you'll know everything you need to know before morning."

"Great. It's a deal." Nice to know that the Mackenzie luck was still in working order, considering that he'd just gotten himself volunteered for something.

When you were doing the burn-in on equipment, you didn't want any trouble with the suppliers. When you were doing some mission of Ford's, you didn't want to be short on information. And when you were working with a woman, you used everything you had, just like with a guy, to get the odds on your side.

If you had something a little extra on your side, like Joanna Pettit, it couldn't hurt. Stacking the odds in his favor, to Mackenzie's way of thinking, was the name of the game.

11

Day 6: Peterson AFB

Cars started pulling up in front of Rowan's place about ten minutes after Cleary got there. One. Two. Five. Ten. Old sedans and station wagons; a street rod; Rowan's wife's subcompact.

Despite the charcoal smoke coming from Peg Rowan's barbecue out back, nobody could call the gathering festive. As the Space Wing pilots saw Cleary, sitting on the stoop, only a couple of them waved.

Rowan came out of the house and said, "I guess we're about to find out what happened, huh?"

"Be a relief to me." Pollock's briefing earlier today had included everybody capable of flying an X-NASP but the two of them. Cleary hadn't seen some of these guys for months. But they'd all seen him. On the evening news.

"Me too," Rowan sighed, sitting down beside him. "I'm hoping like hell this means what I think it does. If they need us, they'll find a way to—"

"Don't count on it. Grounded is grounded," Cleary told Rowan without looking sideways at his copilot, as if they were getting ready to taxi.

But they weren't. And they wouldn't be, anytime soon, unless Ford had pushed some magic button or what Cleary had told the wizards at DIAC had done some special kind of good.

Sonny Cleary was beginning not to care. After all, he wasn't in a D.C. jail. So he was better off than Rowan. Rowan was housebound as well as grounded. Peg had taken one look at her husband and known he'd been dipping his wick where he shouldn't.

Gates, a short-coupled, dog-faced pilot who'd always been Cleary's fiercest rival, reached them first and squatted down, taking off his sunglasses and twisting them in nervous hands. "You okay, Cleary? Rowan?"

"Yeah, I'm okay," Cleary said, "but Rowan's got domestic problems, so tell the guys to take it easy on Peg, hear?"

If this had been a usual get-together, the wives would have been here. But it wasn't.

Gates said, "You ought to take it easy yourself, Cleary. Rowan, Pollock says he's going to drop by."

Rowan got up. "I'd better tell Peg."

"Better tell her you'll be on the roster by morning," Gates called after Rowan's lanky form in the sun as he disappeared around the side of the house.

"So what can you tell me, Gates?" said Cleary cautiously.

Behind Gates, men passed by, headed toward the smell of cooking food, with casual salutes or friendly waves.

"Damndest thing I ever saw. Pollock's talking like this is real-for-real. Walsh says Kirtland Test Center's satisfied that the problem you had was offensive in nature." Gates was going carefully, licking his lips frequently as he spoke and squinting at Cleary as if Cleary were a bogey. "Pollock's been asked for three low-intensity-conflict scenarios—a framework for a forceful response, including NASP assets. So it was a brainstorming session. Colonel Walsh came up with a NASP mission, but it's either you or me who ought to fly it, and everybody knows it."

"So you're flyin' it." Cleary ducked his head. "I got no complaints." A NASP mission? Now? After what happened to Cleary's? Real-time power projection? Cleary couldn't believe his ears. Or his bad luck. But Gates wasn't gloating the way he should be.

Rowan's red-headed daughter, a knockout at eleven, came around the corner: "Sonny, Daddy wants to know how you'd like your meat."

Gates stifled a grin.

Cleary said, "Raw, tell him. Come here, Megan." He put his arm around Megan's waist. "Megan, sweetie, this is Captain Gates. He's a good friend of the family's."

Megan Rowan held out a hand. "Hello, sir. How would you like your meat?"

"Any old way," said Gates.

Megan nodded. "Are you going to fix it so Daddy can fly again, sir?"

"It's already fixed, Megan," Gates said.

Cleary's heart leaped, then settled heavily. Fixed? How? He didn't believe it.

Megan's eyes lit up and she broke away from Cleary. "Outstanding!" she squealed, and went running around the house calling, "Daddy! Daddy!"

"Fixed how? How come I don't know about it? The X-NASP's sure as fuck not fixed," Cleary said dourly. If DIA and DARPA and the Kirtland test facility had all pooled resources and reverse-engineered the problem, all it meant was that they'd been able to determine what had crippled the X-NASP—not that they'd been able to develop countermeasures to keep it from happening again. "And I'm not sure three scenarios mean anything like what you're assuming." Without significant design modifications and some time to make them, the next X-NASP that encountered what Cleary's had might not survive.

"Don't be so negative. Pollock said somethin' that made me think we'd both be flying real high, real soon. They're about to clear you two for takeoff."

"You can't know that. It's too soon to try—"

"I told you Colonel Walsh was at that meeting." Gates was twisting the stems of his aviator glasses into configurations never meant to hook on human ears. "Something's really hot. Look around you. You're up here, cooling your heels. That could just mean that there's no reason for you to be elsewhere. But so are half the guys from Kirtland's squadron."

The Kirtland squadron leader caught Cleary's eye and bore down. "Tell me what really happened up there, Cleary. I've got a feeling I'm going to need to know. Soon. And I want to hear it from you."

"They didn't need to hear from me at that briefing," Cleary said. "I've got all kinds of psychological problems hanging from the trauma I went through, Gates."

"Yeah, we know. Just don't punch me, okay? *You* asked *me* how the briefing went, remember?"

"*You* came out *here* to tell me." Cleary stood up.

So did Gates. "Don't you want to hear the scenarios?"

"Only if there's one I'm going to fly and a retrofitted X-NASP to fly in."

"Well, somebody's X-NASP is going to escort a satellite of ours through the German territorial zone, to make sure they don't claim it as salvage."

That stopped Cleary in his tracks. "What?"

"You heard me. Pollock liked it."

"Couldn't you guys think of anything provocative?"

"You know the job description: preserve free passage in space."

"Your Nomad didn't run away with you. You ever had a space-craft head for the barn all by itself, Gates? With every sensoring package dead? If I were looking that scenario in the face, I'd pack lots of extra oxygen and a pillow for my ass. That's one hell of a high-altitude punch-out."

This was crazy.

"If we go on this one, I'd like to have the benefit of your expertise," Gates said.

Cleary wouldn't have gone to the bathroom as Gates's wingman. He didn't have to. He said, "I'm just sitting out my disciplinary, nice and content. You guys want to start a space war, you can do it without me begging to volunteer."

"I'm not sure that Rowan's going to feel the same way," Gates said. "Are you? We need a veteran on this, so the brass think."

And then Cleary realized that Gates wasn't talking about taking a squadron up there. He was talking about taking one space plane, just him and whoever else Pollock thought could give them the best chance of coming home in one piece.

"It ain't me." Cleary didn't like Gates. He didn't like this mission. "And I hope like hell it ain't Rowan. Somebody who's been through the systems failures we had isn't the right man to take up an unimproved testbed and see if it'll happen again. Not so soon. You tell Pollock for me that if he wants to see if he can finish what we started, and really destroy this program, he can do it with a fresh crew—"

"Tell me yourself, Cleary," said Pollock.

Cleary and Gates both turned and saluted. Their Special Ops Chief had Colonel Walsh in tow and Walsh, the 2nd Space Wing Commander, had a sour smile on his grizzled face. "Cleary, you are one trouble-seeking son of a bitch, you know that?" Walsh said.

Gates said, "If the colonels please, I'm out of here. Cleary, if you ever find your nerve and get back to Kirtland, look me up."

Gates sauntered off toward the backyard barbecue.

"What's this I hear about you not wanting to fly a Nomad power-projection mission, Cleary?" Pollock said.

"Well, sir," said Cleary. "Let's see. I'm grounded. I just got my butt out of jail. I keep getting messages from Carla Chang, the network newsie, about how she wants to take me to dinner. I'm assuming Command was right, that I need some time to think about how to keep what happened up there from happening again."

Walsh said, "Cleary," like he had in the Washington bar that night. Cleary rubbed his eye, which was still a little tender.

Pollock said, "Captain, you were a great help to Ford's folks at DIA. We've been able to give you a clean slate. Everything you thought happened up there can be experimentally supported."

Cleary wanted to sit down, but he couldn't. Pollock was telling him he wasn't grounded anymore. He didn't even feel relieved. How the hell did you tell the USSPACECOM Ops Chief that this mission sounded like a bad idea for anyone to fly? You couldn't. "If you really wanted me, I suppose I would have been at the briefing—sir."

"The results of the teardown just came through. But you might be right—you may be more use to us on the ground for a while," said Pollock carefully. "I like this mission, for the sake of morale if for no other reason. I don't want anybody flying it who's not psychologically prepared. When you get back to Kirtland, Captain Cleary, we want you fit and ready."

Please, don't throw me into the briar patch, Br'er Fox. Something was telling Cleary that the briar patch wasn't a bad place to be right now.

"Yes, sir, when I am, I'll be real glad of it." He could see Walsh's puzzled look. And Pollock wasn't hiding his displeasure.

The Ops Chief said something quietly to Walsh and left them for the group congregating out back.

Colonel Walsh said, "What's up, Sonny?"

"Sir, I don't know. I just don't feel like I'm ready—or that the X-NASP is." You couldn't convince somebody you hadn't lost your nerve. But when you were talking about testbeds as expensive as the X-NASP, part of a pilot's responsibility was to know when he wasn't fit to fly. It wasn't as if this was some kind of insubordination, or grandstanding. . . .

"That's not good enough. You're going to blow your whole career if you keep this up," Walsh said with what seemed like real concern. "We'll tell you when you and your spacecraft are ready. I want you back at Kirtland tomorrow morning. Full physical, including psych evaluation. We need you on the flight line, Sonny. We don't have Nomad-qualified pilots to spare."

"Yes, sir. If you say so, sir." He wouldn't say, even to Walsh, that he was scared to death of what he was hearing about this mission.

He wanted to fly. He even wanted to fly X-NASP. He just didn't want to fly this next mission with Gates. It was a feeling he couldn't explain, but a feeling like that could keep you alive. Or ruin your life, if you let it run you.

Cleary was feeling so badly that he almost went running after Walsh when the Space Wing Commander left him there alone. Then he couldn't bring himself to go join the others.

He just sat there on the Rowans' stoop, staring at the cars parked on the lawn, until Megan Rowan stuck her head around the corner saying, "Son-ny, come and get your bur-ger."

He grabbed Megan and lifted her into his arms.

"Daddy's going to fly again!" Her wide eyes were sparkling. "With Captain Gates. Isn't it wonderful?"

"Yeah, great. Wonderful." They were determined to have somebody on that flight who'd been on the last one. He didn't want to put Megan down. He carried her around the house and over to the barbecue, teasing her so that she was giggling hysterically.

That way he didn't have to look at anything but her happy face. He should have known that if he wouldn't volunteer to fly with Gates, they'd tap Rowan.

Now if he did, it would look bad to the guys—as if he were looking to supplant Rowan.

But he went over to Pollock, who was the ranking officer, and said, between mouthfuls of overdone burger, "I changed my mind. I'll do whatever you want. I'm a little skittish, that's all. I'm fit and ready. I'm just a prima donna. You know that, sir."

"I know that. When I have a mission for a prima donna, I'll be sure to call you."

So it was just one of those days when you couldn't put a foot right no matter what you did. Cleary left early, as soon as Megan went to bed. He couldn't look at Peg, or Rowan. He didn't feel like part of the team right now, and he didn't want any more ribbing about Carla Chang, whose messages were chasing him from Public Affairs office to Public Affairs office.

And most of all, he didn't want to tell anybody, not Rowan, not Gates, not Walsh or Pollock—and especially not Peg, how downright wrong this mission felt to him.

You could do that if you were going to fly it. But not if you weren't. You didn't say one word to curse somebody else's luck.

Anyway, he kept telling himself, when he got back to Kirtland tomorrow he might find out he was flying the force-projection mission after all.

When they needed you for something like this, they really needed you. People's memories tend to get short, and selective.

As Pollock had said, there weren't that many guys qualified on a Nomad. There was a time when Cleary had been jealously proud to be one of them. Now, he was beginning to wonder if he actually had lost his nerve.

His dreams that night in the Peterson motel were full of unresponsive, crashing spacecraft that tumbled end over end and melted slowly around him, while inexplicably working coms showed him the agonized faces of Peg and Megan and Colonel Walsh, back on the Earth below, as he and Rowan and the Nomad began coming apart when they hit the atmosphere.

12

Day 7: Moscow

"Mr. Ford, you have my nation's condolences," said Shitov dolefully as he put down the heavy, shielded Kremlin phone. Ah, Levonov, your curses follow me. Here Shitov had been just about to parade his wonderful trophy of *glasnost,* the redoubtable Dalton Ford, before the democracy-hungry elite of the Executive President's inner circle. And now this. Tragedy. Disaster.

Dalton Ford looked at him unblinkingly and said, "I'll need to confirm with my embassy, of course."

"Of course." This was not Shitov's dingy little KGB office. This was a place to receive foreigners, a borrowed office festooned with Czarist treasures of art and gilt, as if the USSR were a rich and elegantly cultured country, instead of a bunch of terrified men making intricate deals to ensure the delivery of mutton chops and the security of their leases on dachas in safe Great Russian strongholds. Shitov prayed that the phone system, this once, would not betray him as he tried to make the connection to the American embassy that Ford had requested.

Only when he had the American embassy on the line did Shitov look again at Dalton Ford. The taxidermist's stare was still in place on the American's face.

Shitov had seen such stunned looks on the faces of such men many times in the past. Every muscle of Ford's face was straining for an appearance of normalcy. Not a sign was there of anguish or loss—or of any humanity at all.

Therefore, Ford was feeling deep, personal pain. Otherwise, the face of such a professional would have been cunningly arranged to dispel any appearance of shock, of embarrassment, of weakness, perhaps even of personal guilt.

Shitov felt guilt at that moment. He had been too concerned with his own country's need not to appear weak to be doing his job.

He handed Ford the phone and vacated his chair with a beneficent gesture. "Talk. I will wait outside."

Both he and Ford knew that any conversation going from here to the American embassy would be recorded by each side. Ford's remarkable request had not penetrated Shitov's preoccupation, until now.

He had barely reached the door when Ford said, loudly and wryly, "Don't leave on my account, Colonel Shitov," and went back to muttering into the phone.

So Shitov did not leave. He watched the American receive confirmation that one of their most secret spacecraft had crashed into the desert of northern Nevada, first breaking up in the atmosphere so completely that pieces of it were scattered for at least two hundred kilometers.

Ford rubbed the bridge of his nose as he listened. Still, the face showed no sign of tragedy. When he cradled the handset, Ford closed his eyes for an instant before he said, "Thanks. You had more information than my embassy did, but that's not surprising."

"We have . . . common interests," Shitov said softly. "We knew you would need to know this as soon as possible, and that no one would tell you while you were here." Poor Ford. "If you need to make a personal call . . . ?"

"That transparent?" Ford chuckled. It was not a pretty sound. "I should go over to the embassy. I really want to see Baikonur, you know that, Colonel. And I don't want my leaving misconstrued, but . . ."

"But." Shitov moved heavily to the desk as Ford stood up. All his hopes of besting Levonov, finally and completely, using this tame American, were rapidly dwindling. "But," he began again, softly, "you must preserve security, and learn as much as you can. How if we share with you what we know of this . . . incident?"

Stay, Mr. Ford, and work with me. Do not revert to the old ways. "We have much to offer. . . ." Very much, where overhead sensing, especially over the United States, was concerned. So much that Shitov must be careful what he promised, to make sure those promises could safely be fulfilled.

Ford said, "One of those pilots . . . I need to know who was on that plane." Ford's lips quirked. "No use pretending this one didn't happen. It's not that I don't want to stay. . . ."

"If it was our equipment that was used against your spacecraft, then this is an attack on us as well." Shitov took a deep breath and risked his career on his next words. "I am told that we have lost a satellite, at just the same time your space plane was damaged. This satellite was in line of sight of a . . . of the beam weapon trained on your manned spacecraft, my people are sure."

Ford sat on the edge of the marvelous, carved, and gilded desk. He looked at Shitov for a moment before he said, "You DF'd it?"

"Dee Eff'd?"

"DF. Direction finding. You can plot a source from the positions of the two . . . affected spacecraft? You would? Share it, I mean?"

"I am saying that, if our relations are at stake and it will be helpful, we will give you whatever information we can. Within security constraints, I am proving to you that we sold the MHDs without malice, and not expecting them to be used aggressively. This is why you are here, and why I am telling you what I can."

Ford shook his head wonderingly. "I don't know how to thank you." At last, emotion animated Ford's face.

"We are saving our hides, Mr. Ford. If you have a fox in your henhouse, we cannot have it said it is a Soviet fox. If we have a fox in ours, how if we let people think it was an American fox? I have told you, Mr. Ford, our troubles are no longer with one another, if we can only convince our government hierarchies of this. Our troubles are with the New Axis."

Ford rubbed his arms. "Don't call it that, Colonel. It gives me the creeps."

"Then, Mr. Ford, we shall call it the Coalition. But mark my words, it is not what you are calling it, but what we are calling it: the New Axis. You Americans still think that calling a thing by another name changes its nature."

"I've got to go. Come with me, Colonel—to my embassy."

"I must get permission, this is only natural. And you will want more information, I am certain. So I will get you a car, and come along in an hour or so. This is, of course, only possible if you will make it clear that I am not defecting when I arrive at your embassy gates."

Ford tried to smile. But the American was distracted. Someone he knew had been on the space plane, perhaps. Or he was more intimately involved in the technical end of this space plane project than was Shitov with the Cosmos program, whose satellite had been destroyed by what Soviet space scientists were sure was a nonnuclear EMP blast.

Once he got Ford his car, Shitov stood alone on the steps, watching the American depart. If Levonov was in any way responsible for persuading the Soviet government to sell the MHDs to the Germans, then Shitov would be filled with zeal.

In the old days, Shitov might even have laid a trail of crumbs to Levonov's door, linking him with the sale. But these were not the old days. No Soviet malice must be discovered. Because of that, a great deal of cooperation would be necessary.

More cooperation, perhaps, than even the KGB could convince the Executive President was necessary. Those who thought that the President was the KGB's creature were wrong, fools trying to seek solace and continuity where there was none.

Before he went inside to begin wresting from the Soviet Space Agency more information about satellite tracks than he had a right to demand, Shitov looked up at the sky.

The Germans, with their Italian and Japanese cohorts, were becoming so bold they were sloppy. The loss of one Cosmos was not great, not to the Soviet reconnaissance program that had so many. But it was bad luck for the New Axis.

Thus it was good luck for Shitov. He decided that he would have Levonov's movements and meetings over the last year scrutinized, to see if any links with the sale of the MHDs to the Germans could be uncovered—or developed.

But his heart was not in it today. Beyond the white sky was a weapon that had a Soviet power source, but was not a Soviet weapon. This was the coming home to roost of many ill-begotten chickens. The superpowers had given up much, on the ground. They must not be forced to default in space.

Shitov was a man whose sons had not lived to die for their country. But he had had sons once. And he knew loss when he saw it. The American, Dalton Ford, was a man like any other. His personal stake in this matter was written all over his face.

Men who have personal stakes in international crises change the world too radically, too erratically. Shitov must get his *apparatchiki* up and running, to tell him what it was that made his wonderful new asset, Dalton Ford, look as if his own foot were in the grave when he'd heard the news.

In the sky, high above, something glittered. A Soviet aircraft, touched by the sun. Shitov hurried up the steps. Ford would be

leaving for his country, by nightfall, if Shitov was any judge of
men and governments.

Which he was. Shitov must contrive some way to go with him.
This crisis was developing too quickly to try managing it from
behind a desk. He would call Shitova and tell her he would not
be bringing the American home for dinner.

Too bad. It had cost him a great deal to get the leg of lamb
for the stew. And he would make sure that Shitova did not realize
that, secretly, Shitov was relieved.

It was not that Shitova was a terrible cook, or even a mediocre
cook. It was that all Soviet women were terrible cooks, and
that nearly all Soviet food was mediocre, at best, by global
standards.

So this crisis had its blessing: Shitov would not have to watch
Dalton Ford heroically facing a greasy lamb stew with many
potatoes and a few wizened vegetables, or pushing his *plouf*
around his plate and pretending to eat it.

Shitov had been prepared, of course, to tough it out. He had
secured a decent wine. He had sent his aide to the bakery. They
could have filled up on wine and bread. But this way, Shitov
would not have to make robust jokes about his country's econo-
my.

Those jokes were not funny. But Ford would have laughed, and
Shitov would have persevered. Now he did not need to wonder
just how much of what was said in his home would later be
recited back to him at some inopportune time by his enemies
in the KGB.

Now he had only to wonder how he might buy his way onto the
flight returning Dalton Ford to the U.S. It was a matter of dangling
the right tidbits of information before the American. Say the right
thing, and access to the Americans' inner councils—even to Leo
Beckwith himself—would be assured.

Shitov had learned enough about the Americans by now to
know that information could get you anywhere.

But since the information he needed would divulge, as a
byproduct, specifics of Soviet space capabilities, it was not going
to be so simple to get it.

But it still would be simpler than getting decent food on his
dinner table for such a guest—especially if Shitova prepared it.

So Shitov would do what he must do, and be back in the United
States. Even this sacrifice, for his country, would not be too great
a one for Shitov to make. Yes, that was how he would explain
himself to his higher-ups. He would heavily and sorrowfully,

wiping his brow, admit the need for him, Shitov, to keep a personal eye on an escalating incident and his accommodating American agents of *glasnost*.

Changing with the times, Levonov, that's the trick. And if Shitov's minions could find Levonov complicit in this fuckup that had resulted in the New Axis having a space weapon powered by a Soviet source, then Levonov would find that the wheels of change were parked on his face.

Such was the Russian way. The more things change, Shitov told himself, the more they stay the same.

Back in his borrowed office, he began cudgeling the truth into the shape of victory—for himself, for his country—and incidentally, for the Americans.

But not, under any circumstances, for his greatest enemy and that criminal of technology transfer, Levonov.

13

Day 7: Washington

Admiral Leo Beckwith was sweating bullets before the Senate Intelligence Committee. That was a contradiction in terms if Beckwith had ever heard one.

While the Senators grandstanded here, over in another building, Congressmen were pushing the yes/no buttons on their chairs as they voted on a resolution to cancel the X-NASP program's funding.

"And now, Admiral Beckwith, can you give us any salient details to justify the risk to human life—let alone the National Aerospace Plane development program—that you and your people took with such disastrous result?"

Beckwith thought, what the hell? "In a climate of mounting Congressional hysteria, sir, I know you need facts to make the best possible decision."

Behind him, Beckwith's aide slid out of his seat. Beside him, his Special Operations Chief, Pollock, whispered to someone crouching by their table.

Beckwith ignored the distractions. He wet his lips. His pulse was pounding in his ears and the men behind the curved dais all seemed to have faces twice normal size. He kept looking for friendly eyes to rest his on, and couldn't find any. "We're not talking about a test program going haywire here. We're talking about concerted, covert aggression by a hostile coalition of forces, of whom the Germans are only the figureheads."

They wanted to hear it. He was going to tell them. At the end of his table, the Secretary of Defense shifted to stare at him. He almost passed the buck to the DefSec then and there. But he had something he wanted to say—something he'd been burning to say since he'd gotten the news that Gates's space plane had started to tumble.

"This august body is a very special one. We have very special problems right now, with this German territoriality decree. If we allow the Germans to salvage, or destroy with impunity, anything that comes into their unilaterally established zone, we might as well pack up and come home. We have to defend ourselves. If we lose assets"—Beckwith shrugged—"then we lose them. We may not have the backbone or the money to fight a war anymore, gentlemen, but we're about to be tested."

One of the Senators said, "Wars aren't declared by CINCs, Admiral."

"Nor by the Administration without due consultation," the Secretary of Defense put in, looking again at Beckwith. "If I may, Admiral?"

"Please, Mr. Secretary," Beckwith said, and sat back, wiping his face with his handkerchief.

This Administration couldn't afford to lose the ability to fly such missions, not now. Leo and the DefSec were ready to explain to this Senate committee why strategic defense unmanned assets couldn't handle so sensitive a situation. The Executive Branch was ready to do anything necessary, so the DefSec had told him, to keep the Germans from unilaterally claiming space sovereignty.

But Beckwith had heard Administration promises like that before. They'd lost a billion-dollar plane, and two fine men. His heart ached. Especially because, if he couldn't win this battle, the loss of the men and their X-NASP wouldn't serve the purpose that those men and that plane, and everybody who'd slaved to put them into space, were committed to serving.

You couldn't win a battle nobody would let you fight. And you couldn't just roll over. The Secretary of Defense was explaining, patiently and painstakingly, the Administration policy in the face of an equivocal UN resolution and precious little proof that aggression was responsible for the crash of the second X-NASP.

Beckwith was sick at heart. It was hard to breathe in here, and the voices he heard seemed to come and go in waves. He looked at his notes and they blurred. He didn't have a single thing on paper that he could use to win this. There wasn't a clear cause-and-effect relationship between the X-NASP crash and the Germans. Everything he was saying could be interpreted to be an attempt to shift blame away from a flawed program.

You had to try to win with what you had. Beckwith had so little that he was nearly despairing. But he'd been up in one of those X-NASPs. He'd seen the curve of the Earth from space. He understood the technical problems that his science types envisioned. And he didn't blame anybody for what had happened to the second X-NASP. You lost men when you were in the start-up of open hostilities. Some of these Senators weren't old enough to even remember that; not viscerally.

If Beckwith and his USSPACECOM people couldn't find a way to make these Germans back down, many more lives were going to be lost. And if Beckwith couldn't convince these Senators, today, to back him up, then all those subsequent lives lost would be lost because Leo Beckwith had made a bad decision, and moved too early, without enough proof on his side.

Beckwith's aide came scurrying up the aisle and crouched beside him, a memo in hand.

Beckwith took it, read it, and scribbled an addendum.

Then he waited for a chance to reenter the discussion. His heart was thudding now. His hands were trembling. Damn the age spots on them, a constant reminder that nature would cede the field to younger men, eventually.

Beckwith had to find a way to make sure that, when his stint was over, his best had been good enough. He passed the memo to Pollock, who read it and handed it to the Secretary of Defense.

Still talking, the DefSec glanced at it. And stopped in midsentence. "Rather than cede my time to Admiral Beckwith, I'll just tell you that we've received a memo from the field. We've recovered the main CPU and the black box of the crashed X-NASP. Early examinations reveal that the spacecraft was inarguably attacked by a beam weapon of extraordinary but comprehensible power and design, and that we're certain now that we can do a quick retrofit that will make our spacecraft currently on the ground resistant to this kind of attack."

The Senators muttered to each other, hands over their mikes.

The DefSec was relentless: "Of course, the Administration will be discussing all possible responses, overt, clandestine, and covert, and you'll be well informed. At this time, if you have any additional questions about the kind of threat we're facing, I'll be glad to answer them as best I can. I'm sure under the circumstances, you'll be glad to release Admiral Beckwith to his other, pressing duties."

Beckwith gathered his papers in a daze, relief making him clumsy, listening with half an ear to another Senator's questions about electromagnetic pulse and nonnuclear delivery systems.

As he left the hearing room, he was faced with one more crisis in what seemed like an endless stream. His aide was holding the dead pilots' wives at bay.

Why me, Lord?

The widows were in town to be consoled by the President.

For a moment, Beckwith couldn't fathom why they were in this building, and then he understood: Captain Sonny Cleary, the pilot of the first X-NASP to be attacked, was standing by in case his testimony was required by the committee.

Beckwith couldn't have said which of the faces of the three had the most naked anguish on it. The red-haired woman who'd been leaning on Cleary tried to smile when she was introduced to Beckwith.

"Ma'am, you have my deepest sympathy." He looked at the other woman, whose chin was dimpled with the strain of not weeping openly. "Both of you. We're doing our best to make sure that your sacrifices weren't in vain."

Let me out of here. I can't take time for this. . . . He took the cold hand of the red-haired woman in his and pumped it, feeling like an automaton encased in ice.

"Captain," he said, after he'd shaken the second grieving wife's hand, "I need you for a few minutes."

The test pilot paced him, eyes on his face, waiting for whatever Beckwith had to say. Beckwith couldn't hand the youngster the memo; its clearance was too high. "We think you're right about what happened, Captain Cleary. I'm sorry it took two more lives to verify what you suspected."

"Me too, sir. My copilot flew that—" Cleary stopped in mid-sentence and shook his head.

"Are you going to need any help—with those widows, or with that committee, son?" Beckwith stopped and faced the pilot. His aide, sensitive to all such contingencies, was back with the women.

Cleary said, "Sir . . . I really just want to get back up there in a spacecraft that can be expected to do the job. It's not the Nomads. It's just shielding. I know we can lick this. . . ."

The youngster's eyes were red. One was swollen and bruised, and Beckwith remembered that this was the pilot that had gotten into the scuffle with a Congressional aide. "I know you can too, son." Beckwith's voice thickened. "I'm so sorry . . . about your copilot. I know how it feels. Nobody can say anything to you to make you feel better, so I won't try. There's no need to feel better now. Time's got to pass. We'll do our best to get you and that plane you have so much confidence in back up there, I promise."

"Thank you, sir," said Cleary through white lips. Beckwith clapped the pilot on the back, squeezed his elbow, and strode down the hall before Cleary could see how moved Beckwith was.

When his aide caught up, Beckwith said, "What's next?"

"Deputies' meeting, in the White House situation room," the aide said.

"Good," Beckwith grunted. "Let's go." Deputies didn't meet unless the Administration had recognized a crisis. "And while I'm in there, find Ford for me and have him on tap. This is no time for him to be torquing around the Soviet Union."

"He's on his way back now, sir, with 'good news and a surprise,' he says."

"I can use both of those this afternoon," Beckwith said, as he hiked the interminable hallways of power en route to his car.

The eyes of the pilot haunted him. Whenever he came face to face with somebody who was young, and really hurting, and who wanted you to tell him that somehow it would all be worth it—the sacrifice, the loss, the struggle—Beckwith wanted to be God.

But he wasn't. He couldn't promise that pilot more than he had. But if he could have, Leo Beckwith would have promised Captain Cleary the moon and stars.

In point of fact, that was what he was trying to do, for all the Clearys coming up through the ranks, and all the widows and the young wives who didn't want to be widows, and for all the civilians who didn't care about anything more than a good job, food on the table, and unlimited entertainment.

His brief encounter with Cleary sustained Beckwith throughout the painful and explosive Deputies Group meeting, and through another session with the Joint Chiefs, and on into the night.

You couldn't let down someone like that young pilot, who'd look death in the face for you and just wanted you to believe in him, and his hardware, and his mission.

You couldn't. Not if you were Leo Beckwith, and your job was to expedite that mission at the highest levels. Especially not when that mission had gotten boys killed, and one of the live ones looked you in the eye and let you know that he still believed it was worth it.

So it had to be worth it. For all their sakes. Sliding into the back seat of his car, late in the evening, Beckwith decided he'd write his own condolence letters to Mrs. Gates and Mrs. Rowan.

He hadn't written one for a long time. He knew it wouldn't change anything. It was a token of respect. These were his dead. You respected your dead and protected your living.

As the car pulled out past the barricades into the sultry Washington night, Beckwith's aide asked from the front seat if he still wanted to see Dalton Ford, who evidently had Shitov with him.

Maybe Ford had something mitigating. "Might as well. Tell them to meet me at my hotel."

This was going to be a long, lonely night for all of them. When you had casualties, and an incident of such potentially dire proportions, nobody slept much. Meetings came together in a matter of minutes. And it didn't matter how many of you were together. The world seemed huge and empty and fragile as an egg in mid-fall.

14

Day 7: Space Station Freedom

In the main habitat module of the station, Dietrich couldn't get away from the accusing eyes of the other astronauts. Or at least the eyes of Jenkins, the American mission commander, and his Canadian girl astronaut looked accusing.

Maybe they were just worried. Dietrich was worried certainly.

Jenkins rubbed the flat of his hand over his bald spot and said, "I just heard from Santa Rita Control that the Japanese shuttle launched from San Marco Platform without a hitch. That's something anyway."

Dietrich didn't know what to say. He sipped his soup through a straw. He was sure they were suspicious of him. He'd been right here when the MHD had targeted the American X-NASP and fired on it. But he'd sent the message alerting ORTAG to remotely target the X-NASP.

So he'd killed again.

The Canadian woman, Magriffe, was saying, "Maybe they'll have some word when they get here about what's going on down on the ground. I feel so isolated." She rubbed her crossed arms and looked upward, where, beyond the habitat's skin, in the logistics module, her Canadian partner and Jenkins's second-in-command were hard at work.

Dietrich was sure they knew. All of them knew. Not just these two, but the two in the logistics module as well. His own country's science specialist and an Italian were asleep in the parallel habitat module. He was sure they all knew.

San Marco Control was sure they didn't. Nobody knew. The coded assurance had come to him across the light seconds, embedded in regular ORTAG-to-station message traffic. Proceed as planned.

He'd killed again. And he'd dreamed about his father, in his wheelchair—the sunken face, the hands like chicken feet. His mother had been tending Father, and she had both her legs, so the dream was symbolic. But since both were dead and he'd been holding onto his father's hand and looking up at that whiskered face as if he were a small boy, he was sure the symbol represented his own death.

When you consort with the dead in your dreams, what else can it mean?

"Dietrich, are you okay?" asked Jenkins. "You've been pulling a lot of EVA lately. If you're not, you could go back on the Japanese shuttle. No penalty. I'll see to it."

Jenkins thought that because he was the mission commander, he was everyone's boss. "Nah, I am just . . . concerned. As we all are, with the situation on the ground."

Talk about it. Not to talk would be to draw even more suspicion. And too, Americans were terrible liars. He needed to see how Jenkins might react. Now. Before the Japanese shuttle arrived and the planned salvage mission was revealed.

"The situation on the ground," Jenkins said, "isn't our concern. We're a multinational team doing an honest job up here. Whatever's going on down there, we can't let it bother us." He gave Dietrich a reassuring smile that wasn't reassuring.

ORTAG was sure the Americans would stand by and make no outcry while one of their satellites, crippled in the last MHD blast, was salvaged by the crew of the Japanese shuttle in German territorial space. If they did not stand by, then Jenkins's smile would turn into a death's-head grin.

If that happened, Dietrich would flee, over to the MHD station. It was the only safe place to be. There, he had options. Here, he was at the mercy of the others.

This was madness. How could Dietrich stay in the same habitat module with these people once the salvage mission started?

Calm. He must be calm. Everybody up here agreed that politics could not enter into mission performance. No one would know what was going to be done with the satellite once it was salvaged. Since it would be salvaged in the German zone, by a Japanese shuttle launched from a platform of Italian registry in Formosa Bay, its disposition as German salvage would be announced only once it was back on Earth.

All that had nothing to do with Dietrich. Dietrich's job was already done. He had arranged for and performed the destruction of two American spacecraft, as surely as if he had sat on the truss outside the laboratory module and shot at them with a hand weapon.

Without Dietrich, ORTAG would never have known about the second X-NASP's launch in time; without Dietrich, the MHD would never have acquired or fired on its target. He kept looking at the Canadian woman's freckled face, puffy and high-cheeked from so long in microgravity space. Her hair floated around her as if she were one of Shakespeare's witches. She looked like an alien.

She was an alien. They were all aliens, to Dietrich's way of thinking. He sucked his soup and floated there, staring at her. They were all aliens, all these astronauts.

They believed in fairy tales. They believed in lies. They believed in luck. Even his German compatriots believed in luck. Schliemann from ORTAG had sent him a personal message: "Good luck."

Dietrich didn't dare believe in luck up here, or he'd have gone mad. ORTAG had placed a heavy load on Dietrich's shoulders. No one shared it, not even those here to help with his mission— not anyone in Space Station Freedom.

When Jenkins again asked him if he were going to exercise his option to rotate home, Dietrich said, "I'm not sure of my orders yet."

The lie hung in the air between them. Magriffe's Canadian mongrel eyes narrowed as she looked at him.

Women could always tell when you were lying. Dietrich would go aboard the Japanese shuttle, as planned. He would help with the salvage mission, as planned. Beyond that, he dared not speculate.

Violence was not a necessary concomitant of this mission. Schliemann himself had told Dietrich that. The Italians and the Japanese had agreed to going slowly, quietly, carefully. But if the Americans tried to interfere, or if this Canadian woman did not stop looking into Dietrich's soul, then an accident might happen.

Accidents could happen. Projectiles could get loose. Module skins could lose their integrity, depressurize.

Dietrich began to sweat, in the habitat module.

"You'd better get some sleep, Dietrich," said Magriffe. "You don't look too well. Commander Jenkins is right. UN resolutions and politicking on the ground can't be allowed to impact our esprit de corps."

Esprit de *corpse*?

"Sleep? Ya, sleep." Sleep was impossible here. He would sleep after his next EVA—at the MHD.

Nevertheless, Dietrich headed for the supplementary habitat module, where his berth was. The quarters were too close here.

That's what no one on the ground understood. The quarters were too damned close. The Japanese shuttle would deploy the third free-orbiting MHD and then dock here. There would be messages. Orders. The confusion and, hopefully, the oppressive guilt swamping Dietrich's heart would be alleviated by the congratulations of others who at least knew what the real mission up here was.

Beyond the parallel habitat module was a laboratory module dedicated to European Space Agency experiments. Dietrich headed for it. There he would be among his countrymen, his own kind.

And although they dared not openly discuss what might happen next, when the Japanese shuttle docked, at least he would not be standing among the ignorant, damned, arrogant North Americans.

Being around them was like being in the company of ghosts.

15

Day 7: Washington

Cleary knocked on the door of Peg Rowan's hotel room. "It's me, Peg. What's wrong?"

Stupid thing to say. But her message, when he'd gotten back to his own room after a long day of hell, had read, "Need a little help."

The door opened. The woman standing there in a terry robe clutched around her looked like she'd been hit by a truck. Cleary saw red, swollen eyes; streaming tears; yellow-blotched cheeks; and a mouth so contorted in weeping that her teeth and gums showed as if she were some snarling animal.

With a groan of pain and grief, Peg Rowan nearly collapsed against Cleary. She was shaking all over; her arms locked around his neck with desperate strength.

"Let's get out of the hall, Peg." She was incoherent. He couldn't think what to do to calm her.

He shut the door behind him with his foot and stood there, letting her hang on him, rubbing her back with his hands, praying she'd get control.

But she didn't. Couldn't. And her deep wrenching sobs touched off an impulse to join her. Cleary squeezed his own eyes shut and tried to think about something else.

But feeling her shivering against him made it impossible to pretend that everything was all right.

Frank Rowan was dead. Half the Space Wing figured that Cleary should have died instead, that Cleary should have been on that flight. He couldn't believe that Rowan wouldn't come

walking in any minute and catch him hugging his wife, who was
naked under the hotel robe.

But Rowan wouldn't come. Rowan wouldn't ever be there, for
any of them, again.

Peg whined in a choked, impossibly high voice, "Sonny, what
are we going to to do without him? I can't do this. I can't tell
Megan. Who's going to tell Megan? Sonny . . ."

Somehow he had to stop her crying before he lost it himself.
He was beginning to tremble. He caught her up in his arms. She
was heavy; deadweight.

Deadweight. Jesus, what now?

He got her to the bed and tried to tuck her in, as you would
some child. She wouldn't let go of his neck, and then she was
pulling her face up to his.

Her mouth was so distorted with grief it was ugly.

"Sonny, stay with me?"

Her eyes were sucking him down. She let go of his neck with
one hand and it trailed down to grab his belt. Somehow he was
on the bed with her. But this couldn't happen. He couldn't let it
happen. "You don't want this, Peg. You don't know what you're
doing."

He didn't know what he was doing. She knew what she wanted,
all right.

But Cleary's body was in no mood. He leaned down over her
and kissed her forehead. It was clammy. He kissed her swollen
eyes and he could feel them roving beneath her lids. "Hey, hey.
It's okay. We'll get through this. I promise. You let me tell
Megan. We're going to make Frank proud of us, okay, Peg?"

"I can't. . . ." She exploded in a flurry, batting him away, pulling the covers over her head.

He got up and stood there, his breath coming fast, looking at
Peg, who was now in a fetal position beneath the covers.

"I'm sorry," he said, but you could hardly hear it.

At least she wasn't ranting that Rowan's death was his fault.

He got out of there and went straight to the bar downstairs. If
he started drinking in his room, he might not stop. And downstairs, there were live folks who didn't know that he'd lost his
nerve and walked away from a mission he might have been able
to save.

That was the worst of it, he admitted as he ordered a sour mash
and a beer chaser. He couldn't know that he might not have saved
the X-NASP and everybody's ass. Cleary was a better pilot than
Gates or Rowan. If it had been him up there, maybe the X-NASP

wouldn't have crashed. He and Rowan were the best flying team in Air Force Space Command.

How the hell *did* you go on? How did you face the guys? How did you face yourself? He'd almost crawled into the sack with Rowan's wife. But Rowan wasn't dead for him, not like for Peg.

Nobody could be sure that the pilots hadn't punched out, he kept telling himself. For Cleary, Rowan was just MIA. Rowan would come walking out of the desert any minute with a limp and a crooked grin, and then where the hell would Cleary be if he'd fucked Rowan's wife?

Come on, Rowan, be alive.

Cleary knew in his heart it couldn't have happened that way, but you held on to whatever kept you from losing control. Peg didn't understand that. Rowan had been her whole life, all she'd had. So she didn't have anything to hold on to here, with Megan back home, unknowing, shielded by the Space Wing wives and the command structure.

Cleary thought he should have called Gates's wife and told Sally Gates to go see about Peg. But if *he* couldn't stay with her—couldn't take it—how could he ask Gates's widow to stand in for him?

Gates's widow probably blamed Cleary for not flying that mission. Lots of guys did. He could see it in the eyes of the other pilots. And there was nothing he could say.

He should have told somebody when he'd had that bad feeling. Now it was too late. You couldn't explain cowardice by saying it was instinct. He slugged his drink and reached for his beer.

"Captain Cleary, how are you feeling?" asked Carla Chang as she slid onto the bar stool next to him.

Cleary said, "What it's to you? Want to suck my dick?" He hadn't meant to say it. But now, having said it, he stared at her with as much brutality as he could manage. Angry as he was, he managed plenty.

She blinked those slitted, cat eyes and recovered quicker than he expected. "I'll consider it, yes," she said, nodding gravely. "If we can discuss it someplace more . . . conducive."

Out of the hotel, she meant.

Why the fuck not?

He wasn't supposed to disappear without leaving word, was why. He said, "Say the word."

"Let's go."

Her head came up to his armpit. Her butt was low-slung but shapely in that Oriental way. He followed it like a beacon out of the hotel, toward her car, parked on the street in front.

A valet had her keys. Cleary could feel the valet's eyes on him as they got in. The ABC studios were right around the corner.

The car was an expensive German job. As she pulled away, she jerked the stick shift through its gears.

He put his hand on hers, on the gearshift. She said, "Captain Cleary . . ."

"Sonny."

"Sonny, you have my deepest sympathies."

"How deep?" He slid his hand up her arm, and over to her breast. If he fucked her, maybe she'd leave him alone. He needed to fuck somebody—or something. And she was really asking for it. Her breast, once he got his hand under her thin coat, was small and its nipple, uptilted, was already hard.

He couldn't quite believe she was letting him do this, but he couldn't stop either. And she didn't say anything. She just breathed and drove.

When she stopped the car, he looked around and saw that they were parked in a driveway, or an alley. She turned off the key and said, "Sonny, I know I caused you a great deal of trouble."

"Yeah," he said judiciously, running his hand down her arm again. When he reached her hand, he took it in his and calmly, staring into her eyes, pulled her toward him. "But you can make it up to me."

He pressed her fingers against his fly. She didn't blink. Her mouth was partly open. She said, "Okay, cowboy, let's see what you've got."

He leaned forward and kissed her. She didn't close her lips. Her fingers found his zipper and he thought, for one belated, cautious moment, What the fuck am I getting into?

Then she pulled away from him and he thought, Here comes the bullshit.

But she just brushed her thick black hair back from her face and went down on him, then and there, sprawled across the car seat.

He put one hand on the crown of her head and reached over to clutch her ass. He was sure she was going to stop and sit up—demand something or ask some fool question.

But she arched her neck and went right down to the root of him and he lost control of her, the situation, and his cock in one blazing instant.

So of course he had to find some way to regain that control. When she sat up, she licked her lips, tossed her head, and said, "Good as my word, see? Come in and clean up, have a cup of coffee?"

"I'll do better than that," he told her. And he was sure he could, if she'd just give him a couple of minutes.

So he was there a long time. And they talked a lot. Maybe too much. She was amazing without her clothes on. Athletic, like some monkey crawling on him.

When he finally remembered that he hadn't called in, and did so, there was a message waiting for him from Colonel Walsh at the 2nd Space Wing: *Be on the first plane to Kirtland in the morning.* And another from Sally Gates.

He closed his eyes. Morning was only a couple hours off. "Carla, I've got to return this call. . . ."

She rolled out of the bed and said, "You're my source, now, remember? I protect my sources. I'll be in the bathroom. . . ."

Source? He hadn't told her anything. He said, "Thanks." No use discussing what he hadn't told her. She was still a newsie, no matter how good they were together.

Earlier she'd said, "You're safe with me, Sonny. Just relax. I promise. Come here, come on. . . ."

He dialed the hotel and asked for Mrs. Gates's room.

A husky voice answered, as if from very far away.

"This is Sonny Cleary," he said, "returning your call. Sorry to wake you, but I'm leaving in a couple hours. . . ."

From the bathroom, Carla called, "Leaving? You bastard!"

Mrs. Gates said, "Captain, I thought you should hear it from one of us."

Oh, shit.

"Peg Rowan," Sally Gates said, "slit her wrists in the tub."

"God. Is she—?"

"At the hospital. She left the tub running and it overflowed."

"I'll be right there."

"No. Please don't, Captain. Just stay away from us. You've caused enough trouble."

When he hung up the phone, there were tears in his eyes.

Carla Chang was standing by the bed, naked, hands on her hips. "So. Leaving? Hit and run was this?"

He looked up at her and couldn't say anything. His whole body felt like it belonged to somebody else. If he'd stayed with Peg . . .

"What's wrong? You look as if somebody—"

"I just . . . come here," he said, and pulled her down onto him, holding her as tightly as he could.

When he left her, he'd blurted out the whole story of Peg's attempted suicide and she'd promised to keep what he'd told her confidential. He'd promised to invite her out to Space Command and she'd promised to come.

Promises didn't mean anything, he knew. Fucking didn't mean anything either, even though he felt as if this time it had.

All that mattered was getting back to Kirtland and finding out what the hell was up. Because something was.

The 2nd Space Wing was about to test some "retrofit" or other, or Cleary wouldn't be back on the roster. Not so soon, after all that had happened.

But he *was* back on the roster. So it was true. Maybe Peg Rowan and Sally Gates didn't want him around. Maybe there weren't a lot of guys who liked him much right now. But whatever Walsh had in mind was going to get Cleary back into the space envelope, where God could decide who was guilty of what.

That suited Sonny Cleary just fine.

16

Day 8: Formosa Bay

Osawa hated storms. A wild storm was blowing in, toward Kenya, as if nature itself was making a comment on the enterprise underway. The San Marco Launch Control Platform was a modified oil rig, its twenty steel legs dug into the sandy seabed far below.

Osawa could feel it sway. Men outside were being buffeted fiercely, making their way hand over hand along safety rails, hoping to secure equipment against the raging blow.

The wind outside made a deafening roar, pounding against the structure itself. As Osawa watched, a wave crashed over the platform; then another. A man he'd been watching was suddenly gone.

A siren wailed. Lights flashed. Osawa sipped his tea, sitting quietly. There was nothing he could do. Or should do. Everything was in motion. Nature had taken a sacrifice, a worker of some unknown origin. Nature always took sacrifices.

The shuttle had lifted off well before the storm. It was safe, so far. Nearing its destiny. First it would deploy the last of the MHDs, this one responsive to the newest and most sophisticated ground control: a roving policeman of the Coalition's will.

He wondered if the Coalition's German component would survive, politically, all the repercussions of this bold action. He doubted it. As a matter of fact, he hoped it would not. The Japanese Five Hundred Year Plan did not include a German partner as strong as Germany now was.

But Germany would not be so strong once the international community had punished it for its greed and decided it was not

113

trustworthy. Nations had characters. Everyone knew that.

The Japanese character was to slowly move toward a long-range goal, using others when necessary. Up beyond the clouds, the Japanese shuttle was a purportedly unwitting partner in the first test of near-space sovereignty.

So be it. All would go as planned. No one would dare to back out now. And whether the Germans succeeded or failed, Japan would benefit.

The weapons of the future were the weapons of economic warfare. Those who thought this was a state of peace did not understand the nature of war.

Those who thought that the work of the MHDs was not deadly did not understand where power resided in the modern age. Power of the sort that the MHDs provided was the covert sword of the new Japanese hegemony.

After all the squabbling was done, and all the Western resources wasted on internecine disputes, it would be Japanese fortitude, Japanese technology, and Japanese long-term planning that would win the day.

Osawa knew it. This was his plan, a thing of subtle pressure and interlocked repercussions. Schliemann had not understood such thinking, or he never would have succumbed to Osawa's blandishments. As on the night they'd spent at the Palace of Sexual Harassment, Schliemann could not think beyond his blunt-headed cock.

Once the first crippled satellite was salvaged by the Germans, all the dogs would be at each others' throats. But Japan would be quietly selling pulse-resistant technologies.

Japan understood electromagnetic hardening. It understood political hardening. And it would partner everywhere, with each of these xenophobic nations, until all of them were client states of an undeclared but quintessentially powerful Japanese infrastructure.

To conquer the world, these days, one did not use force of arms. One used force of technology, and force of economic muscle, and force of will.

When a huge wave came crashing down so hard upon the launch platform that it smashed the window before which Osawa was drinking tea, he had no time to react.

A piece of glass, borne on the incoming wave, pierced his eye. Another, propelled by the water's force, sliced through his throat and only stopped when his body, flung backward, hit a bulkhead.

The head of Osawa floated in the flooded observation room. The body was sucked out the open window by the receding wave.

Osawa's head came to rest on the decking, by his shattered tea-cup. The head's one good eye looked up and stared out, sightless, beyond the bulkhead, toward the stars.

17

Day 8: Kirtland AFB, New Mexico

"Say again?" Ford asked into the phone.

"I said, we own that satellite. And since we're primarily Agency alumni, we'd really like you to help us get it back down here so we can get it working—before the New Axis salvages it and puts us in the middle of an incident."

"I can see how you'd want that," Ford said softly to the former Deputy Director of CIA on the other end of the phone. Would wonders never cease? He looked out the window of AFOTEC, the Air Force Operational Test and Evaluation Center. It was so hot outside the air wiggled in waves. "We could use some enthusiasm up on the Hill for this salvage mission you want. Second chances aren't easy to get these days."

The heavy hitter on the other end said, surprisingly, "Yes, I think we can handle that here. But you've got to make reclaiming that communications satellite part of the mission."

Ford had been using that as a pretext anyhow. But he bargained for it a while longer. In the end, they had a deal, and Ford could risk saying, "We lost two men trying this once. I want to succeed at it. All of USSPACECOM does. But if this doesn't work, I want some help deflecting the heat."

He got his promise from the reigning monarch of the old-boy network and got off the phone. AFOTEC was working wonders on the Nomad here in record time. Ford had assured Beckwith that he'd keep personal tabs on the technology upgrade in progress, as well as keep Shitov's information channel flowing.

It wasn't your average couple of days, even for Dalton Ford. One of the dead pilots' wives had attempted suicide, which wasn't helping morale where it counted. But everything that could go wrong did, dependably. In a way, it was sort of comforting to Ford.

Ford stopped for a minute to watch when he reached the hangar where the AFOTEC test team and everybody else who had a stake in the X-NASP program were scrambling to retrofit this particular Nomad for a very special operation. A smile quirked his lips.

Nobody could ask for more than these guys were giving this particular emergency. Techs were crawling over the X-NASP like insects. The unit patches in evidence represented every shop with a vested interest.

Considering what they were doing, that included about everybody worth having. Letting Shitov wander around here was impossible, so Ford had left him with the PA officer, who was showing the burly Soviet what he could of the simulated rescue mission that 2nd Space Wing was hoping to perform.

Kirtland had simulation facilities par excellence. Now all they had to do was make the "surrogate-travel" simulation travel for real.

"Hey, Mr. Ford."

"Cleary." Ford's jailbird came toward him with a worried look on his face.

When Cleary reached him, the pilot said, "Sir, are you guys sure about all this C & C gear? I don't get it. I like the new hardening, but I don't see why I need—"

Nobody'd been cleared to tell him yet. That figured. "Come here, Captain," Ford said, and led the worried pilot off into a corner. "You know you're not taking a qualified copilot, right?"

"Yes, sir. Somebody in the seat who's new. I'm not complaining about that."

"Good." Ford took a deep breath. "Then what is it?"

"I've got a lot to do, flyin' one of those. Now they're giving me a laser-spot-tracker targeting system, an automatic target handoff, a sensor-tracking suite incorporating forward-looking infrared and laser-ranging systems, as well as a new global-positioning reference system that I just don't need to fly a rescue mission. They're loading this bird up like she's a Close Air Support fighter. And she ain't."

"Not yet."

Cleary's head jerked up and he looked at Ford askance. "Do you know what's going on? How come I need a handoff? Who'm

I handing off what targets to anyway?"

"You're going to have some weapons capability, if we don't screw this up," Ford said evasively. "Do you mind that? Nothing heavy, a laser pod with unlimited bursts of sensor-blinding 'ammo.' "

"Okay, I'll bite. What am I blinding?"

Cleary was steady as a rock. "Enemy sensors, Sonny."

"Enemy sensors," Cleary said, and puffed out his cheeks. "Mr. Ford, what's happening here?"

"Now about the guy in the right seat . . ." Ford took a deep breath and said, "You'll be carrying somebody who's going to act as your weapons officer, who'll take the target handoffs—if there are any. And who might need command-and-control data relayed to him, just as if he were another aircraft, if he EVAs."

Cleary's eyes widened. "Target handoff to an EV fuckin' A? Everybody doing this, sir? The whole squadron?"

"How many spacecraft do you see in here, Cleary? We'll give you a proper briefing, when we get the rest of the pieces together. But you ought to go look over this equipment. Ask questions. Try to make sure you'll have what you need—the right data at the right time. And keep in mind that you may be acting as a spaceborne relay system for command and control, and intelligence. If you've got suggestions, make them."

"How long do we have?"

"Not long. Go get started. I can't give you, or anybody, final specs until I see what kind of *satellite* interoperability we can deliver."

Not to mention what the Soviets will give me, if I can convince my own brass we should take their satellite tracks.

Cleary looked at him soulfully. "If you guys are trying to worry me, sir, you're succeeding. Is this—I mean, you're serious, right? No joke?"

"No joke. Are you a test pilot, or what? We'll give this bird to somebody else if you don't have the stomach for it."

"I said"—Cleary straightened his shoulders—"I wanted better hardening, some shielding—quicker suicide switches, some sort of defense against pulse. I'm satisfied that's been accomplished. So no, I don't need somebody else to take my place. I did that once. . . ."

The youngster was hurting, but Ford couldn't worry about it. "Then go see how quick you can get spec'd up on this equipment, Captain. Every minute's going to count."

When they flew this sensor-fusion mission, they were going to be burning in hardware that only theoretically worked alone, let alone worked together.

Ford watched Cleary's long, loose strides as the test pilot approached the X-NASP. You could give somebody like Cleary an AMAS (automated maneuvering and attack system), an ATHS (automatic target-handoff system), and a full-capability visor display. You could piggyback data to him from the GPS (Global Positioning System) and various other covert and overt sat-coms of U.S. and Soviet origin. But you couldn't help swamping him with data because, on top of everything that Cleary would be using or handing off to the man in his copilot's seat, he'd still be flying an X-NASP into a lethally hostile environment.

If you got busy enough up there, you could make a deadly error. The Nomads weren't ideally pulse-resistant, even now. The underwing laser pods were countermeasures, designed to kill any sensor trying to target the craft.

It was a whole new bird Cleary was walking around on the hangar floor. It was a whole new ballgame, for everybody.

Nobody'd even tried a simple EVA from one of these spacecraft before.

What was it Cleary had said? EV fuckin' A?

That was about right.

If USSPACECOM got into trouble out there, it was going to be serious trouble.

Shitov was sure that Soviet intelligence-sharing was going to make the difference between success and failure in this operation. And Shitov had been very forthcoming about the nature of the MHDs themselves. So there was a chance. A battle plan for a low-intensity power-projection mission that needn't take a single human life . . . if everything went perfectly.

But things didn't go perfectly, not in quick-reaction missions where the hardware was newly configured and the men weren't familiar with that hardware.

And there were endless political repercussions, things that could go wrong even if all went well.

So Ford was glad he'd had his little talk with one of the owners of the satellite that was now floating, dead in space, pulsed as either a prime or secondary target of the blast that had taken out Gates and Rowan's X-NASP, and incidentally, a Soviet Cosmos.

Ford hoped Los Alamos had their end together. You could never tell, until the last minute, whether people or hardware were really ready and able to perform as expected.

DARPA could balk. Nobody in USSPACECOM could give them orders. They weren't an action agency. Conard had gone down there to see how their preparations were coming.

Ford should have gone, but he was less concerned about the man doing that part of the mission than any other.

After all, if he got a man up there with an exoskeletal powered suit, then that man was going to be James Harry Mackenzie. Mackenzie would look Ford in the eye and tell him, flat out, whether he thought the equipment would perform as advertised— whether Mackenzie could do the job with what he had.

The question was, would the Los Alamos-DARPA team let them try?

If not, then the X-NASP was going to be buzzing around like a wasp up there, hoping to scare the Germans into inactivity the old-fashioned way, with a suppression mission of the sort you'd fly in atmosphere.

What worked in atmosphere didn't always work in the space envelope.

Thinking that glum thought, Ford decided to see if he could get one more, final retrofit, just in case nothing else on this mission went his way. When the chips were down, you could always go kinetic.

Chucking rocks had gotten the job done for mankind for thousands of years. Even in this new, micromanaged environment of low lethality and symbolic action, it didn't hurt to have a rocket in your pocket.

18

"Whither FIFS goeth, I goeth," Joanna Pettit, crossing her arms in a calculated display of determination, told Chuck Conard, the blond Adonis from Consolidated Space Operations Command in Colorado. Pettit was the final authority on whether that suit went anywhere, let alone into a high-risk field situation.

"Huh?" said Conard. A slight frown creased his tanned brow.

He was Army Space Command Intelligence, for God's sake. He couldn't be as stupid as that, Pettit told herself.

The trouble with blond Adonises was that one saw them most frequently in deodorant soap commercials, wearing sensual smiles and rubbing overmuscled bodies in onanistic preoccupation. So when one walked into your office, you assumed that he wasn't smart enough to have anything better to do than maintain his physical perfection.

Pettit tugged at her ponytail. This was a USSPACECOM light colonel and an astronaut. So he couldn't be as dumb as he looked. Or sounded.

She tried again: "I'm not sending that FIFS suit over to Kirtland unless I go with it. You seem to be saying you're going to integrate it into a larger system. For test purposes."

"That's right, Dr. Pettit," said Conard, stone-faced.

She hadn't asked him to sit down in her tiny, private office. She didn't now. "We're the test authority. So far, this suit's come through with flying colors, no matter what we've asked of it. We can't risk a failure caused by unfamiliar personnel who don't know its intricacies. DARPA has too much time and money invested in this program."

121

Say the magic words: DARPA and money. Pettit knew these men referred to her as a DARPA Witch. Or worse. And she was nearly certain that "test," in this discussion, meant "field test": the real thing.

She glared at the Army Space Command officer, daring him to admit the truth, that they were planning to use FIFS for real, not integrate it into some nice, safe test environment.

"Fine," said Conard. "Then would you consider packing an overnight bag and coming with us to Kirtland?"

They *were* planning to use FIFS for real. She wasn't a child. Or a moron. They needn't lie to her. She got up, to continue making her argument at closer range.

Then Conard's words penetrated. "What?" she said. It was her turn to look stupid.

"Come out to AFOTEC and help us put FIFS in the circuit. We can use all the expertise we can get." Conard's blue-sky eyes examined her microscopically and she stopped in her tracks. "But if you're on the team, we expect you to give us one hundred percent."

Get her to Kirtland, and then what? "Whatever you're doing, you people and your Mr. Ford, I want you to know that if you destroy or damage this piece of equipment, in any phase of your 'testing,' DARPA is going to expect you to pay to replace it."

"No problem, Dr. Pettit." Conard picked up his briefcase. "We'll expect you, Mackenzie, and the FIFS at Kirtland by 0800 tomorrow at the latest."

Pettit wanted to tell Conard that he was asking the impossible, just to see some human expression cross his face.

But she didn't. "Fine," she snapped. "We'll be there." At least this way she could keep tabs on what USSPACECOM was doing with FIFS, and make sure that the hardware integration was done correctly.

When she reached the virtual prototyping bay, where Mackenzie was working the suit, she asked the techs to leave. "Tell Jack were're going to take this unit over to Kirtland. I'm going with it. I need everything racked for travel by five o'clock."

Nobody argued with her. She almost wished someone would. Maybe Jack, as senior scientist, would voice the obvious objections.

But he wouldn't. And the rest of them couldn't. She was DARPA's program manager. She who has the gold makes the rules.

Or should. Except, in what was clearly an extraordinary situation, she was being maneuvered into a position where it was going to be extremely difficult to say no to Dalton Ford's next request. Especially because Ford wasn't asking.

Pettit fussed around in the control room instead of breaking into the ongoing simulation.

The man in the suit, out there in the prototyping bay, looked like a man from Mars in some B movie. Mackenzie was going to think she'd lied to him, or at least withheld information.

But she hadn't known for sure that this would happen. If she'd known for certain, she'd never have let him touch her that night. Pettit sat on the edge of the console and stared at the suited man climbing a ladder, ignoring the computer graphics that told her what he saw and measured his performance.

She had every right to be worried about the suit. If they destroyed it, or lost it, she'd make them replace it, all right. Her stomach was queasy. She tried not to guess what was going on at Kirtland. She'd find out when she got there.

So would Mackenzie. This wasn't her idea. Why did she feel so anxious? Because the FIFS program was her personal baby, she told herself. Not because of Mackenzie . . .

She reached down beside her on the console and hit the slate button. "Mac, can you cut this one short and come in? I need to talk to you."

She refused to call him Harry, as he'd asked. She couldn't, and keep him at arm's length. Mackenzie was a grabby, manipulative bastard and she didn't like him at all. If he loved her as much as he loved that suit, he'd refuse whatever this mission was. Balk. He didn't have to go.

She didn't have to let the FIFS suit go. . . .

Nothing was graven in stone. She'd only agreed to take the suit to Kirtland and help interface it with . . . what?

Interoperability tests. That's what she'd call this. She busied herself writing program notes into the computer record until he came into the bay. Might as well have it on file that USSPACECOM, in the person of Conard, had agreed to replace any damaged equipment.

If, when she got to Kirtland, she didn't like what she saw, she could still say no. Only a CINC could argue with her decision. And even that might not stop her from pulling the plug. This was leading-edge test hardware, for God's sake. It wasn't field-ready.

It was barely operational.

If you were a DARPA Witch, and a successful one, you'd taken a lot of crap to get where you were. Taken too much crap to be muscled by a bunch of cowboys.

Mackenzie, still wearing the FIFS underliner, stuck his head in the door. "Yeah, Boss?"

They couldn't seem to keep things impersonal. Her skin tingled, as if lightning were about to strike, whenever he was in the same room.

"Mac, somebody named Conard from CSOC was just here. We're taking the suit over to Kirtland."

"We?" He pushed the door shut, leaned his head back against it, and looked at her through half-closed eyes.

"It's my project. I'm going with FIFS."

He pursed his lips and nodded slightly. "How about my shopping list?"

Did everyone assume that FIFS was combat-ready? Did Mackenzie know more than she did? Had SPACECOM been manipulating her the entire time?

She almost threw a pencil at him. "Take what you want. It's just tests, that's all."

"Right." He pushed away from the door and came over to her. She got up from the console. He was too close. She moved back.

"Look, Mackenzie, back off, okay? We've got too much to do."

"Okay," he said. "Just trying to establish a little rapport here."

She turned around, her back to him. Her neck prickled. Why had she let this idiot grab her like that? She was so uncomfortable around him, whenever he wasn't safe out there in that suit, that she wasn't sure she was making good decisions.

"If you want to establish rapport, why don't you get on the horn to this Ford person and find out what kind of interoperability he's looking for, so that I can bring whatever we're going to need?"

Mackenzie's hand came down on her shoulder, and moved to her throat. She straightened up. She was going to kill this infuriating man, decapitate him with a clipboard. Weapons at hand.

His fingers on her throat were spread wide. He pulled her back toward him and she couldn't say anything. She was frightened, suddenly.

Of him. Or for him. For the suit. The project. Everything.

He pressed against her, from behind, and kissed the top of her head. "It'll be okay. I promise. We're going to do fine."

"We can't do this. . . ."

In the control room, no less. He was impossible.

"Yeah, we can. We'd better. . . . We need to. . . ."

"I don't." She twisted away from him. "What I need is for you to promise me that you won't trash my project." And yourself with it.

They were only inches apart. "Come on," Mackenzie said softly, "don't you trust me? What were we doing this for? Grins?"

"No. Certainly not." Flustered, she got away from him and began stuffing her briefcase.

"Dalton's a good guy. You're going to like him. I'd trust him with my life."

"Good. You may have to." She looked up. "Harry. . . ."

He was staring at her, hands on his hips. "What?"

"I . . . let's do one more run-through of targeting capabilities before we pack it up." She couldn't say what she wanted to say to him, not when she'd just rebuffed him once again. . . .

"Why not? We've got all the time in the world here, right? Hell, it's only a national imperative we're holding up. You want to do it again, we'll do it again. At least there's something you want to do more than once."

He slammed out the door. She was shaking. But she had to make sure that everything was working at top efficiency. There wasn't going to be another chance to tear anything down, or tweak it much, once they got to Kirtland.

And if Mackenzie didn't like it, then that was just too bad. If he lost his life because of her FIFS suit, then it would be too late to wish she'd worked a little bit harder.

Test. Damn. FIFS was ready, and she knew it. The question was whether Mackenzie was ready.

If he and his cowboy buddies asked too much of this program, or made too many last-minute retrofits, then she couldn't be responsible for what would happen.

Saying that would give her precious little satisfaction, if the suit was lost or destroyed or its operator died. Dead in a test was just as dead as any other kind of dead.

So she ran the man and the suit through one more very tough simulation, looking for weak spots, excuses to pull the plug, anything she might have overlooked.

But she didn't find anything. Mackenzie and that FIFS suit were an integral unit, flawless.

She wished they weren't. She wished she had some reason to back out. But there was none. Some days, you just couldn't come off the rails if you tried.

19

Day 8: Cheyenne Mountain

In his underground office, Leo Beckwith was sweating his way through the last of the red tape for the X-NASP mission. And he wasn't liking it. Something was escaping their notice.

The admiral couldn't imagine what it was, but he knew it was there. Years of command had sensitized him to his hunches.

He called the old boy who owned the satellite. "And you're content to let us examine the spacecraft for damage, and make a public fuss if we have to?"

"Leo, we're all in this together," said the worried satellite owner. "As chairman of this board, I can back it up when I say we'll give you all the help we can with this. Just get my satellite back before it breaks up in the atmosphere or the Germans snag it and we're in the middle of an international incident."

The old boys were allergic to the spotlight. Not because they were doing anything untoward. It was simply their nature, combined with years of experience.

"I'll do my best." Beckwith rang off, and punched more buttons. He called everyone he could think of whose voice might sharpen his hunch, or who might say something to clarify the fuzzy feeling he had that something was terribly wrong.

As he sat in his sterile, air-conditioned office, Beckwith's arm began to cramp from holding the phone. He'd used up all the clean handkerchiefs his wife had packed for him. Every one was sopping wet.

At wit's end, Beckwith called Dalton Ford at Kirtland. "Everything going okay, Mr. Ford?"

"So far. Suit's on its way. Spacecraft has got a redundant control suite so we can remote the suit back to us if we lose the operator. Shielding looks good. New suicide switches are all on board . . ."

"And . . ."

"And, Admiral, I ordered a kinetic pod, just in case I need it."

"Mr. Ford, if we needed to chuck lead slugs at this problem, we could have used an SDI weapon—maybe a Brilliant Pebble."

"Well, now we've got a Brilliant Nomad, sir. If we need it, that's all. I'm not saying we will."

"You think the Germans will offer resistance then?"

"I don't know, sir. I do know that they've got men on Space Station Freedom, and a couple more on that Japanese shuttle that's deploying . . . whatever it's deploying." Ford's voice sounded brittle, thin.

"How are you feeling about this mission, Mr. Ford?"

"Not bad. Considering. But not great, yet. We've got a lot of quick fixes to implement, still. And I still need permission to take those satellite dumps from the Soviets, the way Shitov has offered."

"I'm working on it, Mr. Ford. There's a lot of men my age who aren't as psychologically flexible, where old enemies are concerned, as you are. I could use some proof that we'll get more out of this intelligence-sharing than we'll lose."

The Soviet issue was problematical, but not insoluble. Although his words were sharp, his voice was gentle. Ford was a nontraditional thinker. And Ford thought that Soviet data-sharing was a crucial edge in this situation.

Beckwith hadn't factored in the Soviets as crucial. He too was of the old school. He'd been much more worried about the hardware problems. Men his age knew that these youngsters brought you technical fixes they said would work, and then those fixes didn't work.

Technical errors were one way to escalate from "situation" to "confrontation." And Beckwith didn't want a confrontation. Congress had made it clear that the U.S. couldn't afford one. He'd given his word.

Ford said, "Leo, I'll get you what you need. Just tell me I can proceed on the assumption that I'll have permission to take that data when I need to."

"You'll have it, Dalton." Beckwith surprised himself with the flat commitment. But he'd get Ford what Ford needed. Dalton

Ford was Beckwith's secret weapon.

The secret weapon said, "Did you happen to catch Carla Chang's piece on Space Command on the evening news?"

"I'm still in the Mountain," Beckwith reminded Ford, wincing at the thought of what kind of news coverage might be waiting on his VCR.

"You should see it. It was very favorable. Brave men defying death thanklessly in an atmosphere of budgetary constraint and national malaise. Then a piece on Peg Rowan's attempted suicide that would make a stone cry."

"That's good?"

"PR, Admiral. The human face and the human cost. Relieved the hell out of me. Somebody was going to do the Rowan widow. I'm just glad it wasn't a hatchet job."

"Me too."

When Beckwith put down the phone, he was feeling somewhat cheered. And rushed. He began rattling cages on the matter of Soviet intelligence-sharing in this emergency, saying whatever sounded plausible to change minds.

He even called in a few favors. He wanted to get finished here and go watch Carla Chang's piece. A little good press went a long way in times like these.

20

Day 8: Washington

Peg Rowan was walking in the dark and sultry night. She'd been walking ever since she'd seen the evening news.

She'd walked up to the Lincoln Memorial, and stood there, feeling the power of the place. The bandages on her wrists itched.

Foreigners were all around. Japanese took photos with expensive flash cameras on the steps. A group of black-veiled Arab women, some with gold masks over their eyes, streamed by her.

Lincoln looked down at her with his compassionate face. Peg had never realized how much of the nation's strength resided right here.

She wished that strength would come into her. She'd never felt such power—and she was so tired, so weak, so lonely. Lincoln's soul must have found this place and decided it was good. The air was hazy, moist. She turned on the steps, and it seemed she was looking through Lincoln's eyes at all the folks below.

Boys with their fathers in striped summer shirts. Women in white pumps and pearls. Fat men wheezing up the steps, beer bellies hanging over plaid pants.

She fancied she could spot the Americans, that something about Americans set them apart from the rest. A hurried air. A cold selfishness. A callous pride.

Lincoln had been shot by someone who thought his ideas were too dangerous, someone who couldn't believe in the America he'd embodied. Peg Rowan wasn't a highly educated woman. She was an officer's wife, though. So she'd tried to better herself. She'd always tried to do everything precisely right. She'd served tea and danced at parties. She'd endured endless relocations, brutal post politics, and children who cried in the night because as soon as they made friends, their family moved to another town.

She'd loved Frank Rowan, her high school sweetheart, with all the devotion of a religious calling. She'd done everything right. And God had punished her.

She walked down the memorial's steps. She knew that pollution was eating away at the monument, the way time was eating away at America. She felt sorry for the children she saw. They didn't realize that the future wasn't as bright as it had been for the kids of Peg's time.

America was turning its back on Lincoln, just like she was. She knew it. Her father had been in the Vietnam War and died there.

Inexorably, she was drawn to the Vietnam Memorial. Here the names of the dead went on forever. Here the mist hung low and men were working late under bright lights. They had jackhammers, and the sound and the mist and the crouched men and the names all conspired to fill her once more with overwhelming grief.

Her husband's name wasn't here. The news lady hadn't understood that Peg wasn't the hero. Peg was the casualty. She was already dead. She'd died with Frank Rowan, in that second, ill-conceived flight into an airless night.

Peg sniffled and ran the back of her hand under her nose as she walked among the dead. All those names and for what?

So that a fat and complacent generation of Americans who cared only for personal comfort could throw away a second generation of men.

Carla Chang had gotten it wrong. There wasn't anything left to save. There was no heart in the country anymore. That was why Lincoln looked so sad.

Peg Rowan trailed her hand along the monument. The black stone was cool, slick from the humidity. The jackhammers pounded in her ears. The light caught the mist and it writhed as if tortured souls were trying to beat their way into the marble and find the men behind the names chiseled there.

She found her father's name and she knelt down, wishing she'd brought a flag or a flower. But she'd hardly known her father. And she had no flag. She had no flower.

She had a daughter and a son and no husband. Frank's name wouldn't be on any memorial. He was free, not trapped like these men who must stay here for people to find.

She touched her father's name and moved on. She passed an old man crying, and a young child fingering a name while its mother talked to it.

Peg's eyes were so blurred with grief that she couldn't tell if the child was male or female. The news anchor had showed pictures of her husband. Pictures of Megan and of Frank, Jr. And of her.

The whole world knew that Peg Rowan had tried to commit suicide and failed even at that. She should have made Frank stay home. Sonny Cleary hadn't gone. Sonny had moped around the barbecue, trying to let her know what to do to save Frank.

That was why he'd pushed her away, because it was her fault that Frank was dead. Sonny couldn't look at her. She'd sent her husband off to die so that they'd look good in the eyes of the brass and she'd look good in front of the other officers' wives.

She walked and walked and walked, and finally she was out of earshot of the jackhammers and out of sight of the memorial. Then she felt better. Stronger.

She walked until she found herself on a bridge over the river. The Potomac, she thought. She was near Pentagon City. Frank used to talk about this place as if it were the kingdom of heaven.

The Building. Crystal City. The Pearly Gates.

She took off her shoes, put down her purse, and climbed up on the bridge railing. Surely the drop was far enough.

When she threw herself over, she found that she was flying. Weightless. As she imagined she might be in space. In the dark and weightless moment, with the wind in her ears, she let herself weep openly. She screamed her husband's name.

Then she hit the water, hard. And it was black forever.

21

As Ford drove them toward a long-postponed dinner, Shitov said, "Mr. Ford, it is time to get the ghosts out of your attic. People keep dying. We must exorcise the evil spirits plaguing this enterprise." Shitov sighed heavily and watched the expanse of moonlit, American desert speed past the window of Ford's car. "This woman who killed herself, she must be the last to die in this enterprise."

"I'm all for that," Ford said. "But we don't have ghost-busters in the U.S., Colonel."

"I think we should tell your American superiors that our Mir space station is at their disposal, and that this I can guarantee, as well as your satellite links. Any other help you need, you must only ask for."

Shitov was impatient, but not foolish. He understood that Ford was under great pressure to produce. But so was Shitov. None of his people had turned up a shred of evidence linking Levonov to this disastrous technology transfer that had put American and Soviet relations in jeopardy.

Why couldn't the ass who had negotiated this selling of MHDs to the Germans own up to it? The paperwork, what could be found, had the Executive President's name on it, which was merely a formality, and of course the names of various department chiefs, all of which meant nothing either.

"I need some proof of aggression," Ford said predictably.

Shitov sighed avuncularly and reached out to pat Ford on the knee. "Of course you do. This I know you need. I am trying to get it for you. Does the name Tohei, or the name Schliemann, mean a thing to you?"

Ford shook his head. "They're commercial space types. That's all I know."

"You should look into the comings and the goings of these persons. And also, perhaps, into the recent unexpected death of that Osawa person."

"The Japanese industrialist? You think it wasn't an accident? We're not cops or private investigators. They had a bad storm at San Marco—"

"Not for finding sabotage, or for finding murder. Just for identifying the players in a tight group of men who may have been the financing behind the MHD sale. Since it is clearly a problem that they were sold at all, I am having trouble finding out from my government who actually negotiated the deal. We would prefer, of course, to say they were stolen from us, or transshipped as something else—smuggled away from our bosom. But I am adamant that we cannot tell you lies. You must make your people believe we are not telling any lies."

This naked entreaty caused Ford to look at Shitov sideways. "I don't know what you think you're seeing at the test hangar, *Glava,* but we're only cobbling together a rescue mission for a commercial satellite that got fried when the MHD blasted the second X-NASP."

"Before the Germans claim it, yes?"

"Yes," Ford said. "If your people could give us some surveillance on the movements of the Japanese shuttle, or any unusual movements at or around Space Station Freedom, that might be one hell of a goodwill token."

"I will see. I can only ask. Soon you will be inside our pockets, so far as our space-based capabilities go."

"If I'm not mistaken, we've taken you pretty far into our own confidence. At least, my boss is taking a lot of heat for having a Soviet on site here."

"But how else could we do the intelligence sharing in real-time, with interoperating satellites?"

Ford grinned. "Well, if we trusted each other more, we could probably do it in less than real-time. But we're almost there. Let's just hang tough. I'll see if we can do any snooping about those principals you mentioned. You see if you can get your people to give me what they've got on Freedom. You ought to have plenty."

"Plenty, I'm sure." Space Station Freedom was an item of unparalleled interest to Soviet space-based assets. Well, perhaps not quite unparalleled. The continental United States and its coastline still were lucrative surveillance targets. The USSR had more satellites traveling over the U.S. than the U.S. had traveling over the Soviet Union.

So this intelligence-sharing should be helpful in alleviating tensions, if everyone remained calm.

But what Shitov had seen at Kirtland was not indicative of calm. The only bright note was that he, Shitov, was allowed to see these preparations for space warfare.

He knew that Ford was letting him see these things so that he could report back to his country and say that he had seen them. Thus, his nation would not think that these preparations were aimed at it and overreact. Ford was being very careful to keep Shitov informed so that the Soviet military would not jump to conclusions when the redoubtable X-NASP took wing, carrying weapons into space.

Since, among all weapons in space, the Soviet MHD was providing power for the most destabilizing efforts, this was a good strategy on Ford's part.

But Shitov was having trouble convincing Moscow Center that he was not fabricating reasons to stay in the American West. He crossed his legs in the car, to take the pressure off his toes, bruised but proud in his beautiful, if painful, new lizard cowboy boots.

"Mr. Ford, I am not sure how much longer I can stay here without good cause."

Ford nearly stopped the car. He slowed so that other cars honked and raced past. "Colonel, things are going to get very hot here very soon. It's not that we can't let you leave. Of course you're free to leave anytime. But if we need to do all the communicating we're anticipating, about our intentions and coming actions, through embassies and over red phones, something could get scrambled. Please stay."

"I will try, Mr. Ford." Shitov felt much better. He would tell Moscow that the Americans were begging him to stay. "But you must ask my government, and say whatever you can which is most illuminating, without compromising your security—of course."

"Of course." Ford drove faster. "Please, don't bust my butt on this, okay? Whatever you need to convince your people, I'll try to give you. But we can't announce this projected response to your people until we announce it to our . . . other . . . allies."

"You are doing that?"

"Not yet. So we need this back channel. And I can't say any more. I'm already out of my depth. Why don't you have somebody call Admiral Beckwith's office? Meanwhile, I'll ask my boss to have the White House brief your military attaché in Washington. Will that help?"

"Perhaps," Shitov said, concealing his delight. Levonov, you scum, wait until you hear how Shitov has become indispensible to Soviet-American relations. Shitov straghted his broad shoulders, feeling the not unpleasant weight of world diplomacy coming to rest on them.

"When I was a boy, Mr. Ford," Shitov began as Ford pulled his Jeep station wagon into the parking lot of an American steak house, "we used to dream the big dreams. This was when Sputnik was first launched and my father took me outside and showed it to me. We dreamed of great cities in space and a fine new world. Sometimes I think such a world is still within our reach."

"Let's just hope," said Ford, pulling the car into a parking space, "that our reach isn't exceeding our grasp on this one."

"We will do whatever we need to do, Mr. Ford, to make sure that is not the case. My country and yours will find a way to turn even these unfortunate events to our advantage, as we have so far. Are we not survivors?"

Ford grunted and got out of the car.

Shitov followed. Alexander Shitov was a survivor among survivors. Now he would eat a magnificent, marbled American steak cut from the loin of a fat, Kansas beef, and he would savor the *pommes frites* with their skins on, and he would drink good beer made with mountain springwater. Then, thus fortified, he would summon from himself the strength for one more bureaucratic miracle.

He looked up at the twinkling night sky. Here, in the desert, the sky was very clear, not full of pollutants. Here, you could almost see the sat-coms and the piggyback relays and all the other spacecraft.

Shitov had long believed in American-Soviet space cooperation. Since he had seen the might of American technical know-how, he believed in it fervently. When he got home, he was going to try to explain the wonders of Kirtland Air Force Base, where men labored night and day to do ten years' work in a few days, and prepare a special craft for a special task.

Shitov had never seen the like. In his country, nothing moved so fast except a purge or an influenza. If the Soviet Union needed anything, it needed the United States right now.

Shitov took a deep breath of the clean air and followed his American host into the restaurant, smiling.

22

Day 9: Space Station Freedom

Commander Tom Jenkins was a Navy man. He liked things ship-shape. Maybe Julia Magriffe, the Canadian mission specialist, was right to worry about Dietrich. Women had instincts about such things.

But Jenkins didn't have time right now to bear down on Dietrich to see if something gave way. Anyhow, Dietrich was a fool for EVA. Given the amount of EVA time Space Station Freedom required to keep her running smoothly, Jenkins wasn't anxious to confine his best EVA man to sickbay.

Not that they had a sickbay. Sickbay was a designated dual-use for a section of the B habitat module. Since Freedom was getting ready to host the crew of the Japanese shuttle *Edo,* habitat space was at a premium.

So were appearances. Jenkins wanted everything spit-shined and buttoned down. To that end, he was in an EVA suit himself, about to perform a thorough inspection outside the station.

Jenkins had already checked the mobile manipulator arm and everything else he could wiggle or tweak from inside. He'd been up in the logistics module for hours, electronically checking everything he could from inside the station.

From top to bottom, he'd verified the proper functioning of the TDRSS antenna, the upper boom on which the antenna sat, and the Starlab co-orbiting platform which was attached just below Freedom's upper keel. He'd satisfied himself as to the integrity of the transverse boom, with its eight-place solar array, and the power system radiator attached to the boom as well. Even the crucial rotary joint had spec'd out in perfect trim.

Below the transverse boom, where the OTV (orbital transfer vehicle) technology-mission-support structure hung, a huge cube half the size of a space shuttle, all looked fine from the logistics module.

In his suit, he did a final check of his life-support system. Before he ventured outside to get his MMU (manned maneuvering unit), he needed to know that nothing in his suit was malfunctioning. An MMU was similar to an armchair with no legs; it was open to space, providing maneuvering power with jetpacks on your ass and joysticks under your hands. It didn't provide oxygen, or safety. You did that yourself, to the extent that there was any safe way to work in microgravity and near-vacuum.

Dietrich's MMUs were always low on thruster fuel. The guy just wouldn't toe the mark in regard to equipment maintenance. But the German astronaut did so much EVA that everybody cleaned up after him, Jenkins knew. So Jenkins mustn't get the wrong MMU by mistake.

It was Jenkins's turn to spend a long time out there in the cold and dark of space today, on his way to the OTV tech bay. To get to it, he'd be passing by most of the other crucial components of the station—everything but the satellite storage facility on top of which the German-donated MHD rested, hooked into the power system right below the transverse boom and the power system radiator above it.

Jenkins was leaving the station through the laboratory module's air lock, at the very bottom of the keel extension. That way he could eyeball the lower boom, the four-place propulsion module, and the entire keel extension.

On the keel extension, just below the customer-supplied modules from Japan and Germany, was an OMV (orbital maneuvering vehicle), which looked like a screw-on top when it was secured in its housing. The OMV propellant hangar was on the far side of the A habitat module, up where it coupled to the logistics module, right below the two-place radiators and the satellite servicing station.

Dietrich was up there at the satellite servicing station, doing regular maintenance to make sure that everything was functioning perfectly when the new arrivals docked.

You wanted to extend the courtesy of the house. You wanted to make sure that, if the Japanese shuttle had, as they said they would, a satellite to service, you could service it.

Jenkins checked his coms and Di Lella, in the logistics module, answered.

"Where's Magriffe?" Jenkins asked.

"She's off shift," Di Lella reminded him, and went smoothly into a routine that assured module and suit integrity as Jenkins began his EVA.

The lock cycled and Jenkins faced the stars. The curve of the Earth always took his breath away.

He moved out, into the currentless sea, and let the inner lock close. Carefully, he chose an MMU. One missing: Dietrich's. Jenkins was mildly irritated by he didn't know what.

He was mission commander. He hadn't seen Dietrich's EVA logged when he'd logged his own. Or he didn't remember seeing it. Never mind. The German was probably right to be spending extra time on the satellite servicer. Jenkins hadn't seen a recent maintenance report on it.

If the MMUs were smaller, less cumbersome, they could have kept them inside the inner lock. But they were big and awkward.

Big, awkward, and wonderful. Jenkins always felt better when he'd settled into his space-going armchair, the way you always felt better when you had on a life jacket above decks in a storm, or if you could crawl into an inflatable when you'd been washed overboard.

Better adrift with life support and power to direct yourself than falling free. Jenkins could hear his own breathing. Beyond his gold-covered, polarized faceplate, the station looked like what it was: man's finest achievement to date.

The erector-set beauty of the towering keel never failed to impress him. A far cry from the ships of his early dreams, but a ship in space nonetheless. From this vantage, the great umbrella-shaped dish seemed like a spiderweb spun from golden thread. The radiators glittered like fans. A future limited only by imagination and commitment, so the prime contractor had crowed.

Maybe so.

Jenkins hit his right joystick and felt the comforting grab in his crotch as the MMU harness tightened around him.

Di Lella said, "Commander, while you're out there, will you check the OMV? We're getting a funny reading from there."

Funny wasn't a technical term that Jenkins was familiar with. Damn having mission specialists to whom English was a second, sometimes third, language. "Funny how, Di Lella?"

"Funny as if, ah, as if somebody was in there."

Somebody?

Jenkins hit his joystick accidentally, and cursed. He started to tumble, out of control.

End over end. Helplessly. Into and out of his view came first the station, then the distant Earth. For an instant, Jenkins couldn't remember the procedure for stopping an MMU that was tumbling. Two joysticks, with four options each . . .

Blood was pounding in his ears. He could see the veins in his eyes, a trick of hysteria or the polarized light. His breathing was harsh, shallow, quick.

He didn't want to vomit. If he vomited in this suit, he'd wish he were dead.

Spinning, dizzy, Jenkins, hands on both joysticks, coaxed stabilizing bursts from his thrusters. If he could stop himself . . .

He tapped his joysticks and the runaway MMU slowed. A final pair of staggered thruster bursts, and Earth's beauty wasn't strobing by Jenkins any longer. He'd never liked amusement park rides.

Jenkins jetted determinedly toward the skin of the lower laboratory module. Perhaps he was too important to this mission to risk himself on a walk-around. After all, it wasn't part of his job description.

Jenkins snarled at Di Lella, "Tell me more. What, exactly, are you getting?"

"Audio."

"What kind of audio, Di Lella?" Stupid wop. But ethnic slurs weren't going to help the situation. "Tell me exactly what you did and what you heard." Probably a cross com circuit.

"I saw a pressurization light in the OMV, so I ran a systems check. While I was doing that, I had a open com circuit and I heard. . . ."

"What? What did you hear?" demanded Jenkins, as his MMU brought him up against the lock too hard and he braked the impact with his hand. Some Space Command officer! Maybe he'd rotate himself home, before he killed himself. Jenkins slapped the lock plate that would begin the entry cycle. "Well, Di Lella? What the hell did you hear?"

"Snoring," said Di Lella flatly.

"Snoring?" Okay. Dietrich's MMU was out. The laboratory B module was close to the OMV. Right above it were the customer-supplied modules, which included the German parking garage for their manned free-flying platform. "Patch me through to the OMV, Di Lella."

This Dietrich was becoming a real problem. When Jenkins had his patch, he yelled as loud as he could into his helmet mike, "Dietrich, wake the hell up! Now!"

Jenkins heard a snore, a sputter, and a sleepy, "Ya? What?"

"Get back to A module, right now! And don't let me catch you wasting power and life support again. If you want to sleep, you sleep in the habitats like the rest of us."

Idiot. Screwball. Jenkins was so shaken that he had to go very slowly, and very carefully, as he racked his MMU and reentered the module.

One slip out here, and you were in serious trouble.

Jenkins was almost angry enough to tell Dietrich immediately that Dietrich had just lost his slot up here.

But that was a waste of energy. And you didn't want any trouble, especially if you thought you had an unbalanced crew member.

Out of his suit, Jenkins headed directly for the logistics module, where he put in a request to transfer Dietrich. He wanted that bastard out of here so badly now, he couldn't imagine why he hadn't admitted it to himself before.

Off-loading Dietrich wouldn't be that hard to arrange, if the *Edo*'s mission commander would agree to take Dietrich back. Maybe they could fill Dietrich's slot with some Japanese eager beaver.

Or do without a full complement until Germany replaced their man. But one way or another, Dietrich was history.

They'd find other ways to keep up with their EVA schedule. Jenkins was determined. He told Mission Control just how determined. When he got off the horn to Earth, he was still so torqued that he wasn't fit for human society.

He found Magriffe, floating in the B module in shorts with a turkey pack in her hands.

She took one look at his face and said, "I thought you were going to do a walk-around."

So he told her what had happened.

"You're kidding," she said.

"Nope. I'm going to ship him out of here on the *Edo*. I've already transmitted my request."

She raised an eyebrow. "He won't like that."

"We won't tell him until it's time."

Magriffe looked at him once again, this time very hard. "You're worried about something more than Dietrich. What?"

"Beyond inexplicable EMP blasts and the imminent arrival of

the Japanese shuttle—I hope—nothing special."

"While you were asleep, we got a request for some general log information, so I dumped to NASA when it came in."

"If you were concerned about it, you should have asked me first."

"I wasn't. I'm not, really. But I thought you should know that someone wants to look at every EVA we've done: when it was, how long it lasted—for the last ten days."

"Ten days?" The first EMP blast had occurred just about that long ago.

He nodded. "Thanks, Magriffe. I'm sure if there're any more requests of that sort, you'll let me know."

"I found it comforting," she told him. "They're looking out for us. They're trying to find the problem as quickly and . . . carefully . . . as they can."

So it was finally in the open, between them: the danger, so real that everyone had been ignoring it, preferring to think of this crisis only in terms of what it might mean to geopolitical tensions on the ground.

"If we were EMP'd," Jenkins said, "we still might survive long enough for rescue. . . ."

Magriffe was shaking her head at him. Her free-floating hair waved as if underwater. "How?"

"I . . . don't know."

"I could take the batteries out of all the MMUs," she mused. "And out of the OMV and the OTV, and the suits. That might give us enough life support to hold out . . . but if we need them, in the meantime, we'd be forced to reconnect anything we wanted to use in a hurry. It would be very slow."

"I know. I thought of that. Let's hope that we're not EMP'd. After the Japanese shuttle leaves, if we're still thinking this way, I might disconnect some things—after due consultation with Mission Control, of course."

Magriffe smiled at him brightly. She was a wonder and a joy at times like these. He'd heard that women astronauts were more competent over the long haul because they were steadier under continual, low-level pressure. But he hadn't believed it until he'd met Magriffe.

He smiled back, as best he could. "How are the Japs—the Japanese coming with their deployment, have you heard?"

"Not a word. They're still in low orbit, although they've launched their satellite. Maybe they're hanging around to see if their cargo's working the way they want."

Space Station Freedom was prohibited from doing anything that could remotely be considered snooping. Surveillance of national space efforts was not one of the station's missions unless that surveillance was requested. And the *Edo* hadn't requested anything of the sort.

If Jenkins wanted to know more than Magriffe could tell him about the *Edo*'s status, he'd have to go up to the logistics module, clear it of foreign nationals, and ask coded questions of USSPACECOM on a secure channel.

He decided to do that. No matter how much any of them tried, the boundaries of personal security, group security, station security, and national security became blurred.

You couldn't refrain from caring for your own national interests here. No matter what the charter of Space Station Freedom said, Commander Jenkins was an American first—a U.S. Navy Space Command officer.

Something up here was EMPing American space assets. He wished to hell he knew how the guys back at Colorado Springs were faring in determining just what was doing it, and how.

And he wished they'd never find out. He left for the logistics bay without another word, thinking that if the ground did know what the threat was, given security constraints, Jenkins might be the last to find out.

So he'd ask. Carefully. Securely. But he'd ask. Just because he had a peaceful mission up here didn't mean he could avoid responsibility for the security and safety of himself, his crew, and the American investment in Freedom.

Machiavelli was right. A man had to look after his own security needs. Especially when he was floating in space, surrounded by foreigners, who had their own national agendas.

Jenkins chased Di Lella out of the logistics module and locked the door. Then he took a key from around his neck and unlocked the safe. Next, he took a card and potentiated a secure communicator. And then, finally, Jenkins began asking questions.

And he didn't like the answers that came up to him in guarded bursts from Space Command on the planet below. He didn't like them one bit.

23

Day 9: Berlin

Schliemann had a head full of jet-lag misery. He had been on a marathon journey: to the San Marco Launch Control Platform, where he'd dealt with Osawa's death and ongoing complications; from there, to the European Space Agency's Kourou facility in French Guiana, and now here, home to Germany.

At least Berlin was not a place where Schliemann felt like a dinosaur among technocrats.

He had stared at enough computer monitors and huge aerospace display screens to last him the rest of his life.

In a wonderful, dingy, and ancient wursthaus hung with stags' heads and lined with steins, drinking dark beer and eating black bread, Shliemann awaited his compatriot—his quarry, his prey.

He was a dinosaur in this microchip age. But he was a tyrannosaurus of a sort. He ate money; he ripped the hearts from these little companies and digested them, made them a part of his flesh. And he ripped the souls from these bureaucrats and made them extensions of his soul.

With Osawa's death had come an unexpected opportunity for Schliemann to take control. The Japanese were not, as some fools thought, a communal people, among whose high levels all was known and everything shared. Outsiders sneered at Japanese corruption and rampant bribery; but spoke helplessly, as if one Japanese were the same as the next—as if no action against one could alter the performance of the whole.

Wrong. Osawa had been the Coalition's Japanese link. Osawa had held everything in his head; he was the Japanese master planner. Without Osawa, there was no Japanese strong enough to vie with Schliemann for control. There was only Tohei, the financier, who admitted to having no goal but profit in this enterprise.

Schliemann sat back, chewing his bread, as he awaited Tohei. The little Oriental would be easy to spot in this crowd of pale, tall folk.

It was good to be home. It was better to be in a united Berlin. After years of unhappiness, the German people were being given a second chance at greatness. Never mind that their current government was a government of rabbits.

The Tyrannosaurus rex that inhabited Schliemann's body opened its mouth and yawned widely, turning its head from side to side.

One had to move forward. One must take control. One must fill the vacuum. One must always act to control destiny, not be swept along in its flood. Schliemann saw himself as tromping through the swamps of lesser men, his clawed feet splayed wide, sniffing the breeze for opportunity. And rabbits.

He was always ravenous. He was always alert to the kill. He was always victorious.

Tonight, Schliemann's prey emerged from a thicket of German women looking dazed and intimidated. A rabbit frozen in the headlights of an oncoming Mercedes. Schliemann rose to shake Tohei's hand, using his great height as a further intimidation.

"My friend, condolences. All the details are taken care of. You may rest assured that all is well," he told the little man as Tohei sat.

The frail yellow man looked at him from under the folds of his lids and expressed Japanese thanks. Then Tohei said, "And now? What do we do?"

"Split his assets and continue, what else? Otherwise, we lose everything. And I, for one, will not allow that to happen. Have some bread."

Pushing the black bread toward the Japanese rabbit, Schliemann raised his hand for service.

Before the waitress came, the deal would be made, or not.

Tohei fingered the bread. He had a high forehead and a rabbit's nose. "I'm not sure what I can do to ensure success, knowing so little of the plan—"

"I can help you. You know that Osawa and I were in closest communication."

Tohei looked relieved. "I had hoped you were not calling me here to dissolve the enterprise. Everyone will be relieved. . . ."

But the enterprise is now a different one, in which I will gain all and you, if you are lucky, will find a crumb or two to eat when

I have had my fill. "You must continue according to a timetable I will give you. Your people overhead—"

Schliemann paused and looked up, significantly, at the ceiling.

Tohei followed his glance, then looked away. "Yes?"

It was pathetic to see a man so fearful for his assets that he was not capable of thinking under pressure. "Your people . . . overhead . . . must continue to do as Osawa wished. We must honor his wishes, and thus this enterprise will be his memorial."

"Yes," said Tohei, nodding his head. The dark eyes were beginning to glitter with desperation. Confusion was becoming apparent. "But . . ."

"Once the spirit of Osawa is content that we have followed his brilliant direction completely, then we will all have what we need. Isn't this so?"

"Yes. Yes." Tohei couldn't lose face. "Of course, that's what we all want. But . . ."

Schliemann was enjoying this. Information was the key to everything at this moment. And information was what Tohei clearly did not have. Schliemann had had to make sure that his assumptions were correct, that the Japanese consortium had only the vaguest details of the plan. They compartmentalized everything; Osawa had been their guiding light. Without him, they were blind.

"Your people overhead have detailed instructions, which must not be deviated from," Schliemann said sternly, closing his trap and enjoying the other man's discomfort.

When you don't understand the rules, it is always difficult to play the game well. Schliemann almost sympathized. But not quite. Not after his visit with Osawa to the Palace of Sexual Harassment.

"Yes. Yes, of course." Some relief showed on Tohei's face. "We will make sure that NASDA—our National Space Development Agency—performs every part of its mission flawlessly."

"Good. I need your assurance. In that case, I will not withdraw my backing."

Tohei closed his eyes. He had the look of a man about to vomit with relief.

"Once those goals are accomplished, Osawa's timetable for the next phase will arrive in your hands," Schliemann said expansively, as if bestowing a funerary gift upon the little man who was his prey. After all, it was customary to give Japanese intimates a possession of the newly deceased.

"But . . . what is the timetable for?" Broken and miserable, Tohei revealed the depths of his ignorance and became Schliemann's vassal.

The tyrannosaurus might have stood up, beaten his chest with tiny, clawed hands, and blared his deep-throated triumph to the sky. Schliemann did better.

He spied the waitress and said, in his most confidential voice: "The control of a thousand-mile swath of near-space that encircles the earth, completely, and is policed by weapons against which no one's space assets are safe. Then, of course, agreements . . . tariffs . . . you can see where this will go. . . . Japan will be recognized as the mighty nation of economic and technical domination that it is. And almost nothing of this war will ever be known to the general public. The aggressor nations, the old superpowers, our enemies, will capitulate in silence and secrecy, once they realize that Space Station Freedom is our hostage and their passage into space is at risk. . . ."

Schliemann allowed himself to be silenced by the appearance of the fraülein who would take their order.

Tohei licked his lips uncertainly, and picked up his menu with shaking hands. When he put it down a moment later, conceding defeat, Schliemann consented to order for his new vassal.

It was the least he could do for the rabbit. He now had Japan exactly where he wanted it. This space adventure was merely the glue to bind a United Germany and Japan into an unbreakable alliance. With Italy already implicated and involved beyond extrication, there was no way that any nation could back out now.

There never had been. But what Tohei did not know was that, until his death, Osawa had held the reins. And now these had fallen into Schliemann's hands. Thus the spotlight would shift from Germany to Japan, according to a bogus timetable that Schliemann would pass off as Osawa's.

Japan would take its rightful place as figurehead and hated inscrutable enemy. An alliance always needed a hated, inscrutable enemy.

Last time, it had been Hitler. This time, it was going to be the frail little man sitting at Schliemann's side. He who does not learn from history is doomed to repeat it.

Germany would take only economic advantage, and then only as a consortium of private citizens. It was Japan who would salvage the satellite, and cede it to Germany through due legal process. Once that had happened, the curtain of secrecy would fall, and the advantage was theirs.

Schliemann sat back and gave their order to the waitress. He ordered a great deal, many wursts and a mixed grill of venison, elk, and rabbit. He was very hungry, and the swamp was his for as far as his eyes could see.

24

Day 10: United Nations, New York

The flags of many nations waved tauntingly as Shitov waited at the multidenominational church across the street from UN Plaza for the KGB resident to arrive.

In this house of expedient worship, the God in residence could be changed to suit the congregation. They merely took down the cross or the Jewish star and put up whatever symbol of faith was desired.

Only the Americans could conceive of such a convenience. No Marxist rhetoric had succeeded in making such a mockery of religion as this place did. He looked into the church. Beyond its unadorned wooden pews, which suited its sterile modern architecture, was the obligatory altar. Standing in the doorway, with the filthy wind blowing his raincoat around his legs, Shitov wondered what God would look down upon him when he, Shitov, was sacrificed upon that altar today, at the hands of his brothers from the KGB.

Outside, cars whizzed by, spewing pollution. The noise was deafening. Shitov could barely smell the river, and what he smelled, he did not like.

Men crossed the street, against the light, hurrying. Thick, powerful men with hats and purposeful strides.

No one wore fedoras anymore but Russians, Shitov had found out when he'd first come to America. Every time he saw the Executive President on the American newscasts, he wanted to call home and say, "Take off that stupid hat. You look like a character in an old movie to them. They'll never take us seriously until we stop wearing those hats. We might as well wear clown noses and walk about on stilts."

But a man could not tell the Executive President to stop wearing that awful hat, anymore than a man could foresee every possible danger in his actions.

Somehow, helping the Americans, Shitov had forgotten that. The best foxes step incautiously once in a while, and then the trap closes on a leg. But such a fox will often chew off his own leg rather than become a woman's coat. Shitov was feeling like chewing off his leg today. He could defect to the Americans. They would have him.

The approaching men were almost killed by a speeding yellow cab as they dodged their way to the sidewalk. *Die!* he urged them hopefully.

But they did not die. They walked straight up the steps toward him, hands in the pockets of their raincoats, their heavy shoes slapping against the sidewalk like the boots of parading soldiers in Red Square.

Shitov had been called here to face these men and explain himself. Now he must find a way to get his foot out of Levonov's trap. Somehow, because of Shitov's posting here, whatever happened in Soviet-American relations was now his fault.

The first man walked right up to him, so close their bellies almost touched, and said, "Aleksandr Shitov?"

This man had bristly hairs growing out of his nose and blackheads on its bulbous tip. This nose was the nose of a heavy drinker, red and pocked and drooping out of shape as if the nose were wax and melting slowly.

Shitov said, "Ivan Ivanovitch, what a surprise." No surprise. Just recognition codes and go-aheads. Just confrontation.

The other man said, "Let us go inside, out of the rain."

So into the neutralized, sanitized, American church-of-your-choice they went. The second man, whom Shitov did not know, closed the door.

The KGB resident said, "So, how is your posting?"

Shitov propped his ass on the edge of a wooden pew and leaned there. "Because of this posting, whatever happens in the whole world will be Shitov's fault, so how could it be?"

The second man held back, planting himself against the wooden doors to make sure no one innocently walked in on them.

The KGB resident pulled on his hairy nose and said, "Dangerous. To our health. How is it that you are telling Moscow it should be sharing space-based intelligence with the Americans on so massive a scale, just when this New Axis decides to go public? Have you balls for brains?"

Levonov, I will rip your heart from your chest and feed it to your children for this. Shitov had done everything he was told to do, precisely and correctly—perfectly. "I have my instructions." He shrugged. "You are not jealous, Ivan Ivanovitch, that my Directorate trusts me, and not you, to vet the intentions of these Americans?"

"You be careful, you and your Americans, or maybe we will find out your hands are down the front of their pants, eh? I need a full report, one which justifies all you are asking for, before you leave here."

Shitov took the blow stolidly. He showed no emotion. He willed himself not to move or blink, not to let his eyes shift from the eyes of the resident. Now Levonov would be gloating, because all the consequences of being so great an operator were falling on Shitov's head in one awful moment.

"This is my privilege, to tell you how much I have learned, and show you how far into the Americans' confidence I have been taken, Ivan Ivanovitch." Cock-biter. UN flunky.

"Good. We will sit here and I will be for you the father confessor. Then, if everything is as it should be, we will go have a good dinner. Do not worry, Comrade Shitov. By the time we have finished our good dinner, the help you want for your American friends will be assured. If it is to our advantage."

"Comrade," yet. Shitov blinked at the hairy-nosed resident and stood away from the support of the church pew.

Shitov knew a threat when he heard one. He knew a creature of Levonov's when he saw one. This creature of Levonov's was threatening Shitov that if anything, the slightest thing, went wrong with the Americans' plan—which he, Shitov, must now divulge in minute detail—Shitov's career was over.

Worse, his life was probably over. Shitova would be called in the middle of the night and told that her beloved husband had fallen into the East River in New York, and an autopsy would reveal that Shitov had been so drunk it was natural for him to have been clumsy enough to drown himself.

All of this because the Americans needed help. Because Dalton Ford needed help. Because *glasnost* needed help. If not for all the help that everyone needed from Shitov, he would not be facing the New York resident's scornful, arrogant smile.

"So now I am a party to the American plan—by association, is that so?" Shitov demanded.

"Maybe you are. But so what? If it will be a good plan, then my superiors will like it. Come, Shitov, start telling me why you wish to deliver detailed space surveillance data to the Americans. What is worth divulging so much?"

Shitov counted the blackheads on the nose of the resident. These were fascinating. So large. So ripe for squeezing. He said, "If I am not mistaken, Comrade Ivan, when you hear what I have to tell you, you will agree that our superiors will give me anything I ask for—the key to the executive washroom even. But you will understand that I must tape this conversation, for my own records of what is taking place."

Shitov pulled out a Japanese pocket recorder and put it beside him on the pew.

Then the nose of the resident got red, all except for the pocks, which got yellowish white, and the blackheads, which seemed to be about to launch themselves from that hairy nose.

"This is highly irregular, Shitov."

"And this, Ivan Ivanovitch, is no time for mistakes. For misrecollection. Or for misinterpretation."

Shitov sat down heavily on the wooden seat. The resident sat down in the pew across the aisle and propped his head on his hand. "You are an old snake, Shitov. Make sure, while you are shedding your skin, you do not get sunburned."

Shitov knew then that, for the moment, he had won. He would be allowed to make his record of this meeting. Whether he would live to secret it and send it back to Moscow himself was another matter.

Shitov straightened his shoulders and began speaking. If he died, as had many men of his country, because of what he had to say, then Shitova would understand. She would not be the first widow of the new revolution, but she would be a proud one.

Shitov had a vision of Shitova, wearing a black babushka, waddling over to his grave with fresh flowers. Shitova sat on his grave and patted the weeds there. "My bear, I am so proud of you that my bed is warm with it, every night," said Shitova.

So Shitov knew that he was doing the right thing. As he explained about the American space plane in the Kirtland hangar, and about their need to identify the source of the paralyzing pulse, he began to feel proud himself.

These men like the resident, who still clung to the Party and called you Comrade, had not come to terms with the new Russia.

In the new Russia, Shitov might be canonized, a saint. If he lived or died was no longer important to anyone but Shitova, and perhaps to the Americans. So far as the struggle for Soviet-American cooperation was concerned, Shitov was already a hero.

"So you see, we must act now," he told the poker-faced resident, who was trying to conceal his shock at the bonanza of intelligence that Shitov was ably delivering, rapid-fire. "What the Americans need now is virtual proof of hanky-panky that shows how and from where the Germans are doing this. Who are their allies? The Coalition must be unmasked, publicly. Its weapons destroyed. I know we are capable of giving such guidance. I know we can say what is pulsing these spacecraft. And I know we should. But I must have permission. Or else, if the American spacecraft is lost, all our Mir cosmonauts can do is salvage for them the pieces. And this is not enough, not now. Now, we must show our hearts. We must show our might. We must give the Americans what they need or we will never be trusted again."

Almost panting from the effort of making his words carry all the force of purpose he felt, Shitov stopped talking.

He looked covertly at the resident, who was watching Shitov's tape, in the deck, as the wheels went round.

Shitov's heart sank. Could this fool understand nothing? Was Shitov going to fail?

He stood up.

The resident stood up and rubbed his nose ruminatively. Shitov picked up his tape recorder and put it in his pocket, without turning it off.

Shitova, I tried. Levonov, rot in hell. Now these two would take him across the street, douse him with vodka, hit him over the head, and toss him in the river.

These were the tactics of men who still called one another "comrade."

There was no use trying to escape. Shitov looked away, toward the altar. And there he saw Shitova's image. She was floating over the altar as if she were a religious symbol, her huge bosoms rolling out and over him, her inviting thighs draped in folds of white.

And while Shitov was having this vision of his wife as an icon, he heard the resident say, slowly, "If the dinner can wait, I think we should go to my office and file your report, Comrade Shitov. Together."

25

Day 10: Northern Nevada Desert

It was pitch black outside the hangars of the Air Force's most secret test facility. Inside, the lights were daylight-spectrum and exceedingly bright, to help the night-shift workers function at peak efficiency.

Pettit wasn't sure she was functioning at anywhere near peak efficiency. She walked once around the graphite-colored X-NASP and when she was done, she felt as if she'd walked up a steep hill in thin air.

Techs and electronics carts were everywhere. Cables were still snaking out of various parts of the Nomad's anatomy, especially her belly, where weapons pods beneath her aerodynamic skin looked out through open ports whose integrity and flawless operation had to be verified now.

There wasn't any more time. The air in the bay was full of staccato chatter and the clatter of wheels and metal on concrete.

Game time. She rubbed her arms. Los Alamos and DARPA were in too deep to back out now. She saw men she recognized: Chuck Conard, the blond Adonis from Army Space Command, who'd turned out to be an all-right guy; Pollock, the AFSPACECOM Special Operations Chief, pacing back and forth as if his wife were about to have a baby.

Baby. Pettit closed her eyes. Her baby was about to get its first slap on the rump. Premature birth was all she could think about. DARPA had billed the FIFS program as the perfect answer to low-intensity-conflict operational shortfalls, on the ground and in space: minimal logistical problems, maximum efficiency, unparalleled survivability.

But nobody'd ever expected FIFS to earn its stripes, on such short notice, in a deep-space application. And Pettit had never expected to care so much about the man deploying in it.

That wasn't fair. She left the bay and went to the cubbyhole generously referred to as her "office for the duration." Racks of electronic test equipment filled it so that she had to slide between them to find her desk—somebody's desk. She was only here for a few hours.

Then she could go home. And do what? Chew her nails?

The cubbyhole made her claustrophobic. It smelled of dust and overworked circuits. She'd be better off out there, with the plane.

They'd done everything they could at Kirtland to ensure that the pass-through electronics worked—both ways. Theoretically, the pilot could hand off a target to the FIFS operator, or the FIFS operator could call down fire, or transfer targeting data back to the bird. Coms were also directly available to the FIFS operator from relay satellites, just as they were to the Nomad's pilot.

If you could live with the nanoseconds of delay time necessary to relay a message from space to Earth to space again, or vice versa, you could be in direct contact with CSOC or Cheyenne Mountain.

If you could live with the nanoseconds of delay time.

She wanted to go home now. Then she didn't want to leave, even once this final test was done. She decided she needed to talk to the X-NASP's pilot. There was one glitch in the FIFS system that he'd need to fix on the fly, or it could cut X-NASP out of the FIFS com circuit.

She went to find the pilot and tell him. Conard was glad to direct her to him: "Inside." Conard gestured to the open Nomad.

She hurried up the ramp and ducked inside. The insect-eyed helmet of the man on the flight deck turned to her. He held up a hand: Hold on.

When he had his mask off, and his visor retracted, the pilot's drawn face looked familiar as he said, "What can I do for you, ma'am?"

Very polite. He had a midnight shadow and yellow bruises around one eye. Simultaneously, she read the name on the helmet and remembered the public flap: "Capt. Cleary."

"Captain, I'm Joanna Pettit, from DARPA. That's my FIFS suit you'll be operating with up there."

"Glad to know you, ma'am. You people are sure keeping things interesting for us worker bees." His eyes were impatient: What's up?

She said, "I want to show you a trick. Can I?"

He shrugged. "Be my guest."

She scrambled into the other seat inelegantly. Finally settled, she looked over at Cleary in time to see him smother a grin.

The Nomad's control suite was so complex that at first she didn't recognize anything. Then she did. Having found the modification package she was searching for, she said, "Can we turn this on?"

"No problem." Something whined and the flight deck door behind them slid shut automatically as the pilot flicked switches. Her ears blocked.

The cockpit came on line. Seven, plus or minus two, data streams. "One person can fly this?" she heard herself ask.

"I hope to hell so," said the pilot. "What's your trick? Not that I'm anxious to lose your company, but we're on a pretty tight schedule. . . ."

She reached out to touch the targeting handoff, and then stopped. "Okay?"

"Okay."

Her fingers flew. The pilot grunted. She said, "Now, FIFS isn't operational, so you're getting nothing from it naturally. But you could get this error message if he's overloading his AI." Artificial intelligence was only so intelligent. "If you see this, and you know he's out there, then here's what you do."

She walked Cleary through the procedure twice. When the kill screen came up, she hit "K" and the handoff targeter went back to looking for the data she'd just told it was out there. "So you just kill the error on the fly, since you know he's still there."

"Yeah, and if I don't get data the second time, he's not still there, right?"

Pettit stared at Cleary as if he were a worm or an evil omen. "That's right," she said brusquely. "Now, the rest of what you need to know, either your own people or the FIFS operator will tell you." She levered herself out of her seat with the flat of one hand. "Let me get out of your way."

The pilot touched something and the flight-deck door retracted. Pettit was scrambling out before it was fully open.

"Hey," he called after her. "Thanks for the tip. You think of anything else, be sure to come back and tell me."

Pettit was heading for the ramp. "Right after hell freezes over," she muttered. She didn't want to think about what would happen if the pilot of the Nomad got that message for real.

She couldn't think about it.

She concentrated on walking down that ramp as if everything were fine, as if this were a normal situation—as if she weren't scared to death. When her feet hit the concrete, she saw Mackenzie, already wearing the FIFS pressure liner, watching her with a bemused look on his face.

She hurried over to him, saying, "I need to talk to you."

"Okay, where to?"

The cubbyhole was no more inviting than it had ever been. She closed the door. "Mac, you'll want to go over everything really carefully with that pilot of yours."

"Hey, Pettit, it's only a test, remember?" He leaned against one of her rack cases.

"A last test. A final test. There's no time to fix anything. . . ." She was making a fool of herself.

Mackenzie cocked his head. "Look, we're just going to shoot some clay pigeons in the desert. We're only going to zip into the space envelope and out again—test the comms. What's really the matter?"

"I . . ." Decided, she marched up to him. Then she stopped. "I—don't get hurt, Harry."

"Uh-uh. I'm one lucky bastard, remember?" He was looking at her quizzically.

She'd rebuffed him so often, she didn't blame him for being confused. Damn it, she was confused.

They just stood there, a few inches apart. She had to do something. She stood on tiptoe to bring his head down, so that she could give him a good-bye kiss.

"For luck," she said.

"You bet," he said, and as his arms went around her, he pushed her thighs apart with his knee.

Then one of his hands was under her buttocks and her feet were off the ground. His tongue touched her lips.

She hugged him tighter.

He put her down. "Look, we'll finish this when I get back. Understand?"

Flustered, she said, "Certainly. I'd forgotten about the time. . . ."

"Certainly is right."

She was backing away. He caught her by the hand as she was looking at her watch. "For God's sake, the time . . ."

"Yeah," he said. "Even I'm not that crazy. But I'm glad you are. Come on, let's go get me into FIFS and we can both wish it slept two."

She wasn't sure what she'd thought she was doing. But she knew what to do now.

They went over every seal and component of the FIFS suit with one eye on the clock. Mackenzie seemed almost manic.

The wry humor she'd come to expect from him was missing. She said, "So?" when he was fitting the helmet on his head.

Through his external speaker, a tinny voice answered, "So? What do you want for short money?"

"Is everything . . . ?"

"Just the way I like it."

She walked with her man from Mars over to the X-NASP, feeling dissociated, cold, and completely alert.

He took her hand in his gloved one just before he climbed the ramp, and now he had his helmet's visor up. "You did a great job, Pettit. Don't let anybody bust your tail if this turns into a showstopper, hear?"

That was the first moment that she had any inkling just how extensive a test USSPACECOM was planning.

But by then Mackenzie, in the exoskeletal powered FIFS suit, was disappearing into the Nomad and techs were scurrying to pull away equipment.

Carts and hoses and cabling and men were all receding as if blown away by a gale.

The hangar door began opening. The noise was deafening.

She found her way outside as the wheel chocks were removed. A truck started towing the X-NASP into the night.

There weren't many people out here, she thought, feeling lonely in the cold desert night. A couple of dozen, nearly invisible against the black sky except where they were touched by light streaming out the hangar door.

Then the door started to shut and the truck disengaged from the spacecraft. For a minute or two, the only thing Pettit heard were voices.

Then the Nomad came to life with a whine and a roar that made Pettit clamp her hands over her ears.

In spite of herself, she stepped back as the spacecraft started to taxi. The Nomad was awake now, and its voice was deafening.

You could feel its power. The ground shook. Your ears rang. Its exhaust was shielded for stealthiness, but still, as it gained speed, the burn was so hot that heated air chased the desert cold away from it in wild waves.

Then the X-NASP lifted, in a sky-tearing leap that made Pettit take one more step backward. Single-stage-to-orbit.

You didn't understand what that meant until your body told you what sort of forces were involved. And hers collided with someone, in the dark, who'd been standing behind her.

"One hell of a show," the man said as the Nomad became a fiery apparition headed for the heart of night.

"I guess," she muttered, and started to pull away.

The man's hands squeezed her arms. "Nice job, Dr. Pettit. All our hopes are with you."

"Me?" She turned. She'd never seen this man, or didn't think she'd seen him before. Still, it was dark, even though the hangar door was opening to admit the truck.

"Let's hope that suit of yours is all it's cracked up to be."

"Let's hope this test of yours doesn't exceed acceptable parameters," she shot back. Mackenzie, James Harry, was up there now, beyond her ability to protect. FIFS was too. She rubbed her eyes.

The man had a plastic clearance badge alligator-clipped to the pocket of a desert jacket, but she still couldn't read it.

"Let's hope we can stay within whatever those parameters are." His voice in the dark was gentle. "We're looking for a flexible response to a very delicate situation. And I can't tell you how glad we are that you and your program are part of the team."

"Do you mind telling me who you are?" She didn't want to talk to some guy who thought he was the whole U.S. government. And anyway, he was making her nervous.

"Dalton Ford. And Admiral Beckwith asked me to tell you how pleased he personally was to have you on board."

Dalton Ford. Of course. She looked up, trying to find the Nomad in the sky. Her eyes strained to find its shape, but the X-NASP was only a dim spark burning in the dark.

Still looking toward the stars, she said, "Mackenzie told me he'd trust you with his life. I hope he wasn't wrong."

"Me too," said Ford softly, and she heard him walk away.

Pettit stayed out there, watching the sky, until her arms were numb with cold and her cheeks burned.

In the hangar, she could monitor the suit. Why hadn't they told her this might be more than a simple test? She'd have brought more equipment up here.

Well, fine. She could still get more equipment up here. The Nomad hadn't exploded in some horrible, blinding flash; therefore, she should get out of the cold and go to work.

They had a test run under way—maybe the most important test in any of their lives.

Mackenzie, be all right, please? Don't crash my suit. Or yourself.

She tried not to think about EMP pulses. After all, even Ford hadn't exactly said they were going into a combat environment. Flexible testing didn't necessarily mean field test under live enemy fire.

And equipment failure wouldn't necessarily be the end of the world. For her, at least.

She didn't want to think about it. Therefore, she couldn't let it happen. She began to run toward the hangar. It was going to be a long night.

For all of them.

26

Day 10: The X-NASP, Space Envelope

Rowan, this one's for you. Cleary had to keep reminding himself that the guy in the other seat wasn't Rowan. Wasn't really anybody. A place-holder, until Cleary got the Nomad parked.

Cleary's helmet-mounted display kept saying otherwise. Besides monitoring crucial components of his avionics suite, Cleary was using his visor display to keep tabs on how the FIFS system was performing. This was still a test, after all.

Sensor fusion could only simplify by so much the job of flying a spacecraft this complex. Adding pass-throughs and handoff monitoring, then subtracting a copilot, had sounded like somebody's idea of a joke when Cleary'd first heard about it.

Megan Rowan's freckled face and red hair kept ghosting on his visor. Hi, Megan. Be home soon. You pulled a lot of G's, you saw stuff. Nothing to sweat. Cleary's AI pilot's Associate was up and running. AIs—artificial intelligences—were only so intelligent; the man-machine interface couldn't replace Rowan—or any human copilot. But thanks to the Associate AI, the X-NASP could probably reach her matching orbit with the derelict American satellite if Cleary had a heart attack and died at his controls.

He heard a grunt through his com. "You okay, Mackenzie?" You didn't turn your head at these accelerations, unless you turned your whole body from the waist. And Cleary didn't need to look to be reminded what a weird-ass package he was hauling in the other seat.

The FIFS suit looked like a man-shaped coffin to Cleary, but nobody'd asked for his opinion. When Mackenize didn't respond, Cleary imported the whole FIFS helmet display onto his own visor.

Away went his X-NASP navigational data and GPS plotter, to be replaced with a green targeting grid on which Mackenzie was running systems checks with imaginary targets.

Sonny cleared his visor of the import. "Hey, Major Mackenzie, do you copy?"

Cleary's own Associate restored his standard heads-up instrumentation displays. The X-NASP saw the outside through sensoring packages. Sometimes Cleary wished he had a window to the outside, where the stars were. But not today. Today there was nothing relevant to see out there.

The threat was invisible, and too hard to find with the naked eye. He was taking line-of-sight plots to the various possible sources of hostile pulse, for the record. So they'd know down there if what happened to Gates and Rowan happened to him and Major J. H. ("Just call me Mac") Mackenzie.

"Yeah, I'm here, Cleary." Mackenzie's voice sounded breathless. Or sleepy.

"You okay in that tin can?" If there was something wrong with the FIFS, this was the time to find out. If that sarcophagus stopped working, nobody'd bothered to tell him where the can opener was to get Mackenzie out of it. . . .

"Yeah, fine. Just . . . tryin' to scope all this command-and-control data now that it's in a real-time environment."

The guy sounded a thousand miles away.

"You breathing the same air I am, Mac?"

Mackenzie could be testing the EVA mix, which might be a little rich. Or maybe the pressure liner in that thing wasn't—

"Yeah. Sorry. Just checking shit out. I've got a lot of man-machine interfacing to do, and not much time."

Cleary knew that. He didn't blame Mackenzie for being nervous. He just wished the guy sounded more alive. "Weapons checks?" Cleary suggested.

They could fire the lasers mounted in Nomad's belly; they had infinite shots.

"Okay, I'll open the bay doors and you monitor."

"Monitoring."

Cleary didn't like this reverse handoff much. It was disconcerting to see the FIFS suit operate the X-NASP's retractable fire-control electronics. But you had to test it now. Later would be way too late, if push came to shove.

Cleary throttled back, muttering to his Associate, which could execute simple voice commands, and let his head-steered multi-spectral imager know that laser pulses were about to fire. No use commiting fratricide. These belly-mounted, offensive full-spectrum lasers could take out your own equipment if you weren't careful.

Laser pulses were meant to blind the sensoring packages of anything trying to target them. If Cleary were alone up here, considering what had happened to him the last time he flew this route, he'd probably have set the laser pod on intermittent automatic, and let it fire away throughout the flight.

The system was supposed to be able to sense an enemy signal as the X-NASP was acquired by a hostile system, identify the enemy sensor's mode and source, and put the source on the targeting screen so that the lasers could blind it.

All Cleary would have to do, if the counter-sensoring package thought it was about to be attacked, was center the icon in his fire grid and let 'er rip. The doors to all the weapons implanted in the Nomad's aerodynamic belly had opened flawlessly on the FIFS command, their delivery systems deployed now that aerodynamics or low signatures were no longer considerations.

Mackenzie said, "Lasing," laconically.

They sure were. Cleary's visor went to attenuated display mode.

Five pulses later, Cleary overrode the test. No use accidentally blinding some innocent com-sat—or one of his nation's spy-sats. They were too low, still, not to be in pretty heavy traffic. Line of sight in a vacuum is a long way when you're sending out destructive optical pulses at the speed of light.

Anyway, Mackenzie had his own damn laser weapons (and Cleary didn't know what else) racked in the cargo bay behind the flight deck airlock. Like the space shuttle, the X-NASP's cargo bay was top-opening; Mackenzie was going to pop out of there like a Jack in the Box, if there was any trouble, guns blazing. . . .

Mackenzie said, "Lookin' good."

Cleary was too busy reinstating his normal sensoring packages to say more than "Affirmative." When you were shooting laser pulses, you had to protect all your own packages, and that meant cutting down your spectral capabilities.

Cleary's FLIR (forward looking infrared) and ladar (laser radar) popped back onto his heads-up, along with simulated gauges for altitude, speed, gyro displays, and skin temperature. Over that, translucently, his GPS plotted Space Station Freedom, the nearby German power-sat, the Japanese shuttle, its newly released satellite, and the derelict American com-sat.

It was just too much. He didn't care if the next thing he saw was the face of God. He exported everything but regular avionics, giving his AI orders between clenched teeth.

So he'd totally eliminated his visor-monitoring of Mackenzie's packages. Shit, he'd about forgotten Mackenzie altogether when a voice in his ear said, "Did you see that?"

"See fucking what? I'm flying a spacecraft, Mac."

"Something going from the station toward the power satellite. I dunno. You're the pilot. You want it?"

"Yeah, let's see."

Back to the new, cluttered display grid that made his eyes tingle when Cleary stared at it too long. The graph lines were green. The crucial numbers were red. The metering was yellow. The spaceborne objects were white, with orange letter-number designators and coordinates beneath. If these colors don't look right to you . . . Cleary could ask for a time-to-target, or a lock-on for any target, with a flick of a finger, or a few words to his AI.

If he got real busy, he could use the Eagle-eye head-steering mechanism and zero a target visually, or with a combination of voice and data.

Or he could take a nap and let Mackenzie fly this damn bird. Did this ground-pounder think Cleary needed his help?

Then Cleary's heads-up gave him an instant replay of what Mackenzie's system had monitored through the X-NASP's synthetic aperture radar and he whistled.

"Well, lookee there. What do you think, Major?"

"I dunno. Somebody sure goin' over there for something."

"Hold your water, friend." Cleary dumped Mackenzie's scans, sending a secure burst of the last five minutes' worth of X-NASP data to the ground. Then he called Space Station Freedom for a traffic report.

When he'd raised Commander Jenkins, Cleary asked, "You guys flyin' any UFOs out of there? We tracked a weird blip over to that supplementary power station, the one in parallel orbit. And we're in no mood for surprises. Talk to me about it."

The commander, sounding harried, said, "Stand by, Extra Heavy 101. Let me check." The voice was staticky. "Okay. That's the German free-flying platform you saw, with one of our astronauts out to do some routine maintenance."

"Nice of you to let us know. Any other scheduled flights around your coordinates that you'd like to make sure we don't fry accidentally?"

He couldn't really rip the commander a new asshole the way he'd like to. Space Station Freedom personnel weren't informed as to the type of testing the X-NASP was doing. Let alone that Cleary was armed and dangerous in near-space.

"We're sorry to have spooked you," said Freedom's commander dryly. "Extra Heavy 101, it's nice to have you up here. Keep in touch, okay?"

That was weird too. Maybe this Jenkins did know something. Or maybe the EMP scare had made everybody else as nervous as Cleary was. "Good luck to you too," he said, and got off line.

"Hear that?" he asked Mackenzie. Might as well pretend it was a scheduled com check.

"Passed through fine," Mackenzie said as if he were talking about an order of french fries at a drive-through.

Cleary couldn't figure how Mackenzie stayed so calm. But then he thought he understood: Major Mackenzie was still passengering. His mission hadn't started yet. The tests they were performing as they headed toward the coordinates of the derelict satellite weren't the real tests they were here to perform.

The real tests were going to come when—and if—Mackenzie and his special weapons packages went out the cargo bay door to rescue the derelict satellite. Or if they were EMP'd between now and then, or while on station giving the "test" mission a try.

Cleary still had to get a final go-ahead, when he was on range. He couldn't help thinking about the derelict's degenerating orbit as "on range." He'd been a fighter pilot once, and as much as he didn't like considering it, he was feeling like the first of a new breed of fighter pilot.

Firsts always were a little uncomfortable. Sometimes they were downright painful. Cleary finally took a good look at Mackenzie.

Through his visor's heads-up, the bulky, suited figure seemed ominous and powerful. All that weight, all those servos. Technology was taking them all somewhere that nobody was really prepared to go.

Or at least somewhere that Cleary wasn't as prepared to go as Mackenzie was. The guy might be Space Command, but he wasn't your run-of-the-mill astronaut.

Nevertheless, Cleary's orders were to put Mackenzie upside that derelict satellite and hang there while Mackenzie EVA'd in the FIFS suit, and that was what Cleary was going to do.

If he didn't get his ass EMP'd first, like Gates and Rowan had.

When you feel like you're going to be attacked any minute, all the old fighter pilot instincts come rushing in. Cleary kept forgetting that Mackenzie was there; he'd flown single-place fighters an eternity ago.

But those fighters were lots simpler than the Nomad. And every once in a while, when Mackenzie would quietly launch into his test routines, punctuating them with near-whispers and monosyllables, Cleary was glad that Mackenzie was on board.

You got used to the quiet voice; the economical, calm reporting. It made you recall that this guy used to sneak into chemical weapons factories, and snag hostages out of urban venues. So that was why Mackenize tended to whisper.

Cleary told himself that combat diving probably wasn't any more different from combat EVAs than flying an advanced tactical fighter was from flying this modified X-NASP.

He hoped to hell not. The only thing that bothered Cleary half as much as the possibility of getting EMP'd on this flight was having to remotely pilot the FIFS suit back into the Nomad's bay if the operator was nonfunctional.

That's how it had been explained to Cleary: nonfunctional. Not dead. Not floating in a suit full of exploded lungs and blood. Not suffocated or fried or imploded or exploded or any other real way at all.

Just nonfunctional.

Cleary windowed his visor display and let his eyes rest on the avionics suite. It was still there. He was still here.

And Mackenzie, on his right, was still an apparition from the future. Space Command wanted this one bad. It wanted to go clean—to come back un-EMP'd, with the derelict satellite aboard. And to do it as peacefully as possible.

But Dalton Ford had told Cleary privately, "Sonny, this is a force-projection mission. That doesn't mean we start anything. But it means we finish anything that starts. And if we get a good fix on the source of that EMP, you may get some additional orders." Dalton had just ordered the KKD—kinetic kill device—for the X-NASP's belly. "So we're looking for your best shot here."

And Cleary had boasted, "That's the only way I ever play, sir—to win."

Neither of them had mentioned Rowan. Or Peg Rowan. Or poor little orphaned Megan. Cleary wasn't ready to think through Peg's suicide. He was doing a memorial mission here, for Frank Rowan and Gates and Gates's wife, Sally. But not for Peg. Sure as hell not for Peg.

Peg's actions were incomprehensible to Cleary. But he knew it was dangerous to dwell on it. He was too damned busy to dwell on it. He always made sure he was too busy to think about the unthinkable. Suicide was . . . unimaginable to him, to anybody who worked so damned hard at staying alive. He couldn't understand why she'd . . .

"Cleary?" For a moment, Mackenzie was just a disembodied voice in Cleary's ear.

"Yeah, Mac?"

"You want to take a look at that Japanese shuttle and tell me what you think?"

Mackenzie would have made one hell of a copilot—or a weapons officer. He was making himself useful, using his C3I—command, control, communications, and intelligence package—for more than test purposes.

When Cleary zeroed the Japanese shuttle, he saw it was beginning a burn. "So?"

"So, unless I don't understand how to use this shit, he ain't goin' to Space Station Freedom—at least not without a pit stop by the derelict."

"Christ, you're right," Cleary said as he called up the directional plot.

"Well?" said Mackenzie. "Can we beat him there?"

"If I can't, I'll eat that suit of yours," Cleary said. But he had to get permission. Accelerate the timetable. This was a serious complication. And they might be jumping to conclusions.

Still . . . This fit the mission parameters Ford had laid down.

"Mackenzie, how about using your suit-to-ground com? See what Command wants to do about this. Meanwhile, I'm assuming we're going to be needed in that neighborhood."

"My pleasure," Mackenzie murmured.

Cleary kicked the Nomad in the ass and acceleration's hand grabbed his throat and squeezed. Hard.

27

Day 10: Japanese Shuttle Edo

Sekigawa, the shuttle commander, was a man who followed orders.

Now that he had been ordered to match orbits with the derelict spacecraft in the German zone, he was executing those orders without comment.

So why did his German mission specialist feel it necessary to explain to him why this order had been given?

Sekigawa would never understand these Westerners. But as he had accepted the German mission specialist without complaint, he listened to the man's recitation of territorial claim to salvage without comment.

This was not his concern. Sekigawa wanted only to execute the matching orbit perfectly.

He ignored the German-accented voice of Kroeger as best he could. The man was now reciting a list of all the oh, so important people he knew on Earth and how strongly all of them felt about this project.

The Westerners were very strange in their ways, as if they were always on a stage, always in Kabuki, always on display.

This was not Sekigawa's affair, and eventually he said, "Will you pay attention to what we are doing now, please, instead of what we will be doing if we succeed in doing this?"

The German, Kroeger, was better than some, but not so good as a Japanese mission specialist would have been.

Kroeger set to work with a snort. The confines in the shuttle were too close for ill feeling. Sekigawa prided himself on never mishandling a crew.

For a while, he thought he had mishandled this one. Then the flight deck became a busy, efficient unit, and Sekigawa was no longer concerned.

He was not even concerned when his third officer confirmed that there was an American spacecraft headed for very nearly the same coordinates as the *Edo*.

Those who thought space was a vast area were right. But those who thought that politics would not be exported by men to space were wrong.

Sekigawa had been briefed, before he'd lifted off, by members of NASDA, Japan's National Space Agency. He knew what to expect. He was aware that his mission was a difficult one.

He was proud to have been chosen for this mission. They had deployed the German satellite, their payload, without a hitch. Otherwise, the German, Kroeger, would not be so amenable to correction.

But now came the most delicate part of this mission. Sekigawa was clear on his task and his duty. He was to salvage the derelict for the Germans. This was a favor that was not so easy to perform.

Perfectly matching orbits with a piece of space junk was not a simple task. No Japanese had ever done this before.

He wished to perform creditably, with the world watching. And once he did, then he must deploy the new mobile manipulator arm, and two astronauts for safety's sake. Sekigawa wished that there were no foreign components to this mission—no foreign nationals on his flight deck, no foreign favors to be done.

Because of the foreign involvement, Sekigawa felt that he was being watched. This did not help his concentration.

He became very agitated as, twice, small glitches in the CPU, the central processing unit, controlling sensitive attitude-correction jets required subsequent additional corrections.

He was embarrassed to have imperfect control of his ship. He looked surreptitiously over to see if the balding German was leering at him. The German's head was bent to his controls.

Sekigawa took over personally at the most difficult stage, performing the most delicate phases of the final maneuvers himself.

There. Done. He relaxed as the difficult matching orbit was attained.

The German looked across at him and said, "Would you take a look out there, Sekigawa-san?"

He did and he could not believe his eyes. There, beyond the derelict com-sat, was not only the expected American spacecraft, but an American astronaut.

But what an astronaut. Sekigawa suppressed the impulse to rub his eyes.

The figure he saw there resembled nothing so much as a Samurai warrior, hanging in space, his weapons glittering as brightly as the stars at his back.

28

Space standoffs weren't Mackenzie's speciality. He'd tried to tell himself they weren't anybody's speciality as he'd floated out the open cargo hatch of the X-NASP in full kit, with a retrieval line playing out behind him, headed for the derelict sat.

Nearly two hundred miles above the Earth, and it was crowded as hell out here. The Japanese shuttle was sitting on the far side of the little winged com-sat, too close for comfort.

Watching. Waiting.

What the hell did they think they were doing anyhow? This was an American satellite, right? Mackenzie's suit said NASA/USSPACECOM in big letters, right?

Then how come a couple of astronauts were messing with the robot manipulator arm in the *Edo*'s open cargo bay?

If those spacemen wanted to have a tug of war out here, then Mackenzie was perfectly willing to chalk it up to a good day's field test. He was just waiting for mission control to relay a go-ahead.

Waiting for Space Command to make up its goddamn mind.

Running missions with the command component out of the operational loop wasn't Mackenzie's idea of a real good time. What were they doing back at Cheyenne Mountain, having their tarots read?

Mackenzie was whistling a tune softly between his teeth, feeling like a kid trying to decide if he really wanted to rob the candy store or not. But you couldn't act like this was nothing special.

Nobody just happened along in a test spacecraft armed to the teeth, wearing a combatized weapons-delivery platform that only vaguely resembled a conventional EVA suit and openly displaying at least one weapon: A laser rifle looked like a rifle. On the ground or in space, when somebody came toward you with one, the message ought to be clear.

Mackenzie was running what he hoped was an open com channel to the Japanese shuttle. If they wanted to talk to him, here he was. He could see the little lit indicator, at the corner of his vision window, that said all his coms were working. He shifted to the X-NASP's channel and said, "Hey, Cleary, any word from home?"

"No change." Cleary's voice was flat. "Proceed to satellite, secure and prepare to retrieve it."

This was one provocative test. Mackenzie wasn't doing a simulation in a virtual prototyping bay. He hoped to hell he could pull this off. Any of the men on the Japanese shuttle was probably better at space maneuvering than he was.

But at least the FIFS suit didn't weight anything out here. For the first time, its servos and his muscles weren't fighting each other. Its AI kept him oriented straight "up"; it ran its own navigational program, so he didn't have to worry about MMU jets or joysticks.

He'd been in this suit so long that it was almost second nature: He wanted to move and he moved. The FIFS program took neural firing cues, voice commands, and more kinds of sensoring intelligence than Mackenzie needed to see.

All of which meant it could keep him alive, gyro-stabilized, and moving in a direction he wanted to go while both his hands were busy. This space application required an additional power pack for both the maneuvering jets and the laser rifle.

Mackenzie had worried about that, on Earth, because he hadn't trained with it. But the additional pack didn't weigh anything either. And anyway, it made the suit more like a diving rig, and that suited Mackenzie fine.

You wanted to remember how much this was like being underwater. A lot of the risks were similar. But not the same.

Nothing was the same as prototyping combat gear in a real-time environment, especially when that environment was the space envelope.

He shifted, and turned his head in his helmet slightly. FIFS took his cues and reoriented him sufficiently that he could look back at the X-NASP he'd just left.

With her top-opening hatches spread wide, the Nomad looked real comforting, sitting there.

He pulled up his laser targeting grid, picked a direction clearly nonthreatening to the Japanese shuttle, and far out of the light cone that would damage the X-NASP, and let off two trial bursts.

No way they couldn't see that, over there at the upside-down Jap shuttle.

Then he reoriented his line of travel to the sat's coordinates and continued his approach.

The silence in his coms was nerve-wracking. He didn't want to chatter for the record. He wanted to be accessible to anyone with an order, or a warning, or an objection. All he could hear was the nearly subliminal muttering of the suit electronics as they processed. Sometimes he thought he could hear circuits humming, or the display grids booting up.

His visor showed him his approach to the target. The EMP'd satellite wasn't anything special—except that it was about to become a contested prize.

He knew what he was seeing over at that Japanese shuttle. Those astronauts were waiting for their orders, just like Mackenzie was.

At his waist he had three KKDs: smart five-pound missiles he could chuck like grenades if he needed to, and then control from FIFS once he'd powered them up.

But he wasn't in a fire-at-will situation here. He was in a very delicate microgravity dance with a bunch of guys just as nervous as he was.

If they tried to snag the American com-sat with their robot manipulator arm, what then?

Mackenzie wasn't sure that he could stop the robot. Nobody'd given him permission to try. And the smart KKDs would probably be the best option he had. Blinding the sensors of the robot arm meant aiming the focused beam of the laser sniping rifle at wherever the sensoring package was for the arm.

He hadn't the faintest idea where that might be.

Somebody should have given him a short course on the schematics of spacecraft belonging to foreign powers. He toggled to his "mission notes" mode. The light on his com grid turned green. He said into his com: "For the record. Schematics of enemy spacecraft sensoring packages and vital targets would be handy to have on board." Then he went back to standby mode, hoping to hell somebody would goddamned communicate with him.

He'd thought he might get space sick. He hadn't. He should have known better. Mackenzie never hurt at times like these. He never felt a thing, not physically.

He was so close to the satellite now that he fancied he could see the EMP damage on her. But the impacts he saw were only the typical hits from space debris.

Beyond the satellite, the astronauts were moving again. He tried to imagine what they'd thought when he'd test-fired the laser sniping rifle. Even though his faceplate had polarized to full-black to protect him, theirs would have whited out.

He'd carefully aimed in a neutral direction, but he knew they knew what he'd been doing. Shot across your bow, fellas.

No damage, just a simple display of electronic danger. Full-spectrum lasers couldn't be protected against unless you were willing to spend some time as blind as if your head was in a paper bag—in all optical sensoring modes.

Over at the *Edo,* the astronauts were roving around the robot arm's stump. The robot manipulator arm was big. So big that Mackenzie began seriously trying to figure how he could disable it. He'd seen plenty of horror movies in which the hero was picked up by the monster's huge claws and snapped in two at the waist. . . .

You got so jacked up waiting for something to happen that you began making up things that might happen.

It wasn't a healthy state of mind.

"One-Oh-One? Tell me a story about new orders, will you, Cleary?"

"Lots of chatter, no decisions." Mackenzie could almost hear Cleary shrug. "So far, we just proceed to secure the com-sat, but then wait for further instructions."

You could wait around only so long in a space suit, even in FIFS.

Mackenzie said, "I'm proceeding to secure the derelict." Those were his orders. He might as well be where the action was. Anyway, Pettit would have his balls for a wall hanging if he didn't give her toy a thorough shakedown cruise.

Cleary's voice had a ragged edge when the pilot responded. "Okay, but keep in mind I don't want to have to retrieve you from a free-fire zone. And keep your damned head down."

Cleary was reminding Mackenzie to be ready to shut down his sensoring packages fast, to avoid fratricide in case the pilot was ordered to use the X-NASP's greater lasing capability to stun the Japanese spacecraft.

"You bet," Mackenzie said, and headed for the gold wings of the disabled com-sat.

Mackenzie had no intention of getting in the way of the Nomad's firepower. He just wanted to be on the spot, in case he got the order he reasoned he should get.

You didn't come all the way out here to project power and then lose your nerve. You didn't back off, once you'd come this far.

Did you?

Mackenzie had put so much energy into learning this equipment, and so much time into this project, he couldn't imagine any result but successfully salvaging the satellite.

This was a test, all right. A test of nerve.

Abruptly, Mackenzie felt sorry for the astronauts on the Japanese shuttle. It was a multinational ratfuck out here, and the X-NASP was sitting there like a cat in front of the rathole.

If Mackenzie had been one of those other guys, in standard EVA gear, and seen FIFS coming, he'd have wanted to shit on the spot.

You preferred not to do that out here. You preferred to get the hell inside a pressurized spacecraft as soon as you could. And you preferred some goddamned clear and decisive direction from your command chain.

But then, just because this was the space envelope, it didn't mean those guys on the ground were going to perform any better than they ever had.

Mackenzie was beginning to feel a whole lot better about this project, now that he was out here doing it. He'd been determined to do Pettit proud, but that didn't seem to be the point anymore.

The point was that satellite.

As soon as he got to it, he put his hand on one of the wings and began pulling himself around it, winding it in his retrieval line. The line was a pure safety precaution.

FIFS's designers hadn't made an impregnable, unstoppable unit. Mackenzie knew it. Pettit knew it. Space Command knew it. Not even FIFS could operate in *any* environment. If somebody hit the FIFS suit with a KKD, or a hot bath of high-power microwave, or enough EMP, FIFS would go down and that would be the end of the mission for Mackenzie.

So you brought out your lasso and you roped the steer. If they all fucked each other over so bad out here that only the X-NASP was left operational, Cleary could reel in the line with the derelict satellite attached to it. The derelict would end up in the Nomad's cargo bay, just the way it was supposed to.

Mission accomplished. One way or the other.

Mackenzie had just decided where he was going to secure the tow line when Cleary and another voice started talking to him at once. "Hold on, folks. One at a time."

He glanced at the com telltale. Then he chose the communication from the *Edo,* passing it through so that the Nomad would hear and record what FIFS was hearing and recording.

The voice from the Japanese shuttle identified itself as the *Edo*'s pilot and said, "We are asking you not make any attempt to salvage unit."

What the fuck? "This sat is American property," Mackenzie said. Damn, he wasn't used to talking to the enemy. "I have orders to reclaim it for the—"

The incoming transmission clipped his, and then he heard: "—been asked by the German government to secure their rights to this salvage in their territorial zone."

"Salvage, mister, is a first-come, first-served situation." As he talked, Mackenzie determinedly fastened his line to the derelict.

Cleary beeped him with an emergency conference request that came up as a blinking red light on his visor display. Well, the coms worked just fine out here. Pettit would be thrilled when he told her how well.

"Stand by, *Edo,*" he said, and got off line with the shuttle and on with the Nomad. "What the hell is it, Cleary? Aren't you hearing this?"

"I'm hearing it, all right. CSOC says hold it, okay? Don't say anything. Don't do anything else."

"I've secured the tow line."

Cleary sighed. "I'll tell them. You just hang there, Major, until they get it sorted out diplomatically."

Ratfuck was what this was. "*You* want to talk to the *Edo,* Extra Heavy?" Mackenzie suggested. "Somebody'd better."

"Yeah, I'll do that. Listen if you want."

Mackenzie listened. Pretty soon, it sounded like the low end of the United Nations Basketball League arguing technical fouls.

He wanted to shut off the com, but he didn't. That would be irresponsible. Didn't anybody remember that he was hanging out here with only a certain amount of power and life support?

He began to imagine malfunctions, and went to systems checks because they'd better not be more than imaginings. Pettit was going to get the best test report anybody ever had.

He was looking at a long-range, multi-spectral readout on his visor when he saw movement from the quadrant where the

German power station was, about fifty miles off.

He centered the movement on his targeting display and increased magnification, popping through different modes.

Whatever it was, it was coming this way. He got with Cleary: "Remember that UFO? It's coming to the party."

"I can't break out of this loop to deal with it," Cleary told him. "I'm in the middle between Freedom's skipper and the *Edo*'s. You've got ground-to-space. When you've talked to somebody who knows how badly they want this satellite, you get back with me and say what you want to do."

Cleary sounded badly overextended. Standoffs could do that.

Mackenzie got a satellite relay to the ground and began describing what he was seeing, including the bogey headed straight for the two ships floating beside the derelict.

Hell, it was only a fucked satellite. If worse came to worst, they could destroy the satellite there and then, and the territorial problems about its disposition would be over.

Mackenzie was feeling like shooting something. But with so many possible targets out here, he didn't want to pick the wrong one.

That privilege was reserved for those of superior rank. FIFS suit or not, X-NASP or not, somebody on the blue-white Earth had to give permission for an exchange of fire up here.

Unless, of course, Mackenzie could manage to get himself fired upon. But Pettit wouldn't like that. She wouldn't like it one bit.

After all, so far as Pettit was concerned, Mackenzie was only minding the store.

He cleared his faceplate and looked at real-time. There were the *Edo* astronauts, climbing hand over hand along the robot manipulator arm, which was extended about as far as Mackenzie was willing to consider a nonthreatening distance.

And beyond, the free-flying German platform was on its way, coming hell for leather.

Mackenzie cradled his laser rifle and checked its charge, first on his visor display, then manually.

Once he'd fired a quick test blast, he murmured, "And that's the last warning shot for today, fellas. Next time, we shoot for the record." After all, it was Mackenzie's ass out here in the middle of this suddenly contested area.

And he tended to get stubborn when he was hanging in empty space with a full bladder and enough close space support to fry everything in line of sight.

Pettit wanted to know what this FIFS suit could do. Mackenzie knew damned well that if he didn't show her what she wanted to see, he'd never get back into her pants.

He wondered what she'd think if she could see the free-flying platform headed his way, and then realized he could show her.

With a grin, Mackenzie began telling FIFS to dump its last five minutes of recorded scans, via relay, to mission control. In the name of science, the least he could do was make sure she had all the test data she could ever want.

Then, if they got into a scrap up here and FIFS didn't make it home, he could rest easy, knowing that the project wouldn't take the blame.

Because it shouldn't. Anytime you were in a face-off two hundred miles above the Earth and at the center of a diplomatic flap, you wanted to be sure your equipment was up to whatever you asked of it.

And FIFS was. Mackenzie was sure of that now. He just wasn't sure whether the rest of them were.

29

Day 10: Free-Flying Manned Platform

Dietrich was furious. He would put the arrogant Americans in their place. This time, he would not feel blame, or guilt, or have bad dreams.

His feet felt numb in the platform clamps as he headed toward the confrontation brewing at the site of the salvage satellite.

If not for the Japanese shuttle there too, Dietrich could have used the MHD and destroyed the American spacecraft, as well as their astronaut.

He still wished he could do it. But he had been told he must not. So he would go out there himself, as a representative of German interests. No one had said he could not do that. He would ride to the rescue, and they would scatter before him. He would load up the satellite on his free-flying platform and make sure the Americans did not get their hands on it.

If they did, Dietrich was afraid that all would be lost. This satellite was proof of hostile actions in space. Its position plus the time it stopped working, when compared with the position of the second X-NASP when it went out of control, would provide the Americans with enough data to determine from where the EMP blast had come.

It would be the end of Dietrich's beloved MHD station. He would have nowhere to sleep anymore, now that Jenkins had caught him sleeping in the OMV.

They were going to rotate him to Earth anyway. He was sure of it. He must do something to stop it. He must do something now, before things became too desperate.

The Japanese were weak. They could not be counted upon if the situation became desperate.

Dietrich had received a worried communiqué from the ground. They were losing their nerve down there.

He was not losing his up here. He knew what the goals were, for which they all had worked so hard and long. He knew that actions spoke louder than words. He knew that the German, Kroeger, aboard the Japanese shuttle, would support him if he, Dietrich, acted boldly.

And he also knew that Kroeger could not act boldly on his own. Dietrich tapped his control stalk with sharp jabs of his gloved hand.

The platform must be fast enough. It must get there in time. He had to reach the confrontation before Commander Jenkins realized what he was doing. Jenkins would order him to stay away.

Why couldn't he and Kroeger simply take over the Japanese ship, take over the station, take over all of space the way they knew they must?

His feet, in the clamps, ached. Vibration traveled through them, all the way up to his head, and made it ache. This platform was not made for such speed.

But he must get there. He must assert German rights. He knew he must.

He heard a voice in his ears and ignored it.

"Dietrich?" said the voice.

He hunched down, as if he were on a motorcycle headed into the wind.

"Dietrich, do you copy?"

A woman's voice. Nothing to worry about. Magriffe could not force him back.

He pretended that his com system was on the fritz.

It was a long way from the MHD station to the two spacecraft parked by the dead satellite. A long way.

At least the *Edo* had successfully deployed the free-orbiting MHD. Whatever else happened, no one but the Coalition knew that the German satellite launched by the Japanese shuttle contained so powerful a beam weapon.

If some ass on the ground had not asked the Japanese shuttle to recover the American salvage when it entered the German zone, then Dietrich could have handled everything from the MHD. That was why he'd been out there.

But no. Fools on the ground had interfered.

And now . . .

Dietrich saw the American astronaut's tether, attached to the salvage. He punched in a course correction, and slowed the platform slightly. Dietrich's mouth tasted foul.

Something was happening out there. What?

He had to know. If he entered the circuit, if he asked questions, if he showed cognizance, he must then pretend to take orders from Space Station Freedom, if orders were given.

He slowed even further. He stared ahead, at the tiny men and the tiny satellite; at the X-NASP and the shuttle, with its robot manipulator arm extended.

His approach must not be thoughtless. He must not alert them to his purpose. He must not let them decide that he was an enemy. He must not reveal himself. . . .

He had to know what was going on. He had to know.

As he answered Magriffe's call, he saw something explode— a bright light, so bright he could not see.

Hurtling through space, he could not see.

There was a bright white light at the center of his vision. He could not blink it away. It traveled with him everywhere he looked. It obscured his controls.

Dietrich panicked. His finger slipped. The free-flying platform yawed. Only the clamps on his booted feet saved him from separating from the platform.

He kept trying to blink away the spot. He tried to be calm.

He must right his platform. He could see only at the periphery of his vision. Be calm. Be calm.

Don't be afraid. You won't die this way.

He knew these controls so well he could operate them in his sleep. Think, what correction to make?

His eyes were watering. He could feel tears collecting at their corners. One rolled down his cheek. His faceplate was obscured by the bright, white circles—sometimes one, sometimes two, but generally one great white hole beyond which everything was black at the edges of his vision.

Magriffe called his name again.

"Magriffe." He fumbled with his controls. "Magriffe, the Americans have blinded me. I can't see . . . I can't *see,*" he blurted out.

"What? Hold on, Dietrich. We'll get you some help. I'm sure it was some accident. Don't panic."

She was panicked, not him. Dietrich was beyond panic. He would be a martyr. Everyone would know that the Americans had attacked a German citizen in space. An unprovoked attack.

He listened to Magriffe's voice as she tried to help him, and he began to feel the warmth of victory spread over him. He didn't care if they rescued him, not really. Not if he was blind. If he died, he would take the American space program with him to hell.

Magriffe was saying, "—listen carefully. You happened to look at a laser burst, that's all. It's temporary. Do you hear? Don't do anything. Stay on that course. We'll get somebody over to you . . . we'll get you home."

Somebody? Who? An American? A Japanese? Home? Where? Home to Space Station Freedom? Blind, Dietrich careened through space, listening to all the commotion in his coms.

They were sending someone for him. So be it. He was blind, and he didn't believe Magriffe when she said his sight would return.

If he were lucky, he would continue on his present course, crash into the dead satellite, and die. The crash would send pieces of the manned platform and the dead com-sat spinning out of control into the two parked spacecraft.

There would be great damage. There would be a great outcry. It would be the Americans' fault. Justice would be done.

And in the end, no trace would be left of the mission satellite that Dietrich had EMP'd—nothing for the Americans to use to tie Germany to the destructive pulses.

Blindness was a small price to pay for such service to your country.

Dietrich said, in a shaking voice, "Magriffe, do you hear me? Magriffe, I can't hold on much longer. Magriffe, I only wanted to break the deadlock. That salvage belongs to my country, but no one wants any trouble."

"It's okay, Dietrich. We know you meant well. Everyone's so sorry. Please, just hold on."

He would hold on. His boots would hold him to the superstructure of the free-flying platform.

Blind, but with a personal sun in his eyes, Dietrich's platform sped toward the coordinates of the other spacecraft. Magriffe's voice in his ears sounded like the voice of history itself. And somewhere, at the edges of his vision, the stars glittered on a field of black.

30

Day 10: FIFS, Com-Sat Coordinates

"Reel it in, now!" Mackenzie demanded, pushing himself away from the American derelict with one gloved hand. "Extra Heavy 101, do you copy?"

Silence. Mackenzie switched freqs and caught Cleary heatedly explaining to Space Command on the ground: "—FIFS had the German platform targeted, and somehow the target got handed off to Nomad's laser pod. And yeah, I went with it. It's my fault. But you'll be glad to hear that the automatic attitude correction and tracking all works great."

Mackenzie bypassed Cleary. Too busy. There had to be a way for FIFS to initiate the automatic line-retrieval. . . . Then he remembered how to do it. It's always a little switch somewhere, even when that switch is an electronic simulation of a switch.

He was breathing hard as he watched the com-sat. The climate-control package whirred, trying to cool him enough to keep his visor from fogging up. He was floating backward at a pretty good clip. It took him a minute to be sure the derelict was moving as well.

Using his display's plotter, he checked the com-sat's current and most recent coordinates. Okay, it was moving. Cleary was still busy. Mackenzie scanned the other active com freqs.

They were in big trouble now. The out-of-control free-flyer was still coming their way, and the Japanese were chattering a mile a minute to their Santa Rita controllers, ignoring Space Station Freedom's attempts to talk to them.

Freedom was talking about sending an OMV after Dietrich.

Even Mackenzie knew that would take too long. The OMV was about fifty miles above them and maybe two hundred miles downrange, quick guess.

Quicker guess, Mackenzie wanted to get above this multinational screw-up, and fast. FIFS gave him a kick in the ass when he requested upward acceleration.

His heart jumped into his throat. Whee. You didn't realize how fast this thing was until you asked it for fast. Couldn't do that in the virtual prototyping bay.

He hoped to hell he could stop without spinning, but he shouldn't have worried. The maneuvering pack fired retros and made attitude adjustments, putting him exactly where he'd indicated on the visor grid.

Just move the icon and stare. He was glad that north and south weren't interchangeable to FIFS, and then he wasn't sure he was so happy after all.

Into Mackenzie's helmet came a satellite-bounced voice from distant Earth. "Mackenzie, this is Ford. Do you read me?"

Oh, shit. "Yes, sir." There was a two-second time lag on this circuit. "What can I—"

The time lag meant they were going to step all over each other's transmissions. Mackenzie shut his mouth.

"That OMV's not anywhere as near as you are, Mac, to this runaway. Hope you're up on your old Westerns. We've been conferring down here and we think you can hop onto that platform and bring it under control."

Without killing himself, destroying FIFS, and crashing the platform, Ford meant.

Mackenzie said doubtfully, "I don't know, sir. Won't it destabilize if—"

"Mackenzie," said a familiar, female voice. "Just do exactly what I tell you."

What else was new? "Hiya, Pettit. Are we havin' fun yet?"

"We're sending FIFS a routine. Just let the program execute. When you get on board, Station will walk you through the navigating procedures. Or . . ."

A long pause followed, in which Mackenzie's visor did things he hadn't known it could do, throwing up complex multi-colored graphs and some hieroglyphic machine language he didn't like the look of.

Then he received another ground-to-space transmission. Ford again: "If you can't navigate the free-flying platform for any reason, shut it down and use the FIFS self-powering elements to push it to the Japanese shuttle. Their cargo bay is bigger. We don't want you laying a hand on the German pilot, or communicating directly with the Japanese shuttle. And we don't want the Nomad any more involved than it is already. Clear?"

Hand-over. He'd done it on the ground with terrorists and hostages; the labels were interchangeable, depending on whether you were on the dispensing or the receiving end of human collateral.

"I gotcha. Mission understood. FIFS has the dump."

Ford signed off, and Mackenzie concentrated on trying to feel as if he weren't merely along for the ride as he instructed FIFS to execute the intelligence-gathering and logistical portions of the new program.

New screens. New capabilities. A single target centered in a split screen: the German platform. On the other half of his visor, he was getting his own plot data, in relation to everything else cluttering up this bad-luck orbit.

The free-flyer's speed and inclination were constantly tracked for him. His own position was being minutely altered, on the fly, by FIFS as it computed and recomputed the intercept.

He'd nearly forgotten about the outside world. He was watching the bottom corner of the right-hand half of his visor, which was showing FIFS's power and life-support status, and wondering how long this was going to take.

Then Cleary said in his com, "Satellite secure. Those Japs are sure agitated. I heard you're going to snag the runaway. Good luck, Major."

"Yeah, we'll need it. You too."

Mackenzie's privacy com function started blinking. Then Cleary said, "Freedom's commander's chewing some serious tail. You going to fly that platform to the station? If you do, I'm supposed to follow right along—in case you need me."

Cleary was rattled.

"Hey, Sonny. It's not your fault. Maybe these systems are smarter than we are. That platform was coming way too fast. It might have crashed into us or something. I'll back you. We've got plenty of on-the-record."

Then FIFS started demanding his attention. It wanted to do final prepositioning for the intercept.

Mackenzie was glad he didn't know enough to tell how worried he ought to be. Matching orbits was tricky. An intercept was a controlled collision course, as far as he could judge.

He just made sure that all his weapons were secure, safe against loss during the fancy maneuvering, and tried to work with his exoskeletal powered suit.

If he'd had this suit on the ground, he would be damned near invincible in a low-intensity situation. But this wasn't your usual ground low-intensity situation. Ford and friends didn't want any more trouble.

Well, he hoped somebody'd told the German that. He tried contacting Space Station Freedom.

For some reason, he couldn't complete the patch. Then he asked Cleary to help him and found out why: Cleary and Freedom were talking.

When he was in the circuit, he said, "Somebody tell that German guy what's about to happen. He's blind and scared and I don't want to surprise him."

"That's the problem," said a gruff voice with too much of an edge to it not to be Jenkins, the station commander. "He doesn't want an American's help. And it's German property, so it's German territory."

Mackenzie stared at the com light disbelievingly, as if it were the face attached to the voice he was hearing. "Well, shit, let him kiss—"

"We're taking care of it, Mac. You just execute your orders," Cleary said in a half-pleading voice.

"Mackenzie out."

What was he, a robot janitor?

He clocked his velocity. He double-checked the match with the target. His real-time view shifted, as FIFS made another fine course correction.

He could see the shuttle and the X-NASP now. He was a little above them. The com-sat was invisible—probably inside the X-NASP by now. The Nomad's payload bay was closed. The Japanese shuttle, upside down, was retracting its manipulator arm. He monitored their com, and couldn't make much of the foreign-language chatter. But they didn't want their robot arm to get hit, that was for certain.

He didn't want to collide with the platform himself. He heard breathing, but it wasn't his own.

What the hell was this? Then he realized. "Cleary, what the hell are you doing?"

"Just trying to make sure that if you need some help, somebody hears you."

"Well, don't breathe at me, okay? You want to monitor this circus act, take it on pass-through."

"Yeah, I'd like that."

Cleary was really taking this hard. Or maybe the pilot had more sense than Mackenzie did. But Mackenzie was used to jumping down onto things, and not worrying too much about how hard he hit.

He figured he had two things in his favor. If he didn't watch the visor display too closely, he didn't have to think about how fast he was moving. In space, you didn't feel a thing.

And he didn't mind jumping or, in this case, executing an abrupt acceleration toward moving coordinates that happened to be inhabited by another moving piece of hardware. He didn't much care if the blind guy wanted him on the runaway platform or not. So far as Mackenzie was concerned, it was a target. Repercussions of actions had never been his concern, as long as those actions were clearly delineated.

So when it came time to drop—he couldn't help thinking of it that way—"onto" the platform, he thought of it in airdrop terms, and it felt real familiar.

In fact, nothing had felt so damned familiar since the night he'd seen the FIFS suit for the first time.

If this had been a real high-altitude low-opening jump, he'd have had to worry about whether his chute would open. Instead, he had to worry about whether FIFS had computed the right instant and degree of jet-assisted braking to employ.

Until the moment of impact (ignoring the indicator which was telling him in red how fast he was going), he felt as if he were still floating, just as he'd been throughout this EVA. Then he got grabbed in the crotch and slammed upward toward the top of the FIFS helmet, just before he was kicked in the ass.

But now he could see the platform. It was long, flat, and sure enough, it had a guy up front, clinging to a podium-type control stalk. He hoped somebody'd bothered to program this tin can not to land him on the other guy's head.

Blind guy or not, space envelope or not, if he killed the subject of this rescue mission, it wasn't going to go down well on the ground.

He hit pretty hard, he thought. But he hit amidships, behind the blind guy, on top of the generator housing or whatever it was that doubled as cargo area.

The platform tipped straight "up" in relation to its previous inclination.

Mackenzie swore and grabbed for the blind guy, who began to struggle wildly.

"Cleary," he called into his com as the guy's arms pinwheeled and the platform began spinning lazily, "get me a channel to this fool. Fast!"

He didn't care about anybody's rules of engagement now. He had his arms around the blind guy, who didn't realize that there was no way to elude the embrace of somebody in a powered exoskeletal suit.

But Mackenzie couldn't hold the blind German with both hands and stop the platform from tumbling end over end.

The German was locked securely onto the platform with boot clamps, so that was something.

Through his visor, Mackenzie could see the landmarks of the Japanese shuttle and the Nomad kaleidoscoping slowly into and out of his view. He could hear his own breathing.

He could feel the lurches of the man his arms were imprisoning— but only barely, as FIFS compensated with more power.

He wasn't hearing anything in his com. And then he heard Cleary and the station commander arguing, because Cleary wanted him to hear it.

In his whole life, Mackenzie had never been so uniquely fucked over by colliding command imperatives.

Cleary was saying, "—then you tell the platform pilot to stop fucking with this rescue attempt. Or we'll let him go on his way. And then you people can try your luck."

Pretty hard-ass.

The station commander said, "Captain, you'll do exactly what you're told. Stand by."

So then they were all standing by, while Mackenzie was hugging the German from behind and the platform tumbled lazily toward disaster.

You didn't have to think quick, in the space business, unless you were out here on the business end.

He seriously considered ripping the German's life support and saying the guy did it while he was struggling. But that would never play. FIFS was recording everything.

He tried to see past the back of the German's helmet. But he couldn't very well.

What he could see confirmed what his visor display was telling him: They were tumbling toward the Japanese shuttle. You didn't want to crash into anything, not at this velocity. Not tumbling . . .

With a muttered command to his AI, Mackenzie shut down his coms completely. He pulled up his kinetic kill deployment package, and programmed KKD #1 of the three on his belt remotely.

Then he took a chance. Still holding the German, Mackenzie dropped to his knees, undid the boot clamps, and jumped with the blind guy under one arm.

Holding the German by the MMU, he reached down with his left hand, unclipped the KKD from his belt, and chucked it hard, at the platform.

He was guessing where to throw it. He was hoping it had enough smarts to find its target.

He'd sent it seeking the heat of the platform's power source.

It flared angrily to life, then disappeared under the platform.

Please don't blow us both to shit.

FIFS gave him all the speed it could.

He needn't have worried. The KKD was smart enough.

Mackenzie and the struggling blind guy were still accelerating when the German platform veered crazily and began to come apart in a silent burst of strutwork, metal, and electronics.

31

Day 10: Space Station Freedom

Commander Jenkins said, "You what? You idiots." Space Station Freedom, around him, looked the same as it ever had. Nothing in evidence in the logistics module indicated that World War Three might just have started. On his watch yet. He had to think.

It didn't matter why the Space Command pilot and FIFS operator had disobeyed direct orders. That was for a subsequent inquiry. It mattered that the situation not be exacerbated.

"Stand by, 101 Extra Heavy." Jenkins licked dry lips, and hailed the Japanese shuttle.

When he'd finished abasing himself, Jenkins felt as if he needed a shower. But he had a solution to at least the most immediate of their problems.

He called the Nomad back: "Have your FIFS operator hand over the German national to a Japanese astronaut who'll come out to get him. Tell your man not to talk to the Japanese. And not to try to talk to the German he's got in tow. *I'll* do that. The German's in shock. We'll make that clear to everyone. Once the German is handed over to the Japanese astronaut, your FIFS operator returns to your ship and you two get on about your business. Is that clear? Get away from those coordinates. Make sure all your communications are secure. And don't involve Freedom any further in your adventure—not in any way whatsoever. Do you understand me, Captain Cleary?"

The voice of the Nomad pilot replied, "Yes, sir. Thank you, sir." Crisp. Controlled. Jenkins heard no sign that Cleary understood what a mess he and his shipmate had made.

Well, Jenkins understood. He pushed up from the com station and away. When he unsealed the lock, Magriffe was waiting there, curled up in midair, making notes on her clipboard.

"I wanted to be here if you needed me."

"More than ever," he told her. "See what you can do to smoothe things over, will you? My lips are sore from all the ass I've been kissing."

"We're still hosting the Japanese contingent?"

"We are."

"And they'll take Dietrich back with them?"

"As soon as he's fit to travel." The Italian space physician would have to make that determination. "Where is Di Lella, anyway?"

"Talking to Dietrich—or trying to, from the A lab module. Poor Dietrich. It must have been terrible, to go through all that and be blind while it was happening."

Terrible. This was one terrible mission, that was for sure. In a stellar career, Jenkins had never been party to such a mess. "Ah, Magriffe, any suggestions on damage control, before this error chain stretches all the way to the ground?"

Her hair waved lazily around her face. "Try not to worry, Commander. Dietrich's alive. According to Di Lella, who's been discussing the blinding with someone knowledgeable on the ground, he should be fine in a couple of days. If we wait that couple of days, all we'll have to account for is a lost platform. Dietrich will have a wild story to tell, but he's fatigued from his time up here in any case. If I were you, I'd go back through his record and list any aberrant behavior. After all, what did he think he was doing?"

"Would you do that for me, Magriffe?"

"I . . . of course."

If it weren't so unprofessional, Jenkins would have kissed her. But it was. And he didn't. Instead, he said, "I feel much better. Considering that I'm about to host that Japanese delegation, you've performed quite a feat of magic in these last few minutes." He'd showed weakness, and before a woman. He had to make her believe that he was in control. He had to make her feel useful, make her believe that they could do something to restore the status quo ante.

Now if only he could make himself believe it . . .

He let Magriffe accompany him back into the secure com station atop the logistics module, and pulled himself up to the console with a new sense of purpose.

He could host the Japanese, calm the Germans, and make things right with the ground, all before dinnertime. After all, damage control up here was his job.

But as long as he lived he would never forget the moment when that FIFS cowboy reported destroying the German platform as a necessary concomitant of saving Dietrich.

He wondered how much of what the FIFS operator had done was now being viewed at Santa Rita Control, the Italian launch-control platform which was mission control for this Japanese shuttle.

When you had a bad day in space, it was a really bad day.

32

Everything that mattered to Schliemann was orbiting with the space station, two hundred miles overhead. The tension he felt made his whole body ache unbearably.

And from that space station so far above Schliemann's head, Jenkins, the idiot commander of Space Station Freedom, was giving him a typical American hard time. Schliemann wanted to speak to Dietrich, not to this boorish American who was obsessed with his own "command responsibilities."

He *needed* to speak to Dietrich.

Schliemann was hunched over a com system in the Santa Rita facility, hands cupping the headset he wore as if, by that means, he could hear the transmission better. And his left thigh was cramping. He rubbed it with sweaty fingers.

No one here at the control platform understood the implications of what had happened up there at the coordinates of the derelict satellite. Not yet. None of the men around him knew that the failure of the joint Japanese-German salvage mission and the destruction of the German free-flying platform might have signaled the destruction of the Coalition—or cared. These were unwitting men, at Santa Rita Control, working for pay, concerned that their performance was acceptable.

But nervous. International conflict over a space derelict had made everyone nervous. The Japanese were worried about their precious shuttle, which had taken a few paltry shrapnel hits.

The Italian members of the Coalition were positively mutinous. Osawa's death in a freak accident at the San Marco launch platform, 920 kilometers away, linked to Santa Rita by twenty-three cables, had made the Italians, always superstitious, panicky and defensive.

Luckily, no Italian Coalition member was on site here today, only workers. These technicians and ground controllers were not political. They might know, but certainly didn't care, that the German government was about to fall because of what had happened. They didn't even know that Schliemann had been asked to resign his post in the German Space Agency. Not yet.

So they did not know how important this conversation was. If they could have found someone in the Italian or German governments whom they could ask whether this transmission to Space Station Freedom was permissible, the answer might have been no. But they had no reason to ask. They had been paid. Schliemann had been here before. He was still technically an ORTAG functionary.

These Italians knew only that a German official wished to express a personal message of comfort and sympathy to a German astronaut, blinded in a terrible accident.

That was what the Americans were calling this—an accident.

Schliemann cleared his throat and tried again.

"Commander Jenkins, I understand your concerns. They are our concerns as well. But I need to speak to my—to Astronaut Dietrich. He deserves our best wishes for a speedy recovery."

Schliemann patiently waited out the time lag, his eyes defocused. His fingers traced the bumper of the communications console at which he sat. He was in danger of losing everything. The Coalition was in a rout. Why had this fool, Dietrich, gone charging the American-Japanese standoff, as if he were some cowboy from an American movie?

Why?

Jenkins's voice finally reached him: "We're getting him. You can imagine, sir, that he's somewhat shaken up. Everyone is agreed, up here, that this was just the most unfortunate series of mishaps. We'll get Dietrich down as fast as we can, on the *Edo,* as soon as it's made some minor repairs. I—"

"I'm not sure that's necessary, are you, Commander? As you say, the *Edo* took some damage—from shrapnel due to the American destruction of a German space asset, our free-flying manned platform. So we wouldn't want a German astronaut's life to be risked unnecessarily. Perhaps our man can wait for the next scheduled space shuttle."

Having cut off Jenkins's transmission, Schliemann could only wait again to see what effect his veiled warning might have. One couldn't insist that a blind man—even a man blinded temporarily—stay in space. One could merely point out that all precautions must be taken.

"Uh, sir," Jenkins said at last, "we don't think the Japanese shuttle has any major problems. But we'll take all necessary precautions. Maybe Dietrich *should* wait for a later flight. We'll see. I'm sure your government will receive a more official statement, but we're sorry about this—about the lost equipment, as well. We've got one hell of a mess up here, with all that new space junk so close to the station. So you'll excuse me if I seem brusque."

Did Jenkins intend to insult and obstruct? Did the American know that Schliemann was in trouble because of this? That the whole German government was in trouble? Jenkins must know, of course, or he'd be speaking more respectfully to a high official of the German Space Agency.

"I'm sure we're all sorry, but not as sorry as Dietrich," Schliemann nearly growled. One must say something. Dead air was costly. How long could it take to get the fool to the logistics module?

Time lag again. A few seconds can be an eternity.

The next voice he heard, mercifully, was Dietrich's. The man sounded weak, disoriented, and angry. "Herr Schliemann? This is an honor. I'm . . . I was attacked by the Americans."

No, no. Do not be overt. Schliemann had to calm this man enough to deliver a coded message. "We are all sorry for your pain, my friend. You will see again soon, I am assured. But tell me how bad it is. The Americans think you should come home on the Japanese shuttle. Is this what you want?"

Another two-second lag, while Dietrich, a low-level operator, decided whether he was fit to proceed. It was now up to this space monkey whether the plan could continue on schedule in its primary form. Schliemann had no time to search for any irony that might lurk in this turn of events.

He must control this situation, or go to a backup plan, using remote control from Santa Rita to follow through, in spite of Japanese reluctance in the wake of the salvage misadventure. But then Schliemann would be exposed, his complicity clear.

In the open. And now, with so many political problems on Earth, he was frankly afraid to try. So everything hung on this wounded man. Schliemann picked at a hangnail until his finger bled and Dietrich's answer reached him:

"I'll be fine, Herr Schliemann. I promise. I want to stay here and do my job."

Schliemann felt as if he had just ejaculated. He eagerly spoke the simple, coded message that would tell Dietrich how to proceed: "You have until the Japanese shuttle leaves to decide, of course. By noontime, tomorrow, you should know better how fit you are. I'm sure the Americans will let you finish your tour if that is what you request. After all, they are at fault here, not you. Things will go fine, in the end. Take heart." *Noontime tomorrow.* This was the projected deadline for international compliance with the demands Schliemann would make. *Go fine, in the end* meant *Get ready to EMP the station.* Schliemann added: "We will announce this to the world," to make sure Dietrich understood, and also for the benefit of the Americans. Then he said, "Our faith in you is unshaken, Herr Dietrich. Your country will hail you as a hero."

And he ended the transmission.

33

Day 11: Space Station Freedom

Dietrich could see a little better now. He was still groping. The light was still living in his eyes: sometimes one circle of light, sometimes two. But now he could see something out of the corners of his eyes.

If he looked carefully. If he turned his head just right. If he moved his eyes as little as possible. If he breathed deeply and blinked away the salve that Di Lella had applied to them.

Di Lella had brought him the news where he floated in sickbay. The mission was falling apart. Someone had changed the plan, because of the trouble over the derelict. Or they were lying to him. The Italians and the Japanese were going off on their own. They weren't staying with the timetable Schliemann had determined for announcing a threat to the station. They were trying to gain some political advantage. There was trouble down on the ground. Fighting between the factions in the Coalition.

He hung in his sickbay webbing, fuming, waiting for Di Lella to send Kroeger to see him.

Di Lella was treating him as if he were extraneous. "I called the ground," Di Lella had said to him, puffed with importance and sharp-tongued with power. "I spoke personally with the Ministry, and told them what happened to you. Then I spoke with Sekigawa, from the Japanese shuttle. We decided to use your injury as a pretext, and avoid trouble."

In his undamaged mind's eye, Dietrich could see Di Lella's sanguine, oily face. The olive skin, the coarse hair, the thick lips and Roman nose. And Di Lella was gloating. The Japanese and Italians wanted to back out!

"Avoid what kind of trouble? The plan is set," Dietrich fumed. "You cannot deviate." They *did* want to back out! But today Schliemann would announce, anonymously, the threat to the station's survival.

"This is not your decision," said Di Lella. "You just rest. We will do what we must. We are working closely together, the Japanese and ourselves, to make sure that the German weakness does not overwhelm us."

"*What* German weakness?" Dietrich had almost shouted. "*We* have a plan." Dietrich needed to find a way to execute his part of that plan, despite the recent debacle over the derelict satellite. He had promised Schliemann he would. While Jenkins and everyone else remained distracted by what had happened, Dietrich could still save the plan. Schliemann was counting on him. "We must follow through, Di Lella."

"We have a problem in your government. This is no time to discuss it. We will take a different tack. Be assured, all is going well. I am talking to the very highest levels. And—ssh, here comes the Canadian whore."

So Di Lella had medicated his eyes, telling him it was an antibiotic, and made his vision even worse.

But Dietrich had seen the blur of movement that was the Canadian woman as she swam over to him through the air. "Don't worry, Dietrich, you'll be okay. We're going to send you down on the Japanese shuttle. Your eyes will recover fully, so NASA says."

No!

"They ought to know. It was their weapon that did this to me. I don't want any help from the Americans."

"Hey, Dietrich, it was a mistake. The Americans are sorry. Commander Jenkins talked to you, didn't he?"

"Ya, he talked to me." Arrogant slut. She was the whore of the American commander. And Jenkins had come to Dietrich after Schliemann's transmission, telling Dietrich not to worry—that no international tensions would result from this unhappy accident if everyone worked together.

As if that were a desirable result. Dietrich wanted desperately to palm his eyes, to get the sticky salve out of them. Where was Kroeger? The Japanese shuttle crew was performing maintenance, but Kroeger, his countryman, should have been able to find time to see him.

Dietrich would go find Kroeger, he decided. He knew the station well enough. He could see—a little. And he could hear very well. The station normally slept six, and now the crew of the Japanese shuttle was aboard also, so there were nine of them, including Dietrich.

Schliemann himself had spoken to Dietrich on a pretext of concern for his health, and given Dietrich the signal to go ahead with the plan. Dietrich had confirmed that he was able. Now he must be true to his word.

He would find Kroeger. Out of his berth, floating free, he heard Kroeger's harsh, "Dietrich, what are you doing?"

He turned his head to the left, to the right. He could see Kroeger, just an arm and a leg in shorts. But he knew where Kroeger was.

He said, in that direction: "Coming to find you. We must talk. Privately."

Better not reveal that he could only see a little bit.

"So, talk. Now."

Therefore, there was no one else within earshot. "The Italians and Japanese are going off on their own. We are in a power struggle and I am not willing to lose it."

"Ya, I know this. But what can we do? Down below, they are losing their nerve. Osawa is dead. The chancellor resigned. Schliemann has been asked to resign from the ORTAG board."

Dietrich knew all about Schliemann, more than Kroeger could possibly know. Schliemann was even now preparing to announce to the world that Space Station Freedom was the Coalition's hostage. Dietrich must hurry.

"We can do what we must." Dietrich pushed himself toward the voice. "I cannot see entirely well, but well enough. We will go to the OMV together. You will help me. We will carry through the plan."

"How? We cannot, just the two of us."

"We can," Dietrich said. "We will. We must."

"But how will we survive if we—?"

"The original plan. The *original* plan. We will hold these fools to their word. Everything we have said will happen, shall happen. I have provisions, for rescue. In time. Don't worry. Just help me. We must defeat these cowards, or all is lost." He hit something soft: Kroeger's shoulder.

"You can't see at all." Kroeger's hand came down on his shoulder. "How can we—?"

"You can't refuse me." Dietrich's hand grasped Kroeger's arm and squeezed. "I can see a little. Enough. Now help me get into a suit. Once we are at the OMV, I can handle myself. I can do this in my sleep—blindfolded, so to speak." And he grinned. A wide, confident grin, because he was confident, now that everything was at risk, that he would find a way to make sure no one won if he did not.

There were winning situations, and there were losing situations. If he, Dietrich, did not win, then what he lost would be only a pittance compared to what the others lost. These Japanese all thought they were performing in a theater, that they could change their roles at any time. These Italians had no balls; Di Lella was proof of that.

And as for the station personnel, Dietrich had always hated all of them. Once Germany was clearly in control of space, his brothers on the ground would recover their courage. And Dietrich could deliver that control, as long as Kroeger was here to be his eyes. He had promised Schliemann. Dietrich always kept his promises.

With his hand on Kroeger's arm, clamped tight, he said through gritted teeth, "Come. Lead me. We must suit up and get to the OMV."

The orbital maneuvering vehicle was Dietrich's safe haven. In it was all the additional capability he needed. With it, he could get to his MHD station. If anyone tried to stop them, Dietrich had another option.

It was a terrible option, so he did not tell Kroeger about it. It was a frightening option, because it could mean Dietrich's death, as well as the deaths of the others.

He could make an EMP bomb of the auxiliary-power MHD that was a part of Space Station Freedom, and kill the station without leaving it. A frightening option, but a tempting option to a blind man. If Dietrich was truly forever blind—if the Americans, Japanese, Italians, and Canadians were lying to him about his eyes—then Dietrich had nothing to lose. His life was already over.

Kroeger was arguing with him intermittently, every time there was a place to argue where no one would overhear. In the interconnecting modules, this was not frequently. But it was frequent enough to annoy Dietrich.

He kept blinking away the light. He kept trying to see from the sides of his head. He kept trying to make the glimpses he got of the station modules around him into a real return of vision.

He needed to see.

He must see. But when they reached the suit storage area and began to prepare for an EVA to the OMV, he still could see very little.

Worse, Kroeger could see very well and Kroeger was talking to someone. The Japanese shuttle commander, Sekigawa, was there.

The two men argued over Dietrich. Kroeger said, "Dietrich needs to show me the OMV, Sekigawa-san," which should have been enough to say.

But Sekigawa wanted explanations, and felt that he could give Kroeger orders.

So now there was more trouble. The Japanese, who knew the plan, and should be helping, were backing out. If only Dietrich could see! It was hard to keep his mind on what the two men were saying. These Japanese were trying to spoil everything. What right did the Japanese commander have to tell Kroeger what to do?

Kroeger might be a mission specialist attached to Sekigawa's crew, but he was still a German astronaut.

And Dietrich was not under Sekigawa's control at all.

"Is there anyone else in here?" Dietrich hissed, twice, to Kroeger, before the man snarled, "No," and continued talking to Sekigawa as if Dietrich was unimportant.

So Dietrich let go of Kroeger and, pretending that he could really see instead of see only a little, began to get into his EVA suit.

He was not sure he could make this EVA on his own, without a helper. But he would try.

Sekigawa had no control over him. Dietrich was his own man.

He heard the other two, arguing more and more heatedly, but he was concentrating on getting into the suit. This was not a simple task for a man half blind. Not simple at all.

But the plan had time-critical steps, which must be accomplished. He had promised Schliemann that, despite his blindness, he could still meet the schedule.

Then someone said, "Dietrich, what are you doing?" and that someone was Magriffe, the Canadian whore.

"I'm going out," he said gruffly, without turning his head. He blinked as hard and as often as he could. After each blink, it seemed, the light was growing dimmer. Vision was returning. "We have an EVA schedule to maintain," he reminded her. "Especially with so much new space debris so close to the station, that schedule is crucial." Space debris from the American destruction of the German free-flying platform. Dietrich's hatred stuck in his throat. "I thought I'd show Kroeger the ropes, but now we have a dispute." He shrugged without looking over his shoulder at her.

What good would that do? He could barely see. By tilting his head, he could manage to confirm his hands' knowledge of what he was doing, but it was a slow process. She must not know how slow.

Dietrich was almost ready. He had done so many EVAs that he could do this one now. He dreaded only the moment when he must put his hands in their gloves. From then on, his tactile knowledge of his surroundings would be reduced. But still, by looking to the left of what he wanted to see, he could see at least half—well, a small portion—of the object.

Magriffe came around in front of him, saying, "Oh, Dietrich, that's wonderful—that you're so much better. But are you sure you can manage?"

Magriffe was a shape, an arm and a curve of hip, a jellyfish of hair with a bright white light for a face and no far side. But she was discernible. It was enough. The Americans and this Canadian slut were off their guard, too distracted by the problems created by Dietrich's misfortune to think of their own safety. So Dietrich's blindness was lucky—if Dietrich could overcome it.

"I am perfectly capable. We are far behind schedule, I know. But I'm not doing anything too difficult this first time out. I'll just be checking the auxiliary power source, which, you'll remember, Germany donated to the project." To get there, he had to pass the OMV. "I thought I would take Kroeger and show him his nation's pride. And if all goes well, we will take a ride over to the free-orbiting power plant, so that Kroeger can report back about it. This is a part of his mission." He smiled at the light that was Magriffe's face. "Of course, if Herr Sekigawa will not let Herr Kroeger accompany me, then I will go myself. But I will not send a good report about bad cooperation."

Let them think he was all healed. Let them think that he had perfect vision. Let Magriffe think that this argument was about simple matters of command, not the larger power struggle. She didn't know anything about that. But she soon would. Now, she and Jenkins and the other Americans aboard Freedom thought that averting an international political incident was their greatest concern. Very soon they would learn differently.

It was a good thing that the Japanese commander and Kroeger had been arguing in pidgin German, and not in English. It was a good thing, also, that Sekigawa's English was good enough that he realized when all arguments must cease.

The Japanese said, from somewhere behind the light in Dietrich's eyes, "I was only questioning the wisdom of allowing our German friend to let his sense of duty override his caution. He has been so recently injured."

"I am a German, I am not a Japanese." Good. From the sound of it, Dietrich was winning the argument.

He would have given anything to see the Japanese's face. So much could be learned from facial expressions.

But not everything. Magriffe began smoothing over the rift she perceived between Kroeger and his Japanese superior. All for the good of international relations. All for harmony on the station.

She would not dare forbid Dietrich his EVA. Not now.

And so he got his help, his spare pair of eyes, and out they went.

It was easy enough, with Kroeger to help him into the inner lock, to cycle the lock, and to help Dietrich into his MMU.

And maybe his eyes were getting a little better. He pretended they were. The joysticks under his gloved hands felt good. The MMU cradled him in its wonderfully competent embrace.

Kroeger had insisted on a safety line between them. This demand he'd acceded to, as much because Kroeger was not a man who was accustomed to EVAs as because it was good to have a line to someone whose eyes could see more than the edges of things.

And it was good to hear Kroeger's breathing, as they climbed up the strutwork. Beneath the station was a long fall to Earth. Dietrich was not foolish enough to lose touch with the framework of the station. He could not afford to lose his grip.

But climbing was effortless, as always. Out here, you didn't need to see so much, unless you were operating controls. Dietrich was only climbing.

His inner eye knew exactly where he was. He envisioned himself as a surefooted spider on a web, and even Kroeger was fooled.

"You really are better, Herr Dietrich," Kroeger puffed into his com mike.

And Dietrich said, "Better every minute, Kroeger." You could not discuss anything sensitive in these helmets. Everything could be monitored, so close to the station. He must hope that nothing went amiss.

They had only a little more climbing to do when Dietrich misremembered where the next crossbeam was. His hand closed on nothing.

His foot was already pushing him out of contact with the last strut.

And he was floating sightless in the abyss.

He yelled, "Kroeger!" He tried to see where the strut was. He turned his head wildly in his helmet.

"Yes, yes?" Kroeger's voice said in his ears. Kroeger's safety line tugged at Dietrich's waist.

But Dietrich saw the strut, just in time. His accomplished hand knew exactly how much course correction to apply with the joystick under his right hand. His left grabbed the strut again, and Dietrich responded in a loud voice, "You be careful back there, Kroeger. You are becoming careless."

"Sorry," Kroeger said uncertainly, not sure why he had been so brusquely critiqued.

And then Dietrich glimpsed the round underside of the OMV. Glimpsed it! *Saw* the curve, out of the corner of his eye.

He was transported with joy. He scrambled faster, and Kroeger had to beg him to slow down.

But Dietrich was not uncertain any longer.

When he reached the OMV and crawled inside, he made room for Kroeger. It was tight. But it was done.

"Come here." He crooked a finger at Kroeger, who could see, and signaled that the other man turn off his com gear. They touched helmets, and the sound of their voices was conducted by the contact.

"Now we are going to the MHD. I will tell you what to do to help me. We must take the OMV out now, before anyone thinks to stop us." Before the announcement, on Earth, precipitated a state of heightened alert on the station.

"As you say, Herr Dietrich."

Herr Dietrich indeed. As he was directing Kroeger, he smiled to himself. They would separate the OMV from the station, take the OMV over to the parked power sat. From there all things were possible.

Dietrich could have chosen to continue up the keel and make an EMP bomb out of the auxiliary power station that the Germans had donated to Space Station Freedom. But then he too would have been a helpless prisoner inside the space station or the *Edo,* awaiting death or possible rescue by an undamaged spacecraft.

This way, he would have the OMV. He would save it, and his suit, and Kroeger's suit, from the crippling EMP that would destroy everything electronic on the station and on the Japanese shuttle, as soon as he and Kroeger were safely out of range at the MHD satellite. The Japanese deserved no warning, no exemption.

Then he and Kroeger could come back, innocent of blame and safe. Come back to the station and do as they wished, once the EMP was past.

Or stay there at the MHD, ready to EMP whatever might threaten them, until everyone on the station and the shuttle was dead. Dietrich had enough life support on the MHD station to do that. And from there, he could remotely command the free-orbiting MHD satellite that the Japanese had just put in orbit for Germany. He could, if worse came to worst, put it on automatic target-acquisition. If he wished, he could hold the entire world at bay, once he reached the MHD station.

He could even, if Kroeger was trustworthy, get some sleep. When he woke, his eyes would be better. But until his eyes were better, he needed Kroeger to execute the fine commands and read the tiny letters and numbers and touch the complex control panels. So Kroeger would live. His fellow German would live awhile, anyway.

Long enough for Dietrich to decide whose man Kroeger really was, and whether he could spare the additional life support to keep Kroeger alive.

He tried to see Kroeger, but Kroeger's head was a light—a light on big shoulders in an EVA suit.

He began giving concise instructions, and Kroeger seemed to be following every one.

When the OMV was separated and launched, Dietrich had thought he would feel better.

But he didn't. They had a long way to go. Kroeger was not as familiar with the controls of the OMV as was Dietrich. And Dietrich was not fully assured of Kroeger's loyalty.

Kroeger said, "Once the Coalition makes the threat, on Earth, you know, the station will be on full alert. So will the shuttle. The *Edo* sustained some damage, enough that it cannot depart early. So they are already hardening their craft as best they can. Secretly. In case the, ah, event cannot be postponed. And they know too much about the plan to be trusted."

"So?" Traitor. Kroeger was helping the Japanese to back out of the plan; helping the Italians.

"So, it will be good to go carefully."

"The threat will be made on schedule. If there is no response by the designated hour, the threat will be carried out. If the Japanese are still at the station, too bad. They knew what might happen. They know how to prepare. The factions will fall into line when the time comes."

Ahead, somewhere beyond the white light in his eyes, was the MHD platform, where Dietrich felt happiest.

From there, all things were possible. There, he would decide the fate of Kroeger. Of Space Station Freedom. Of the *Edo*. And of all the space-faring world.

34

Day 11: Northern Nevada desert

"We *did* every fucking thing right," Sonny Cleary said defensively, snapping his visor up and squinting at Mackenzie.

"Not quite," Mackenzie reminded him. "We blinded a guy."

"Temporarily. It's probably worn off by now."

"Yeah, probably has. But these folks don't care about that. And we trashed that German free-flyer." The FIFS suit made Mackenzie's steps ponderous. Beside Cleary, the FIFS operator loomed huge in the bright hangar lights as the two of them left the Nomad to the mercy of a swarm of techs in white coveralls.

More mercy than the two of them were going to get. Cleary took off his helmet. He could feel the waves of heat coming off the Nomad, even though the desert night that had concealed their landing was bitterly cold outside.

Waiting for Cleary and Mackenzie was a formidable knot of brass whose facial expressions ran from cold to hot. Either kind of hostility could burn you pretty good.

Cleary tried to decide what Ford's appraising stare meant, then decided he liked Colonel Walsh's proprietary flush better. Maybe the Space Wing Commander was there to take Cleary's part. But that DARPA witch, Pettit, was purely overheated.

She broke away from the brass and came at the two of them like an angry wasp, taking Mackenzie by the exoskeletaly powered arm. Dorothy and the Tin Man, twenty-first-century style.

Pettit said, "Major, I need your report. Right now. In private."

The Tin Man probably didn't have a heart, Cleary thought as Mackenzie said, "Later. Whatever's going to happen here, I need to tell my side of it. Whatever shit's handed out, half of it's mine.

I don't need any special DARPA interference run for me, hear?"
He moved his arm, just a little, and the DARPA rep, thrown off
balance, shook loose as if he'd swatted her.

Not a great start.

Mackenzie knew it and caught her before she fell. Cleary hadn't
realized that overpowered personal tank could move so fast.

The waiting crowd was watching them in utter silence. Pollock,
the Special Ops Chief, tugging on his bushy mustache, had some
white-haired guy with him whom Cleary didn't recognize. Maybe
Space Command thought that Cleary needed a lawyer.

After all, Sonny Cleary had fired on a foreign national in
peacetime. Or at least, the X-NASP had. Never mind that it was
a laser burst meant to blind optical sensors, not people. How did
you claim technical error without killing the whole program? You
couldn't.

Maybe Pettit and Mackenzie were trying to come up with an
answer to that very question, huddling together and whispering in
plain sight of the waiting brass.

This was getting more awkward by the minute. Cleary squared
his shoulders and marched right up to them, helmet under his
arm. No use putting off the inevitable or making angry people
any angrier. Cleary had no doubt that he was going to catch
hell, sooner or later. The Space Station Freedom skipper had
been madder than a wet hen.

"Mr. Ford; Colonel Walsh; Colonel Pollock." He figured somebody would introduce him to the other, white-haired guy, who was
beginning to seem like the leader of this firing squad. "I just want
to say how—"

Ford's cold eyes reflected a distant concern. "Don't say anything yet, Sonny. Just listen. Colonel Walsh?"

Cleary hadn't remembered Walsh's face as being so deeply
lined. In these harsh lights, it resembled the Grand Canyon.

Walsh, who'd protected Cleary throughout the Washington
hearings, said, "Sonny, you remember Admiral Beckwith, I'm
sure."

Oh, Jesus. Admiral Beckwith. How could he have forgotten that
face? The admiral's pep talk outside the hearing room? But Peg
Rowan had been there, and Sally Gates. . . .

Cleary stood there, stunned, his senses so acute that the heavy
footfalls of FIFS coming up behind him sounded like thunder-
claps, but his body so distant that he wasn't sure it was going
to respond to the commands of his mind, which seemed to be
floating near the hangar's ceiling. Beckwith, CINCSPACE. Ignore

the Commander in Chief, Sonny. Great start. He remembered the square-jawed face—now. And the frank stare. "Sir," he managed, and almost choked on it.

What the hell was the admiral doing here? Oh, man, if what Cleary and Mackenzie had done up there was bad enough to get CINCSPACE out of bed, then Cleary should have kissed the X-NASP good-bye while he had the chance.

Walsh was introducing Beckwith to Mackenzie.

"It's a pleasure to meet you, Admiral," said Mackenzie in that cool, whispery voice as he held out his mechanized, gloved hand and Cleary stepped out of the way so the two could shake hands.

The admiral put his hand in the exoskeletal glove and said, "I assume you have fine control of your equipment, Major Mackenzie."

"Most of the time, sir," Mackenzie said, and performed a creditable handshake.

Whatever bomb this bunch was about to drop, they were taking their time about it.

The admiral's voice was dry. "You two had a little trouble up there, I hear."

"Yes, sir, we did," Cleary said, surprised that the words actually came out of his mouth audibly. "Or I did. It wasn't the hardware. The target handoff program worked fine. So did the counter-sensor package. It was my fault. I . . . overreacted."

"In what way?" said the admiral. "Simply, in English."

Everybody was watching him, including Mackenzie and Pettit.

"FIFS—the exoskeletal suit's electronics, sir, identified the approaching free-flying platform as a target and handed that target to the Nomad. My spacecraft pinpointed that target automatically, because the target sent an optical signal that the X-NASP's counter-sensor system recognized as offensive. The counter-sensor system's mission was to blind any optical sensor of a hostile target-acquisition system trained on it. The X-NASP thought it was about to be attacked, maybe EMP'd. So I let the counter-sensor package fire a laser burst to blind the enemy sensor." He shrugged. "There was no way to determine fast enough that the unidentified sensor was a range-finder for navigational purposes only. It could have been hostile." He was sweating. "We'd been EMP'd out there once. Maybe I was a little trigger-happy, but it was just bad luck that the guy happened to be looking right into an optical range-finder when we fired the laser burst."

He wasn't lying, but he was trying like hell to save everybody's asses. He'd been thinking what he would say, all the way home.

Cleary didn't dare look away from Beckwith, no matter how much he wanted to see how his story was playing for Walsh, or Pollock, or Dalton Ford. Shit, he should be used to this by now. All he did these days was testify to one bunch of witch-hunters or another.

Beckwith's eyes disappeared in crinkled skin, then popped back out. The admiral said, "Are you saying you don't regard this . . . misfire . . . as a major technical problem with the X-NASP's defensive systems, Captain?"

Cleary blinked. He wasn't good at playing chicken. Now he did look away from Beckwith, to Pollock, to Walsh, to Dalton Ford, who should have been a professional poker player. Then back to Beckwith. "No sir, I don't see any problem." What was he supposed to say? It was as much his fault as the Nomad's. "Not a significant one anyway."

"Good."

Everybody in the group seemed to take one step apart. Cleary felt lost, alone, adrift. Had he said the right thing or the wrong thing?

The DARPA woman touched Mackenzie's arm. Mackenzie leaned down so that she could whisper to him some more.

Maybe this would be the end of it. Maybe Beckwith would go away. Maybe Cleary had done okay.

But Beckwith didn't leave. The admiral said, "So in general, Captain Cleary, you're content with the performance of this modified Nomad. Would you say that this reconfigured spacecraft is capable of meeting any real-time or near-term space-based threat—including the threat of nonnuclear pulse? These folks are telling me it's the best we've got, but you're our on-site expert on pulse."

"Yes, sir, it's a great system, an incomparable spacecraft." At least they were giving him a chance to save the program. "The weapons systems we tested—they're defensive, but they're everything you could ask for."

Beckwith looked the way Cleary's father should have looked, but hadn't. The man had this knack of making you think that he cared about you, and what you thought—and that, somehow, he would save your ass.

"Good," said the admiral paternally. "So, what about your personal feelings? You're the most competent pilot we have on this spacecraft, Captain Cleary. Would you take her up again, into a hostile environment, with no significant changes?"

"Any time, sir." *Just give me a shot.*

"How about in ten, twelve hours?" Now Beckwith wasn't paternal at all. He was hard as nails. His eyes glittered. "Your space wing commander tells me it will take that long to turn her around."

What? Ten, twelve hours? All you could do to the Nomad in ten or twelve hours was refuel her, resupply the life-support system, and make sure that her brakes worked.

Cleary felt as if he were falling free. *Okay. I'll bite. Dying for something was better than dying for nothing. If it was kill either himself or the program, then there wasn't any good choice.*

So he said, "Ah, yes, sir. I'd be confident that the Nomad could perform another mission with minimum turnaround time."

Everybody in the huddle breathed, deep breaths that you could hear as if a wind were blowing through the hangar.

Beckwith let Cleary out of his stare, and Cleary felt as if he'd been physically freed from a restraint. He slumped and rubbed his eyes.

When he finished, Beckwith was saying, "Colonel Pollock, you heard the man. Colonel Walsh, you've got your orders."

"Yes, sir," said Walsh, and left the group at a half run.

Beckwith turned to Mackenzie. "Major, how about you? Are you too tired to settle a hostage situation for me, up there at Space Station Freedom?"

Hostage situation. Now Cleary knew what Pettit had been whispering to Mackenzie about, because Mac didn't flap or look stupid or vacant-eyed, the way Cleary must have looked.

Mackenzie said, "We can turn FIFS around by the time the bird is ready. If Mr. Ford wants to brief me while we run our systems checks, it'll save time."

"Fine. Dalton, you're ready to go, I know. Major Mackenzie," Beckwith said, "I really want this situation resolved without casualties, but I'm no fool. You do what you need to do, and we'll back you."

Hostage situation?

Beckwith eyed Cleary again. "Thank you, Captain." Then, to Pollock: "Walk me to my car, Colonel." Beckwith smiled a grim smile. "Good luck, gentlemen. I wish I were young enough to go with you. Colonel Pollock here took me for a ride in an X-NASP once. I don't think I ever fully understood our role in space before that moment."

Then the two men walked away and Cleary said, "Somebody tell me what the hell's happening. Doesn't anybody care about the satellite we brought home?"

Pettit was standing on tiptoe and Mackenzie was stooped low to hear her, his helmeted head bent to hers.

Dalton Ford said, "We care very deeply about that satellite you two brought home, Sonny. So deeply we're not going to give it up. It's the proof we need that somebody's got an EMP device up there. And we're not the only ones who know that."

At least Cleary and Mackenzie had done something right.

Ford was still talking: "We've received a threat to destroy Space Station Freedom, the Japanese shuttle, and everyone on board if we don't deliver that satellite to something called the Coalition, via the Italians at Santa Rita, by noon tomorrow. We're not going to do that. We're also not going to do anything else this mysterious Coalition has demanded. We're not going to publicly apologize for an attack on a German citizen or pay damages or acknowledge any territorial limit around German space assets. I'm sure you understand our policy on hostage-taking," Ford said, as if it mattered what Cleary understood.

"Yes, sir. I understand." What did you say?

"Good. The German government's split over this, so we don't have clear lines of communication. They say the German space agency went off on its own with that announcement of territorial sovereignty, but they're not backing off it either. There's nobody to do that. Their chancellor has resigned; they're looking to form a new government. Politics." Ford nearly spat the word. "Meanwhile, we've got a deadline, people up there in jeopardy, and we don't know exactly who's made the threat. It was phoned in to a German newspaper, as well as one of ours, an Italian daily, and a Japanese TV station simultaneously. We can't tell whether this Coalition can or will carry out its threat. But we've got to act on the assumption that they can, and will, do what they say they'll do."

"What about the Japanese shuttle? Can't we evacuate the station personnel that way?" Cleary wished to hell this had happened while they were still up there. He felt numb all over. You didn't turn around a complex spacecraft in a few hours. But he'd agreed to it. He wished there was another EMP-hardened Nomad with weapons capability. But there wasn't. And you couldn't send an American space shuttle into what might be a combat environment.

But the Japanese *Edo* was already up there. It was docked by now, on the spot.

Ford was shaking his head and his lips were drawn so tight they were white. "The Japanese shuttle's got maintenance problems. They say they'll be at the station for at least thirty-six hours. And we can't let whoever this is force us to evacuate on the basis of a threat. We don't want to panic those folks up there. We can't be seen abandoning Space Station Freedom for no reason either. We looked for an alternative, and you're it."

"Power projection? Just go sit up there?" Cleary murmured. Sitting duck. What had he gotten himself into?

"That X-NASP of yours is the most hardened thing we've got. If you get up there all right, and you need to, you can bring our personnel home in your cargo bay in EVA suits. But we don't want that. That's not winning. Winning is eliminating the danger, if there really is one."

"There really is one," Cleary muttered. He couldn't help it. Ford didn't understand EMP in space the way he did; Ford had never been EMP'd in space. EMP the station, and the folks up there didn't have long to live. All the crucial life-support components were battery- or power-dependent. "Better have the station commander disconnect everything that runs on batteries, and pull the plug on everything he can do without."

How long could that many people survive on the available air in those modules? Even with what was in the EVA suits, without powered life support, there wasn't much.

"We've already sent Jenkins some emergency procedures. Cleary," Ford said, "are you ready to deal with this for us? Able? If you aren't, say so. Walsh will go. He's offered. But that Nomad's going. You heard the admiral."

Cleary spread his hands and looked at them. They weren't real steady, but they weren't real shaky either. "That's my bird. I'll fly her to hell for the admiral, no sweat, even if it's EMP all the way." He wished he felt as gung-ho as he sounded. "But you said winning was eliminating the threat. I suppose you know just how you want us to do that?"

Mackenzie hushed Pettit and took a step closer. Ford looked between them. "We have some new data. So we think we know the sources of the EMP."

"Sources?" Mackenzie asked in that quiet way he had.

"They don't know what they're talking about, not yet," Pettit said in a sharp, accusatory voice, watching Mackenzie, not Ford.

Ford ignored her and answered Mackenzie. "You'll have a full briefing, I promise, Mac. I need to see someone first. Right now, you make sure your technical capability's the best we can manage—both of you. We're aware that the KKDs on the X-NASP are still untested, but we may have you test them on the EMP sources . . . as soon as we've confirmed this new data with our own."

New data? Cleary wanted to sit down. "I . . . we'd better get started."

"Go get out of those suits, gentlemen. Have some coffee. Make your checklists." Ford was as cool as could be. "As Ms. Pettit says, I've got some last-minute homework to do. Just be sure that all your gear is up and running and you're as rested as you can manage. We don't have a hell of a lot of time. Okay, Mac?"

Mackenzie said, "You know I won't let you down, Dalton."

Pettit said, "Mackenzie!" as if she'd wanted Mackenzie to balk.

Ford said, "Thanks, Mac." And: "See, Sonny, maybe next time you won't be so eager to have me make everything all right." Ford winked at Cleary and clapped him on the shoulder before he walked away, just an average-looking guy in chinos and a windbreaker.

"I gotta go sit somewhere," Cleary told the woman.

Mackenzie, still wearing the FIFS suit, waved him off. "Do that, Sonny. I'll catch up with you."

Cleary went. Time to scratch your nuts. Sit on a real toilet. Eat a sandwich. Take a nap. Call your girlfriend.

A grin spread slowly across Cleary's face as he left the hangar area. Behind him, at the Nomad, technicians were unloading the satellite. And he was going to unload a little too.

He thought he'd call Megan Rowan. The kid was stashed with strangers; she could use the sound of a friendly voice. Or maybe he'd call Sally Gates, touch base. But then he decided, what the hell.

He didn't have to say why he was calling. He could call Carla Chang if he wanted to. And he wanted to. Just say hi and tell her how much he missed the feel of her, how much he wished he had her climbing around on him tonight.

This morning. It was morning back on the East Coast. He'd give her a wake-up call.

Next to the Nomad, she was his favorite lady, even if she was only a little less dangerous.

Somebody wanted to EMP the station. How come the clowns in intelligence weren't sure who, even after the Germans had made a public, unilateral decree? What if the Nomad wasn't hardened enough to withstand a second, full-out EMP attack. What did Ford mean by "sources," plural?

Cleary could end up like some embassy guard in front of a diplomatic mission, gun loaded, with orders not to shoot even though a hostile horde was charging his position.

He didn't want to think about it. So Carla Chang's voice would be the perfect tranquilizer, until it was time for the briefing— and he had to think about how he was going to get himself and Mackenzie through this suicide mission alive.

Nobody knew like Cleary what it meant to be imprisoned in a dead hunk of machinery.

He kept seeing the station, an erector set in space, and hoping to hell there'd be somebody alive up there when they got there.

Because they were going to get there. He knew because Carla Chang was home when he called, and sleepy enough to make him feel as if he had everything to live for.

You didn't get that lucky and then die. Not on a rescue mission. You didn't.

35

Day 11: German MHD Orbital Power Station

Almost as soon as he and Kroeger had parked the OMV beside the MHD station, it occurred to Dietrich that he had been very lucky. Even now, hours later, his luck was holding.

Jenkins was a tinny voice from a far distance, saying, "Come back, Dietrich. Dietrich, do you read? Kroeger, do you copy?"

Dietrich was lucky because Kroeger, once removed from the influence of the multinationals, had remembered that he was a German. At least he was that.

Dietrich had told Kroeger that they must simply ignore Jenkins's calls. And so far, Kroeger was obeying him.

Dietrich had no intention of answering Jenkins's calls—yet. When Dietrich contacted Space Station Freedom, it would be on his terms.

"Don't be nervous, Kroeger. They have no way to get out here to us. We have the OMV, and the free-flying platform is destroyed. The orbital transfer vehicle assembly remains incomplete. It's too far to come in an MMU. Soon enough, we will talk to them."

Kroeger said, "I don't know. They sound angry. And worried. They must have heard by now about the threat. What if they decide we are a part of that threat?"

"What if they do? We have the weapon. They are at our mercy. But they won't. I come out here and sleep in this station all the time. They are used to it. They will assume we fell asleep out here. And that is what we will say, if we need to. But I don't think we will need to."

Dietrich could not see the MHD station around him—or anything else—very well yet. But he knew by heart every inch of the

215

simple module that housed his beloved Magneto Hydro Dynamic generator.

He knew it precisely. He remembered every inch of it, every nut and bolt. And he remembered, also, the long argument that Kroeger had had with Sekigawa back on Space Station Freedom. The Japanese did not want to take the chance that their beloved shuttle might have to be sacrificed to the plan.

Dietrich had no way of knowing Kroeger's mind. He had no way of knowing Kroeger's heart. And he really had no great need of Kroeger any longer.

While they'd EVA'd from the OMV into the airlock of the pressurized MHD module, Dietrich had decided that he would kill Kroeger if he must. Kill him as soon as they were inside.

But he had not killed Kroeger then. Kroeger could see. He decided to let Kroeger live awhile longer. Dietrich would kill Kroeger if Kroeger balked even a little at Dietrich's orders. Or at his new idea.

Because he had a new idea. He could not trust any of those fools on the ground. He could not even trust Herr Schliemann. He could not trust anyone back at the station, or anyone aboard the Japanese shuttle.

Their lives were in his hands and some of them knew it. Others must be guessing by now.

Schliemann had tried to help, but it was clear now that Dietrich was on his own. If he lost heart, he would be sent back to Earth on the *Edo*. And he could not allow that.

So he could not wait, as Schliemann had ordered him, until noon tomorrow. If he did, the Americans might capitulate. The Coalition might strike some sort of deal. And he, Dietrich, would be shipped back to Earth, where he would face an uncertain justice.

If the Coalition failed, he was doomed. If they lost heart, he was equally doomed. If some deal was struck and he was given over as a sacrificial lamb to American justice, as sometimes happened, then also was he doomed. He had EMP'd two American space planes. He was responsible for that.

They would punish him. And if the German government had fallen, then how could Schliemann, or anyone, protect him? He would be treated as a common terrorist, a criminal.

So he must act quickly. Act definitively. Take everyone by surprise.

But hours had passed and he still was not certain quite how to proceed.

He had Kroeger. He had telemetry that would allow him to set the second, lower-orbiting MHD satellite, which the Japanese had launched, to kill any spacecraft emitting an exhaust plume. But he couldn't see well enough yet to operate the equipment. He must make Kroeger do that for him.

Blinking rapidly, Dietrich tried to make out Kroeger's face. The man was right beside him, performing a routine maintenance task exactly as Dietrich had instructed.

But Kroeger still had a light where his head should be.

At least it was a smaller light. Vision, Dietrich was almost certain, was returning in increments. In the meantime, Kroeger would obey Dietrich. Dietrich had let Kroeger live. He'd let him inside the MHD station.

From the first moment they'd entered the lock, Kroeger had become increasingly more deferential. Once they'd stepped inside, into the pressurized module, and taken off their helmets, Kroeger had been on Dietrich's spacecraft.

They both knew it. Kroeger was fascinated by the Soviet-made MHD, which looked like a turbine of unremarkable manufacture. He'd asked many questions and Dietrich had answered them proudly.

Kroeger might, by now, be the world's second greatest expert on utilization of Soviet MHD technology in space. Kroeger touched Dietrich's arm and said, "All finished. I will recite what I have done, ya? And you can make sure it is correct."

"Ya." Dietrich had made certain that Kroeger had no idea what he was doing. Beyond what Dietrich had told him, Kroeger knew nothing.

Dietrich listened, and nodded, and when Kroeger was done, Dietrich said, "Ya, good. Now you will follow these instructions even more closely."

Dietrich directed Kroeger as Kroeger sent the command that would enable the Japanese-launched MHD to fire at will upon any spacecraft with an exhaust plume.

When that was done, and verified, Dietrich said, "This is very good. Now we must do our targeting for this station. And you must listen even more closely."

Kroeger said, "I—are you sure?"

"We must be ready. We must be able. This station was built to putatively beam power to Space Station Freedom in case of a power emergency there. If we were to decide not to do any-thing, we must still correct for orbital decay and make minute adjustments in relative trajectories, in case we need to perform our primary function."

"Of course. Well, in that case, tell me what to do."

If Kroeger wished to pretend that he didn't understand the implications of what they were doing, then Dietrich would go along with that. So maybe Kroeger was not so stupid as he seemed. If all went wrong, Kroeger could later claim ignorance of the hostility of his acts, and Dietrich could not truly contradict him.

"You must follow my instructions to the letter, Kroeger. Any misalignment could result in disaster."

Dietrich wished he could see well enough to do this himself. But he could not. If Kroeger did not do exactly as he was told, then Kroeger was a corpse.

Dietrich could see well enough to kill the man with a light for a head. He had no doubt of that. He could do it with his bare hands.

But Kroeger did not balk, and Dietrich played his cards very close to the chest. He did not tell Kroeger that he was doing more than a realignment. He did not tell Kroeger anything but what operations to perform, until the station vibrated, and moved underfoot.

Even Dietrich could tell that the lights flickered as the demand for power surged.

Kroeger said in a strangled voice, "It's . . . I did something wrong. It's *firing*."

And it was. Dietrich had heard the pitch of the generator change. He'd heard it before, when he'd fired on the American space planes.

He knew the sound. He knew too that the lights should flicker, so he wasn't afraid, the way Kroeger was.

Dietrich said, "You must have initiated the sequence somehow." Then he clapped Kroeger on the back. "So, we're a little early. A few hours. What does it matter? We were going to do it anyway."

A sob came out of Kroeger. The man doubled over, so that his body was primarily a light.

Hands came out of that light toward him, and grabbed him by the shoulders. "What have we done? What have *you* done? What will we do? What will we do? We've destroyed the station. I never thought we'd . . ." Kroeger's voice trailed off into a hiss of panic. " . . . do it."

Those two words hung in the air between them until the generator's pitch returned to normal.

"Do exactly as I say now. Carefully." He began directing Kroeger to return the MHD to a benign mode. Then he had the other man change the attitude of the MHD station, just slightly, just enough to put the beam-focusing element out of direct line of sight to Space Station Freedom.

When all that was done, Kroeger was panting as if he had run too far. He kept asking questions, dully, as if he couldn't think at all.

"What now? What do we do next, Dietrich?"

And when Dietrich did not immediately answer, Kroeger grabbed him and shook him, screaming: *"What? What now? What do we do?"*

Dietrich considered trying to strangle Kroeger, but the man was very strong in his hysteria.

Dietrich said calmly, "We will try to establish radio contact—first with the station, then with the *Edo,* and finally with the ground. We will then know how much damage has been done."

"God, God, my God," Kroeger chanted. "How long can we stay alive here? Will they send a rescue ship for us?"

Once again, Dietrich tried to see past the light. He could see parts of the MHD station now; he told himself he could see Kroeger's shoulders, shaking.

"We can stay alive here, or in the OMV, long enough to make sure of what has happened to the others. We will go back there, after establishing that we have no idea what happened to them, or how. So we will hide among the victims—if you can convince me that you're calm enough to play your part."

"I'm calm. I am."

"Of course you are. We will go back, then, after we do a few things here and we are certain that it is safe to go back. After all, we have an undamaged life-support system. Ground control may ask us to stay here. We will contact them from the OMV and see. But we must be very calm."

Otherwise, Kroeger, you will die. You will die along with anyone else who interferes with me.

Dietrich floated before the man who was mostly light, trying to decide just how he should proceed, now that Space Station Freedom was crippled in orbit. Kroeger must not know it, but Dietrich had no definite plan, from here on, beyond making sure that he survived.

"It's all over," Kroeger moaned. "We're all going to die."

Dietrich ignored this whining. A man could last a long time, using the undamaged life support of the MHD station, especially with the OMV for backup and the whole station to loot. The station wasn't destroyed. It was only powerless. Its crew might die, true. But supplies could be ferried over here, using the OMV, once that happened. In that way, perhaps, two men could survive until rescue came.

Dietrich must think. Kroeger's panic was contagious.

Over on Space Station Freedom, all the lights had just—gone out. All the air-purifiers and central processing units and auxiliaries had stopped working—everything and anything that hadn't been turned off or stripped of batteries.

So, he must find out how much of the station was capable of being put back on line. Going back and hiding among the other victims might be best.

But then he would need to kill Kroeger. Kroeger could never carry out a demanding charade. And too, there was the matter of timing.

Dietrich must pretend that both of them had fallen asleep over here. He must not call in too early. He must not seem to be concerned. He must continue, using Kroeger's eyes, to keep the plan working.

"Kroeger, get hold of yourself. We must act as if we are doing what we came here to do. And then we must proceed normally, in all things. Normal emergency procedures are still normal procedures. Do you understand?"

"Ya," said the light before him. "Ya. There is no choice now."

Had there been before? Had this Kroeger been here to await his moment and then kill Dietrich, to prevent what had just happened? If so, it was too late now.

Dietrich had won. Even though his eyes could not see very well, his mind showed him the panic and the chaos that must be reigning now on Space Station Freedom and on the Japanese shuttle.

And no rescue was possible, by shuttle or aerospace plane, unless Dietrich was alive and well to interrupt the automatic firing sequence that would begin when the Japanese-launched MHD, in an orbit fifty miles below, sensed any approaching spacecraft with an exhaust plume from rocket engines.

So Dietrich truly had very little to worry about. He had foolishly allowed Kroeger to make him nervous. No one would dare to harm Dietrich in any way. Not if they wanted to rescue anyone, or to bring home their dead, or tend to the funeral of Space Station Freedom.

Precious shuttle. Precious station. Rest in peace.

36

When Ford's helicopter arrived at the coordinates Shitov had set for the meet, the sun was rising over the desert.

Levonov, you will never know what it is to stand in the American West while the desert turns lavender, and orange, and gold, with the fate of the world in your hands. Shitov walked away from his rented white Cadillac, toward the gold cloud of dust from which Ford emerged.

"Did you get it?" Ford asked without preamble, squinting at Shitov, an odd look on his face.

Perhaps Ford's odd expression was in reaction to Shitov's black, beaver-felt ten-gallon, purchased at an emporium in Albuquerque, a huge place that claimed to be the world's largest Western store. Or to the magnificent chased silver tips on Shitov's lizard cowboy boots and on the collar of his new Western shirt, which was plaid with black piping and pearl snaps. Or maybe Ford disapproved of Shitov's tooled leather belt that said ALEX in raised letters, which also was bound with silver wire and had a bucking horse on its buckle.

But perhaps Ford was reacting to none of these things. Ford was under great pressure, due to circumstances. So were they all. Shitov said, "My friend, of course I have got it. Otherwise, would I ask you to meet me in so inconvenient a place?"

In this desert, no one could sneak up on you. Shitov could literally see for miles. Shitov had determined the exact coordinates himself, so close to the time of the meeting that no one could have planted electronic bugs in the cactus or disguised them as rocks lying on the ground.

"Look, Shitov, you said you had—"

"I have the proof you need, Mr. Ford." Shitov reached into the pocket of his new shirt and pulled out a small optical disk. "And more."

"What's on this? I haven't got time, Colonel, for your games right now. What do you mean, 'more'?"

Shitov allowed his face to take on a hurt expression. He was enjoying himself. The sunrise was not yet over. He did not wish to hurry this moment.

"More. Proof that the electromagnetic pulse attacks on your spacecraft came from the German auxiliary power station in orbit near Space Station Freedom. Intelligence that unequivocally identifies the satellite launched by the Japanese for Germany as another MHD, this one with no other purpose but for using as a weapon." Shitov sighed deeply. He was still holding the optical disk. He would not relinquish it to Ford until the time was right.

Ford's hand was out, but he was not yet touching the disk. "I'm on a tight schedule, here, *Glava*. I wish I could tell you how tight."

"We are sharing this intelligence on certain conditions, Mr. Ford." Levonov, you have stepped in the bear trap this time. Among the names and dates that Shitov was giving Ford, Levonov's name came up as a facilitator of the MHD transfer. Levonov, your career is shit. And you have never even seen the American desert at sunrise.

"What conditions, Colonel? I'm not in any position to bargain on the spot, and you know it. You said you had everything I needed. I need it now. And I need it without strings."

"You will have it, Mr. Ford. All you asked for and more. The coordinates of the hostile MHDs, both of them. Proof enough to destroy either, or both if you wish. One has surely behaved aggressively, but this one may have a person or two on board. The other, the new one, is purely hardware."

"Great." Ford started to take the optical disk.

Shitov snatched it from his grasp, holding it high in the air. "Ah, ah, Mr. Ford. Not yet. First, we have a concern that must be addressed. Citizens of ours were involved in this transfer of the MHDs to the Germans. We are offering this intelligence on the understanding that you will help us minimize embarrassing knowledge of Soviet participation in this misadventure. We, in turn, are disciplining our own people. We will not have our favored-nation trading status endangered. We are helping in this effort, and we are giving much information, with this packet, that is top-top secret. From this, you will learn more than we might like about our surveillance capabilities."

"We've been through all this, Colonel. You know we're ready to play ball."

Shitov, holding the optical disk just out of reach, continued implacably. "So you must not disseminate this information, even among your allies. We are entering, with the transfer of this data, into a privileged intelligence-sharing arrangement, the agreement for which must follow, but will be worked out in specifics between our government and yours. This is, as they say in your country, the down payment."

"I understand. I've already talked about this with my higher-ups, as you requested. If your information gives us, as you say it does, proof of aggression, and the ability to act, then we'll be more than glad to protect you and your country as its source. After all, we've got our pride too." Ford's expression was sour.

"And if, despite our best efforts, this does not go your way, Mr. Ford, you must not blame this on us. Our MHD is not the problem. No technology is hostile, only—"

"Men, yes, we know. Can I have it? Or is there something else?"

Levonov, this is the stake I have been wanting to drive through your heart for years now. "Yes, but it is a personal something else." Now Shitov lowered the disk, in its plastic case, until Ford's fingers touched it. For a moment, they both held the disk, which contained a landmark transfer of sensitive intelligence revealing Soviet capabilities in space. And on the ground.

"Tell me what you want, Colonel. I've got to get this data processed. Fast."

"I would like Shitova to be granted an immediate visa to come here and spend some time with me, since I am staying on for a time."

"I'm sure we can arrange that."

A ray of sun hit the clear plastic cover of the disk, between them. "And I would like your personal assurance that our Soviet justice will be sufficient where Soviet citizens were involved in this mischief, since none of the actions of these citizens of ours was malicious. And we do not want to be painted as dupes of the New Axis, not in public or in private. Every nation has its fools."

"Done, Shitov. I promise you, we'll cover your ass."

Shitov let go of the optical disk. Ford put it in his pocket. "Thanks, Colonel. If you'd be willing to go back to Kirtland and make yourself available, in case we have questions, or problems regarding this disk, I'd appreciate it."

Ah, the Americans counted more and more upon the help of Shitov every day. This he had said to Moscow Center, but now he had proof of it. Levonov, I will have your balls in a jar on my shelf. And any time you give me even the slightest bit of problem, I will take down those balls and slice off a chunk and feed it to my dog.

"Mr. Ford, I am at your disposal during this crisis. Whatever help you require, if it is within my power to deliver, then I will deliver it."

"Great. Gotta run, Colonel."

And Ford did run, back to his waiting helicopter, whose blades, now in slow rotation, glinted in the sunlight.

As the helicopter whined and lifted into the bright new day, Shitov walked back to his rented Cadillac. In the back seat was a pocketbook shaped like a Western saddle that he had bought for Shitova. It was a large bag, commodious, with a secure latch.

He was sure she was going to love filling it with America's bounty. She would enjoy it almost as much as Shitov was enjoying the thought of Levonov's imminent demotion.

If all went well—if the Americans, with Shitov's help, were able to save their space station personnel in a daring rescue— then Shitov would be a hero of two governments.

This enviable position, he admitted as he slid carefully behind the wheel of the white Cadillac, was due in part to his great enemy, Levonov.

So Shitov would be lenient when he wrote his report. And if he were asked what he thought should happen to Levonov, he would not suggest the Manchurian border as a suitable post for the fool.

After all, if Levonov had not helped sell the MHDs to the Germans, then none of this great good fortune would have befallen Shitov. And if Levonov and Shitov had not been mortal enemies, then Shitov might never have uncovered so much detailed information that the Americans now could use to such great advantage.

Not only did Dalton Ford have intelligence on the behavior of certain satellites, but Ford now had in his possession the names of all the major players in the Coalition: of Osawa, of Schliemann, of Tohei, and the rest.

A Russian who knew so much would have brought each and every conspirator under his personal control. What the Americans would do, this was still uncertain.

So the Executive President himself had remarked, Shitov had been told by the UN KGB resident. Only this veiled warning, delivered over a phone line, clouded Shitov's joy as he drove over the desert, toward the road.

These roads in America were endless. This one could take him to Las Vegas, to Kirtland in New Mexico, or to oblivion.

But Shitov had been in intelligence a long time. He knew that no outcome was ever assured, nor was any damage-control complete.

So he had asked to have Shitova join him. If things went wrong, which they well could, then Shitov would work as quickly as possible to remove Shitova from harm's way.

Once she was safe in America, out of the reach of Levonov, then Shitov could relax.

But by then, whatever was going to happen, high above all their heads, would already have happened.

Thus he was driving very fast, over the American roads, so that he could find a phone and call Shitova to arrange for her visit. While he could still count on the goodwill of the American government, and of his own government, he must bring Shitova out of Russia.

If things went wrong, he wanted her with him. And if things went very well, still, she should be here.

He would take Shitova to the Grand Canyon, and they would ride down its walls on mules. He would buy her a cowgirl hat and a shirt with fringe over the breasts and a pair of leggings, and off they would go.

Surely in America there was a mule stout enough for Shitova. Somewhere. And if there were not, then he would drive her around in a Cadillac just like this one, and not even the UN resident would dare question his expense-account receipts.

His friends in the American government would see to that. If their mission was successful, that is.

Driving the Cadillac down the endless highway, Shitov looked up at the wide sky. Beyond it, a space station was hostage to terrorists. This was an inevitable result of political conflict in space. But now Shitov's fate too was hostage to these same terrorists. As was the fate of American-Soviet cooperation.

Levonov, in the old days we would have taken you out behind a rural police station and shot you in the back of the head. I would have done it myself.

But these were the new days, and things were not so simple. In the old days, you only had to worry about the capitalist enemy, and ghosts in the attic.

Now the attic was full of stars, of spacecraft and space habitats. Now the men were not as important as the technologies, some thought.

Now the Americans were about to attempt a bold and a dangerous rescue of men. To do so, they must destroy the machines that threatened them.

To this end, Shitov had done all he could. The Soviet government had done all it could. If the Americans were successful, the back of the New Axis would be broken, and Shitov's place in history would be made.

Otherwise, like the fallen German government, he would be cast out, a failure, a man whom no one wanted any longer.

So the stake was not yet driven into Levonov's heart. The game was not yet over. And everyone had risked more than they could afford on the outcome.

Even Shitova, though she didn't know it yet.

37

Day 11: Space Station Freedom

It was like a grave inside Space Station Freedom. Most of the station was still dark. The *Edo* wasn't in much better shape. Jenkins kept trying to calm down the six people under his command, but he couldn't seem to do it.

"Magriffe?" he called. "Magriffe?"

No answer. He pushed himself along in the dark, a flashlight in one hand, through the logistics module. He'd come up here to try to raise Kroeger and Dietrich one more time. Used precious power, battery power.

He wished he hadn't. It was as spooky and silent as a mausoleum in here, with only a few red lights to indicate that any systems at all were functioning.

He pushed himself down, toward the lock, and beyond, into the A habitat module.

Something bumped him. He couldn't imagine what, but there were plenty of things floating around loose. Everyone had panicked. People had run for EVA suits. It had taken all of Jenkins's leadership skills to sort out the melee over the suits.

Later, they would need what suits they had. Now, Jenkins needed a damage assessment. Sekigawa had agreed, but that was all Sekigawa had agreed to. Again, the soft thing bumped Jenkins.

This time, he shined his light on it.

Magriffe's hip. She'd rebounded off the wall and was floating toward him again.

This was no place to sleep. This was no time to sleep. Jenkins grabbed her by the arm. "Magriffe, wake up. Wake up, damn it! This is no time to—"

She was flaccid in his grasp. He pulled her toward him. Was she in some sort of shock?

The flashlight in his hand shook. Magriffe's head was at an unlikely angle, even for someone sleeping in microgravity. Her neck was black and blue. Her eyes were wide open.

The flashlight in Jenkins's hand shook so violently that he wasn't sure of what he was seeing.

So he pulled the woman's body up against him and tried to see if she was breathing.

"Magriffe?" God, Magriffe. He'd sent her off to Di Lella, to get a tranquilizer shot. She'd been sure that Dietrich had known this was going to happen.

She'd been sure that Dietrich had taken the other German and gone off in the OMV to the relative safety of the MHD station, to avoid being EMP'd.

"Di Lella!" Jenkins called. But nobody answered. Towing Magriffe's body by the hand, he pushed himself toward the lock that led into the docked Japanese shuttle.

Then he changed his mind. Maybe Di Lella, the station physician, was in the laboratory module, still, trying to save some of the experiments. Or maybe in the sickbay area, giving shots to more of the rattled crew.

Jenkins suddenly didn't know where to go. What had happened? Had the shot been too strong? Had Magriffe somehow broken her neck in a freak accident?

It was hard to break your neck in microgravity. Jenkins couldn't think.

He wanted to cradle Magriffe in his arms and rock her, but what if somebody came?

The dark station was little more than an oversized coffin, if no rescue vehicle made it here before their air ran out.

He had to find the others. He pulled Magriffe along, toward the laboratory module, where Di Lella probably was.

Everybody was working to restore power wherever possible, that was all. Magriffe, behind him, thudded against a bulkhead.

Di Lella and Jenkins's two remaining crewmen were probably working their tails off, trying to get the Japanese crew to cooperate. Sekigawa had looked at Jenkins with soul-less eyes and said, "So, you were not properly prepared for this emergency, Commander? This is not something that I am pleased to hear."

As if Sekigawa had been better prepared. As if anybody could be better prepared.

"Di Lella?" Jenkins called as he made his way toward the logistics module. With the flashlight in one hand and Magriffe in tow, he was awkward.

He heard a sound, behind him.

And a voice said, "Commander Jenkins? What's wrong?"

Where had Di Lella come from? "Di Lella, look at Magriffe." Easy. His voice was shaky. "She's dead. Di Lella, I think she's dead. Broke her neck or something. I sent her to you for a trank—"

"Let me see," said Di Lella, out of the dark.

Jenkins shined the light on Magriffe and Di Lella came up beside him.

Then something hit him, hard, in the temple.

Stunned, he couldn't even grunt with pain. Colored lights exploded before his eyes. Something floating loose, he thought. Then he wasn't sure what he thought.

Hands were around his throat. The flashlight was gone. Its beam bobbed dizzily. He couldn't scream or even groan. He began to struggle, to claw at the hands. But then he felt a sharp pain in his neck.

Jenkins heard Di Lella say, very softly, "There just isn't enough air for everyone. I'm sure you understand."

And then nothing. The dark of death, when it came, wasn't much different than the dark of the station.

38

All Pettit could do was wait now. Wait in the tracking facility. Wait outside it, watching the sun go down. Wait to hear that the X-NASP had successfully passed the halfway point. Wait for Space Station Freedom to make contact again. Wait for Ford to decide to tell her something that would mitigate the foolishness of this mission.

Waiting was the hardest thing. The deadline wasn't until noon tomorrow. None of this had had to happen. The Americans could have made some kind of deal. Somebody could have negotiated a solution, somehow. Admiral Beckwith could have threatened the terrorists with SDI smart weapons such as Brilliant Pebbles, or economic sanctions, or found some other way.

But all these Space Command honchos had been sure there wasn't any other way. Pettit, outside in the sunset, knew that FIFS had been one of the factors in their decision to send the Nomad back up into space. So whatever happened was her fault, as much as anyone's.

She'd sworn FIFS was ready. She'd chosen Mackenzie. She'd trained him. And she hadn't protested loudly enough when testosterone clouded logic and these bastards decided they could turn the X-NASP around in twelve hours and go head-to-head with disaster.

It was all her fault. Walking in the New Mexico dusk, wherever Pettit looked, she saw the X-NASP, black and uncaring, swallowing up Mackenzie and Cleary before it leaped into space like a startled hawk.

She saw Mackenzie, slow and careful in the FIFS suit, stomping up the ramp into that black bird from hell. He'd looked tired.

Hell, he was tired. They were all tired. You shouldn't do this kind of mission with fatigue wastes clogging your brain, not when your survival hung on precision.

She kept seeing Mackenzie in that suit, and the Nomad, and she wanted to cry, or throw something, or burst into the control facility and demand a progress report.

But it wouldn't help. And anyway, if the X-NASP crashed during its ascent, someone would hurry out here to tell her.

There was nothing to be gained by hanging over the men in there, who were trying to work.

Nothing at all. She scuffed dust with her toes, until she couldn't see the dust eddy because it was getting dark.

When it got dark out here, it got cold. She didn't want anyone to come looking for her. She was afraid that if someone did, they'd be bearing bad news. She couldn't handle any bad news.

So when Ford came toward her, she froze in her tracks. She didn't say anything. She just watched the man come.

He had a jacket for her. "Here," he said. "It's cold out here."

She didn't take it. "Is everything all right?" What a stupid thing to ask. Of course everything wasn't all right.

"They're doing fine, if that's what you mean." He held out the jacket again. "Put this on."

She did. "Thanks. Do you need me in there?" Her voice sounded as vulnerable as she felt.

"They're doing fine. But why don't you come in? In case Mackenzie has a question, we won't have to come looking for you."

Earlier, they hadn't wanted her around. Earlier, there'd been some sort of secret huddle over targets and intelligence. She'd been glad to leave.

No, she hadn't. She'd been angry.

Pettit said, "Okay," and went with Ford, back toward the control room.

But she kept seeing Mackenzie, in the suit. And out of it. She'd never meant to make things harder for him. She should have said . . . something. Told him how she felt, at least. But she'd been so jacked up, so concerned about the suit's performance. So concerned about his ability to function during a second mission, back-to-back with a first . . .

When he'd touched her, she should have responded. When he'd put his arms around her, she shouldn't have pulled away. But she was so tense. So much was riding on the performance of FIFS, she couldn't feel anything.

Or what she felt was inappropriate. Mackenzie's life might hang on FIFS's ability to perform in a hostile wave bath. How was she going to make love to a man she might be sending to his death?

She'd tried to be civil. But she could barely talk to him. She could hardly look at him. If FIFS malfunctioned, Mackenzie would die up there. And it would be all her fault.

FIFS wasn't ready for this. Nobody was ready for this. Terrorists with EMP weapons, altercations in deep space . . .

Ford said, "Hey, Ms. Pettit, I know Mac real well. He always comes back."

She stopped still, barely containing the impulse to slap Ford across the face. How dare he tell her about Mackenzie? How dare he comfort her? How dare he make promises that he couldn't keep?

But she didn't slap Ford. She said, "I certainly hope you're right, Mr. Ford. My program will never survive a failure of this magnitude."

And she brushed by him, blindly. Indoors, at least, she wouldn't be so cold that her whole body seemed numb. Inside, she'd hear for herself how they were doing up there.

Anything was better than listening to her own regrets and Ford's inane attempts to lift her morale.

Morale was for men. She was a woman, and she faced the truth squarely. Only this time, the truth was a man named Mackenzie, James Harry, in an exoskeletal suit of her devising.

She'd never meant FIFS to be a battle suit. She hadn't. She'd only been trying to give a technological edge to someone facing a hostile environment. FIFS was a command-and-control triumph.

But it wasn't meant for space combat. Nothing was. Especially not a human being.

If she could have, she'd have called the X-NASP back down. She'd have refused to let FIFS take part in this suicide mission.

But she couldn't, not now. When she could have, she hadn't thought to say no.

And now there was an ominous silence from Space Station Freedom. She hurried.

The terrorists were supposed to wait until noon tomorrow. Maybe they had; maybe they would. Maybe these Space Command soldiers were wrong about the meaning of the ominous silence from Space Station Freedom and the *Edo*.

She wanted them to be wrong. Mackenzie had said to her, when she'd been helping him back into the suit, "Don't look so down.

Unlucky in love, lucky in space war."

"That's not funny," she'd said.

"Let's hope it's true," he'd shot back.

She could still see his face, in the FIFS helmet, its raised visor shadowing his tired eyes.

She couldn't live with herself if he got killed, in her suit. She'd shut down the program. She'd quit.

She stumbled into the control room and heard Cleary's voice, scratchy and distant, on the loudspeaker.

Her heart leaped. Relief ran over her from head to toe as if she'd just stepped into a shower.

The cool, macho pilot sounded as if he did this every day, as if this were nothing special.

She suddenly needed to sit down. In that instant, rebellious, she hated them all: Mackenzie, Cleary, Admiral Beckwith, Pollock, Walsh, and Ford.

Especially Ford, because he came up and squatted down by the chair she'd taken against the wall. "See?" he said, fixing her with a level stare from bright eyes. "They're fine."

"Fuck you, Ford," she wanted to say, finally. She'd wanted to say it for a very long time, ever since that first night he'd come around with his intelligence community arrogance and his cloak of inscrutability. But she couldn't say that. She said, instead, "So far."

Which was a better thing to say. A clear indictment of his infallibility. Ford couldn't manipulate this flight, the way everyone was saying he'd manipulated the Soviets into helping him gather intelligence for the mission.

That was what they were calling it in here. The Mission. In capital letters.

But the mission was now beyond any manipulation from the ground. Everything hung on the performance of two overtired men and a space plane that should never have been sent into space again so soon.

Ford got up and said, "Can I have my jacket back?"

She gave it to him. She nearly threw it at him. Then she leaned back and closed her eyes, willing him away.

But when she did, there was Mackenzie, in the FIFS suit, disappearing into the Nomad again.

He hadn't even waved good-bye.

39

Day 12: The Nomad, Space Envelope

Cleary wasn't sure anybody back on Earth understood what they were asking. But he'd agreed to give it to them. Now, on his way to a two-hundred-mile-high rendezvous with the unknown, he wished he hadn't.

Mackenzie had been at the same briefing. "Hey, Mac," Cleary said.

The suit still startled him when he glimpsed it out of the corner of his eye. Rowan, who used to sit in that seat, seemed like a memory from his childhood.

"Yeah, Cleary, just a sec."

Mackenzie hit a declutter mode. Cleary could tell because his own heads-up display simplified as it subtracted Mackenzie's green and red data streams.

"Okay," came the quiet voice in Cleary's ears. "What's up?"

"We are," Cleary reminded him sourly. "We've got about an hour to decide whether they're right, and we should play sitting duck, or whether we can be a little more cautious."

The cockpit voice recorder would save all this for posterity, but Cleary was thinking about survival. Sometimes being letter perfect could get you killed, while a little improvisation could save you.

"Cautious?" Mackenzie chuckled. "My mother was in labor with me for forty-nine hours. You can't get much more cautious than that."

So maybe Mackenzie had been thinking over Ford's briefing too. This high, this far into the flight, you had plenty of time to think. Acceleration wasn't strangling you. You weren't so acutely aware that most critical failures took place within the first few minutes of lift-off. You still felt the hand of fate, but it wasn't over your eyes.

"Cautious, yeah. I dunno about you, but I'd kind of like to deploy my weapons now, just in case we need 'em in a hurry."

In a hurry. The last time Cleary'd been EMP'd, he hadn't been much higher than he was now. Ford had said, "We want you to know that there's probably a second EMP source out there, orbiting about fifty miles under Space Station Freedom. We'll give you the exact orbit, time-specific coordinates, everything you'll need. But you've got two possible sources to worry about. The other one's the MHD station."

And Cleary had said, "Which one do you want us to take out first?" Depending on relative position, one would be a better initial target.

"Not so fast," Ford had replied, and Mackenzie had groaned knowingly, and yawned, saying, "Here comes the catch."

Now, miles away, straight up, Mackenzie said, "Let's do it, Captain. Ready to deploy weapons."

Space physicians said that when you yawned, you were preparing for action. Cleary yawned, and began retracting the doors that shielded the KKD cannon and laser pods in the Nomad's belly.

Then he said, "Take the laser."

"Got it," Mackenzie murmured, and began extending the weapons-delivery platform on which the laser pod rested.

Cleary forgot about everything else as he did systems checks. The colored grids came and went. Numbers flickered across his display. And meanwhile, he kept the X-NASP on a steady course for an intercept with Space Station Freedom.

Sometimes you forgot that Mackenzie was a major. Right now, he was Cleary's weapons officer, and Cleary was damned glad of it.

He knew where the Nomad was in relation to the ground and he knew that an EMP weapon could reach him here. One had reached him here before.

You couldn't keep the Earth's curvature between you and the EMP sources, because those sources were near the Nomad's destination. One of them was parked right next door.

The X-NASP wanted to fly, that was one good thing. The Nomad didn't seem to mind the quick turnaround. He'd worried about that, the way he had about everything else since he'd been briefed.

If he could get back that feeling of invulnerability he'd had when he'd been talking to Carla Chang, then he knew he'd come through this all right. But he didn't seem to be able to convince his body that it wasn't dog-tired.

And that made him worry about the X-NASP. If he was tired, what about all these crucial systems, any one of which could kill you just by failing.

He made a course correction, and vibration came up through his seat.

Mackenzie said, "Shit."

Cleary said, "What's shit?"

Mackenzie didn't immediately answer. Cleary demanded, "Look, what's shit? Don't say that and then not tell me—"

In answer, Mackenzie ported a schematic onto the program window that center-punched Cleary's visor display, dumping his flight data with an override.

"Shit," Cleary whispered as he looked at the graph showing him that the laser pod had jammed, half deployed.

"Can we shoot it from there?" Mackenzie asked after too long, while they listened to each other breathe.

"Yeah, sure. We just can't aim it more than thirty degrees in any direction."

"We can aim the Nomad, can't we?"

"You can go out and free it up, once we park, can't you?" Cleary countered. "Probably a cable fouled it." As he spoke, he was trying everything he knew to free the laser pod.

But so was Mackenzie. The system froze entirely.

"Just hold it, okay? Before we crash the software?" Cleary snapped.

"I'm holding."

Mackenzie didn't bother reminding Cleary that Mackenzie was the weapons officer.

"Okay. Try again. Wiggle it every which way. Up. Down. Left. Right. See if frees up. I gotta fly this thing."

Great. The laser pod was their best shot at blinding anything targeting them.

He would send Mackenzie out to free it manually, but he couldn't do that yet. He flipped through his data screens. He was seventy-five miles below the space station, and closing.

And he hadn't been EMP'd yet. He brought up a patch to the ground and reported the problem.

They told him, "Good luck."

He didn't bother to thank them. He was searching all the

satellite data he could access, looking for the purported low-orbiting-threat source.

If that thing caught wind of him, and was really what Ford said it was, his ass was fried.

He found it, and it was doing some sort of attitude correction. He could see the representational icon move on his visor.

"Mackenzie, look at this. You think this thing is trying to get into position to shoot at us?"

He ported the data to Mackenzie's display, and simultaneously began targeting the low-flying source with one of his KKDs.

A kinetic kill device took time to reach its target, not like laser or EMP bursts. Still, he wasn't willing to wait.

Maybe he hadn't really seen what he thought he saw.

But Mackenzie knew what Cleary wanted him to say: "Looks that way to me. FIFS thinks it's a good target too. Wants a handoff."

"Go ahead then. Try your luck."

Mackenzie needed to test the KKD cannon's ability to take targeting and fire-control orders from the FIFS's electronics anyway.

"Test under possibly hostile conditions," Mackenzie muttered for the record. Then, on Cleary's visor, in the upper right corner, a targeting grid appeared, with the low-flying EMP source centered on it and a red circle around the source.

When the cross hairs locked onto auto, Mackenzie sighed, "Oh, yesss."

The KKD cannon under the X-NASP's nose fired. Cleary went to tracking mode, to see if it was going to hit.

He was sure he could feel the KKD fire.

The Nomad gave a little buck. Then she gave a bigger buck.

Then all his visor scans dumped and he was staring at a clear screen.

Cleary's mouth dried up. He was seeing the redundant control suite. He still had lights. But that suite was going crazy and Mackenzie was swearing a blue streak.

Cleary said calmly, "Possible EMP attack from Target A," for the record.

Cleary's visor display came back, and the target was still on it.

He kicked his laser pod, hard, with three commands in succession, trying to zero it on the target. At the same time, he said, "Here we go," and began bringing the X-NASP into direct line of sight to the A target.

The KKD was nearly there. But Cleary was pretty sure they'd taken a glancing EMP hit; if he was right, they couldn't afford another.

"Mackenzie, fire at will. Laser pulses, these coordinates."

He was too busy to do it. Even with computational and targeting computers, he was asking the X-NASP's systems to stay locked on that target while he was engaged in evasive maneuvers.

"Laser bursts. Three at one-second intervals, three at half-second intervals. On my mark," Mackenzie warned.

Cleary barely had time to shield the Nomad's optics. Then he got even busier, tending to his own part of this little war.

He'd almost forgotten about the KKD when it hit the target, straight on.

Mackenzie's laser was still firing when the icon representing the low-flying target dropped out of position, in fragments. "Hey, Mackenzie, you can stop now."

"I got infinite shots," Mackenzie reminded him.

"And we got a damage assessment to do." On the fly. While returning to their original heading and making their way to a higher orbit.

"See if that laser's really freed up or not," Cleary suggested, as his body let his mind believe that he wasn't dead.

He wanted to retch, for a minute. Then he wanted to flip up his visor and go with his cockpit displays.

So he said, "Going to real-time suite," and retracted the visor. If he had to check every system on this bird, he could do it easier this way.

But what he saw made him flip the visor right back down again. They'd taken a glancing bath, all right.

"Mackenzie, I gotta fly for a while, so you're going to want to replace some suicide switches here and there."

He began naming the systems. He was lucky the weapons still worked. Some of his coms weren't so lucky. His GPS relay was flashing a warning signal. He probably couldn't have found Earth right now if he tried.

"Mackenzie?" he said again. "*Mackenzie?*"

No answer.

What the fuck?

Then he thought it through. He turned his head and tapped on the outside of the other man's helmet, right in front of Mackenzie's eyes.

If Cleary's systems had taken some damage, then Mackenzie's coms might be shot too.

What the fuck were they going to do then? If there were no coms between these two systems, they'd need to do some major on-the-spot reconfiguring to complete any part of this mission, let alone an EVA to look at the laser pod or a visit to Space Station Freedom.

But when Mackenzie retracted his visor and said, "What? I'm talking to the ground," Cleary realized he was overreacting.

"Then tell them I've got some minor com damage. That we were definitely EMP'd. But we're able to continue."

"I was doing that," Mackenzie said.

"Well it's not your goddamn job to make that decision," Cleary said, but very softly, so that Mac couldn't hear him.

At least they'd gotten a chance to test the X-NASP's KKD delivery system. Now if they could just avoid another EMP attack, maybe they had enough snap-in replacements to get through this mission with all their systems intact.

Otherwise, it was going to be a long, slow fall to the ground below.

And Cleary was absolutely positive that he didn't want to go through that again.

"Hey, Mac*ken*zie," he said, louder. "Tell 'em that EMP hardening they did was about eighty percent. Not bad for seat of the pants."

Mackenzie gave him a thumbs-up and snapped down his visor, but there was something jerky about his movements in the FIFS suit. And Mackenzie hadn't made a single smart remark since they'd been hit.

So maybe FIFS had taken more damage than Mackenzie was letting on. Just like an operations officer, to fake his way into combat, even if he had technical problems.

Cleary was going to have to talk to Mackenzie, seriously, about whether FIFS was up to this mission. Just as soon as he got the Nomad parked at Space Station Freedom. After all, if FIFS wasn't perfect, then neither was the Nomad.

But they'd come this far, and they could probably make it the rest of the way.

Mackenzie could use one of the standard EVA suits in the Nomad's cargo bay, if he had to. They had nine of them, in case they were needed for the hostages.

Funny, this was the first time Cleary had thought of the Freedom and *Edo* crew as hostages.

But this was the first time Cleary'd thought about what was going to happen if the FIFS suit malfunctioned.

It didn't have to be that way. Maybe Mackenzie was just tired, or Cleary was just hyped, or whatever was wrong could be fixed.

Like the laser pod, anything could be fixed, if you were lucky enough and tried hard enough. Cleary was sure as hell going to fix the Nomad, the best he could, with the spares he'd brought along.

After all, you couldn't turn tail and go home just because the enemy shot at you. Especially when you'd knocked that enemy out of orbit. Cleary had had worse days, even if, right now, he couldn't remember when.

Those guys up on that space station deserved a ride home, that was for sure. And if Cleary got to give them that ride, he was going to thank Ford for getting that Soviet intelligence about the low-orbital EMP source.

It was the least he could do, considering that Ford had probably saved the whole mission with that data.

If he'd had a goddamned working space-to-ground com, he'd have done it himself, right then. Coms were the most vulnerable to EMP, because EMP could get inside even a hardened box, using any antenna as a pathway.

Later, he decided. He'd call Ford later. After everything that could be fixed was fixed. After he got home, with his passengers. After they'd trashed the other EMP source, if it fired on them.

Which, at this point, he was damn well sure it would.

"Hey," he said to Mackenzie, and rapped on Mackenzie's visor again.

"What?" Mackenzie replied, still manually pushing his faceplate up.

"Ask Ford if we can fire at will on the second EMP source, since the first one shot at us."

"Nah," said Mackenzie. "Too much chance he'd say no."

And Mackenzie grinned at Cleary, an ugly grin inside his helmet that made chills run up and down Cleary's spine.

If you didn't know better, and you saw that grin in there, you'd have thought you were looking at Death himself, twenty-first-century style.

40

Day 12: Space Station Freedom

As soon as Kroeger had helped him with the tricky docking procedure that secured the OMV to the keel extension of Space Station Freedom, Dietrich knew the time was right.

He could see much better now. If his sight had returned while they'd still been at the MHD station, Dietrich might have decided to stay there. But it had not. So here he was, with a traitorous coward clambering out of the OMV into space beside him.

While still holding onto the OMV assembly, Dietrich groped for the MMU that must be somewhere behind the small light at the center of his vision, beyond Kroeger's head.

Kroeger's voice in his ears was surprised, concerned: "Dietrich, what's wrong? Dietrich?"

"I'm dizzy. I can't see," Dietrich said pitifully, at the same time jumping onto Kroeger's back like a lion jumping onto the back of an antelope.

"Dietrich! God, man, be careful."

Dietrich was solidly anchored to Kroeger's back now, holding onto the other man's MMU.

"I'm afraid," Dietrich whined. "I can't see." And he kicked them away from the keel's strutwork.

He was lying to Kroeger. He could see better than he'd been able to since he'd looked at the laser.

They were spinning in space now, tumbling slowly, and Kroeger was babbling at him: "Be calm, Herr Dietrich. Be calm. I will get us to the station. Just hold on."

Dietrich was holding on. But only with one hand. With his other hand, he was disengaging Kroeger's MMU from the fool's

EVA suit. The MMU had twenty-four thrusters. It carried twelve kilograms of gaseous nitrogen and had a Delta-V capability of twenty miles per second.

Kroeger was wildly mashing his joysticks, trying to right them, not knowing that he was held to his MMU only loosely, by Dietrich's grasp and his own grip on his joysticks.

"You crazy man," Kroeger was saying. "Be still. It's only a little distance. Be still and I will piggyback you to the station!"

But Dietrich had no intention of going to the station. He applied full acceleration when they were facing away from the station.

Kroeger screamed, "Dolt! Wrong way, wrong way!"

But it was the right way, so far as Dietrich was concerned. When they were far enough from the station that Kroeger could never make it back without his MMU, Dietrich applied reverse thrusters as hard as he could.

There was a moment when Kroeger held on to his joysticks. And then the force of the braking thrust him out of his MMU harness altogether.

The traitor was floating free in space, helpless! Ha!

Dietrich, holding Kroeger's MMU, continued reverse thrusting, ignoring Kroeger's voice in his ears as best he could.

At first the other man was sure this was an accident. "Dietrich, stop! Dietrich, can't you see me? Dietrich? Come back. I've lost my MMU."

But the truth soon dawned on Kroeger. After that, Dietrich was forced to listen to the threats, and the whines, and then the screams coming out of the traitor as Dietrich jetted away, Kroeger's MMU in his grasp, toward the space station.

He could barely see Kroeger, gesticulating. Kroeger was only a light anyway. A small light with a terrified voice, begging him to save a traitor.

"*Please,* Dietrich. *Please don't leave me out here!*"

Unimaginative words, simple words, words of a fool who thought that Dietrich gave a damn.

Dietrich wished he could silence Kroeger's voice, but that was impossible in the EVA suit. When he was sure Kroeger could not, by some freak chance, reclaim the MMU, Dietrich sent it spinning away, into the blackness of space.

He would say Kroeger had had an accident and he, Dietrich, had been unable to see well enough to save him. Poor Dietrich had to listen to Kroeger's pathetic cries all the way back to the space station.

Only as he was climbing in the lock did Dietrich think to wonder what good his story would do if someone inside had been listening on the EVA channel. He told himself that couldn't happen.

All their electronics would have been destroyed by his cleansing EMP. But someone might have cannily saved an EVA suit or two.

So by the time he had gotten out of his MMU, racked it, and used manual defaults to let himself in the lock, pushing hard on the manual inner lock wheel to open it, he was terrified that someone had heard them.

He wasn't thinking as clearly as he should. He was exhausted, traumatized from his injury, and still half blind. Schliemann would not blame him if he failed, but Dietrich must not fail.

He must succeed. So he would have to kill anyone in here who was still alive, anyone who might have heard what went on outside the station.

He could do that. No one would expect him to be on his guard. He was poor, blind Dietrich, the pathetic man who'd gone blind.

Once he'd closed the inner lock, he looked around, squinting, and nearly died of fright.

The empty EVA suits seemed like men lined up there to confront him. But they weren't men. They were empty suits.

And that gave him an idea. Who knew how many of the astronauts might have been out on EVA, repairing damage from the explosion of the manned free-flying platform, when the EMP blast struck the station?

No one could say for certain that such a scenario had not taken place. If Dietrich took anyone whom he might have to kill, and put that person in an EMP'd EVA suit, and spaced the corpse, then no one would know that Dietrich had killed someone. Or more than one person.

He could dispense with any number of enemies in here, if he had to. So he went looking for those enemies, the Americans and the Canadian bitch, still wearing his EVA suit, because he might need it to beat a hasty retreat.

The center of his vision was still a white light, but it was a small light. The station, however, was dark almost everywhere. A few battery-powered emergency lights studded the darkness with red.

He looked for a long time before he found anyone. All over Space Station Freedom, it was dark. He couldn't find Jenkins. He couldn't find Magriffe. He couldn't find either of the other two American crewmen.

When he did find people, they were all in the Japanese shuttle.

He might have missed them entirely, if he hadn't taken off his helmet so that he could hear any possible sounds. He might have thought he was alone here, and spent hours concocting stories about how he had become the only survivor.

But beyond the A habitat module, he heard a noise, and another. His ears had become so good, in this short interval of visual impairment, he thought he might miss his newfound aural acuity when his vision had fully returned.

When he went through, into the belly of the shuttle, he already knew that Di Lella was in there.

He recognized the voice. And Di Lella was saying, "We must decide what to do, Sekigawa-san."

"Yes, we must," said Dietrich, straightening his shoulders and looking around. He knew there were only three people in here. He could see that much. One was Di Lella. Sekigawa was a second. The third was probably the other shuttle crewman. "Where are the rest? The Americans, the Canadian?" he asked.

"Where is Kroeger?" asked Sekigawa, when Kroeger did not follow Dietrich into the shuttle's midsection.

"Kroeger met with an accident. A terrible one. He is lost in space."

"Interesting," Di Lella said, and a face with a white ball where the eyes and mouth should be swam close to his. "But you survived."

"As you see," said Dietrich. "Something is very wrong here." He could feel it. He had come back here to hide among the survivors.

"And you are the reason for that," Sekigawa said, a disembodied voice dripping scorn.

"All of you knew what was to happen," Dietrich said, taking a step backward. His voice trebled defensively. "Where are the others? The Americans? The Canadian?"

"Dead. We had to kill them, to save the air," said Di Lella flatly.

"Why?" Dietrich said, horrified despite himself. He had killed, but that was different. These men had killed the station personnel in cold blood! And Di Lella was a doctor! "Why?"

"Why, idiot?" said the Japanese-accented voice of Sekigawa, as a small, blurred figure rose and came toward him menacingly. "Why? Because, fool, you acted so far before the deadline that we were not ready. Do you understand? The *Edo* was not prepared. So now we are helpless, here, until some ship comes to rescue us. Because of you!"

Dietrich continued retreating, toward the mid-deck lock and the relative safety of the empty station beyond. "You are not safe. You have killed all the others. How will you explain it?"

"What's to explain? They died as a result of the EMP, didn't they?" said Di Lella.

He was watching Di Lella as closely as his damaged eyes would allow. Was it Dietrich's imagination, or was Di Lella trying to edge around behind him?

He scrambled back until his hips and shoulders touched the lock. He doubled over and backed through it, his heart pounding, calling out, "You may have to wait a long time."

He couldn't lock them out quickly enough. Di Lella was right behind him, his hand keeping the lock from closing.

Dietrich slammed the lock against Di Lella's hand, yelling, "Stay away from me! You need me! If you kill me, any rescue craft will be destroyed before it reaches you by my EMP satellites! Stay away from me! If I die, you all die!"

But Di Lella kept coming. His other hand, now his shoulders, were pushing the lock.

Dietrich, terrified, pushed off into the darkness. In the darkness, he would be safe. He had been living in darkness longer than they had. And if he didn't have his MMU, he still had his EVA suit, his helmet, his OMV. He could climb up the keel to the OMV and escape.

If he could make it to the OMV, he could flee to the MHD power station. He could abandon these fools to their deaths. He could wait there until all of them had died.

"Dietrich," he heard, behind him. Di Lella was calling him. "Dietrich, come back. We must talk, get our stories straight."

But Dietrich would not be fooled by Di Lella again. These men were all as dead as the men they themselves had killed. If Dietrich could make it to the OMV, he would leave them here. Once at his precious MHD station, he would not stop the EMPing of rescue vehicles until all of them were dead.

It wouldn't take so long. A few days, a week or two.

He could hold out that long, if he could elude Di Lella long enough to get to the OMV and escape.

Dietrich swam through the darkened station, counting red lights, settling his EVA helmet on his head as he fled.

He knew he should never have left the MHD station. He knew it. And now, if he did not make it back there, he'd die here.

He hit a dark console, and rebounded. He pushed off again. His breathing was ragged, amplified in the confines of his helmet. At least he couldn't hear Kroeger screaming anymore.

If he could find his way to the OMV, he would be safe.

But where was he, now, exactly?

He wasn't sure. Panic overswept him. You couldn't get lost on the station. You couldn't. He knew every inch of it.

But he was lost, and Di Lella was close behind.

Dietrich pushed off a wall, blindly, and his groping hand touched a lock.

But which one?

Praying that it was the one leading into the laboratory module, he pulled himself through.

He locked it, manually, turning the wheel until his arms ached.

It began to turn from the other side: Di Lella!

But this was the laboratory module. From here he could reach the OMV.

If Di Lella didn't catch him first.

41

Day 12: MHD Station

This EVA was giving new meaning to the term "midnight creep," Mackenzie thought as he dropped out of the Nomad's open cargo bay, laser rifle in hand.

Clipped to his waist, this time, he had a soldering gun and a tool kit as well as his smart KKDs.

"Mac, you okay?" said Cleary into his ear.

"Okay, yeah. Proceeding to laser pod. Keep your fingers crossed."

Okay was a relative term. The FIFS suit was glitchy. He wasn't ready to admit how glitchy to Cleary, or to the ground. He'd satisfied himself that the glitches seemed to be mostly in the power mode for the mobility servos, not in the life support. Mostly. He was trying not to think about what would happen if the servos froze up entirely.

If that happened, Mackenzie was going to wish he'd come out here in one of the low-tech EVA suits instead. Because if the servos froze, the only muscles that Mackenzie was going to be able to move were the ones in his face.

Compared to losing mobility, a few com glitches that were intermittent in the space-to-ground mode didn't seem like anything. And if they didn't get that laser pod fixed, then their only option was to chuck KKDs at the MHD station below.

That was the compromise that Mackenzie had worked out with mission control. The ground wanted him to do a walk-through of the MHD station. They wanted an on-site. And if possible, they wanted a crippled but generally whole station to show the world: proof of aggression.

Cleary and he had already trashed the other EMP source, and

Ford was real clear about not wanting to be in an our-word-against-theirs situation.

If the laser pod had been trustworthy, maybe you could have considered the MHD station disarmed by now, since they'd lased the fuck out of it, coming in from above.

But lasing was effective only if an optical sensor was trained on you and you hit it, straight on. And their gear was too twitchy to know if one had been.

So they lased anyway, despite the laser pod's impairment, trying to position the X-NASP to compensate for the pod's problem. They had infinite shots. They couldn't risk another EMP attack on the Nomad. The MHD station had easily discernible beam-focusers.

Next, those geniuses on the ground had decided that Cleary ought to go around wide, get above the target, where any EMPing of Nomad was less likely, and fix the laser, so you didn't have to aim the whole X-NASP at the target.

Once Mackenzie fixed the laser delivery system, he was supposed to drop down onto the MHD station, trusty laser rifle in hand, and knock on the door.

Knock, knock, said the big bad wolf in the exoskeletal powered suit that was a little slow taking commands from Mackenzie's body these days.

While Mackenzie was looking around inside the station, Cleary was going to be safe "above" the beam-focuser, parked out of its range. They hoped.

Only if Mackenzie got into trouble was Cleary supposed to fly down and face the beam-focuser, laser pod blazing.

Who the hell thought up these dumb-ass tactical requirements anyway? It couldn't have been Ford. Ford knew his ass from a HALO jump.

But they were writing the book on LIC (low intensity conflict) missions in space as they went, and if Mackenzie knew the signs, this part of his mission had been designed by committee.

On the fly. In response to reduced capability reports from the field. Damn Pettit. She asked too many questions.

As Mackenzie jetted toward the laser pod on the Nomad's belly, which was "up" to his senses, he kept wishing that those folks on the ground didn't have such a good take on how the suit was performing.

But fucking Pettit could use FIFS to give him a remote sperm-count, and she'd been all over him while he made his damage report.

Space didn't do much for your sense of direction. In relation to the MHD station, the Nomad was standing on her nose, at twelve o'clock to the orbital power module.

In the distance, farther away than it looked, Mackenzie could see Space Station Freedom, part of it brightly lit, part in shadow. Or destroyed.

He asked FIFS for a magnified view, and got it. Most of his FIFS systems seemed fine. Fuck Pettit. She worried too much.

The EMP bath that the Nomad and FIFS had taken had probably screwed up the ground dumps, more than anything else. Cleary had said his GPS link was fried about the worst of anything.

Except the coms.

The jets on the FIFS suit vibrated his butt as he made a correction that sent him around the Nomad's nose. If the X-NASP had had windows, he could have waved to Cleary. It had sensors, so he waved anyway, in case Cleary was taking a visual. Waved the best he could with the laser rifle in his hand.

He liked the laser rifle. He didn't expect to need it. But he was perfectly willing to climb down the MHD's face and stick its muzzle right in the beam-focuser and pull the trigger.

He hadn't told anybody he was going to do that, but he was determined to try it.

Before he knocked on the door.

Maybe they could ask him to refrain from chucking KKDs at the lethal power platform hanging there, quiet and smug, but they couldn't ask him not to cripple its ability to kill him. At least they hadn't thought to ask him.

He'd been afraid Pettit would figure out what he had in mind. But Pettit hadn't. And since she was determined to fuck him every way but physically, he didn't mind fucking her back.

Shit, he'd have fucked her back physically, if she'd only given him a chance.

Cleary's voice came again. "Progress report, Mackenzie?"

"I'm almost at the laser pod. Everything's nominal."

The com sounded funny. He couldn't hear himself, the way he usually could during a transmission. He waited a minute and said, "Cleary, do you copy?"

Cleary said, "Mackenzie, do you read?"

Oh, crap. Cleary couldn't hear him. If Cleary couldn't hear him, Cleary might not be getting any FIFS com data.

Mackenzie told FIFS's AI Associate, "Shift, Com Two." Then he resumed transmitting: "Here's a running commentary. I can't tell if you can hear me, Sonny, but I'm almost at the laser pod. I can see it. I think I see the problem. I'm jetting a little under it, so I can disengage the cable. I don't need to do anything extensive. I can fix it by hand." Or foot.

He shifted the laser rifle to his left hand and used his right to tap in an emergency patch to the Nomad on the cuff keypad system. He'd never had to use the cuff before.

He pulled up a com status grid and it looked fine, green and happy. At the same time, Cleary said, "Where the fuck were you?" in his ear.

"Hawaii. R and R," he said, and he could hear himself. He had a live circuit.

He tensed his body and cued the jetpack to give him a little thrust, up and to the left. Simultaneously, he pulled up a schematic of the laser-pod deployment assembly.

He could see the cable that had fouled the swiveling belly turret; he just didn't want to pull on anything until he knew whether he might pull something loose.

"I'm going to manually slip this cable, Three-Three, off to the right. I think I have the slack. Then I'm going to pull it a little tighter underneath. I'm afraid to cut and solder it. We'll just hope it doesn't happen again. Okay?"

Cleary must have been looking at the same schematic. "Yeah. But then you'd better get clear; the targeter's got some backed-up commands in its buffer. You don't want it to hit you in the face when it starts moving. It ought to be pretty anxious to execute a bunch of orders. And you'd better shield for laser pulses."

"Roger."

Cleary was sharp. Mackenzie was worried about exactly that scenario: getting lased when the frustrated pod was free to cut loose.

All he needed was to blind himself, or crash his own optics when the laser fired.

When it was freed up, that laser pod was going to go off like Fourth of July fireworks.

He tried to get FIFS as ready for those fireworks as he could. But he needed to see sharply to work. He couldn't see as well as he liked if he shut down too many band-widths.

You shut down three, you were blocking out most of the available spectrum. You shut down four, you might as well be in total darkness, but you were totally protected.

Mackenzie shifted the laser rifle to his shoulder and pulled himself in against the delivery platform. It was going to surge forward some when the system was freed.

He felt his right-hand glove servo stall, then restart. Great. Perfect time to get clumsy.

He just hung there, looking at the problem laser pod. He examined the cable fouling the deployment mechanism in every possible signature mode.

Then he pulled himself up onto the pod.

No use taking a single extra chance. He straddled the laser pod as if he'd climbed onto a horse. He was weightless, like everything else around here. He couldn't hurt the pod. Much.

If the guys on the ground knew he was sitting on their precious laser pod, they'd probably bill him for the cost of the unit. But he couldn't imagine how else he could avoid frying his own sensoring packages when the pod started firing, and still see what he was doing as he unsnarled the cable.

There wasn't room for FIFS inside the deployment port. As it was, he had to bend down real far, from on top of the pod, to reach the cable.

And the glove on his right hand wasn't particularly responsive.

With his other hand, he grabbed the top of the opening in the Nomad's belly. He settled his foot on the targeting assembly and pushed backward. Then he reached down and carefully tugged the looped cable loose.

The pod surged forward, under him. He pulled himself up, flat against Nomad's belly, his helmeted head pressed to the hull. *Now, don't crush me to death, okay, pod?*

"Jesus," Cleary muttered in his ear. "Look at that thing go."

Inches below Mackenzie's back, the laser pod was weaving and spitting bright, destructive pulses that Mackenzie couldn't see because he'd gone to full blackout on all systems.

He felt the pod whack him in the ass—hard. And in the back, harder. For a minute he thought FIFS was going to crack open like a lobster shell.

Then the pod stopped moving, as suddenly as it began, finished executing the routines stored in its buffer.

If the "cancel" command had been working right, then Mackenzie wouldn't have been lying on his back on a firing laser weapon with all his sensoring packages shut down.

He said, "Cleary, are you going to tell me when it's safe to come out, or what?"

"Yeah, in a sec. I make it three more delayed pulses to go."

The pod spat three times, weaving its snout.

Then Cleary said: "Okay, come back on line."

Mackenzie started to slide out, carefully, from between the laser pod and the X-NASP's skin. His right arm wasn't working right. He pushed harder, to kick the servo into motion.

It wouldn't kick.

He hung there a minute before he decided, what the hell, and pushed himself awkwardly free with his left arm.

Then he brought up his sensoring packages and considered the situation.

He flexed his right arm again, trying to raise it. The arm felt as if the suit he was wearing were made of concrete.

Terrific.

And Cleary wanted a status report.

"Nominal. Proceeding to MHD station. You going to be here when I get back?"

The pilot had a choice. He could hang where he was, or fly around and try to distract the MHD station's attention. Nobody knew whether that attention was automated or human-directed.

"I'll be right here, friend. I don't want to risk you missing your taxi."

Not even the ground was sure if this station would reorient itself to focus its beam on the X-NASP, if the X-NASP taunted it. Cleary meant that they'd try it later, together, if they needed to.

"Thanks. Proceeding to MHD station now." The prospect of being adrift out here if the Nomad got itself fried wasn't one that Mackenzie favored, even though the ground thought he could make it to Space Station Freedom if he had to, using the powered suit.

Let them fucking try setting personal transport records in space using partially EMP'd equipment.

They were pretty sure that the other beam source had responded to the Nomad's exhaust plume. So they were equally sure that the MHD station, if it behaved like the lower-orbiting EMP source, wouldn't zero FIFS as a target: no hot exhaust.

Mackenzie, at this moment, didn't find that assurance as comforting as Mission Control had meant it to be. As Pettit had meant it to be.

Those guys down there were always better at telling you what had happened than they were at telling you what would happen.

Nobody knew what the fuck this MHD station was capable of, or whether there was any resistance waiting inside it.

Nothing for it but to go answer some of these nagging questions. Since the wrong answer could get Mackenzie or Cleary killed, he wasn't going to defer any part of this mission until later.

His FIFS jets were working fine. Mackenzie told himself he had plenty of drop time to try to get the right-arm servos back on line. If he couldn't, then he'd shoot left-handed, if he had to shoot.

He wondered if Cinderella had felt like this when her clock struck twelve. Probably not. Finding yourself inside a pumpkin at midnight beat finding yourself inside a sarcophagus.

He pushed against the stalled servos with his right hand until he grunted. The arm didn't budge.

Cleary said, "Mackenzie, what the fuck's going on? If you've got a problem, then I want to know about it."

Mackenzie considered pretending he couldn't hear Cleary. But just then, the right arm of the suit freed up. A little. Enough that he could, pushing hard, raise the arm.

He said, "No problem, Cleary. Just trying to get pumped up enough that I don't fall asleep up here. It's a long drop."

"Did I ever tell you about the time I got head from America's favorite newsreader, Carla Chang?"

"Nope." As he listened to Cleary's chatter, Mackenzie worked the suit arm.

Then the hand. The thumb was the hardest. His whole arm ached from the isometrics he was performing. Push against an immovable object. If a FIFS suit could rust, it might feel like this.

When he had the thumb working, he was almost on top of the power station, and Cleary was telling him how glad Carla Chang had been to receive an obscene phone call from Cleary right before this mission started.

Mackenzie said, "Cleary, shut up. You want this on the record? They're going to go into full damage control when they hear you called a newsie from the base. Next thing you know, it'll be my ass too, for not reporting a breach of security."

Cleary said, "Jesus, Mackenzie, I was just trying to help you stay awake."

"My dick doesn't have much room in here, asshole. And you're going to step on yours if you keep on this way. Making contact with the purported power station module. Now."

His booted feet touched the module skin. He let them glance off, and slid down its side, carefully, still working the arm as he looked for the lock.

You had to be able to get into this thing somehow. It was logged as man-supportable. Only when he found the lock did he try taking his laser rifle in his malfunctioning right glove.

At least you didn't have to squeeze hard on this trigger.

"Sending handoff data; target is airlock."

He went past the airlock. "Sending handoff; target is beam-focuser."

Cleary said, "Got it." If something happened to Mackenzie, Cleary now knew just where to shoot a KKD.

He slid along the hull of the module, trying to keep as close as he could and use his thrusters as little as he could, as he approached the beam-focuser, a recessed port with a wide aperture.

He hung above it for a minute, upside down.

"Lasing. On my mark."

Then he pointed the laser rifle at it. Synchronized the rifle with his own optics so he could shoot. Advised Cleary. And shot.

Three times. Each time his visor polarized almost to blackout. But still, this close, his view whited out from the backwash.

He prayed he hadn't damaged anything. He said, "Lasing complete. Let's hope the thing was on."

"No sign of change," Cleary said, a crackly sound in his ears with too much static.

If the beam-focuser had no continually running optics, lasing it wouldn't have done any damage.

But on the other hand, if no optics had been damaged, anybody inside might still be oblivious to his presence.

"Goin' in," Mackenzie said, and approached the lock.

The electronics of this station were working fine. He hit the lock-plate. It cycled.

He swung in, feet first. It closed. He had to float there while the inner lock cycled, then hit the plate to open it when the light turned green.

Not exactly a total surprise to anyone inside.

Still, he went in firing three bursts a second. His faceplate reacted as if he were trying to blink dust out of his eyes.

When he stopped firing, he realized that nobody was in here. But the Magneto Hydro Dynamic generator was.

"Damn," he said. "Cleary?"

No answer. For a moment, he clutched the rifle. Then he reasoned that this was a shielded environment; normal space-to-space coms wouldn't work. The station had its own com system. He trashed it with one blow of his armored fist.

He looked for a control panel, and found it. When he did, he shouldered his laser rifle and took out the tool kit.

Then he removed the main panel, and started pulling circuit

boards. He fused a couple of connections, destroying the fire-control circuitry as he went. Then his fine control in the right hand of the FIFS suit went again.

Okay. So what? He used the FIFS right glove as a bludgeon and crushed whatever he could find that looked crucial and irreplaceable.

Then he thought to check if the beam-focuser had had optics up and running. He couldn't tell. So he trashed another control panel. For good measure, he blew the life support, evacuating all the stored oxygen into space.

When he left the MHD station, it was powerless and wide open. It made him feel real good to know that.

As soon as he was outside it, he started hearing Cleary's voice again: "Goddamn it, Mackenzie, fucking say something. Anything!"

Say what? "Mission accomplished. Module intact. Mission capability destroyed. Nobody's going to put that fire-control system back together again from what's handy up here. I'm coming home."

"Next stop, Space Station Freedom," Cleary reminded him. "Pick up the pieces. See if anybody from the *Edo* wants to hitch a ride."

The ground's assumption was that the Japanese shuttle and the space station had already been crippled by EMP. He and Cleary were empowered to evacuate all personnel, if that assumption was correct.

Nobody on Earth knew what to expect in the way of damage there. Or whether there would be casualties. Or survivors. There were simply too many variables. And Freedom and *Edo* weren't talking.

"Yeah, I'm hurrying."

There had to be some survivors, Mackenzie reasoned. A few. But at least they weren't hostages any longer.

Mackenzie was jetting straight "up," toward the X-NASP poised on her nose overhead, when his right hand spasmed, the glove splayed wide, and he lost hold of the laser rifle.

It floated there, in front of his eyes.

He grabbed for it with his left hand. Caught it.

But just in time. Now the left servos were fritzy too.

At least they'd waited to give him shit until he could deal with it.

He said, "Cleary, you copy?"

"Right here, Mac."

"Call Mission Control and ask Pettit what I'm supposed to do when the mobility servos in this thing freeze up."

"Oh, man. Are you telling me you need a pickup?"

"Nope. I'm telling you I don't want a long discussion. I want a quick fix. By the time I'm back there, I want to know if there's anything they can do from the ground that will help." He wasn't going to try talking to her himself right now. Even if his space-to-ground link worked, he didn't need the grief.

"Workin' on it."

Maybe there was something they could do, from Earth. And maybe not. If it weren't starting to get scary, this intermittent systems failure, Mackenzie wouldn't even have mentioned it.

He knew Pettit wanted FIFS to get a clean bill of health. But if he died up here in it, her program was going to die with him. And he didn't want that on his conscience.

"Mission accomplished" reports usually cut you some slack with your rear-echelon commanders.

If there was any time to report this kind of problem, it was now, when the problem clearly hadn't impacted perfect mission performance.

Shit, FIFS was everything you could ask for in a space battle suit.

When it was working. If you were asshole enough to ask for a space battle suit in the first place. Mackenzie watched the comforting nose of the X-NASP grow larger as FIFS took him home.

Even the fact that the ship was on her nose, pointed at him, didn't bother him anymore. He was getting the hang of this microgravity combat crap. Better not tell anybody that, or he'd end up with a specialty he didn't want.

Right now, he just wanted to get in that nice, pressurized spacecraft. Then he wanted to visit the station, pick up anybody who needed a ride, and get the hell out of the space envelope.

Every time FIFS glitched on him, his gut did a flip. It was one thing to find out you had problems in a simulation bay. It was another to find out you had them in space.

Mackenzie wasn't a fool. The closer he got to the X-NASP, the more he wanted to be safe aboard her. Then this part of the mission would be over. Then he could take a deep breath. Then he could get out of this suit, maybe, even.

If they couldn't fix it from the ground.

But at least the rough stuff was over. The MHD station was an automated system, so you didn't have to worry about hostile personnel. All you had to do was get to some folks who were going to be real glad to see you, pack 'em into the cargo bay, and go on home.

He was glad he couldn't see the Earth from this angle.

He kept focused on the nose of the Nomad. He'd never seen anything as beautiful in his life.

42

Day 12: Space Station Freedom

Dietrich was curled up in the OMV, shaking. He couldn't keep the image of Di Lella's face out of his mind.

If only Dietrich had been a little more blind, a little while longer.

Di Lella had asked for it. Di Lella was going to kill him, Dietrich reminded himself.

But all he could see was the horrible popping of Di Lella's eyes. And the blood coming out of his mouth. And the way his body had seemed to turn inside out when the air had rushed out of the module and sucked Dietrich and Di Lella with it.

Di Lella should have been wearing an EVA suit, not a T-shirt and shorts, Dietrich thought dreamily.

Then he might not have looked so awful when he died.

If Di Lella had not chased Dietrich all the way through the station, then Dietrich would not have opened the outer lock while Di Lella was forcing the inner one open. It was the fool's own fault.

They were all fools, all traitors.

But now there was only Dietrich left. Only Dietrich, alone in the OMV. How had it happened?

He couldn't quite remember.

He had been very angry at what Di Lella had done. And so he had gone through the entire station, emptying out the air by opening each lock in turn. The safety systems were all down, EMP'd.

And the two Japanese were not quick enough, not smart enough, to avoid Dietrich's revenge. If they had stayed in their space shuttle, instead of chasing after Dietrich, they might have lived. If they had worn their EVA helmets, they might have survived. But they had not.

And now, the station was cleansed of most of the horror. Most of the blood and guts had been sucked out into space with the air.

Every so often, Dietrich was sure that he could see one of the bodies floating by. But this was not likely. His eyes were not good. He was probably imagining the bodies.

The corpses were on their way to Earth, or to the sun, or to oblivion in deep space.

Dietrich was all alone out there, and his eyes were bothering him again now.

He had cried for a time. Perhaps that was why his eyes were sore.

He had cried when he saw what he thought was Di Lella's body floating past the OMV. How could it have established an orbit around the station? It couldn't have, except by the most unkind coincidence. So it wasn't there.

He was afraid he was losing his mind.

He had been under a terrible strain.

As soon as he recovered his strength, he would take the OMV over to the MHD module. There he would call the ground and tell a terrible tale of madness and death.

Space psychosis was not unknown. He would be believed. He was the only survivor of a terrible disaster.

He would be believed. He was the single surviving hostage to terror among the stars.

All the dead astronauts danced outside the OMV, waving to him, each with a face like a bright, white light.

He had an MMU. He could go out there and clean up. There shouldn't be such a mess around the station. The corpses must be tidy. He could go out and catch each one, and wipe its ruined eye sockets. He could clean the blood from the open mouths, and the bits of lung from their noses. He could put them inside, and close up the station.

He wished there was air left in the station. He wished there was enough life support to go back inside. But even the *Edo* was dead, airless.

And the corpses were right outside the OMV, waving at him.

He blinked and looked again. Now there was only one corpse.

That was better, anyhow. One corpse, with only one small light for its face.

Soon he could see clearly enough to be on his way.

He could uncurl himself. He could stop floating here, in a ball. He could leave this place of death forever.

But first, he must take care of the single corpse. He must.

He wasn't wearing his MMU. He must get into it.

Decided, he uncurled to do that.

But again he saw the corpse. And it was coming closer.

It was much more horrible now than any of the corpses had been before. Its head was oversized. Its shoulders were very broad. It gleamed all over.

And there were voices in his ears. He could hear voices, as if there was someone using the EVA channel.

He slapped at his helmet, as if he could slap some sense into what he heard.

But the voice was still there. It was saying, "Attention, any survivors on this channel. This is Rescue Mission. Come in, please. We are instituting a thorough search. So if you can't respond, don't worry. We'll find you. We're coming."

Dietrich was horrified.

"We'll find you. Just relax and respond if you can. Executing broadband com sweep. Any survivors, do you copy?"

Dietrich wished he could turn off the EVA helmet, but he couldn't.

He was sure it wouldn't have helped, anyhow. He was imagining this.

It was a reaction of his mind to all the death. Any rescue mission would have been destroyed by his orbital EMP satellite. He had put it on automatic. It would search out and destroy any ship approaching.

Therefore, what he was hearing was the voice of a ghost.

It looked like a ghost, all distorted and gleaming with a supernatural effluence, floating there without an EVA suit.

Nothing could maneuver in space as this ghost was doing, not without an MMU.

Therefore, it was just poor Dietrich's eyes, playing tricks on him again.

Or it was a real ghost, coming to get him.

He began to shake. His mouth grew sticky. His stomach threatened to throw up bile. His pulse hammered his ears so that he could hardly discern the words of the ghost.

But it was coming closer, this thing with a voice for a head.

Maybe it was a Japanese ghost. It looked like a Samurai warrior. Or maybe it was a German ghost, from feudal times. It looked like a knight in armor. Maybe it was Dietrich's ancestor, a ghost come to save him from this loneliness.

But he was shaking too terribly for this to be a benign ghost.

This was a horrible ghost. This was a vengeful ghost. And it was sailing through space, right for him.

It was coming toward the OMV and it had a weapon in its hands.

Dietrich knew a weapon when he saw one. Maybe there had been someone else; maybe it was not a ghost at all.

Maybe the Japanese had had a secret ally, someone else who'd remained alive aboard their shuttle.

But no, no one could sail through space like that, with no MMU.

No one was that big. No one came at you, armed and armored, sailing effortlessly through space, but a ghost.

Dietrich yelled "No! Stay away from me!"

And the ghost answered: "Hold on. I'm coming. Can you give your exact location? Repeat: If you copy, give your location."

"No!" Dietrich screamed again.

"I'll home in on your signal. Just keep talking. Repeat, keep talking."

Dietrich couldn't find the saliva to respond. His mouth was a dessicated dead thing. He tried to get into the MMU, to step into the harness, but he couldn't. He was too clumsy. He couldn't see well enough.

He couldn't remember quite what to do.

It didn't matter. He knew his way around the station. He knew the keel like no one else. And anyway, what good was an MMU against a ghost?

He pushed the MMU away and scrambled out of the OMV. No time to go through separation procedures. No time. He hung from the circular OMV and swung onto the keel's struts like a monkey. Let this ghost catch him now!

He began climbing, toward the upper keel. He couldn't let the ghost catch him. He couldn't.

The ghost was talking to him now. He tried to ignore the taunting voice.

"Easy, fella, I'm on my way. Just stop where you are, okay?"

Dietrich had no intention of stopping. He climbed and climbed. He watched his hands, not the ghost. He grabbed the struts and he climbed.

His feet were assured as he climbed. He was headed for the OMV mission-support structure. He could hide in there. It was a big box, with places to hide inside. Unfinished, it was the perfect place.

He would get in there, and then he would be fine. The ghost couldn't go into the box. It was a ghost. It wasn't real.

It lived out in space, where the corpses lived.

Dietrich started singing as loudly as he could, in German, to drown out the sound of the ghost.

He sang and he climbed and he climbed and he sang.

His foot slipped. He hung by his hands. But he was weightless. His eyes were pounding. He could see the veins in them. The white spot centering his vision was marbled with veins.

He could see little lights inside the big light in his eyes as he climbed, singing as loud as he could.

Then, suddenly, the ghost was right before him.

It was reaching out for him.

It had no face. Its huge helmet was empty.

And its hand was a gauntleted horror that grabbed his shoulder with crushing force.

The ghost pulled Dietrich from the keel as if he were a child. It had a rifle. It was going to kill him.

Dietrich, screaming so loudly he couldn't hear the ghost's shouts, grabbed for the rifle.

They struggled there, the rifle between them, man and ghost.

Then the rifle disappeared in a flash of white light and Dietrich was floating free.

But there was something in his mouth. It tasted like blood. And he couldn't breathe. There was something in his nose. Or there was nothing in his nose. He tried to catch his breath and realized that he couldn't.

He felt as if he were spinning wildly, going very fast. His shoulder hurt and he grabbed it with his gloved hand.

Something was spurting out of his shoulder. Blood, air, everything.

Life was spurting out of his shoulder, where the ghost had grabbed him.

The ghost had crushed his shoulder. The ghost had torn open his suit.

He couldn't sing anymore. He couldn't breathe anymore. He was drowning, choking, smothering all at once.

Something grabbed him again: the ghost. He knew it.

But it was too late. Too late for the ghost.

The ghost couldn't hurt Dietrich anymore. Dietrich was becoming a ghost himself.

If it didn't hurt so much, he would have laughed at the ghost. If he could have seen the ghost, he would have defied it.

But he could see only white, slowly fading to black, everywhere. And he couldn't hear anything at all.

43

Day 12: Berlin

Schliemann was not afraid. Everything was under control. Everything was still his to manipulate. As he slid into the same table in the same wursthaus to await Tohei, he was optimistic.

Even though the German government had fallen, new elections would prove that Schliemann's Coalition had been right. By noon, the Americans would capitulate. Afraid for their precious station and its personnel, they would hand over the derelict satellite and accede to the Coalition's demands.

Tohei would see that Schliemann had been right. He opened his menu. The eyes of stags dead two hundred years looked calmly down over his shoulder as he read. Soon enough, Schliemann could reveal himself as leader of the Coalition.

He would be a hero to the people, to the German, the Italian, and the Japanese people. Never mind that he had been removed from the ORTAG board. Never mind that the fish was fighting on the hook.

The more it fought, the deeper the hook was set.

No word had come from the Americans, or the Canadians, as yet. Nothing on the news reflected the progress of events. But all would be well. Schliemann's man in space would see to that.

He spied Tohei, through the thin crowd of late morning. The little Oriental had a face like a walnut. He had come in with a crowd of bigger men, Germans who went to the bar and laughed loudly as the tense little fellow looked uneasily around for Schliemann.

Schliemann waved. The Oriental saw him and bowed his head, coming toward him like a servant.

In contrast to the crowd in the wursthaus, the Oriental seemed even more frail and more unimportant than usual.

When Tohei reached his table, the little man did not sit.

Schliemann said, "Sit down. Sit down. We will soon have something to celebrate."

"What can we have, Schliemann?" asked Tohei morosely, not sliding into the booth. "It is all over. Done."

Behind Tohei, some of the men from the bar waited to get past him.

"Nothing is over. We will win in the end. This silence of theirs is just a bluff. Now sit down, let these men get by."

Tohei looked over his shoulder and said, "This is the man. This is Herr Schliemann, who masterminded everything."

For the first time, Schliemann focused on the men towering over Tohei.

There were four of them. They were big, dour men of his nation.

He considered trying to run. He considered lying. And then he sat back and said, "Gentlemen, I will finish my beer first."

Then he would go with them. He would say nothing without his attorney present, of course.

One of them said, "No, you won't, Herr Schliemann. You will get up now, and come with us quietly, or we will be forced to take steps."

The voice of his countryman was very threatening.

"Surely, this is premature," he couldn't help but say, as he rose. "I have many friends left in—"

As he was sliding out of the booth, one of the men grabbed his arm, yanked on it. He felt the handcuff click around his wrist.

He was so embarrassed, he was nearly unable to move. His other wrist was handcuffed too.

As they walked him out through the crowd, Schliemann wished that he had not set the meeting here, where so many people knew him.

Before him, the disgusting little monkey of an Oriental seemed to scamper delightedly as Schliemann was hustled toward a waiting police car.

The man holding his right elbow was telling Schliemann that he was under arrest for terrorism, sabotage, and the murder of nine people aboard Space Station Freedom.

"That's ridiculous," he snapped. One of those nine was his agent, Dietrich. He almost told them so, but caution prevailed.

Something had gone wrong. It was not even yet the moment of the deadline. He must secure legal counsel, and find out what had gone wrong. Nine dead? That meant everyone, including the Japanese shuttle crew.

And then he knew what had happened. The fierce pleasure in the Oriental's eyes made sense.

For Schliemann, the whole world telescoped into a black tunnel, at the end of which was Tohei, the monkey man.

"Traitor," he hissed at Tohei.

"Fool," the Oriental hissed back.

In that moment, Schliemann decided to cooperate as fully as necessary, to make sure that Tohei and his Japenese cohorts suffered hideous disgrace.

After all, Osawa had been the real mastermind of the plan, of the Coalition. The Japanese, and the Italians, would rue the day they failed to protect Schliemann, who had all of Osawa's notes.

The police car was a bullet-proof BMW. As one of the men holding Schliemann put a hand on his head to push him down into the back seat of the car, a shot rang out.

Then another, bouncing off the BMW's glass.

Schliemann never heard the third shot. It went through his right temple, directly into his brain.

The last thing he saw was the frozen smile on Tohei's yellow face.

44

Day 12: Northern Nevada Desert

"Touchdown," Cleary sighed and sat back for a minute before he looked over at Mackenzie and smiled at the man in the FIFS suit.

Sonny Cleary had never been so tired in his life. His whole body was trembling. So he thought he could imagine how Mac must feel, in that glitchy suit. "They'll believe you, Mac. I believe you. It's going to be okay."

"Whatever," Mackenzie said. His visor was up. According to Mackenzie, the suit was still fritzy, and it seemed as if it was, whenever Mackenzie moved. But he hadn't gotten out of it.

Maybe that was because Cleary had a corpse in his cargo bay, where the standard EVA suits were. If he hadn't seen the scuffle himself, he didn't know what he'd have thought. But the Nomad had recorded the whole thing: the chase up the keel, the struggle—everything.

"Let's go. Face time." Cleary shut down the Nomad, taking his time.

Mackenzie's movements were jerky, awkward as he stood, head bent.

Mackenzie claimed that the suit's glove had glitched, and spasmed shut when he'd grabbed the crazy guy. He'd still had part of the dead guy's suit—and some bone and flesh, clutched in his right glove when he'd come in.

At least nobody had insisted they stay around and hunt for more bodies. Maybe you could have found some, with intense sensoring sweeps. But maybe not. Space was a big place.

Cleary had never been so glad to get out of the space envelope. Still, leaving the Nomad, he felt a little regretful somehow.

Outside, it was dark, still. The moon was down, the stars faded.
You could see a swathe of purple, lighter sky in the distance where
dawn was going to break. The fresh air sure smelled nice, even
with exhaust fumes in it.

He followed the slow-moving FIFS suit down the ramp. Cleary
was damned glad he wasn't in Mackenzie's shoes.

Accidentally killing the sole survivor on the station, even a
crazy survivor—it probably wasn't playing real well down here.

But it wasn't anybody's fault.

They were going to tell that to endless committees, Cleary
figured. His life had turned into a series of hearings punctuated
by death-defying stunts in the space envelope.

The hangar door was open by the time they got down the ramp.
Now Cleary could see past Mackenzie to where Pettit, Ford, and
Walsh were waiting.

Cleary reached out and waved a hand in front of Mackenzie's
face. "It's okay. We both know what really happened."

"Yep," said Mackenzie. His visor was up. His voice was
scratchy. His steps were slow and heavy. Cleary had a sudden,
urgent need to protect the other man.

Funny. Mackenzie was probably the most dangerous sucker
that Cleary'd ever shared a mission with. But inquiries were hell.
Cleary could attest to that.

Pettit came running over, paused a few feet in front of them, and
walking backwards, said: "Don't worry. We have all the dumps.
FIFS was just damaged when the laser pod hit it in the seat. All
the servo controls are back there."

"So?" Mackenzie croaked.

Cleary left them there. He could move faster, in his standard
EVA suit.

By the time he'd reached Ford and Walsh, he had his helmet
off. It was cold out here. The breath came out of his mouth in
white puffs. "Colonel; Mr. Ford."

"Good job, Cleary," said Walsh. "We're all proud of you. The
admiral sends his compliments. Come on in and let's get started
debriefing."

Walsh turned on his heel and walked hurriedly toward the
hangar, pointedly leaving him alone with Ford.   .

Behind them, the ground crew was getting ready to tow the
Nomad into the hangar.

Cleary looked Ford straight in the eye and said, "Mac wasn't to blame for what happened out there. That guy was so crazy, even if FIFS hadn't torn his EVA suit, we'd have never gotten him inside alive."

"I looked at what you dumped. Don't worry. The Germans picked up the ringleaders, and the corpse you have there, Dietrich, was named as one of the conspirators. So were some of the others up there."

"Oh." Relief flooded Cleary so that he felt weak. "So Mac's not—"

"Mac's going to get lots of points for this. So are you, Cleary."

Ford had this way of making you believe anything he said. "But what about FIFS—?"

"Cleary, have I ever lied to you? This is a win. For FIFS too. Relax. Look at those two. Does Pettit look unhappy to you?"

He turned around and said, "No, sir. She doesn't look exactly unhappy."

In the predawn light, Pettit was hanging from the FIFS suit, her arms around its neck. Could they kiss through the visor opening?

Cleary turned back. "I wish you guys had told us how happy you all are while we were still up there."

"Come on, I'll buy you a cup of coffee from the machine."

Cleary paced Ford, until Ford said, "You've got a friendly reporter waiting for you. It threw us at first. Now we want to coach you on how to handle it."

Oh, shit. "Uh—I bet I know who. I just called her, off the record, to say—never mind."

"And she had a number reader on her phone. So she found us eventually. But we can use the right kind of press on this. I assume it's a *very* friendly relationship?"

"Far as I'm concerned, it is." For all Cleary knew, they'd monitored the whole Carla Chang story he'd told Mackenzie during the EVA. "When am I supposed to talk to her?"

"We're going to give her an exclusive look around, in the wake of an eminently successful power projection, and have her sign a non-disclosure agreement. Then you two can fuck your brains out, for all we care. Just make sure that we get to vet any story she's going to write."

"I'll try." Carla Chang.

"She'll be here right about the time your debrief's finished, so I'll be around if you need me."

To make everything all right.

Cleary looked back again, at Mackenzie and Pettit, who were still talking on the apron.

Behind the huge figure of the space-suited man and the girl, the black Nomad was rolling slowly toward the hangar.

Ford was right, again. Everything was going to be all right.

45

When the military jet's door opened, Shitov's heart skipped a beat.

There she was. Shitova, in a black babushka and carrying a huge net bag.

He could not run up the stairs to her. He was, after all, a diplomat of some standing. He waited where he was as she waddled down the stairs, carefully, heavily, her body swaying.

Levonov, you will never know how much joy you have brought me. At your new desk in the Agriculture Ministry, think of me. Envision me, with my beloved Shitova beside me, riding around in the white limousines with the long horns of cattle on their grills.

Imagine what I am eating, the marbled Kansas steaks and the strawberries in champagne. And envision Shitova, in Neiman Marcus, shopping, while your wife makes you sleep on the couch because you have lost your seats at the ballet.

Shitova's little eyes roved, bright in their plump cheeks, looking for him as she came toward the building. Beside her and behind her walked American soldiers, half again her height and half of her breadth.

In her raincoat and her babushka and her thick-heeled black shoes, she was fooling all these Americans.

She had cleverly disguised herself as a frumpy matron. They could not know what a princess of passion had set foot on American soil.

After all, the blood of the czars ran in Shitova's veins. Shitov squared his shoulders and stepped forward, arms wide, to embrace his wife.

271

"Ah, my husband," said Shitova, the light of love ennobling her round face. "I am hungry. I have had nothing but crackers since we left Moscow."

She reached up for him, and they kissed. Her endless breasts pushed against his chest, his stomach. The warmth of her was like a great pillow.

When he could finally bring himself to release her from his bear's embrace, he took her immediately to his waiting white Cadillac. And as he did, he told her of all the wonders awaiting her in New Mexico, especially about the Western store.

"There you will get the boots like these," he told her, showing her his. "And the cowgirl shirt with fringe. And the silver belt. And a hat to keep the sun out of your eyes. And we will ride down the Grand Canyon on mules. Together."

"Yes, yes, my bruin. But first," Shitova commanded, "something to eat."

If you enjoyed COBRA, turn the page
for an exciting excerpt from
Daniel Stryker's first book,

HAWKEYE

Follow Dalton Ford in his first
adventure into the world of
high-tech sabotage and terrorism.
Now available from Jove.

Day 18: Homs Gap, Syria

Free-falling from the Learjet with Saudi markings, through the still night, Ford had plenty of time to think.

He didn't like thinking in free-fall. He liked floating, stretching out, kiting with his body and listening to the wind. But that was what you did when you were skydiving for fun, not when you were HALOing into hostile territory from 22,000 feet, wearing a black motorcycle helmet to which the mask feeding from your oxygen bottle was attached.

Ford couldn't hear the flap of his clothes against him; he couldn't really feel the peace that he knew was up here.

Down below, there wasn't much in the way of peace to be had, either. And above him . . .

The Learjet they'd borrowed from the Saudi moderates was gone now, shadowing its way along in the radar image of a charter, bound for Turkey out of Cairo West, on a regular route. Seti hadn't missed a trick, making himself useful.

If there'd been any way that Ford could have gotten in here without Seti knowing about it, he'd have felt better. But Seti had been bound to find out anyway, no matter how Ford played it, when he didn't show up with Quantrell's team for the nap-of-the-earth insertion.

He shouldn't keep worrying about it. He should watch his step out here—keep an eye on his altimeter and his descent curve. *Jabal* meant mountain, and Ford's drop between the Jabal an-Nusayriyah range and the Anti-Lebanon mountains wasn't the easiest he'd ever tried.

275

Strange things happened with air currents when you had the ocean so close, two mountain ranges that almost met, and a river flowing through the gap between them.

The Israelis had known the area like the backs of their hands—what radars to watch for, where the airstreams tended to get tricky. Meri Soukry had gotten him everything he needed.

Ford was falling into the moisture-laden sea winds of the Jabal an-Nusayriyah's fertile, western slopes in the scruffy battle dress of one of the private militias of the Lebanese Maronites. He had a Soviet AKM-15 paratroop sniper rifle, instead of the AK-47s being carried by Quantrell's forces, but the rest of what he carried was calculated to identify his body, if captured, as belonging to a mercenary out of Lebanon.

Since you could see into the Bekáa Valley from his projected landing zone, and the Lebanese border was on the "Go to Shit" plan (if everything went to shit, you walked down into Tripoli and met at a bar there), Ford was comfortable enough with the legend. He had a British-made Racal PRM4735 Covert Personal Radio system, complete with earpiece and lapel mike, for communicating with Quantrell's troops on the ground; a couple hand-emplaceable jammers on his web belt, along with three Soviet butterfly mines, C-4, three concussion grenades and three thermite grenades of East European manufacture.

The only telltales that marked him as what he was—an American purple suit bulling his way into a Special Forces mission because, years ago, he'd led A-teams out here—were his custom electronics, and that couldn't be helped.

Ford wasn't going to miss this chance to field-test his black box. Hell, that was what he'd been doing here in the first place. He'd stripped the box out of its hard case and stuffed it into his pack, along with his other necessaries.

Like the Jack Crain survival knife he carried, it didn't fit well with his image as a low-tech mercenary. But then, neither did his high-tech dental work or his cyanide pills. If he decided to get dead, he'd blow the equipment first; if he had time before getting dead accidentally, he'd set the booby trap on the black box, although if you did that and forgot . . .

Everything seemed hypothetical, free-falling in a helmet while you breathed bottled oxygen. He checked his wrist-strapped altimeter again; mustn't forget to bury it with the helmet, oxygen bottle, and mask.

He wanted as low a chute opening as he dared attempt. The landing zone he'd chosen on the mountain's slope was one where he could hunker down and keep watch on the facility with his naked eye, just upslope of the radar signature.

He wanted to see the damned dish, if he could, from where he was going to dig in and wait for Quantrell's people.

You didn't want to wait long. Not if the other signatures they'd picked up were accurate. Not if Meri was right about troops and artillery massing just southwest of the Gap, for a push down through Lebanon.

But before Ford could worry about anything as peripheral to his current situation as being discovered on the ground, he had to land—on his feet, not his head, and preferably without breaking anything.

He wanted to think about it in terms of controlled descent. And he wanted his timing to be just right. But he couldn't help trying to see into the murk down there, as it came closer. And he couldn't help counting to himself as he got ready to pull his cord.

He pulled it.

He could feel the chute billow out. It was a kind of sixth sense you acquired, as if you could see through the top of your head; the same kind of sixth sense that would prompt you to step just to the left of a mine or to bend down to light a cigarette just when the bullet was coming your way out of the trees.

If you lost that edge, you were dead. Until he pulled his cord and knew his chute hadn't streamed, Ford wasn't sure he still had it. But he did, and when the comforting jerk of the chute pulled him up short, he was humming to himself, already disengaging one of the Velcro tabs on his mask so that he could breathe the salty air.

From here to the ground, Ford would get to find out if he was still the lucky bastard he'd always been. All the while he kept glancing at the global positioning handheld, while controlling his descent, part of him was remembering Vladimir Matiosov's *Soviet Military Review* article on tracking techniques for shooting paratroopers from the ground: *"When firing at paratroopers, the lead is taken in paratrooper length reckoned from his waist-band . . ."*

Ford put the GPS handheld back in his jacket pocket. If he'd calculated his drift right, he'd be well within the grid square marking his optimum position.

" . . . the lead must be one less than the slant range expressed in hundreds of meters, and two less for weapons using rifle and 5.45-mm cartridges. . . ."

A downdraft caught him, and tried to suck him south. He wasn't about to end up in that valley, sitting on a railroad car, trying to explain what the hell he was doing there. . . .

" . . . *the aiming point must be displaced . . . in the direction of the parachuter's movement, which depends on the direction and speed of the wind. . . .*"

There. Better. You could see the rough edge of the range now, dark against the sky to his left. Its average height was 1,211 meters. "Average" didn't mean much if you were walking terrain because you'd screwed up. What had made him say he could do this without night-vision goggles?

" . . . *After the first long burst, the sight setting or aiming point can be changed, after which the weapon should be set to the previous position and firing continuously until the target is destroyed.*"

Whap! Up out of the night came the trees as if they were reaching for him. Ford cursed as he yanked on his chute. He didn't want to be hung in the trees. A leafy branch caught in his half-disengaged oxygen mask and broke off, snapping him across the face, under the eye, as it did so.

Then the ground slapped him, hard, under the feet and his knees weren't good enough to keep his ass from hitting a bunch of sharp rocks. *Don't want to be dragged . . .*

Pulling in the chute, trying to get his balance and run with it while he squeezed out the air, he kept feeling a jagged pain in his leg. When he had his arms around the parachute silk and it wasn't fighting him, he still couldn't stop to worry about what might hurt.

The leg held him. Out of his harness, he gathered the chute into a ball, stripped off his helmet, altimeter, and oxygen bottle, rolled them in the chute, and then began digging a hole to bury them, using his Crain knife.

The soil was rocky, but if you don't care how hard it is to do something, your adrenaline will do it for you.

Sometime after he'd gotten the hole dug, stuffed the damned parachute in the hole and shoveled dirt and small rocks over it with his hand, he remembered that his leg still hurt.

By then he was rechecking his position with his GPS handheld. *Walk half a mile uphill? Why not?*

Because it hurt, now that he thought about it. He stopped to check out the leg, and when he put his head down it hurt to breathe. He could feel his pulse pounding behind his eyes like something in there that wanted to bust out.

He couldn't find anything broken, although he thought he probably had one hell of a hematoma. *Walk uphill, you bet*.

Nobody'd shot at him, he thought, about the time he noticed that the quarter moon was rising over the mountains.

Half a mile straight up, it felt like.

He hiked, turning on his Racal PRM4735, in case it could pick up anything from Quantrell's party this early.

He didn't hear a thing, once he got the inductive loop played out and the button earpiece in his ear. He took the little palm-sized Racal remote unit out of his belt and hit the control which generated a short tone burst that would signal, if Marconi was listening, that Ford was on-site and in position.

Well, close enough, anyway. He put the palm-sized RCU in his breast pocket; the batteries would give him four active-duty hours before he had to change them.

He hoped to hell that was going to be enough. Maybe he wandered a little off course because his leg hurt, and he was instinctively taking whatever looked like the easiest route. Or maybe he was still as lucky as he needed to be, because while he was climbing toward the grid coordinates he wanted, a little upslope of the area where the space-tracking radar signal had been, he hit something with his sore leg.

And then he looked again. And blinked in the moonlight.

If he hadn't been climbing around in the dark, he probably never would have banged right into one of the dish supports—or, more exactly, the concrete piling into which the support was set.

Even right on top of it, he couldn't see it for the overgrowth, and the dish itself was camouflage-painted to match the environment, set into a handy hollow.

He stepped back three paces, very carefully. If there were any seismics here, he'd just tripped one.

Then, trusting his instinct, he kept backing up, ten paces, in what he hoped and firmly believed were his own footsteps.

He was right on top of the goddamned thing.

Hunkering down there, he considered his options. And then he reached for the C-4 he was carrying.

It was going take him a few minutes to pack the supports of the dish and set timers, but it was an opportunity he couldn't let pass.

For all he knew, he could end up the only guy who made it to the site. Anything could—and did—happen on lateral insertions. Something invariably went wrong.

The timers he had with him were radio-controllable, if he wanted to delay them later, so he set them to maximum and then started backing up again, still using his own tracks as best he could.

His leg was burning like thermite from all that kneeling and scrambling, and he was very conscious that, if there had been seismics or motion detectors emplaced around the dish, he'd be getting a bullet in the brain any minute now.

But he managed to retreat from the dish far enough to detour to his left before he heard voices.

He flattened in the underbrush, while his mind was still telling him that you wouldn't want seismics or motion detectors out here, because of plant, animal, and other nonhostile intrusions: you'd be running back and forth on false alarms all the time.

But his ears were listening. The voices were upslope, a little to his right. He kept trying to see their source, or make out the words. But he couldn't.

There was a dark regularity up there that might be a building, or an entrance to an underground building, because the edge, from his vantage point, was so regular.

Two men were talking, and it was an Arab dialect, he was nearly sure. That wasn't surprising.

What was surprising was that the voices started receding, and then there was a sudden square of light, which narrowed before it disappeared.

Okay, his intelligence had been better than he'd given it credit for; or he'd misread his GPS. One way or the other, he was right on top of the ground station that, an hour ago, he wasn't sure was out here.

Damn his leg. He grabbed his thigh as he got up and headed off to the left of the station. Still had to make the rendezvous. Still had to make contact with Quantrell's team. At least, now, even if he bought it, the dish might still blow on schedule, if the plastique wasn't discovered.

It was Bulgarian C-4, he reminded himself. He'd have to remember to thank Ignatov for that. Without it, all Ford's suspicions that Seti/Hatim was setting them up to take a fall might really have been bothering him as he limped his way toward the SAG drop point.

It wasn't until he was almost there that he began thinking about setting up his black box. He had lots of intel to gather, yet. And if he could do it, without being discovered, before Quantrell's team dropped, so much the better.

Since he'd almost screwed everything up back there—blown the whole mission by getting discovered prematurely, just the way Quantrell would be worried he might, he ought to have a little something more than a few preset detonations to tell Quantrell about when next they met.

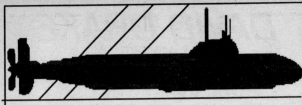

Tom Clancy's

#1 *New York Times* Bestsellers

____THE HUNT FOR RED OCTOBER 0-425-12027-9/$5.95
"Flawless authenticity, frighteningly genuine."
—*The Wall Street Journal*

____RED STORM RISING 0-425-10107-X/$5.99
"Brilliant . . . Staccato suspense."—*Newsweek*

____PATRIOT GAMES 0-425-10972-0/$5.99
"Marvelously tense . . . He is a master of the genre he seems
to have created."—*Publishers Weekly*

____THE CARDINAL OF THE KREMLIN 0-425-11684-0/$5.99
"The best of the Jack Ryan series!"—*New York Times*

____CLEAR AND PRESENT DANGER 0-425-12212-3/$5.95
"Clancy's best work since *The Hunt For Red October*."
—*Publishers Weekly*